I dedicate this book to my husband.
He supports me in everything I do.
He's a keeper.

SCHOOLING OF A MIDLIFE WITCH

J.C. YEAMANS

RSP

REED SHORE PRESS

PRONUNCIATION GUIDE

Gwynedd: GWYN-eth
Cockburn: CO-burn
Nain: NINE
Taid: TIDE
Aberystwyth: AB-uh-RIST-with
Shailagh: SHAY-la
Aonghas: ANG-us
Gorawen: GOHR-a-when

CONTENTS

CHAPTER ONE

WHERE TO GO FROM HERE?

AGHHH! I RAISE MY hand to summon the amber glow and activate the spell. The edges of the plastic bowl melt toward the center, turning the ingredients into a brown, poop-colored blob! My best friend Ronnie Baldwin came across this spell, and I hoped the incantation would unlock the charm on my mother's letter. The rustle of the door lock and handle sends my heart beating into overdrive, and I break out in a hot flash with beads of sweat dripping into the gelled mess. I rummage through the drawers to find a kitchen towel to cover the bowl. It's a bitch not having a secret magic space. How the hell will I explain this?

The door creaks open as I fan myself, and Tyler enters with disheveled hair and clothes. "Hi, Mom. I didn't expect to find you awake this early. You're all sweaty. Hot flash?"

"Yeah. And I got up early to do bodyweight exercises." While I gape at his hazel eyes and chestnut hair, I blink several times, hoping he doesn't notice the covered bowl.

Tyler squints at me. "Don't say anything. I stayed at Zoe's again last night. You don't need to judge."

I try to appear innocent. "I don't care if you stayed at Zoe's." Except for the whole hanging-with-a-witch may bring out the witch in you, too. "I'm happy for you."

"Then why are you acting so weird?" He walks toward me, and I shift my body in front of the bowl as my heart palpitates. "Are you hiding something, Mom?"

I can't lie to my son anymore. "No, I had an accident with your plastic bowl." I squish my lips together, and my chest tightens.

Tyler uncovers the bowl and groans. "Damn it, Mom. How many times have I told you not to put this bowl on the bottom rack of the dishwasher? Why did you try to use it in that condition?"

I push my lower lip up, and my chest relaxes. "I'm sorry. You didn't have any other bowl, so I had to make do. I'll buy you a new one."

"What the hell were you making, anyway?" He examines the brown goop in the bowl, glancing at the mortar and pestle my former Scottish lover Archie gave me the morning of the Winter Solstice.

My mouth drops open, and I search my angsty brain for a quick answer. "A new recipe. It didn't turn out right." This was the first time I concocted a spell since I sold my house in March and moved into his apartment, and I worried I'd forgotten everything.

"It looks like shit." Tyler takes the bowl and throws it into the trash. "I've got to shower and get to work." He stares at me with a tense mouth. "You've been doing so well since you sold the house, but you've also been a little...scatter-brained."

I scowl at my son and recognize the resemblance to his father, my late husband, Richard Wolfe. "Well, it's not the best situation...me living here in your apartment. Sleeping on your sofa bed and working from here, and I start my graduate degree in the fall. I think I'm getting on your nerves. Maybe I should look for a place again."

Tyler lowers his eyes. "I still worry about you, Mom. Something happened at the Winter Solstice Celebration you won't talk about. Zoe changes the subject every time I bring it up. And you haven't spoken to Archie since he gave you his dirk."

He's right, of course. I can't tell him about the hidden coven and what happened that night. It's been six months since The Bearsden Coven banished the evil Sluagh fairy back to the Otherworld, and I left the coven. I've procrastinated about all of it—dealing with the Fellowship and Dr. Archie Cockburn, the prior chair of the Celtic Studies department and coven leader. I miss his humor and tenderness. And I can't lie...I miss the sex, too. I bite my lower lip and stare into my son's concerned eyes.

Tyler rolls his head around and sighs. "I've gotta take a shower and get to work. What do you have planned today?"

"After I clean this up, I going to Ronnie's to help her with something." In reality, I'm going to go through my mom's family steamer trunk.

"Tell Ronnie I said hi, and I'm glad she's home from the rehab."

I nod. "I will. She'll appreciate the concern."

Tyler heads into the bathroom, and I clean up the mess I made. Something has to give. Being in limbo these past few months has me so frustrated. I couldn't go through my mom's magic trunk while Ronnie was in rehab and her boyfriend Derek Young was living at her house. And I can't practice magic in Tyler's apartment. That failed miserably.

I throw on a loose V-neck t-shirt and a pair of jean shorts and slip on some flat sandals for my trip to see my best friend at her house. The guilt over the Sluagh attack eats at me so much I baked her chocolate chip cookies. And I hate to bake. I grip the steering wheel of my metallic-blue Prius, and my stomach flutters with anticipation. I'm eager to see Ronnie, but I've waited three months to go through Mom's trunk. When I arrive, Derek's car sits in the driveway, so I park in front.

As I wait on the small porch of Ronnie's cape cod house, a warm, gentle breeze flits through my long, chestnut hair. A whiff of lavender passes by my nose and calms me. The door opens, and a cheery grin lights up Derek's rugged face. His tousled brown hair is still wet from a shower.

"Hi, Gwyn. Come on in." He motions me into the house and closes the door behind us. I follow his burly physique into the kitchen.

Ronnie's quaint cape cod has a large living room and dining room on either side of a central stairway with a compact kitchen in the back. The walls are a pale blue hue, and she's decorated the house with accents of aqua and red. Painted, white furniture gives the house a beachy feel and is comforting. She needs that now. I find her sitting at the kitchen table with her legs propped up and a mug of syrupy coffee in her hands. Her crimson hair hangs in ringlets across the back of her chair, and the patch of white hair at her forehead line has grown about three inches. Her freckled, heart-shaped face has a rosy glow. I place the plastic tub of cookies on the counter.

Ronnie raises her arms. "Come over here and give me a hug!"

"It's so wonderful to see you out of rehab," I say as I give her a squeeze.

"I slept like a baby last night. Rehab was a terrible place to recover." She winks at me out of Derek's line of sight. "Honey, you can leave now. Gwyn will watch me for a while."

Derek walks over to kiss Ronnie goodbye. "I'll see you later, babe. Thanks for hanging with Ronnie for a while." He kisses my best friend one more time. "You're sure you don't want me to stay home from the gym today?"

"I'm sure." Ronnie stares him down with azure-blue eyes.

"OK. I'm outta here. See you around six." Derek heads out through the kitchen door.

Ronnie wipes her hand over her cheeks and sighs. "I was afraid he wouldn't leave. If I wasn't ready, the doctors wouldn't have sent me home."

"I agree," I say. "I still have so much guilt around the Sluagh's attack."

"That's obvious. You never bake." Ronnie presses her lips together. "It wasn't your fault, Gwyn. Audrey summoned the Host of the Unforgiven Dead from the Otherworld."

Audrey Kenilworth. We never figured out why she infiltrated the Bearsden Coven and called on the Sluagh to kill me. She must have left Bearsden by now, but where would she go? Her parents had kicked her out for being a pagan.

"Has Derek pressed you any more about what happened?" I ask.

Ronnie shakes her head. "No. He let it go after a while. I told him I don't remember. It's not a lie, because I blacked out. But I decided I'm gonna tell him I'm a witch in a coven. Waiting for the right time. And I'm not asking permission from the Fellowship. If they expel me, so be it."

"Leslie needs to understand things need to change. The coven members should have more say in the direction it takes, considering how it affects their daily lives." I finish my tea. "Well, I'm a little anxious to...you know." I hike my eyebrows and turn my head toward her home office.

"Of course, you are." Ronnie grabs her crutches to stand.

I hop out of my chair and dart to her. "Are you OK to walk? I can go in there alone."

"Would you rather I not be there while you sort through the contents?"

"I've got nothing to hide from you."

Ronnie leads the way into her office, where the steamer trunk has collected dust for three months. She pulls a chair toward my family heirloom with a crutch and drops onto the seat while I sift through my purse for the key. When I broke the trunk's locking spell, I didn't know how to reset it and had to buy a metal lock. I turn the key, remove it, and lift the lid. My best friend gasps at the contents. Archie's ancestral dirk rests on top, reminding me I'm not safe while it's stored in the trunk. I pull out my mom's charmed letter from my purse.

"If you examine the surface under bright light, you can see a flickering of letters on the page." I shift the paper slightly, and shimmering letters appear to float above the paper.

Ronnie's mouth falls open. "Oh, Gwyn. Did you have any success with the spell this morning?"

"No. It was a disaster. I melted one of Tyler's plastic bowls."

"Oh, shit. Why did you think you could use a plastic bowl?"

"It's all he had. And I ran out of time. He came home earlier than I expected. He saw the bowl but figured it had melted in the dishwasher."

"Good save." Ronnie pulls out one of the black capes. "Oh, my gods. Leslie said the coven used to wear these, but they gave them up over the years. Students considered them outdated and creepy. They wanted t-shirts. They put F.A.P. for Fellowship of Associated Pagans on the first set, thinking it was funny. Leslie was NOT amused."

I chuckle, imagining the expression on Dr. Leslie Hughes's face. The acting chair of the Celtic Studies department and coven Elder has a stiff demeanor. "But the capes are pretty." As I brush the embroidery on the front, a frown appears. "I've forgotten a lot of my magic skills, Ronnie. My skills have gone to the shitters. I need training."

My friend stares at me with a flat mouth. "You know I can't. When you withdrew from the coven, you lost all connections. None of us can teach you. It's against the order."

"I know. It's not fair to ask you." I pull out the tray, and Ronnie gasps at the piles of witchcraft and personal items. "I don't even know where to start."

My friend eyes my mom's leather-bound book. "Is that a spell book? Can I see it?"

"I think so, but it's all in Welsh, so I don't know for sure."

Ronnie flips through a few fragile pages and gives the tome back to me. "There has to be someone who can translate this for you, but you'd have to lie about what it is."

"It's why I came today. DUB hired a new assistant professor for the Celtic Studies department. He's American but studied in Wales and speaks Welsh. I have an appointment with him after lunch."

She raises her crimson eyebrows. "Are you sure you should show an Unremarkable your family's spell book? He could get suspicious." The Unremarkable name still has a terrible connotation for someone who isn't *in the knowing*.

"I'm gonna tell him it's a collectible book I found in my parents' mementos," I say. "Since I didn't want to chance running into Archie, I waited until the semester was over. He won't be there since he's not the chair, but the new professor is settling into his office."

Ronnie frowns. "You can't keep putting it off, friend. I only saw him once while I was in rehab. He didn't talk about you, but I noticed a sadness in his eyes."

"I didn't mean to wait this long, but the months passed so quickly. Now it feels so awkward to talk with him." I lay the grimoire on the floor next to me.

"I know you have reasons not to trust him, not being forth-coming about all the witches he slept with, but he must have strong feelings for you. After all, he gave you his family's dirk for protection. Why would he do that if he didn't care deeply about you?"

I recall when he handed me the heirloom the day I sold my house. "Procrastination is my forte, you know."

"I do. Of course, the dirk isn't protecting you from anything locked in that trunk." Ronnie grabs her crutches and stands. "I'll go get lunch ready while you sort through your mom's stuff. You don't need me spying on you."

"You shouldn't be preparing our meal. I told Derek I would wait on you."

"For fuck's sake. I'm hobbling around with no issue. I can make lunch!"

"OK," I say. "But you better yell if you need help."

"Remember, you're the stubborn one, not me." Ronnie hobbles out of her office.

When I first discovered the trunk had all my parents' witch stuff, I didn't have the time to inventory any of the items. A huge grin forms on my mouth when I find the picture album, and I take a few minutes to flip through the pages filled with photos of my parents and me. I come across the picture of Leslie holding me on her hip, laughing as she tickled my tummy. She appeared to be so happy. What made her so arrogant and bitter? Is it connected to my parents' departure from the coven?

When I get to the last few pages, a couple of photos fall out and onto the floor. The first one is a picture of me sitting on a small bed in my old bedroom, and a tall Black girl in her teens sits on another bed on the other side of the room. My parents took a second picture during the Yule holiday. They're standing next to each other, and the Black teen holds my three-year-old hand.

Ronnie yells from the kitchen. "Gwyn, lunch is on the table!"

I stuff the pictures in my purse as my stomach tightens into a ball of what-the-fuck?

CHAPTER TWO

INCOMPETENCE CAN BE DANGEROUS

I PARK IN THE South Campus parking lot of Delaware University at Bearsden and stroll through the *Kissing Arch,* where Archie first kissed me on the cheek and ignited my witch powers. It's a perfect June day to walk on campus—upper 70s and low humidity. The aroma from rose bushes floats in the air, and a warm breeze frolics with my hair. When I pass the Old Men oak trees, the vision of the Sluagh returns, but I don't shudder or shake. The Host of the Unforgiven Dead no longer scares me.

When I arrive at Stewart Hall, I admire its red brick topped with the big white dome before entering through its large double doors. As I descend the stairs, I'm hit with the musty air of the basement where the Celtic Studies department has offices. I pass the main office, noticing the department chair's plaque now reads Dr. Leslie Hughes. She can't be happy about her temporary assignment, especially since she spends summers in Great Britain, and she's in her mid-70s.

The office two doors down displays a plaque with the name Dr. Archibald Cockburn. I stop abruptly and pass the tips of my fingers across his name. Ronnie's right. It's time to call him and hash things out. The new professor's name doesn't appear anywhere, so I turn the corner and walk until I reach the last door on the left. The plaque holder has no name. I tap on the blue metal door but get no response, so I knock again with my bare knuckles.

"Wait a minute!" yells a male voice from inside. The door flies open, revealing a slender man of medium height in his late 30s wearing jeans and a DUB t-shirt with *Go Highlanders* on the front. He has short, dark-brown hair, deep-set brown eyes, and a picture-perfect smile. "Hi! You must be Gwynedd Crowther." He shakes my hand with a tight squeeze. "I'm Nick Evans. Come in. Please excuse my office. It's a disaster. I hate moving." He motions for me to sit and drops into his chair behind the desk.

"Thank you for agreeing to meet with me, Dr. Evans. It's fantastic DUB hired someone who can speak Welsh. I don't know where else I could have gone. Thank you so much for agreeing to translate the old tome for me. And I'll pay you whatever you want," I say.

"Nonsense. This qualifies as research for me. No need to pay," he says. "And frankly, I'm more than a little excited. Can I see it?"

"Oh, sure. Of course." I pull out the leather grimoire and pass it to him, hesitating for a moment. "You should know this antiquated book has been in my family for many years. It's fragile."

"Don't worry. I'll keep it in a safe place." He reaches for the tome, but I don't release my grasp. "Mrs. Crowther, I promise I've handled antiquities older than your family's tome."

"Of course you have. I'm sorry. And it's not Mrs. I'm a widow, but I kept my maiden name, anyway. And please, call me Gwyn."

"Sure, Gwyn. I'm sorry about your husband. And you can call me Nick."

"OK, Nick." I don't know what to share. You don't tell a person at a first meeting your husband was a cheating liar. "My husband, Richard, passed away over a year ago. It was hard, but I'm plodding along."

"That's good to hear." Nick pulls the leather strap out and opens the tome to the first page. He reads the first few lines and peers up at me. "Do you know what's in here?"

I swallow. "No idea." It's not a complete lie. I don't really know.

"At a first glance, the words appear to list ingredients—a recipe. But they're written oddly. Sort of like a rhyme." He reads a few more lines, running his youthful fingers under the words as he reads. "I mean, it's old. People wrote stuff in prose. Still odd for a recipe book."

"Yeah, makes sense." I glance at the framed diploma hanging on the wall behind him—a Ph.D. from Cardiff University in Wales. "How long do you think it will take you to translate it?"

"Oh, it could take a few months. I've got to get organized here and at home. And prepare syllabi for the fall courses. But I'll chip away at it."

"I appreciate your time. Well, I guess we're finished." I stand with a sigh and throw my purse over my shoulder.

Nick pushes up from his desk chair. "Let me get the door for you."

"Thank you. You have my cell number saved in your phone?"

Nick nods as he opens the door. "I'll call you when I've got a few pages done. See if you want me to continue."

"Sounds like a plan." I leave Nick's office, and the door closes behind me.

I receive a text from Tyler and read it as I shuffle down the hallway, hearing the murmur of students chatting in the distance. Summer Session classes must have let out. And bam! I run into someone and drop my phone on the floor. When I raise my head to identify the nitwit who ran into me, a set of icy-blue eyes stares down at me from a foot above. My lips part, but I'm too stunned to speak.

"Gwyn. What are you doing here?" Archie asks in his soft Scottish accent. His ash-blond hair is cut shorter, but he still has a neatly trimmed goatee.

"I...I had a meeting with the new Celtic Studies professor," I say.

"Nick Evans? Why on earth would you meet with him?" I glance at my phone on the floor as he bends to pick it up and passes it to me. "Actually, I was on my way to speak with him."

"Well, I won't keep you." I shove my cell into my purse and take a few steps.

"Stop, Gwyn. I've not seen you for months, and that's all you're going to say?"

I force myself to turn around. Damn, he is a handsome man. Running into him did not cross my mind as even a remote possibility during Summer Session.

Archie squints at me. "You didn't expect to see me, did you?"

"You said you never taught Summer Session," I say, fiddling with an earring. "I meant to contact you sooner, but the months passed in the blink of an eye, especially visiting Ronnie in rehab so much."

He smiles, never taking his gaze from me. "You don't owe me an explanation. Leslie asked me to teach so Nick wouldn't have to jump right in. And I wanted to keep busy this summer. I don't need to speak to Nick right now. Please, will you come to my office and talk?"

The beating of my heart pounds heavier with each pulse. So much for procrastination. "Sure."

"My office isn't far. Follow me." He looks more like a professor in his DUB polo shirt and chinos.

"Yeah. I saw your name plaque when I passed by," I say, blushing.

He opens the door. "Please excuse the piles. It's tough to stay on top of assignments during Summer Session."

The small office has a desk and a wall of shelves. A beam of sunlight breaks through the high basement window, highlighting the stacks of open books laying everywhere. Papers clutter the surface of his desk. This isn't like him. His office and home never had an item out of place. He closes a book and removes it from a chair, motioning me to sit, and pulls up another one for himself.

"You cut your hair shorter. It gives you a distinguished appearance."

"Heh, makes me look like a middle-aged man."

"Well, you are a middle-aged man." I arch my eyebrows and chuckle.

He sighs and leans back in his chair. "Apparently. Tell me how you've been."

Damn. Where do I start? We've not spoken for six months about what happened—only briefly three months ago when he gave me his dirk.

"I've been living with Tyler, working for the insurance agency, and visiting Ronnie in rehab," I say. "It's about all I could handle."

"But you're all right?" Archie asks.

"I am. I'm sorry I left you hanging like I did. At the time, I wanted nothing to do with magic anymore. And then..."

"What? Did something happen?" Fear captures his eyes, and he leans forward.

"Oh, no. Nothing bad. I want to tell you something. I finally opened my mom's steamer trunk. You were right. There were items in there."

His eyebrows jump. "Aye? What did you find?"

A huge grin brightens my face. "My parents' magic stuff had been collecting dust in the steamer trunk for decades."

"I'm so happy for you." Archie smiles and extends his hand but pulls it back. "Did you find any answers? Why they left the coven?"

"No, but think I found a family grimoire. Unfortunately, it's all in Welsh."

His eyes grow big. "Is that why you met with Nick? Gwyn, you don't know what's in that book. What if he gets suspicious?"

"About an old family book of recipes? That's what he thinks they are so far."

Archie stares at me with pressed lips. "I know enough not to argue with you. All I ask is you recognize the dangers of exposing the coven to an Unremarkable."

"Why would translating an old spell book matter, anyway? He knows it's old and not relevant."

"We'll see, I guess." He averts his eyes for a moment. "Thank you for trusting me enough to share this information. You must have concerns, considering how we parted."

Here we go. I wasn't prepared to talk about us. "Saying the events of that day overwhelmed me hardly touches on the shit storm of emotions I experienced."

"I understand. I've missed you. Not a day has passed without imagining how you were getting on. I recognize the mistakes I made, but I can't change my past." Archie leans forward and grasps my hand. "Would you reconsider? Give me a chance to prove myself?"

The touch of his warm skin sends my heart pumping into overdrive. "Things would have to be different. I'm not the naïve, vulnerable woman you met in August—I've changed." I search for truth in his transparent-blue eyes, but I've been here before.

"I know you have, and I'm so impressed with the woman you've become. Could I call you sometime? Meet for lunch or dinner? I'd be chuffed to bits to meet for a cuppa tea."

"That would be nice." I pull my hand from his and grab my purse.

He leans back with hope in his eyes. "I'm a wee bit swamped with school right now, but I'll call soon."

"You seem happy to be back in the classroom," I say as I stand.

Archie follows me to the door. "It's been a lot of work after being chair for so long, but I wanted to be busy." He opens the door, and I take a few steps. "Gwyn?"

When I turn and gaze at his chiseled face, I glimpse the slight scar on his right cheek.

"I didn't say it before, but...you truly look wonderful."

"Thank you, Archie. We'll talk soon." I walk into the hallway, and the door shuts behind me. That went better than expected, but why does my heart want to break through my ribcage?

The next day, I drive to Main Street and park near Ronnie's restaurant, the Sunshine Garden Café. I jaywalk across the street to the Mystic Sage, where Shane Murphy's occult and witchcraft store exists between an ice cream shop and a local Methodist church. I haven't seen my coven friend since the Winter Solstice Ceremony.

A young college undergrad with short brown hair and dark, soulful eyes waits behind the counter. "Hello, may I help you?" he asks in a tenor voice.

"I'm here to see Shane. Is he here?" I pinch my nose to keep a sneeze at bay. The mixture of herbs in the Mystic Sage always tickles my nostrils.

"Yeah, he's in the back going through boxes delivered this morning." The young man's shoulders hang low, as if someone has beaten him down all his life. "I'm familiar with the products in the store. Maybe I can help you find what you need?"

"Oh, I'm not here to buy anything. I used to work here." I glance at the skull mug full of pens on the sales counter. Some things never change.

His eyes become animated. "You're Ms. Crowther?"

"Yes. But you can call me Gwyn," I say.

"Shane said you were returning to work. I'm Jeff Williams." He reaches over the counter with a fist.

"Oh." I raise my hand and fist bump in a slightly awkward movement. "Nice to meet you, Jeff."

He points to the doorway. "There's the boss."

Shane's face lights up, and a wide grin peeks through his long white beard as he gives me a hug. "You're a sight for sore eyes and all the others in-between. I hope these months helped to clear your head."

"They have, but I'll share more later. I missed you so much, Shane."

"Darling, I missed you more than apple pie." His hair is as white and wiry as ever and tied behind his head. "You've met my newest addition to the store?"

"Yeah. Jeff introduced himself. Do you still want me to start on Wednesday?"

"Definitely. And if you're willing to listen, I have a big idea for new merchandise I'd like to bounce off you." He wrinkles his nose. "If you're up to it."

"Sure, Shane. I'm ready to establish a routine before the fall semester begins."

"Perfect," he says in his North Carolinian accent.

"Well, I'll see you on Wednesday." I wave at Jeff and exit the store.

On the way back to my parking spot, I pass a city building undergoing renovation. The structure is mostly gutted and has a chain-link fence surrounding it. I notice construction workers waiting in line at Bennie's vending truck. Main Street has construction cluttering the otherwise quaint downtown all the time, and they're starting renovations on Mitchell Hall soon to convert it to a community center. Progress is messy.

A bright light shines in my eyes, and I peer up at the building, lifting my hand to block the glare. I notice movement on the top of the structure. Without warning, my witch energy radiates, seeping out as if a magnet is pulling my magic toward the building. A vibration captures my hand as the ground rumbles, and the sounds of cracking and splitting fill the air. Pieces of the building crumble until the entire structure collapses as I shove my vibrating hand into my armpit to hide the amber glow. I become lightheaded and tumble to the pavement, blocking the fall with the palms of my hands.

Panic sets in as people around me shout and scream, scattering away from the crumbling concrete and brick. I stand with a wobble and cover my mouth and nose with my t-shirt as I run down the paver sidewalk but trip and fall again—this time scraping my knees. Someone leans over me and huddles as the remaining rubble rolls into the street, crushing cars. When the catastrophe ends, people cry and shout exclamations of horror. I uncover my face to find Jeff Williams kneeling beside me.

"You OK, Ms. Crowther?" he asks.

A cloud of dust floats around us, and the Bearsden Fire Department sirens blare in the distance.

"Yeah. Thank you for putting yourself in harm's way for me." My hands shake as I glance at them—no amber glow. "I've only scraped my palms and knees a bit." I stand and lose my balance.

"Whoa…maybe you should get checked over by medics," he says, grabbing my arm.

"No. I'll clean the scrapes at home." The EMTs and police may ask questions. What would I say? *I'm sorry. My unskilled magic obliterated the building. My bad.*

"Suit yourself. A few people have blood on their faces. I'm going to see if I can help."

Jeff dashes to an area where several passersby crowd together, attending to their wounds. I notice Shane has joined him, and I wave to him, signaling I'm OK. A couple of ambulances arrive, and paramedics rush to the injured. As I stare at the pile of rubble, I cover my mouth with a trembling hand, and a rush of guilt latches on like the teeth of a bear trap. What the fuck have I done?

Chapter Three

A Trinity of Witches

I'm so rattled, I have to grab the door handle twice to open my Prius. As I pull out of my parking spot, several fire engines and police cars have arrived, and they've put orange cones out to block traffic. What if the movement on the top of the building was a person? Nausea builds in my stomach, and I pull over to vomit. I'd planned on being gone all day, but I've got to get home and clean the abrasions on my hands and knees. And brush my teeth.

I wanted to stop by the Bearsden Shelter to visit Elijah Jackson and help serve lunch as a surprise. I miss the kind Black man who resembles a giant. If I'm going to return to work at the Mystic Sage, I might as well volunteer at the shelter again, too. I can't take the route my parents did—cut myself off from magic and my witch friends. There must be a way I can move forward with my life without isolating myself. My parents were wrong to withdraw from magic and raise me as an Unremarkable.

My hand trembles as I push the door key in, and it drops to the floor. I scoop up the key and open the lock on the second try, plopping onto a living room chair for a minute to calm down. It was a mistake to believe I could go about my daily life harboring uncontrolled magic. What if I glimpsed a person on the roof? A worker not taking his union lunch break?

I go to the bathroom to clean my wounds. It stings like a bitch. The box of adhesive bandages is only that—an empty box. Tyler keeps a first-aid kit in his nightstand. I walk to his closed bedroom door, a reminder his room is off limits, but he should be OK with me getting bandages. I push the door open, and my eyes pop out when I see my son's bare back.

"Hi, Gwyn!" Zoe waves from underneath my son.

Tyler's head twists around and shouts, "MOM?"

"Oh, my gods. I'm so sorry!" I rush out of his bedroom, slamming the door behind me.

My entire body tenses up while I hyperventilate. What else can go wrong today? I dart to the kitchen and rip off a paper towel to blot the blood on my hands and knees. When I turn around, Tyler is standing in his gray robe, his mouth displaying a smirk.

"I don't know what to say." I push my lower lip up.

"You said you'd be busy all day." He glares at me until he notices the abrasions. "Mom, what happened to you?"

"I was about to explain. You know the small city building housing the parking division? The one being renovated?"

He rocks his head. "Yeah?"

"The building collapsed to the ground. The rubble scattered around and into the street. Didn't you hear all the sirens blaring?"

"What? No, I didn't." Tyler's face distorts with worry as he walks over to me. "You got hurt?"

"I ran as fast as I could and tripped on the paver sidewalk. It looks worse than it is. I went into your bedroom to check your nightstand for bandages."

Zoe comes into the kitchen with her signature tooth-filled grin, wearing a wrinkled light-blue t-shirt and shorts. "See Tyler, this isn't awkward at all." She pouts with concern in her big brown eyes when she sees my scraped palms. "What happened?"

"The city building on Main Street imploded," Tyler says. "Mom, fell. I'll go check my nightstand."

I'm not feeling as embarrassed since Zoe has dressed and acts like I didn't walk in on them having sex. "How are you? I haven't seen you since the two of you started dating."

She gives me a hug. "I've been great, but I missed you, Gwyn."

"I missed you, too, Zoe." I want to return the hug, but I'm afraid I'll get blood all over her pretty t-shirt.

She whispers, "Have you been practicing magic? My body tingles as if you've been dabbling with the mojo?"

"You can sense my use of magic?" I whisper, not denying the obvious.

Zoe steps back and snickers. "Oh, yeah…" She places her index finger on her lips.

My son walks back into the kitchen wearing his work clothes and presses extra-large bandages on my palms and my knees.

"They should keep you from bleeding on everything," Tyler says.

"Or doing anything else!" I try to make a fist. "How am I supposed to hold stuff?"

"I guess you'll have to let others do for you for a day or so."

"Don't be a smart ass. I'm gonna make lunch. You want me to make sandwiches for you both?"

Tyler crosses his arms. "Are we even gonna talk about the fact you walked in on Zoe and me naked and…"

"NO." I stare him down. "Let's call it even-steven and move on." I roll my eyes at him, and he bursts out laughing.

Zoe laughs but gets quiet. "Wait. You walked in on your mom having sex?"

After lunch, I pull myself together and decide to stop by the shelter, anyway. I can't put the images of the imploding building out of my head. Police still have Main Street blocked, so I take a roundabout way to get there. The rainbow sign *All Are Welcome Here* hangs above the double entry doors, and I recall my first visit—the first time I met Sebastian, a sweet, homeless man who sobered up only to be killed by the Sluagh. I close my eyes and swallow.

I enter the double doors with a soft spot in my heart, remembering the times I volunteered here. But the curve of my mouth fades as I recall Frank Walker's bloodied body on the floor of the dining hall—another homeless man. I shake it off and glance around the room, searching for Elijah, the social worker who runs the shelter. The kitchen doors swing open, and he walks to the serving line with an arm around a student volunteer who's wearing a DUB t-shirt displaying the mascot of the Scotty dog in a kilt on the front. Elijah gestures to the dining table and his mouth drops open. He pats the young man on the back and meanders around the line toward me. His light-brown eyes always radiated with an electric quality.

"I imagined I was seeing things." He bends down and wraps his massive arms around me.

"It's so good to see you, Elijah. I'm sorry I stayed away for so long. Needed to clear my head," I say, fighting back the tears.

"That's all right. I'm thrilled you're here. What's up with the bandages?"

"You heard about the city building imploding? I fell on the pavers. Not a big deal." But it is. *It might be my fault.*

"Oh, Gwyn. I'm so glad you weren't hurt too bad. I sure hope they figure out what happened. News reports say they don't think anyone was in the building when it collapsed."

"That's a relief," I say as my shoulders relax.

"Something I can do for you?" he asks with a chuckle. "Or are you here to work?"

I laugh, too. "Actually, I was going to surprise you and help with lunch until I fell. I went home to clean up...well, to Tyler's apartment."

Elijah receives a text on his phone and types a return message. "Have you seen Trinity?"

"No. Not yet," I say with darting eyes.

"Well, I hope you want to see her, because she's about to walk through those doors."

The entry door bangs open, and Trinity Johnson, the director of the LGBTQ support group Family for All, rushes in, eyeing me with a beaming smile. The tall, curvy Black woman rushes to me with her long, burgundy hair flowing. She grabs me and squeezes so hard my ribs flex.

"Trinity, I can't breathe," I say. "I'm happy to see you, too."

"I'm sorry. I'm beside myself you've come back to us," she says, releasing me from her grasp. "I know you had a tug-of-war going on inside that head of yours, but you made the right decision."

"I'm not returning to the coven, Trinity. I'm here for a different reason." My eyes drift back and forth between them, recognizing their disappointment.

"Oh. It was wrong for me to assume. But I'm glad you came, anyway." She points at my hands.

"Gwyn was on Main Street when the building imploded," Elijah says.

"The bandages are overkill. Only minor abrasions," I say. "Elijah, I don't mean to be rude, but can I chat with Trinity alone?"

"Yeah. No problem. I gotta get back to work. Don't be a stranger." He strolls back to the serving line.

"Can we find a spot at a table away from prying ears?" I ask.

"Sure," Trinity says. "Let's go to the far side of the dining hall."

We sit down on a bench next to each other. I reach for my purse and remove the picture I found in my parents' steamer trunk, passing it to Trinity with a blank face. Tears well up in her eyes as she closes them, pushing a single tear onto her velvety skin.

"That's you in the photo, isn't it?" I ask. "Please explain to me what this means. And don't pull a Leslie on me."

"It's me. Damn, I was thin." Trinity wipes her drippy eyes and laughs through the tears. "When my parents kicked me out, it wasn't all because I was a lesbian. Before my grandma passed away, she had taught me magic, and my parents forbade it. I had no place to go but the local shelter. I met Leslie there, and your parents, Rhys and Lowri."

My lips part. "So, you came to live with us?"

"Yeah. Your parents offered me a bed in your room. I even babysat when they had class or wanted to go out, but eventually, they told me I had to move out."

"Because they withdrew from the coven?" I ask.

"They gave me a choice. I could stay, but I'd have to give up magic, and I just couldn't do it."

I understand how Trinity must have felt, given my recent magic sobriety. "Why did they leave the coven? You don't quit for no reason. Out of the blue, they decide they won't practice magic? It doesn't make sense. And Leslie has zipped her lips."

Trinity squints at me. "Something happened on Samhain that put you in danger. Rhys and Lowri made their choice to keep you safe. It has something to do with the first time the coven opened a large portal on Samhain. Your parents weren't there. I remember thinking it was freaking odd after I told your mom Leslie was going to do it after all. We made no contact with the Otherworld that night, because the ceremony ended when your mom came crashing into the Celestial Gardens. She took Leslie aside and screamed at her, but I couldn't make out their conversation."

I rub my thumb into the palm of my injured hand. "Do you remember who else participated in the circle?"

"Oh, my gods," she says. "It was so long ago. Most of those witches left."

"So, only Leslie knows what really happened?" I ask.

"Well, her and that old coot, Agnes." Trinity smiles and waves to a student volunteer as she passes.

My eyes bulge out. "Agnes Pritchard was in the coven with my mom?"

"Yeah. I figured you knew. There was a time Leslie, Agnes, and your mom hung out together like peas and carrots. I was only fifteen, so they didn't let me go to the Raven with them late at night. Too many drunks and potheads. And the Heathens biker gang. Wasn't a good place for a young Black teen to be in the '60s, you know."

"I imagine it wasn't. I guess I should've put two and two together. That's when you went to live with Leslie?"

"Yeah, I lived with her until I went to college and moved into an apartment with a girlfriend. Not Charlie, by the way," Trinity says. "That cheating floozy was a colossal mistake."

"We all make them," I say.

"That's for damn sure." She stares at me, and sadness lingers in her eyes. "You have no idea how much it hurt to leave you and your parents. I'd grown to love all of you like family, one who didn't care I was different."

"I don't remember you living with us, and I wish I did." As more people arrive, our secluded chat has to end. "Trinity, I still care about all of you. That's never been the issue. I'm not sure I can

ever return to the…Fellowship. I need to figure out my life first."
And find out what's in my mom's letter.

Trinity gives me a hug and whispers in my ear, "Every witch has
to discover their own path. I won't pressure you, but I can't say
Leslie won't." She stands and adjusts her blouse. "But you don't
have to deal with her until she gets back in August."

"Thank you for being honest with me." I push up from the
bench and gaze at her with a deeper sense of trust but… "Why
didn't you tell me all this after Samhain? When I discovered…you
know."

"Leslie asked me not to. I trusted her to know what was best.
But after what happened at the Winter Solstice Ceremony, I'm
questioning her judgment. I promise you I've told you everything
I know. I don't want to lose your friendship. Not after losing you
for all these years." Her eyes have a sincerity I'd not seen before.

"You don't need to worry about that," I say.

I hug Trinity goodbye and wave to Elijah, who's been eyeing our
conversation from the serving line. When I get to my car, I turn on
the AC and sit back for a minute, allowing the cool air to caress my
exposed skin. Leslie, my mom, and Agnes Pritchard were friends.
What the hell happened? I plan to find out.

CHAPTER FOUR

WHAT'S IN A TOME?

I LIE ON THE sofa bed and pull my knees to my chest to stretch. I guess I'm not exercising today. Since I fell on the paver walkway, my lower left back pinches like a bitch. I must have strained a muscle, or it's the weakness in my hip joint. Who the hell knows? Certainly not my PCP.

While I stretch, the vision of the city building disintegrating returns to me. As I lift my hand, a faint amber glow emerges, and I can't pull it back in. I stuff my hand under the sheets with my chest tightening and heart pounding into my ribs.

The shower stops running, and a few minutes after, Tyler walks out of the bathroom and notices my fetal position. "Still hurts?"

"Yeah. Don't worry about it. It's happened before. I'm doing the PT exercises from the last time I strained the same muscle." I check my hand under the sheets before rolling over until my feet hit the carpet. "This sofa bed doesn't help either."

"Let me sleep on the couch for a couple of nights. You take my bed. I don't mind." He gathers his keys and wallet and heads toward the door.

"Nah. It just needs time to heal." I stand and straighten my back. "See? I'm fine. Go to work."

"You're so stubborn." My cell phone rings playing the tune of *Don't Stop Believin'*, and he sighs. "I really hate that song, Mom."

"Don't push your luck." I open the door and push him out like I'm sending him off to high school. Archie's name flashes on my cell.

"Hello," I say while I make my tea.

"It's so wonderful to hear your voice," he says. "Would you be interested in dinner? I could pick you up, and we could go to the Raven Pub? Or Ronnie's café, if you like?"

I take a moment to think about it. Might be nice to eat at the Raven for a change.

Tension leaks into his warm baritone voice. "Are you there, Gwyn?"

"Yeah. I was thinking I've not been to the Raven for a long time." Not since we ate there last, when I learned about the Seelie and Unseelie Fae. "But let's not make this so formal. I can meet you there." And I can say goodbye to him from the restaurant. I don't trust myself to be alone with him yet. Sex deprivation is real.

"Cracking. Meet you at 6:00 p.m?"

"Sure. I'm looking forward to it, Archie."

I swipe the red circle on my phone screen and walk into the bathroom. As the shower water warms up, I strip down to my birthday suit. *Don't Stop Believin'* rings on my cell again, and I assume Archie's forgotten something.

Nick Evan's name appears, and I swipe the green circle. "Hello?"

"Hi, Ms. Crowther. I wanted to let you know I've translated a few pages of the antiquarian journal you gave me," he says in a pleasing tenor voice. Students must love listening to his lectures. "But I've discovered some unusual things I'd rather not discuss on the phone. I know it's last minute, but could we meet sometime today?"

Unusual things? That's disconcerting. "Does late morning work for you? I've not showered yet." Standing naked with only a cell phone in my hand, I cross my legs and try to cover my boobs with the other.

"I've got meetings in the morning and have to get to the DMV in the afternoon," he says. "Any chance we could meet around five?"

Hmph. So close to dinner. "I could meet for about thirty minutes. I'm meeting someone for dinner at six."

"Awesome." He sighs into the phone. "If I spend one more minute in my office, I'm going to snap. Could we meet at the Raven Pub? I've heard it has a unique history."

My body freezes. "Could we be done by 5:30?"

"Sounds good. See you soon, Ms. Crowther." The call ends, and I place my cell on the vanity. As I step into the shower, it occurs to me the young man can't get past my motherly vibes. But I wish he'd stop calling me Ms. Crowther.

Worried about parking, I arrive extra early and grab a spot in the Raven Pub's small lot. I used to walk to the restaurant from my home on Mulberry Lane. I don't miss the house, but it was a convenient stroll to Main Street. The city needed a parking garage, but Mitchell Hall will make a wonderful community center. It's only 4:30 p.m., so I decide to take a stroll and check on its progress.

The red-brick Federalist mansion resembles a haunted house in its dreary state, with vines growing over the exterior and a few shutters hanging by a single screw. The city hasn't installed fencing yet. With the collapse of the city building, I'm sure they'll push back the renovation. Since the purge of the Sluagh six months ago, I've stayed away from the Celestial Gardens. But now, I want to go in—see if the Seelie Fae boy and girl will appear. And with luck, share with me what they remember about my mom.

Main Street is fairly empty for a Tuesday afternoon, so I walk to the side gate to sneak in. When I reach the opening in the iron fence, I hit my head as if I've bumped into a concrete wall. While I rub my forehead, I step back, befuddled. I raise my hand and push at the air, stopping when my fingers touch a hard, flat surface. Damn. A protection barrier spell. But who cast it?

I'm furious and determined to get in. I check around for passers-by and summon my witch energy, chanting the only spell I remember to crack the invisible wall. The amber glow sparks and ricochets onto a section of the iron fence, heating the metal to a dark orange hue, and it wilts like a plant needing water.

"Shit!" I glance over my shoulder and shake the glow from my hand. No one saw me, but I rush toward the sidewalk in my flats, running until I reach the Raven parking lot. I tap my chest to calm the thumping and try to catch my breath, but I break out in a hot flash, sweating buckets in the June heat. "Great." I sift through my purse, find a crumpled tissue, and blot my face and neck. It's almost 5:00 p.m., so I comb my sweaty fringe of bangs and enter the restaurant.

When I approach the hostess in the main room, I'm about to ask the young woman with short blue hair and face piercings if Nick Evans has arrived. But he motions to me from a booth in the back room. I've worn capri pants to hide the abrasions on my knees, but the bandages on my palms are obvious.

"Hello again." I slide onto the padded booth seat and touch my flushed cheeks with my fingertips. My chest rises and falls as I steady my breathing.

"Thanks so much for meeting here. I was suffocating in my office." Nick lowers his eyebrows and crouches over the table. "Ms. Crowther, are you OK? Your face is the shade of ripe strawberries." He gestures to the bandages on my palms. "And your hands?"

My mouth falls open as I stare at his warm brown eyes. I can't talk to this young man about my menopausal hot flashes, and I can't tell him I ran from the Mitchell's mansion after I melted the fence. "I was late and ran in here. My hands got scraped when I fell on the sidewalk a couple of days ago."

Nick leans back against the booth and smiles. "Let's hope you heal fast." A waiter comes to our table and offers us menus, but Nick raises his palm. "We aren't ordering dinner, but I'd like a beer. Ms. Crowther, what would you like? My treat?"

"Oh, I don't want a drink. Water for me," I say. "If you keep calling me Ms. Crowther, I'm going to address you as Dr. Evans."

Nick chuckles. "I didn't want to be disrespectful."

"Did you ever think I may not deserve respect?" I lift my eyebrows and blink twice.

"Aren't you sassy?" He bursts out laughing. "Working with you is gonna be way more fun than I planned."

I glimpse the time on my phone. "We've only got about twenty minutes. You said there were some odd things about the tome?"

"Yeah." Nick's face turns more serious, and he pulls out a tablet from a backpack. "I saved the translations in an online document. Your family told you this was a journal of home recipes?"

I stare at him with puzzled eyes. "They didn't tell me anything. I was guessing."

"It's not a book of cooking instructions." Nick hands me the tablet.

The first entry is a type of protection spell, although it's not written as one. I say nothing as my eyes drift from the screen to his eyes.

"I'm uncertain, but my best guess it's witchcraft related." He taps the table with his fingertips until the waiter shows up with the beer and water.

I swipe the screen, and the next spell appears to be instructions for a love potion. "Interesting, don't you think?" I pass the tablet back to him.

"It's probably valuable—a collector's item. Some rich dude would pay thousands for an old tome about witchcraft." Nick swallows some beer and places the glass on the table. "Let me show you some examples of what others sell for."

For the next thirty minutes, he shows me sites where I could list the tome, and how much I could "fetch" for an antiquated book of witchcraft—like I would ever sell it. I nod while he wastes his time, but I thank him for his research.

"Would you like me to keep translating?" Nick asks.

I take a sip of water. "Do you want to? I mean, you're working for free."

"Absolutely." Nick looks away for a moment as if he's contemplating a major decision.

"Something wrong?" I ask as I lean toward the table.

"Not exactly." He stares at me with a glint in his eyes. "You're gonna think I'm being creepy, but I've gotta ask. The next time we meet to go over the translations, could we do dinner?"

I sit up straight with bulbous eyes. "Are you asking me out on a date?" I glimpse the time on my cell. It's 5:40 p.m. Archie will arrive soon.

"Yeah. I like you. You have spunk. You're completely different from other women I've dated."

"Because they're probably twenty years younger. Nick, I must be old enough to be your mom."

"I don't think so. I'm thirty-eight." He examines my face. "You're maybe ten years older, max."

"Ugh...no." My eyes roll around while I calculate the age difference. "I'm fifteen years older than you."

"Wow." Nick takes another drink of his beer. "I don't care. Would you at least consider it? It's just dinner."

While I stare at those warm, brown eyes, I mull it over. "I'll think about it. At least you're calling me Gwyn now." My phone displays 5:50 p.m. "We've gone way past 5:30." I tap my fingernails on the table in morse code for *you've-gotta-go.*

"Oh, I'm sorry. You go ahead. I'll stay and finish my beer. I'll call you when I've got more translated, and we'll meet for dinner. My treat."

"I'm eating here." I glance over his shoulder at the door, and Archie walks in.

Nick cocks his head. "Even better. We can chat until your dinner guest arrives."

My former lover locks eyes with mine and grins. As he meanders through the main room to get to the back, his eyes veer to the head of my booth mate.

Nick turns his head. "Hi, Archie. You meeting someone for dinner?"

Archie peers at me and smiles. "I am."

I sink into the booth bench. "He's meeting me for dinner, Nick."

The young professor presses his lips together and slides out of the booth seat, grabbing his beer. "I'll call you soon. See you tomorrow at Stewart Hall, Archie."

Archie nods. "We'll go over the new research you found."

Nick takes the last sip of his beer and gets up from the booth. "Enjoy your dinner." He heads toward the exit.

Archie slides onto the padded bench. "He kept it warm for me, I see? Why do you have bandages on your hands?"

"I fell on the sidewalk. It's only minor scrapes. We only met to discuss the translation of my mom's tome."

"His expression showed a little more interest than a professor doing research on a tome. But you don't owe me any explanation. Not with my past."

I've got to be open with him, or we have no chance at all. "We met to discuss what he translated, but..." My glass of water calls to me, and I take a sip to wet my dry mouth. "He asked me to eat dinner with him."

He glances at Nick's empty glass. "And what did you tell him?"

"I said I'm too old for him." The waiter who brought my drink passes by, and I flag him over. "Can we get some menus?"

"He's only a few years younger than I am, Gwyn."

"I shouldn't have said anything." The waiter brings our menus, and I scope the list of food as if it's the first time.

"It's all right." He lays his warm hand on mine. "I have no hold over you. See whomever you want."

His touch sends tingles up my arm. I gaze into his eyes, and my breathing stops. Oh, how wrong you are. We order and chat while we wait for our food. I want so badly to tell him about the incident surrounding the implosion of the building and melting the iron fence at Mitchell Hall. And how I can't control my magic. Instead, our conversation floats freely describing memories of happier times.

Archie chuckles and whispers, "Your expression when Ronnie and I told you we were a coven, and you're a witch. I wish I had a photo to frame."

"Well, what were you expecting? Do you know how crazy it sounded?" I snicker, but the laughter fades. "The night of Samhain changed my life forever. And Mabon." I stare at him with longing in my eyes, and he grasps my hand again.

"Gwynedd, I want you to know. No matter what happens to us, I will always care about you." The waiter arrives with our food as Archie leans back against the booth seat.

My cheeks inflame from the heat of his gaze. "Now that you're back in the classroom, are you happy with your decision?"

"Aye. I hadn't expected to jump into the pit of Summer Session, but Leslie insisted I take on the class with the hire of Nick Evans."

"I guess Leslie's a little miffed she had to take over as Interim Chair for one year?"

"More than a wee bit." Archie takes a bite of his beer-battered fish. "You're aware Trinity is leader of the Fellowship now? Truthfully, she always was. And it's well-earned."

"Yeah. Spence and Tanner told me after they bought my house. I found a picture of her in my mom's trunk, so I met with her at the shelter. Apparently, she lived with us when I was little. I don't remember her, but she shared some things about my mom, Leslie...and Agnes Pritchard."

"Hmph. Really? Leslie told me about your mum and being good friends. She never went into details, and I didn't press her on the matter. I knew Trinity lived with her for a while. Shane once mentioned Agnes Pritchard was in the coven around the time it formed in the mid-'60s. No one knows why she left."

I jab my kale salad with a fork. "I don't know what happened. But I'm gonna find out if I have to drag it out of Leslie using a pair of pliers."

"Well, she doesn't return until August, so you can keep them in your toolbox for now."

"I don't want to talk about the Fellowship now. Can we have a normal dinner without bringing them up?"

"Of course. Whatever you want, Gwynedd."

CHAPTER FIVE

A WITCH'S CONFESSION

THE NEXT MORNING, I spend a bit of time at Ronnie's sifting through my mother's trunk full of magic items—so many jars full of ground herbs. Did Mom think they would be useful after several decades? I should probably toss the gross contents but decide to store them and finish for the day.

Ronnie calls me from the kitchen. "Gwyn, tea is on the table!"

I close the lock and dash to join her while my tea is hot. I sit down and take a sip of my Earl Grey while my best friend hobbles around with a walking boot on her left foot.

She fills her mug with her death coffee and shuffles to her seat, spilling coffee on the way. "Shit."

"Sit down. I'll wipe it up," I say.

I dart to the sink and grab a damp sponge and share what Trinity told me about the coven's past regarding Samhain and the friendship Leslie, Agnes, and my mom had.

"That adds more questions than an explanation," Ronnie says. "What happened to your hands and knees?"

"Fell on the pavement. I plan to find answers somehow." I bend over to mop up the drips of coffee. "Last night was so awkward. After Nick Evans shared what I already suspected...that the journal is an old book of witchcraft and not a recipe book, he asked me out on a date."

Ronnie cackles and slaps the table. "You go, girl. Is he even forty?"

I toss the sponge into the sink and sit down to finish my tea. "No. He's thirty-eight. And literally, right after, Archie entered the Raven."

"You planned that poorly. Did he seem jealous?"

"He raised an eyebrow or two but said he has no hold over me. Dinner was fabulous. It was as if nothing ever happened. When he accompanied me to my car, he didn't even give me a peck on the cheek. He said goodnight and walked home."

"Archie must really want you back and doesn't want to fuck up. I haven't seen him since he visited me in the hospital. How is he?"

"He seems happy to be teaching. But his office was in a bit of disarray—books scattered, stacks of papers. Unusual for him."

"Well, he hasn't taught for a few years." Ronnie's phone vibrates. "It's a text from Derek." As she reads, her eyes bulge out like a Panic Pete toy, and she types frantically into her phone.

"What's wrong? Did something happen to Derek?" I ask.

Ronnie places her cell on the table. "Oh, he's OK. Can't say the same about Lindsey Hope."

The councilwoman had voted to side with the community on stopping the demolition of Mitchell Hall and supporting its transformation into a community center. But not without a spell of influence cast by the coven.

"What do you mean? Did she get kicked off the city council? Did she resign?"

My best friend gapes at me. "Derek says they found a body in the rubble of the fallen building on Main Street. A next of kin identified the body. It's Lindsey Hope!"

I gasp for air, but it's caught in my throat like a lump of cotton. I grab my neck and pull at the skin.

"Gwyn? What's wrong?" Ronnie jumps out of her chair and darts to me, her injured foot sliding behind.

"I...can't...breathe..." My face must be the shade of a pomegranate as my friend panics, grasping my shoulders and shaking my torso.

She smacks my back, and air enters my lungs with an airy hiss. "For the love of all the gods and goddesses, what's the matter with you?"

As my breathing stabilizes, I glance at my friend. "I think I may have killed Lindsey Hope."

Ronnie frowns. "What the hell are you rambling about? They found her body in the pile of concrete. Are you daft?"

"I've gotta tell you something, Ronnie." I raise my hand, and the amber glow emanates from my fingers.

She smirks as she falls into her chair. "Show me something I don't already know."

"I'm not summoning my energy, Ronnie. It happens when I lift my hand. I can't control it. I was walking past the building to get to my car. A light shone in my eyes, and I looked up at the building, raising my hand to block the glare. My witch energy emerged and my hand vibrated. Then the ground rumbled, and the building collapsed." I shake my hand, and the amber glow dissipates.

"Oh, shit. If she was on the roof, it doesn't mean you killed her. It was an accident. It wasn't your fault."

"I may not have murdered her, but it's definitely my fault." My eyelids close, and I imagine Lindsey Hope falling to her death as the building disintegrates into a pile of brick, concrete, and metal.

"You've gotta tell the others and get this under control," Ronnie says with angst in her voice.

I snap at my friend. "I am NOT going back to the coven. They used me. Well, Leslie at least. I can't go back to those conditions. Things have to change."

Ronnie falls back against her chair. "You've never spoken to me in that tone of voice."

"I'm sorry." She sticks her tongue out at me, and I chuckle. "You understand, right?"

"Yeah. Everyone understands why you left, and they support your decision. But they're family. They...we can still hope for your return. Without training from the coven, what will you do? You can't roam around with magic sparking at random."

"I'm hoping the translation of my mom's grimoire will help me figure that out. But I have knots in my stomach over Lindsey Hope—accident or not."

"Don't beat yourself up over it." Ronnie pats my hand.

I bite my lower lip as I recall the incident at Mitchell Hall. "It happened another time, too."

"What?" Ronnie straightens her back. "Did you implode another building?"

"Nooo. I melted part of the iron fence, trying to get into the Celestial Gardens. Did you know a special protection spell was cast? I wanted to see if the Seelie Fae children were there."

"Oh, my gods, I hope no one saw you. I was gonna tell you, eventually. The coven worried Audrey and whoever was controlling her might try to use the mound portal, so they cast a spell to keep out witches who aren't members of the Bearsden Coven."

"Oh." I stare at her with disappointment in my eyes.

Ronnie gets up from her chair. "I hate to kick you out, but I've gotta get to the café."

I pick up my teacup and place it in the sink. "Derek must be freaking out. I can't believe you're going back to work so soon."

"Well, he can flip out. Sitting in this house has tested my nerves. I can take it easy there as well as here. What's on your agenda?" She grabs her large tote and swings it over her shoulder.

"Lunch with Spence and Tanner at my house—their house. I haven't seen my old homestead since they moved in." I secretly hope they will consider training me. Tanner wasn't happy with Leslie withholding the existence of the Seelie and Unseelie Fae.

"Please, give them my best." She falls into the seat of her small SUV and frowns. "You're my best friend, but I can't keep this to myself for long. If you can't get your magic under control, you'll tell the Fellowship...or I will."

The harsh words from my friend are hard to swallow. If I'm careful, what could go wrong?

The mid-June temperatures have risen, and I'm forced to use the AC in my Prius. I'm not excited about the sticky, humid temps of the Delaware summer as the heat triggers my hot flashes. I park in front of my old colonial home and observe the improvements my friends Tanner Jones and Spence Huxley have made since moving in. They've replaced old scruffy shrubs in the front with crimson azaleas—my favorite.

It's strange to knock on the front door of the house where I raised my son and spent the last few years with my late husband. I scowl, thinking back on the last words I spoke to his spirit the night of Samhain, when I confronted him about his cheating with Cassandra Parnell. No one answers, but I notice a yellow Post-It note stuck to the door. Spence's handwriting says to come in if he doesn't answer the door, because he's upstairs in the magic room practicing the craft. So, I enter.

Tanner and Spence have done a wonderful job creating a welcoming ambiance in my old home. A mirror with hooks for coats and jackets hangs on the wall to the left of the door over a small mahogany table. I place my purse on a hook, slip off my sneakers, and head upstairs. On the way up, I notice the lack of creaking in the stairs. The young men fixed those as well. When I arrive at the top of the stairs, I observe only one room with the door closed.

I don't want to startle him, so I tap on the door lightly. "Spence? Are you in there?"

As I turn the doorknob, the muffled voices of Spence and Tanner ring out. "NO! Don't open the door!" A few items crash onto the floor with a whump, whump, whump, and Spence laughs.

Tanner yells through laughter, "Gwyn, wait for us in the kitchen. We'll be down in a couple of minutes." He speaks in a barely audible voice, "I told you we didn't have time for a quickie."

I release my grip on the knob and cringe. "OK. See you downstairs." They say things happen in threes, but I dodged this one.

I shuffle into the kitchen and lean against the new concrete countertop, admiring the light slate-gray walls. They contrast well with the newly painted white cabinets—Millennial and Zillennial touches to a '40s home. Soon after, heavy footsteps thump down the stairs in uneven patterns.

Spence dashes in and embraces me with his lanky arms. "It's been too long, sis." He's wearing an old, wrinkled F.A.P. t-shirt, the purple ones Leslie made them throw out. The purple stripe in his jet-black hair has faded.

"I missed you, too," I say.

He steps back, noticing the bandages on my hands and knees. "Woah, sis?"

How many times do I need to repeat the same damn story? "You know about the building imploding, I assume. I ran and tripped on the pavement, but I'll take these off tonight."

"I'm relieved you're OK, but I'm beginning to think there's a curse on you."

"You and me both. Are you attending summer courses?"

"Nah. Last year was so messed up. I needed a break. I'm gonna work in the garden and concentrate on the craft. Tanner said I should, and you know me. I never argue with my better half."

My brow crinkles. "Since when do you do what Tanner tells you?"

"He doesn't," Tanner says, entering the kitchen. "Hey, Gwyn. It's so awesome to see you." He gives me a peck on the cheek as he tucks in his dress shirt and messes with his brown hair. "Sorry, it took me a while to come down. I had to get cleaned up a bit." His eyes veer to my bandages, but he says nothing.

Spence snickers. "Are we gonna talk about it, or pretend you didn't almost crash in on us in the throes of passion?" The doorbell rings, and Spence flashes his palm. "Hold that answer. I'll be right back." He darts into the foyer.

"I love what you did to the kitchen, Tanner," I say. "A little modern for me, but it suits you both."

"Thanks. Spence chose the colors. He has a creative side."

Spence shuffles through the doorway. "Look who's here!"

Skye McGowen enters the kitchen wearing a tank top and jean shorts—her wavy, fire-red hair as bouncy as ever. My other Celtic Studies classmate from the fall semester and a Fellowship member approaches to give me a hug.

"It's so awesome to see you," she says in her husky voice. "I hope it's OK Spence invited me for lunch."

"Of course," I say. "I'm glad you came. It's like a mini-reunion."

She stares at my wounds with her sky-blue eyes. "What the fuck happened to you?"

"I'll explain later," I say, sighing.

Spence guffaws. "Skye, Gwyn almost barged in on Tanner and me doing it in the magic room. Would have been the second time she walked in on a couple doing it, too."

I grind my teeth. "Third actually. Second time this week, though."

"What?" Tanner laughs while getting food out of the fridge. "Who? And where?" Spence joins him to make sandwiches.

"I've gotta sit down for this." Skye pulls out a chair and settles in, crossing her legs.

"I went home early after I fell. It happened when the city building imploded." They gawk at me as I continue with my recollection. "There weren't any bandages in the bathroom, so I figured I'd check Tyler's nightstand."

Spence snickers. "Oh, my gods. You walked in on Tyler and Zoe? Wish I'd been there."

"It was so awkward. Zoe waved to me from the bed." I laugh and shake my head.

"Zoe cracks me up," Skye says. "I remember when you told us about the first time—the couple screwing in a study room in the basement of Stewart Hall."

Tanner places sandwiches and a bowl of chips on the table. "Oh, yeah. Spence told me. Well, you didn't know them, so not as awkward."

I stop laughing abruptly. "Actually, I knew the couple."

"You told us you didn't see their faces," Spence says, giving us our drinks.

"I didn't, but I found out later who they were." I finally sit down and load my plate with a cheese sandwich and chips.

"No, you don't," Skye says. "You can't tell us you know who they were and end the convo."

"Exactly," Spence says with a mouth full of PB & J. "We're not gonna stop until you do. Spill the tea."

I glance at Tanner's midnight-blue eyes and press my lips together.

"I think Gwyn would rather keep that to herself, dude," Tanner says.

"Not a chance," Skye says, chewing. "Spill it." She leans toward Spence, and the two of them stare me down.

"Oh, fine." I hold my breath for a bit before the air escapes in a puff of *I-give-up*. "It was Archie."

"And Courtney?" Spence exclaims with bug eyes.

"Of course, it was Courtney. Who else?" Skye says.

"Maybe we should change the subject," Tanner says. He gets up from the table and retrieves the bag of chips. "Are things going OK?"

"Not exactly. I found a letter from my mom in the trunk, but she placed a charm on it. My skills are too weak to break it, and I think it's connected to my ancestral witch past, so no one else can either." My eyes circle the table. "I need to train again."

Tanner leans back in his seat while Spence and Skye lock their eyes. All three of them say in unison, "Nope. Not happening."

"Seriously, you're suggesting we train you?" Tanner asks.

"Dr. Hughes would expel all of us in a heartbeat." Spence crosses his arms and flutters his eyelashes. "We love you, but yikes. The coven Elder would kick us out without a second thought."

"I'm sorry. I shouldn't have hinted at the possibility." My eyes fall to the floor.

"We're sorry, Gwyn." Skye leans her elbows on the table. "This wouldn't be an issue if you returned to the coven."

I sit back, observing the hopeful expressions on their faces. "I can't. If I go back now, groveling, Leslie will hold it over my head forever. I'll never have a say in the coven. Don't worry about me. I'll figure something out. Forget about it."

We have a great time reminiscing while we finish our lunch, and I regret not doing it sooner. Spence tells us to leave our plates on the table, and we all go to the front door.

"It was great seeing you all. Let's do it again," I say.

Spence kisses Tanner. "Have a productive afternoon, hon." He gives Skye and me a hug goodbye. "Wait...wait just a minute." He cocks his head and grimaces. "Archie has a Horned God tattoo on his ass?"

CHAPTER SIX

TRYING NEW THINGS

"Your hands and knees are healing well." Tyler finishes the last bite of the veggie omelet I cooked and sets his plate in the dishwasher.

"Yeah, I had to remove the bandages," I say, wiggling my fingers. "I couldn't get anything done with them on."

He rushes to the bathroom to brush his teeth and returns, grabbing his car keys off the hook. "What are you doing today?"

"Insurance agency paperwork in the morning and the Mystic Sage in the afternoon. Tyler, I should start looking for a small place for myself—an apartment, condo, maybe a townhome. You deserve to be on your own again. I appreciate your concern and supporting me through this horrible year and a half, but I need to settle into a life of my own, too." I touch the side of his handsome face. "So, you can have yours."

Tyler chuckles. "You're right. This is because you walked in on me and Zoe."

"Of course, I'm right. I'm the mom. Your relationship with Zoe is only part of the equation. Now get to work. And I'll do the same."

"Have a good day, Mom." He kisses me on the forehead and heads to his software development job.

After cleaning the kitchen and taking a shower, I set up my laptop on the kitchen table to work. I search for news about the building's implosion and discover the city has closed Main Street to through traffic while construction crews continue to remove the rubble. No mention of Lindsey Hope yet.

Don't Stop Believin' plays on my cell, and the vibration causes it to shuffle across the table. It's Nick Evans. "Hello."

"Hi, Gwyn," he says. "I've got more of the family journal translated. Thought you'd like to have dinner and go over my findings. I love the food at the Raven Pub. Reminds me of the pubs in Wales. Would six o'clock work for you?"

"Sure," I say with a pound of trepidation. "I'll meet you there."

"I can't wait. And Gwyn?" he asks with confidence in his tenor voice. "Remember, it's only dinner."

After a quick lunch, I change my clothes for work and dinner. I opt for skinny jeans, my favorite teal V-neck blouse, and heeled sandals—nice but not too sexy. As I drive up University Avenue, the street that runs parallel to Main Street, I hope to find a spot in the parking lot behind Shane's store. I have to pay when I arrive, but what other choice do I have? I walk through the opening between the Mystic Sage and the camera shop.

Main Street is a mess. Front-loaders scoop up chunks of concrete and dump the ruins into trucks. Construction workers and firefighters sift through the pieces of the city parking building, most likely searching for more bodies. As I rub the center of my left palm, I hope they don't find anyone else in the remains. I check the time on my cell phone and find I've only got a couple of minutes before my shift starts.

I enter the store with a ding and notice Jeff cleaning up the herb jars. "Hi. Busy day? Any rude shoppers?"

"Hi, Gwyn," he says sporting a somber face. "No. Shane got a shipment in, and I'm putting out new stock."

"Stop. Your shift is over. I'll take care of it."

"Thanks. I ran out of time." Jeff's cell phone rings. "Excuse me. I need to answer this."

He strolls into the crystals room and talks while I set my purse behind the counter. His voice becomes agitated, as if he's arguing with the caller. I try not to eavesdrop. Instead, I concentrate on setting out the new shipment.

Jeff ambles back into the front of the store, scowling. "Sorry. I hope you didn't hear any of that."

"No. I don't eavesdrop, but the other caller sounded angry. Are you OK?"

"She's always yelling at me. Telling me what to do. I hoped to get away from it by going to college."

"Your mom? I hope you don't mind me prying?" I ask.

"Nah," he says. "My aunt. She raised me when my parents died, so she's overprotective."

"Give her some slack," I say. "We mom types can be that way. She's only showing she cares."

Jeff's frown morphs into a cheery grin. "Thanks. You must be a great mom."

"Hmph. You'll have to ask my son, Tyler. He may not agree," I say.

He laughs, which appears to be a rarity with his demeanor. "I hoped attending college two hours away would release me from her clutches, but it's only gotten worse. She..."

"She what?" I ask with those dreaded elevens between my eyes.

Jeff averts his eyes. "Nothing. I've gotta get going. I'm late for a study group for my chemistry lab."

"Enjoy your afternoon. Get some studying done."

"I will. Thanks for the pep talk. See ya later." Jeff exits the store, and for a moment, I relish in my good deed for the day.

I continue stocking the shelves of herb jars, which takes about twenty minutes, and park my butt on the stool behind the counter for the next few hours as shoppers come and go. Occasionally, the store is so quiet the hum of the large machinery up the street breaks through the glass front, reminding me of my magic failure.

The door dings, and I jump, turning my attention to the lone customer. It's Agnes Pritchard, the local "out" witch. I've not seen her since right before the Winter Solstice Ceremony. She hinted she knew about the Host of the Unforgiven Dead, buying extra herbs to produce stronger protection spells, I assume. As she heads straight for the herbs, she doesn't notice me behind the counter.

Agnes appears irritated as she scoffs at the jars I've arranged. After examining a few of the herb-filled containers, she places them back on the shelf in a huff. She approaches me in her long black skirt and short-sleeved blouse, exposing the pagan tattoos on her wrinkled arms. Her long salt and pepper hair covers half her face until she gazes up at me with pale-gray eyes. As her hair falls back, she purses her lips and squints at me, giving me a once-over.

"Hmph. You're back in the store," she says.

"Yup. Can I help you, Ms. Pritchard?" I ask.

Agnes scowls. "I doubt it. Did you rearrange the jars?"

"Yeah, I did. Shane received a new shipment, and I had to make room for the extras."

She scowls again and pushes the long bangs aside, revealing her entire face to me for the first time. Although her skin has the wrinkles of an octogenarian who's spent a good deal of time in the sun, the remnants of an attractive young woman with a slender nose peek through. "Well, you made a fucking awful mess of it. I couldn't find anything."

"I'm sorry?" What made her so bitter and grumbly? Does it have anything to do with my mom and Leslie?

Agnes grimaces and steps toward the entry door, stopping for a moment. She turns around and glares at me. "I never got a good look at you before. You remind me of someone I used to know. Hmph."

She exits the store, and the door slams with a clank of the bamboo chimes. Soon after, Shane arrives wearing his standard Hawaiian-print shirt, baggy cargo shorts, and sandals.

"Thanks for manning the ship alone this afternoon. Any issues?" he asks.

"Only one. Ms. Pritchard stopped in to buy herbs, but my organizational skills don't suit her. I guess she doesn't like change."

"No. She does not." Shane shoves his hands in his back pockets as I walk around the counter to join him. He observes my heeled sandals, and a gleeful grin peeks through his whiskers. "Gotta date?"

"Sort of. I'm meeting the new Celtic Studies professor for dinner to discuss the translations of my mom's grimoire. I'm hoping to find some answers."

Shane twirls strands of his beard around a finger. "Do you think that's wise, Gwyn?"

"Probably not, but what other choice do I have? I told him it was a family collectible. It's not a lie."

"I know it's not my place, but as your friend, I'm gonna give you a piece of advice. Be careful of those you confide in. It could come back to bite you in the rump." He opens his mouth and bites into the air.

I laugh at his southern way. "I'll keep it in mind." As I grab my purse and throw it over my shoulder, the hum of the trucks in the distance invades the sanctuary of the Mystic Sage. "Shane, you mentioned a while back Agnes used to belong to the coven but left. And Leslie never said why?"

"That's correct. Whenever I brought up the idea of Agnes joining the coven again, Leslie chopped my head off like a cleaver on a fresh slab of beef."

"Thanks for the vivid description." I blink a few times. "Trinity shared something with me. She said Leslie, Agnes, and my mom were friends."

"Interesting. Isn't it, darling?" he asks.

"Sure is." I pull the door open and stop. "Has Agnes ever had apprentices? Teach the craft on her own?"

"Oh, I don't rightly know, but I doubt it. She's a hedge witch and keeps to herself."

"What's a hedge witch? Sounds like she gardens."

"Agnes practices witchcraft in solitary with a daily routine and connects with plants and the natural world. The name comes from the days of the wise women who lived outside the villages beyond the hedge." His eyes open wide. "If you're thinking...what I think you're thinking, I don't wanna know."

I chuckle. "Bye, Shane. See you on Saturday."

As I stroll down Main Street for dinner, I pass by the scene of my crime and guilt takes a sharp bite out of my gut. I stop and observe the responders as they continue sifting through the rubble. A shudder travels through my body, shaking me to my core. I can't let this happen again or Ronnie will tell the coven.

When I arrive at the Raven Pub with its two-story Victorian wrap-around porch and three-story turret, I notice Nick waiting for me on the porch outside the double doors. He's wearing Levi jeans, a tight-fitting polo shirt, and Vans sneakers. He lifts his head in my direction and removes his dark sunglasses.

I wave as I climb the steps of the porch. "You didn't have to wait for me out here? It's so hot today."

"Eh, it's nice out. You look great." He gestures toward the double wooden doors. "After you?"

Wednesday evening has fewer crowds, and the hostess gives us a choice of seats. We ask for a booth in the back room. I can't stand eating at a table in the room where the stuffed raven glares at you from behind the display glass. The aroma of fresh popcorn permeates as usual. I love Ronnie's bright and modern vegetarian restaurant, but the Raven has a vintage charm with its dark-stained wooden walls and booths. The waitress brings our water and takes our order, leaving us with an awkwardness in the air. When we finally speak, we both talk at the same time.

Nick laughs. "Please, you go first."

"I was going to ask where you're from originally. Obviously, not Wales," I say.

"No, but from a very Welsh area. I grew up in Bryn Mawr, Pennsylvania. The strange spelling of the city's name fascinated me as a kid. In high school, I read everything I could find about Wales and the language. When I finished my undergraduate degree, I went to Wales for my master's and doctorate. I studied at Cardiff University but spent a lot of time traveling to the National Library of Wales in Aberystwyth."

"I went to school right here at DUB. And I took my first grad course last fall after thirty years. I'm going halftime in the fall—working on a master's in public relations. I've never even visited Wales. My parents said I had a great-aunt living there, but I've never met her. She's probably gone by now." I tap morse code for *I'm-drowning-in-small-talk* on my water glass.

Nick leans over the table. "Gwyn, it's only dinner." He gazes at me with dark-brown eyes, rich like espresso.

"I'm still uncomfortable with it. What could you possibly find attractive? I've got laugh lines and crow's feet."

He leans back against the booth and grins. "I don't know exactly. Your Welsh heritage, similar interests in antiquarian books, the way you carry yourself. You have so much confidence."

"Good thing you didn't meet me a year ago." I chuckle and knead my hands. "Let's just say a lot happened this past year."

"Well, you seem to be handling things well now. And you obviously don't realize how sexy you are," he says with alluring eyes.

"Are you trying to embarrass me on purpose?" I ask.

Nick crouches over the table again and whispers, "Is it working?"

I stare him down. "You're quite the smartass yourself, aren't you?"

"So, my mom keeps telling me. And before you say anything about being old enough to be my mom, you're not. My mom's in her early 70s."

"Well, she raised an intelligent, handsome man. Even if he's a smartass." I examine his youthful, handsome face. "Still, what else do we have in common? Like our tastes in music, for instance. I bet we don't even listen to the same type."

"Do you listen to White Stripes? Strokes?" He chuckles when I shake my head. "Radiohead? You've got to know Radiohead."

"I've listened to Radiohead." He's nerdy, but I love his humor. At the least, I've made a new friend—an Unremarkable friend.

"See, I'm sure there's more we have in common, too."

Our dinner arrives, and we discuss his time in Wales while we eat. But we haven't discussed the translations of my mom's grimoire.

"You forgot to show me what you found in the old tome," I say.

"Oh, I didn't forget." He takes the last bite of his medium-rare steak. "I was in such a rush to get here, I forgot to carry my tablet with me. My apartment is down the street a bit. I rent a place over the Roots of the Earth, the store that sells artsy pottery, clothes, and jewelry."

"I've bought earrings there." It's also across the street from the pile of rubble from the city parking building. I stick a fork into my kale and goat cheese salad.

"But it's a bit of a mess in front. The collapse of the building left dust and bits of concrete everywhere."

"I saw coming here." It's like Karma is spying on me, waiting for an opportune time to strike me down.

He frowns. "Yeah. Rumor is a city councilwoman died when the building disintegrated."

I jab my salad again and insert the last of my healthy greens. I swallow hard. "Can we change the subject?"

"I'm sorry. We can go to my apartment, and I can show you what I found. If that's OK with you?"

"Sure. And I won't be far from my car."

"Excellent." The young professor tosses his napkin. "Waitress? Can I have the check, please?"

We stroll up Main Street for about ten minutes until we arrive at the Roots of the Earth specialty shop. I follow Nick behind the store to a set of stairs that lead to his apartment door. It's a roomy one-bedroom apartment, and I'm guessing it's quiet at night. Better than renting above a bar. A black modern sofa sits against one wall with stacks of half-open books. He has a lamp sitting on a large box.

"You'll have to excuse the mess," he says. "I only moved in two weeks ago and have a lot of unpacking to do."

"It takes time to get organized," I say. "I sold my house in March and moved in with my son, Tyler. I've got a ton of stuff packed away in storage at a friend's house until I figure out where I'm going to live."

"Oh, that was nice of them, but selling must have been hard." Nick's dark eyes draw together.

"My husband passed away over a year ago. Selling the house was the best decision I ever made. Losing my husband was challenging, but I'm managing well." If you discount the *I-can't-control-my-magic* issue. "You had to show me something in the journal?"

"Oh, yeah. Over here. It's on my coffee table." He sits down and lifts a few papers, revealing the tome. "Please, sit down. I don't bite."

I chuckle and sit beside him. "What did you find?"

"It wasn't the translations. Every couple of pages there are new entries and directions for what appear to be spells for witchcraft. That's not the interesting part." Nick opens my mom's grimoire to the first page. "Notice the script. The antiquated use of a quill with ink. Lots of inkblots on the page where it leaked or dropped." He flips a bunch of pages and stops. "Now examine the handwriting on this page. The script has different turns on the rounded letters. It changes like this quite a few times." He flips to my mother's entries. "Don't you think this is odd?"

"What's strange about it?" I ask, staring at my mom's handwriting.

"The ink. You don't find something unusual about it?"

I shrug and avert my gaze. "You're the academic researcher."

Nick flips to the first page, gestures to the inked words, and flips back to the page with my mom's script. "Notice anything now? It's modern ink, like an old ballpoint pen. The other page entries were written using a quill."

"What are you suggesting?" I ask, knowing damn well what he's getting at.

"Not only were the entries written by different people but also during different time periods. The last few…I'm guessing the '50s or '60s." He closes the tome and places it on the table. "There's more going on with this journal than either of us imagined. I'm so stoked to complete the translations and discover its secrets."

"Well, good luck," I say. "Remember, it is a collectible my family owned. Who knows where it came from? I was hoping for family recipes."

Nick tilts his head and leans into me, grinning. The closeness makes me uncomfortable, so I push off the sofa. "I should get going. Thank you so much for the time you've spent on this journal. And thanks for dinner. I had a great time."

He stands and follows me to the door. "See…I told you we'd get along fabulous. I'd like to kiss you before you go, but I didn't want to presume."

"I guess it's OK," I say, smiling coyly.

"And if I kiss you and it feels like you're kissing your…a family member, then we'll know it wasn't meant to be." He bends to kiss me, but in this first awkward attempt, he can't quite find my mouth. "I'm sorry…I haven't done this in a while."

"I haven't either," I say, blushing like a schoolgirl.

"Believe it or not, I don't date much. Women find me a little nerdy, being an academic." Nick locks his dark eyes on mine and leans into me. This time, he finds my mouth and presses his lips against mine. They're soft and warm. I like it, so I press back. He smiles as he pulls away. "Works for me."

My face flushes. "I didn't mind it either. I guess I'll talk to you when you've completed more translations?"

"Yeah. Or sooner, if that's cool with you?" he asks.

"Sure," I say, smiling. "Why not?"

Nick straightens his back with a grin of accomplishment. "Awesome. I'll call you later this week."

"Thank you for a lovely evening, Nick," I say.

"You're welcome, Ms. Crowther." He peers down at me and snickers.

On the stroll back to my car, I touch my lips with my fingers, recalling Nick's kiss. Dating two men at once is outside my comfort zone, but Ronnie's advice hit the nail on the head. I have to spread my wings and keep my options open. I still have a strong desire for Archie, but what if my emotions were all caught up in the magic or the newness of my first man after losing my cheating husband? And Nick is an Unremarkable. How awesome would it be to have a bit of normalcy in my life, especially after this past year?

When I arrive at my Prius, only a few cars dot the parking lot. As I touch the handle, the car beeps to unlock, but I'm distracted by a flashing light from the roof of the Mystic Sage building. I glance up, blocking the light with my right hand. My witch energy radiates from my fingertips as my hand vibrates, slithering like snakes until it attaches to the body of a shiny, black Porsche three spots away. The top of the luxury car turns orange like molten lava and melts into the body of the car. I gasp and pull my hands until the amber glow springs back at me like a rubber band.

A quick glance around the parking lot confirms no one has observed my inadvertent destruction, but what do I do? A responsible person calls the police and reports the damage. But what the hell would I tell them? "I'm sorry. It was an accident. I couldn't control my magic and liquified the roof of the car."

I jump into the car seat, start my Prius, and drive off with my hands glued to the steering wheel and shaking uncontrollably. If the police find out, they'll arrest me for hit and run. Strike that—*hot magic and run.*

Chapter Seven

DESPERATELY SEEKING A TEACHER

As I LIE ON the sofa bed, I peruse my social media for any post referencing *the incident* in the city parking lot behind the Mystic Sage. It's been three days. You'd think something would show up by now. And bingo. I find an article in the Wilmington Daily News. Authorities continue to investigate the "vandalism in the parking lot on University Avenue and have no explanations for how the roof of a Porsche could have collapsed into the body of the car. No witnesses have come forward." I drop my phone onto my stomach.

Tyler's bedroom door opens, and he comes out in a t-shirt and underwear, rubbing his eyes. "Morning, Mom. I'm surprised you're in bed at 9:00 a.m."

"Yeah. I've been awake for a while, reading my email and the local news." I gather my messy hair and smooth it out.

"Oh, yeah. I meant to ask you if you heard about the vandalism behind the Mystic Sage." My son walks into the kitchen and pulls out a pan. "It's really strange. Investigators say it looks like someone used a blowtorch or something similar to melt the metal of the roof. Who would do that?"

I stare up at the dingy-white ceiling above the sofa and lie through my teeth. "I don't know, but I need to get ready for work. Shane expects me at ten."

"Why don't I make breakfast while you shower?" he says while removing eggs and spinach from the fridge. "You've cooked breakfast almost every morning since you moved in."

"Sure. I appreciate it, dear." As I sit up, my lower back pinches, reminding me I forgot to stretch. I pull my knees to my chest, groaning as I count to thirty.

Tyler grimaces. "I wish you would let me sleep on the sofa bed a few nights, at least until your back has healed from the fall."

"It's not a permanent solution, and I don't have time to discuss it now." I roll off, arch my back, and head into the bathroom for a quick shower. When I'm finished, I throw on a V-neck tee and jeans and eat breakfast. My son's omelet hits the spot. "Thank you, dear. Will you see Zoe tonight?"

"Yeah, but I'm going to her apartment." He glares at me as he flips his egg.

I chuckle. "It may take me a while, but I'm gonna search for an apartment or a room near campus. It would be great to walk to school in the fall."

"I feel like I'm pushing you out."

"This was supposed to be temporary. You don't need to worry about me anymore. I'm getting along just fine." Except for destroying buildings and cars at random, I'm good?

Tyler plops into his chair and places his eggs on the table. "Have a great day, Mom."

"Bye, dear," I say.

I grab my purse and leave for the Mystic Sage. It's a near-perfect June day for Delaware with low humidity and temps in the upper 70s. When I park, I notice the damaged Porsche is gone and knots form in my stomach. I can't go on like this. Someone might notice the next time I screw up. How will I explain the oddity?

Shane is packing a paper bag with items when I enter the store. The bright red and yellow Hawaiian print shirt he's wearing nearly blinds me.

"Good morning! What are you doing?" I ask.

"Good morning to you, too, Gwyn," he replies. "Agnes Pritchard phoned in an order. I don't mind delivering to her, but she never even gives me a *how-do-you-do* for driving all the way out to her farm."

My eyebrows leap as an idea lights up like a bulb in my head. "I've still got my purse on my shoulder. Why don't I deliver the items to her? I can grab the bag and drive it over to her right now?"

"I know why you're volunteering. It's fine by me, but you'll get nowhere with her. She won't even as much as spit in your direction." He guffaws as he shakes a finger. "Actually, she might."

"I'll take my chances." I pick up the paper bag and turn toward the door. "You don't think this is a good idea, do you?"

"You must discover your own path," he says. "But you'll need her address, yes?"

"Oh, yeah," I say as I hand him my phone. "Can you type in the address to Google Maps?"

"Certainly. Knock on her front door and leave the bag. She's not likely to open the door. But you can try," he says, passing me my cell. "I wish you all the luck of the gods."

"Thanks, Shane. And thank you for not trying to talk me out of it."

He shoves his hands in his back pockets. "If I've learned anything about you, I know you're gonna do what you will. And don't worry. I won't share this with the coven."

I wave goodbye and exit the store. The directions take me to the outskirts of Bearsden, where the town becomes less dense and transitions to farmland near the Maryland border. The GPS tells me to turn right. Overgrown fields of grass and wildflowers blanket both sides of the old gravel road, obscuring the house most of the way.

I park my Prius in front of the old clapboard farmhouse with a small porch. The house desperately calls out for tender loving care. Dingy-gray paint chips flap in the June breeze, breaking off and falling to the scruffy shrubs below. The red metal roof has faded, and patches of rust have formed a starry pattern. I imagine a maze of buckets scattered on the floors of the upstairs bedrooms, collecting water every time it rains.

As I get out of my car, I notice chickens running around freely in the distance between an old, dilapidated chicken coop and a small barn that's seen better days. I recognize the woods near North Basin Creek Park. There's a bog in there. I bet the gnats and mosquitoes swarm here in July and August. I grab the bag of witch supplies and step up the creaky, worn wooden steps of the porch, knocking on the faded purple front door with a rat-a-tat-tat. No one answers, so I knock using a heavy hand.

"Ms. Pritchard? Are you home? It's Gwynedd from the Mystic Sage." A curtain moves in a window to the left of the front door, and half a wrinkled face peeks out and disappears. "I have your delivery."

Agnes shouts with a gravelly voice from the other side of the door. "Leave it on the porch and go."

"Ms. Pritchard, I would really like to talk to you. Can I come in for a minute?" I wait for a bit and listen to the crickets chirping.

"Hmph. I'll come back another time when you feel like having company."

I set the paper bag full of herbs, candles, and crushed crystals onto the porch floor and return to my car. The door creaks open. I turn around, hoping to catch her, but she's grabbed the bag and shut the door in the time you could say *catch-the-witch*.

On the way back to the Mystic Sage, my cell phone rings over my car speakers. Archie's name appears on the dashboard screen. "Hello."

"Good afternoon," he says, filling my Prius with a light Scottish brogue. "I hope you're enjoying this glorious day full of sunshine."

"I dropped off a Mystic Sage delivery to Agnes Pritchard. She wouldn't even open the door, so I'm driving back to the store." The AC in the car cools my frustration.

"I'm not surprised. She's more of a hermit. I know it's short notice, but would you like to have dinner with me tonight?" he asks.

"Sure. Where do you want to meet?" I ask.

"I hoped you would come here to my house." Archie hesitates. "Are you comfortable eating here? We could go out again if you like, but the loud music in most of the Bearsden restaurants makes it difficult to hold a conversation without shouting like a drunk."

"That sounds fine. I finish work around six."

"Perfect. See you in a few hours."

I arrive at the Mystic Sage parking lot about the time the phone call ends and rush back to the store. As I enter, a sense of defeat overwhelms me. I'm in deep shit if I can't convince Agnes to train me.

Shane walks in from the crystals room as I store my purse behind the counter. "How was Agnes? Was she happy with the merchandise I sent?"

"I don't know," I say, exhaling. "She wouldn't even open the damn door to talk to me. It's not like she doesn't know me."

"It's different when she comes to the store. You invaded her privacy by going to her home, and I'm sure she'll chew me out like bubblegum and spit the next time she shops. Agnes doesn't get close to anyone I know. I'm probably the closest to a friend she has, and I'm only a delivery boy to her—well, delivery old man," he says with a belly laugh.

I chuckle. "Well, I'm not giving up. I can be stubborn, too."

"I'm not touching that one, darling," Shane says.

The door dings, and Jeff enters with the gloom of doom on his face. "Hi, Gwyn. Hi, Shane."

"Why so glum, Jeff? Did you get a poor grade on an exam?" I ask.

"No. Family stuff. Don't worry about it," he says. "Shane, I came early like you asked to help stock the shelves."

"Thank you, Jeffrey. I've never had such a dedicated undergrad work for me. You're always on time and do anything I ask." Shane pats him on the back. "If you ever need an ear to vent, you can bend mine anytime."

"Goes for me, too," I say.

"Thanks for being so supportive." He grimaces at Shane. "Can you call me Jeff? My aunt calls me Jeffrey whenever she's angry."

"Of course," Shane says. "I'm sorry I caused you any discomfort. Jeff, it is."

The hippie and the undergrad go to the storage room while I spend the afternoon behind the cash register or dusting the shelves. My heart aches for Jeff. His aunt sounds like a supreme bitch—not the motherly type. What a horrible childhood he must have had.

A sense of familiarity rises from the pit of my stomach when I park my car in front of Archie's cottage home with the four-window dormer and brownstone facade. I lock my Prius with a beep-beep and saunter up the flagstone walkway to the door. It's open, so instinctively, I grab the screen door handle but remove my hand and tap instead. As I wait for him to come, I remember the key to his house still hangs on a DUB keychain in the zippered pouch of my purse. I should have returned it.

Archie approaches sporting a cheerful grin and pushes on the screen. "Why are you waiting on the stoop? You know you can come right in."

"Walking in without knocking didn't seem right." He's so damn handsome. Always at ease in his home, he's wearing jeans and a black t-shirt.

"Nonsense. Come in. I'm finishing up dinner. Make yourself comfortable."

As I slip off my sandals, I drop my purse next to his oak hall tree and stroll over to the fireplace. I examine the painting of the young woman with chestnut hair and hazel eyes who resembles me. Reaching toward the coming storm of dismal clouds, she stands in a field of wildflowers while the winds clutch the finger-like strands of her hair. Archie kissed me in front of this painting after I commented on the likeness.

I search for the painter's name in the bottom right corner. I'd not checked before, but it doesn't matter—no artist's signature. Out of the corner of my eyes, a faint shimmer of light appears to emanate from the canvas—must be the sunrays sneaking through a window.

"The likeness still amazes me," he says.

I flinch. "Damn, Archie. Stop sneaking up on me."

"I promise you I was not sneaking. I'm in my bare feet, after all."

"If you weren't so meticulous about fixing the creaks in the wooden floors, I'd have a clue you were coming."

He leans into me and chuckles. "Would you like to eat dinner, or would you prefer to argue about my apparent crafty behavior?"

I stare up at him and blink. "Do you really think you can win me over with snark?"

"It worked before." He moves closer and strokes my cheek. "Of course not. I hope you don't mind eating in the kitchen. I thought it'd be more informal—intimate."

My heart flutters as his finger titillates my skin. "Sure. I loved eating in there."

I follow Archie to the table, and he pulls out a chair for me. While I get comfortable, he retrieves the vegetable lasagna from the stove. I missed his cooking and the conversations we had here. And the sex—I chuckle to myself.

"You find my lasagna comical, do you?" he asks.

"No. I remembered something that happened in here." My face flushes, and I fan myself with a paper napkin. Or is the memory of fucking in the kitchen chair raising my temperature? "The heat in here is triggering a hot flash."

Archie stares at me with lascivious eyes. "Would you like to move into the dining room?"

"No. I'll be OK in a minute." I peer up at him with rosy cheeks as I continue to wave the napkin. "The kitchen does heat up a bit when you...cook."

"Aye, it certainly does." As he places a serving of lasagna on each of our plates, his eyes narrow. "We are talking about my cooking?"

I avert my eyes and snicker. We have a wonderful chat about the planned renovations on Mitchell Hall to transform the old mansion into a community center. And I recall the memory of the Seelie Fae children. What if they appear during the renovations?

How can the city proceed with the mound there? What is the coven's plan?

"Ronnie told me about the protection spell on the gardens. I tried to enter and ran into an invisible wall." I glare at him as I shove a bite of lasagna into my mouth.

"It wasn't to keep you out." He stops slicing into his lasagna and peers at me. "We needed to preserve the area in case Audrey returns. Connecting exclusivity of the spell to the coven ensures the safety of the space. Why did you want to go in there?"

"I wanted to see if the Seelie Fae children would appear," I say. "Ask them about my mother."

"It's probably best to limit your contact with them. And the mound portal. But you know the solution to gain access." He finishes the last morsel on his plate.

I roll my eyes at him. "I'm not returning to the coven. Rules have to change for me to return. And I'm sure Dr. Leslie Hughes won't approve of them."

"Hmph. One never knows about the future." Archie collects our dinner plates and sets them on the counter. "Why don't you go into the living room, and I'll put away the food."

When I enter, the ticking of that annoying mantle clock grates at my ears. I shuffle over to the Celtic weapons display on the wall and examine the flintlock pistols, swords, and dirks. I notice him entering the room but turn my interest back to the historical wall of violence.

"It's hard to imagine men, and some women, defending them-selves with these weapons," I say. "Then I remember stabbing the Host of the Unforgiven Dead to save Ronnie."

Archie shifts closer to me. "There's no telling what a person will do to save the ones they love." He gazes down at me, and his magnetic eyes capture mine in a moment of silent yearning.

My heart thumps in my chest, reminding me how much I still love this man. I turn my head toward the dirks. "Your family heirloom rests safely in my mom's trunk at Ronnie's. I couldn't store it in Tyler's apartment."

"It's not providing you much protection there." He places an index finger under my chin, barely stroking my flush skin. "I want you so badly. But I know the physical intimacy would confuse you while you're figuring things out."

"One kiss would be OK," I say.

"If I kissed you after these months apart, I wouldn't be able to stop." His eyes burn with the lust of a chaste man. "Gwynedd, I wish I could go back and change things—be more forthcoming about my past. Part of me knew you'd not want a man who tossed the feelings of a woman around like a football, knowing your husband treated you so badly. I meant it when I said I want to be a better man—a better witch. And I owe that to you."

I stare at his transparent eyes, and they shine with sincerity. "I believe you."

"Phew," he says. "What would you like to do? Chat more? Play some checkers?"

"Sure. A few games of checkers would be fun." As I throw my right hand up, the amber glow of my witch energy emerges from my fingertips, and I pull it back.

Archie takes my hand in his and rubs the skin. "What is this? I sense this was not intentional."

"No. Since I stopped training, I've lost many of my skills." I wrestle with telling him the truth about the collapse of the city building—that it's my fault. "And a couple of weeks ago, I lost control of my witch energy."

He continues to stroke the back of my hand. "You need to start instruction again."

"Don't you think I know that?" I yank my hand from the warmth of his palms. "I can't train with anyone in the coven. What am I supposed to do?"

"Aye. It's against the Regional Book of Shadows. If any of us trained you, Leslie and Trinity would expel us from the coven."

"Ronnie reminded me of the coven's little rule. Don't worry about me. I'm sure the problem with my witch energy will pass." Who am I kidding? I need help. "I'm thinking of asking Agnes Pritchard to train me."

"Gwyn, I don't think that's a good idea. That old hedge witch practices in solitary. But I won't try to talk you out of it. I'd be wasting my time."

The mantle clock dings 8:30 p.m., and I flinch. "Actually, I'm going to pass on checkers. I should get going. As usual, dinner was fabulous. I'd love to reciprocate, but Tyler's apartment is a tad small."

"Why don't I walk you to your car?" he asks.

I slip on my sandals and grab my purse from the hall tree, and we stroll to my car. After I settle into the driver's seat of my Prius, I push the button to lower my window. "Thanks again for dinner."

"I would love to do it again soon, but I realize you may have other commitments." Archie raises a corner of his mouth.

My heart sinks since I know what he's inferring. "I'll let you know when I'm free."

"Before you go, I want to say something." He rests his arms on the rim of the car window and stares into my eyes. "If you need anything, want anything...my allegiances go beyond the rules of a coven."

I gaze at his gorgeous face, and my face flushes. "Goodnight, Archie."

"Sleep well, Gwynedd." He strokes the tip of my chin and walks back toward his house.

I head for home with the AC blasting, thinking about Agnes Pritchard. She better want company the next time I visit. Ready or not, I'm coming, Agnes.

Chapter Eight

How to Snag a Hedge Witch

"So, how was dinner at Archie's?" Ronnie hobbles on her foot brace to her kitchen table with a cup of her death coffee. "The water in the teakettle should be hot in a couple of minutes."

"Thanks, Ronnie. I could have done that." While I wait for the whistle to blow, I grab an Earl Grey tea bag from the cabinet. It's relaxing to spend a few minutes with my friend on a Saturday morning like I used to. "Dinner was fabulous, as usual. Archie's trying to make amends, I think. But the whole *he-slept-with-the-witches-he-recruited* thing hangs out there like a..."

"Big dick?" The whistle on the tea kettle blows, and she cracks up. "On cue!"

"Oh, my gods, Ronnie. I've never talked about the size of his...package." Steam rises like a mini-tornado as I pour the boiling water into my teacup. My back muscle pinches as I sit down, and I rub the area.

"I know, but I'm all ears. Your back hasn't healed from the fall yet?"

"No. I was already aching there. The fall exacerbated it. It sucks to get old, friend."

"I hear ya. Speaking of dicks, have you seen Mr. New Professor's royal gems yet?" she asks with wide eyes.

"For fuck's sake," I say. "No. Dating two men at once already takes me out of my comfort zone. Sleeping with two at the same time is more than I can handle. Besides, Archie won't even kiss me. He's afraid he won't be able to control himself."

Ronnie snickers. "Well, that's probably true if he hasn't seen anyone since the two of you took a break. But what about Nick?" Her crimson eyebrows jiggle like Groucho Marx.

"He kissed me." I sip my tea. "At first, his attempt was awkward, but the second try was...an improvement."

She takes a sip of her coffee. "I think it's a good idea you're giving this man a chance. Don't worry about the age gap. If he doesn't care, why should you? You know how much I like Archie, but maybe he was a rebound. Nick could be a better match. Is there anything about him you like?"

"Yeah. He's an Unremarkable. There's no talk of the purging of the Sluagh. Or worries about rogue witches and fae sneaking into our world. We talk about regular stuff—nothing concerning magic. Shane was married to an Unremarkable. Perhaps I need a similar balance."

"True, but he is translating your mom's family grimoire, right? That's hardly avoiding magic."

"I know. But he was the closest person I could find, and I didn't expect him to be attracted to me. I certainly wasn't looking for anything. I can barely handle one man."

"Hey," she cackles. "We've switched places. Here I sit, committed to one man after sleeping with so many I lost count. And you're playing the field, a woman who only dated a handful of men before marrying her college sweetheart."

"I don't think dating two men equates to playing the field." I sip the last drops of my tea. "This was fun, friend, but I've got to get what I came for and head to work."

"Oh, yeah, your mom's letter." Ronnie leans back and props her healing foot on a chair. "What do you need it for? You said you don't have the magic to break the charm."

I bite my lower lip but decide to tell her my plans—sort of. "When I got to work on Wednesday, I offered to deliver merchandise to Agnes Pritchard to give Shane a break. I'm thinking..."

"Oh, my gods. You can't ask that old hermit for help. I hear Agnes is a self-learned hedge witch. She's all over the place. Doesn't always mask her magic. Shane says she and Leslie had a blowup back in the day, and Agnes left the coven. Might be dangerous putting any faith in her. She could obliterate your mom's letter."

Ronnie's got a point, but I don't have any other solution. "I'll be back in a minute." I walk into her office and unlock the trunk. My mom's letter rests in the tray, waiting for my return. I grasp the envelope, close the lid, and set the lock. When I enter the kitchen, my friend is loading the dishwasher.

"So, you're adamant about asking that old coot for help?" she asks with a disapproving gaze.

I give her a hug. "Don't worry. She wouldn't even talk to me the last time, and I have little faith in my chances this time, either."

"Well, good luck." Ronnie smiles, but the curls of her mouth fall flat. "Wait. You're not thinking of asking her to train you, are you?"

I stare into her anxious eyes. "No comment."

"This has to be the nuttiest idea you've ever come up with, but I know I can't change your mind. I hope it works out. Keep me informed about your dating progress. I have to live vicariously through you since I'm in a relationship."

"Don't hold your breath. How is Derek? I haven't seen him around. Is he being less overprotective since you got rid of the crutches?" I ask.

"Yeah. He's back to a normal work schedule. I know you're not dating Archie exclusively, but we could still do dinner some night. Would you be interested?"

"Let me think about it. I've got a lot going on in my head right now."

"You sure do. And training from a hermit will only add to the clutter in there." Ronnie taps me on the head.

"I'll be in touch." I give her another quick hug and make my way to the Mystic Sage. On the drive there, I consider Ronnie's advice but refute her concerns. Agnes is the only solution to my magical ineptness.

I'm stocking the herb jars section when Jeff arrives for work. He enters the store whistling to the tune of Mozart's "A Little Night Music."

"Hi, Jeff. You seem jovial," I say.

"Yeah, I am." He grins as he places his backpack behind the counter. "My research paper grade in an upper-level Econ course posted online today. Got an A!"

"That's great! Economics courses are tough, especially at DUB." I hesitate to ask but do it, anyway. "Your aunt must be proud?"

"Not really. She expects it. If I get anything below an A, she freaks out." He strolls over to join me.

"I'm sorry to hear that. What matters is you did your best, and sometimes our best isn't A work." My magic training was mediocre at best. Luck was on my side when I attacked the Sluagh. "How about your uncle? Does he support you?"

"Eh. He does whatever my aunt wants." He bends over to open a box. "Do you want me to take over for you?"

"Actually, I was hoping you could handle the store while I make a delivery to Agnes Pritchard."

"Sure. Have fun. That old woman gives me the creeps."

I chuckle. "Because she professes to be a witch?"

"Nah. Lots of people say they're witches these days. Doesn't mean it's for real. It's the way she drags her feet across the floor when she shops. And she barely says a word. When she does, it's so curt."

"Ms. Pritchard is in her 80s, Jeff. She could have lots of reasons for appearing so bitter." And I plan to find out why. I grab the paper bag full of herbs and crystals and head for the door. "I'll be back in about an hour, hour and a half."

"Why so long? Will the traffic be bad on a Saturday?" Jeff asks.

I need to make up an excuse in case Agnes decides I'm worthy of her company. "Her farm is outside the city limits in the county. Bearsden traffic can be awful, and one lane of Main Street is still closed. I promise I'll be as quick as I can. But call me if there's a run on the cinnamon sticks."

"I'll text you." Jeff bursts out laughing. How wonderful to see him in such good spirits. I imagine his aunt wants the best for him, but it's not doing anything for his self-esteem.

The drive to Agnes's farm takes only ten minutes, thanks to making every light on Manor Road. I pull up to her house and park my Prius. Resting in the car for a couple of minutes, I mull over a plan of action. I'll try to sweet-talk her and refuse to leave until she talks to me, even if I have to stand on her porch for the remainder of the afternoon.

I fling my purse over my shoulder and scoop up the delivery bag. The porch steps creak as I approach her door, and I tap the screen. No response. I open the screen and knock lightly on the front door. "Ms. Pritchard, it's Gwyn from Mystic Sage. I've got your order."

The sun beats down on the porch, and the leaves on the trees have the stillness of an oil painting. As insects buzz around my head, I knock repeatedly to the rhythm of a classic rock song I can't remember the title of. Still no answer. I leave the bag in front of the door and walk around the front of the house to a weathered picket fence flaking chips of paint. Peeking in the back, I observe an extensive herb garden surrounded by high chicken wire fencing. The plants are barely visible through the tangled mess of vines and weeds. But the view glistens with enchantment. A kaleidoscope of butterflies flutters above the garden in colors of the rainbow while the bees buzz and dance about. The sun creates a magical halo bubble encompassing them all.

No evidence of Agnes exists, so I turn around and return to the porch. As I take the first step, I notice the Mystic Sage paper bag is missing, and my jaw drops. I snap my mouth closed and march up the steps to the door. With my fists drumming, I shout at the door, "Ms. Pritchard? I know you're in there!" I wait a minute or two and pound on the door again. "Ms. Pritchard, I just want to talk to you. I need your help."

"Go away!" she yells in a throaty voice through the door. "Be gone with ya!"

Agnes holds my last hope of training outside the Bearsden Coven in her fragile, elderly hands. "Ms. Pritchard, I know I don't have the right to ask, but I have no one else to turn to. I need your expertise." Crickets. Crickets. A fly buzzes by, and I slap the side of my head, squishing it flat against my skin. Ugh. "Agnes, if you refuse to speak with me, I'll keep coming back!"

Desperation floods my heart, sending it into minor tachycardia. I grind my teeth on a thumbnail, agonizing over what to do or say to convince her to help me. I only have one option—divulge everything and take my chances.

"Agnes, my last name is Crowther. You knew my mom, I think." I lay the side of my head against the wooden surface and place my palm flat on the door. "Actually, I know you knew her. Her name was Lowri."

I sense no movement on the other side of the front door and stand back as the screen door slaps shut with a clap. This was a pipe dream, believing this old woman would give two shits about my problem. I start down the steps, and the door creaks. My head snaps around. I can view the foyer of the farmhouse and a long hallway that ends at the back.

A head with salt and pepper hair bends around the door. "Well? For fuck's sake. Are you fucking coming in or not?"

My eyes pop out, and a huge grin stretches across my mouth as I open the screen door and enter. "Thank you, Ms. Pritchard."

"Yeah, yeah, yeah." She slams the door shut and scowls. "And don't call me Ms. Pritchard. My name is Agnes. I'm not your fucking grandmother. Let's go to the kitchen."

I follow her down the hallway as dusty particles swim through the rays of sun shining through the back storm door. She drags one foot along the floor, dusting up the faded wood, leaving streaks of a clean floor in her wake. The walls have fifty-year-old wallpaper with orange and pink sunflowers. The hallway ends at the entry to a massive kitchen containing dingy-white cabinets from the '40s, I would guess. A massive pine table with mismatched hardwood chairs rests in the center.

"Pick a chair. Doesn't matter which one, 'cause they're all hard on the ass," she says. "I just put a kettle on. Would you like some herbal tea?"

"I would love some tea." I glance around the outdated kitchen with beat-up wood cabinets, and my gaze lands on the vinyl flooring, an old pattern with a black and white geometric pattern. The flooring creates an optical illusion of never-ending swirls, and I get dizzy.

Agnes slides her feet across the floor and sits in a chair across from me. Brushing her hair from her face exposes a woman with wrinkled, leather-like skin. But she has a heart-shaped face with a dainty narrow nose and unusual pale-gray irises. "So, Lowri Crowther was your mom. I thought you looked familiar. Makes complete sense now why the Bearsden Coven would go after you. I hear things, but it never occurred to me you were Lowri's daughter. 'Cause she withdrew at the same time I did."

"My best friend Ronnie joined the Fellowship, and they convinced her to lure me in. It was quite a shock when it happened." I glance at my purse on the vinyl floor, my mom's letter protruding from the top.

"I bet it was. You have the coven. Why hound me for help?" The whistle blows on the teakettle, and she shuffles over to the counter. "Peppermint or my personal blend?" She winks at me.

"Your personal blend sounds intriguing, but will I be able to drive after?" I ask.

Agnes belly laughs with a sinister tone and pours the water into the cups. "Come and get it. I don't serve people anymore. I had forty years of that bullshit."

"Of course." I jump up and walk to the counter for my cup, and we both return to the table. I pucker up and blow on her special tea and take a sip. "Oh! This is fabulous! A bit of cinnamon I detect? A hint of lavender and mint?"

"And mugwort. To help you think more clearly, improve your insight. I sense you need clarity." She waves a hand, prompting her spoon to dance freely in her cup. "You never answered my question."

I retrieve my mom's letter from my purse and pass it across the table to her, admiring her overt use of magic. "When I broke the spell on the lock of my mom's steamer trunk, I discovered her witchcraft mementos. I found this letter in there, but it's charmed. I sense the letter requires an incantation to unlock the charm, but I didn't get far enough along in my training before I left the coven."

"Ha! You left, too. Not surprised. I tired of Leslie's bullshit back in the '60s." She eyeballs me with a witchy inspection. "Your mom did, too. Lowri and I didn't always see eye to eye, but we agreed on that."

With a fling of her hand, the spoon flies out of the cup and onto the saucer. She takes a sip of her tea. Passing her withered hand over the paper, the trapped letters glimmer but can't escape the charm. She grimaces and tries one more time.

I inspect her glassy, gray eyes and ask her the question that's made a home in my head for months. "What was the tipping point that made my mom and dad leave the coven? I asked Leslie several times, but she refused to answer. Trinity was a teen at the time and doesn't know."

"I don't know the actual reason. Leslie wouldn't tell me. She was only a novice when she joined the coven, and Lowri was an ancestral witch with potent powers. The two of them were best friends, and frankly, I resented it sometimes. Leslie's power grew stronger over a couple of years, and she'd learned about opening a portal to the Otherworld on Samhain. Lowri was dead set against it. I overheard them arguing about it one night. She told Leslie she wouldn't take part in the ceremony and would never speak to her again if she tried to open a portal."

"Well, shit. And she opened the portal last year on Samhain, too." A sigh slips through my lips. "Then what happened?"

"No shocker there. Headstrong, Leslie is. She opened the portal without Lowri. She had become the leader of the Bearsden Coven by the time Samhain rolled around, and she had the support of everyone else. The others didn't know why Lowri was against it, because she only told Leslie—some huge fucking secret she wouldn't share with anyone else. Fucking pissed me off, to be honest. We'd become good friends."

"But you went along with Leslie, anyway? Why? If you respected my mom as you did?"

"You don't say no to your lover. Not if you wanna get laid later." She guffaws and leans her head back, exposing her tonsils.

I gape at Agnes and can't bring myself to respond.

"Why are you so shocked? Got something against lesbians, do ya?" She glares at me with an evil eye.

I blink several times. "Uhh, no. Leslie never mentioned she ever had a relationship. I figured she was asexual."

"Hardly. She was just inexperienced when I met her. I was with someone when I met Leslie, a really passionate woman named Judy. But something about Leslie made me...sssizzle." A lecherous look captures her eyes. "I remember the first time I kissed her. Pressed her against the wall of my living room, and..."

Oh, my gods. She isn't going to actually tell me what happened, is she? I roll my lips inward as my eyes bulge out.

She continues, "...slid my hand up her slender thigh and lifted her DUB plaid skirt..." *Yes. Yes, she is.* I mash my teeth together as Agnes recalls her first time with Leslie. "...the minute I touched her, she was like hot, molten lava in my hand."

I continue to grind my teeth with froggy eyes and clear my throat.

Agnes laughs at me in a deep, alto voice. "Are you a fucking prude?"

"No. I just can't imagine Leslie being passionate about anyone." I stare at her with a flat mouth.

Her face turns somber. "Well, that was a fucking long time ago. Before we split up. After we opened the portal on the night of Samhain, we got into a huge fight. I demanded she tell me what the big secret was that kept Lowri from the ceremony, and she flat out wouldn't. I guess I was jealous of their friendship and felt betrayed, so I left in a huff." She twists her mouth into a bundle of wrinkles. "Never spoke with her again."

"You left the coven, because you broke up." I lock eyes with hers and lay my hand on her knobby fingers. "I surmised you were a mean, bitter woman who reveled in being a curmudgeon. You're just a woman with a broken heart."

Agnes's eyes become wet, and she clears her throat. "Fuck that." She snaps her hand from mine. "I don't regret my decision—not one day."

"You keep telling yourself that, Agnes," I say. "I've learned you can repeat a supposition as much as you want, but it doesn't make it true."

She stares me down with pursed lips. "So, what do you want from me, offspring of Lowri Crowther?"

"I want you to train me. Teach me everything you know. Once I've developed my skills, I hope to break the charmed letter, so I can finally discover what my mom wanted to tell me."

"I haven't trained a witch since I left the coven, or as they refer to their ruse, the Fellowship of Associated Pagans—no patience for that group."

"I have another reason," I say.

"Oh? In trouble with the law?" she asks.

"Not exactly." Air escapes my lungs as my shoulders fall. "My skills have deteriorated so much, I'm having accidents."

Agnes raises her salt-and-pepper eyebrows. "Now I'm intrigued. What the fuck did you do?"

I swallow and blurt it out. "I accidentally imploded the city building on Main Street."

"No fucking way." She breaks out in laughter, grabbing her belly, but stops when I tear up. "I imagine Lindsey Hope's death weighs on you. I'm not saying she deserved it, but she was in the wrong place at the wrong time. It wasn't your fault." She grasps my hand.

"And it's happened a couple more times," I say. "There's no one else to turn to. I don't want to return to the coven until I'm competent, so Leslie doesn't hold all the cards. I'm begging you. Will you help me, Agnes?"

"When you put it that way..." she says with a smirk. "I'd love to see Leslie meet her match for once. I'll help you, but I've got conditions."

A smile erupts on my mouth. "Anything, Agnes. Whatever you want."

"I'd like a trade. You do a little work around my house. Some painting, repairs you can muster, help with the garden. If you agree to my terms, you've got a deal."

"Sounds reasonable. Thank you, Agnes."

"Don't thank me yet. I haven't given you the fucking list."

CHAPTER NINE

THE COST OF TRAINING

As I sip my Earl Grey on this lazy Sunday morning, a news story in The Bearsden Chronicles appears on my social media feed. The cleanup of the collapsed city building continues, and an investigation ensues to discover the cause. I have faith Agnes will train me well enough that it never happens again. I've got on my old, frayed jean shorts and a red tank top for the day's activities. The first day of July has hit us with temps in the upper 80s and high humidity. It's as if June opened a door, and July crashed the party without an invitation.

Tyler's bedroom door opens, and he staggers out in a t-shirt and boxer briefs. "Good morning, Mom. You're up early, and you closed up the sofa bed already."

"Yeah. I'm going to help an old woman who visits the Mystic Sage regularly. She's in her 80s, and her house and yard need upkeep." I take the last sip of my tea and place my cup in the sink.

"That's nice of you." My son spies the freshly made coffee and grabs a mug from the cabinet. "You made coffee? Thanks, Mom."

"You're welcome." I gather my purse and packed lunch.

Tyler cocks his head. "You're gonna be gone all day?"

"Yeah. It's a farm near Maryland, and I don't want to lose time coming back for lunch."

"Before you go, I promised Zoe I would ask." He pours coffee into his mug. "And please, don't shoot the messenger. Zoe and the other members of the Fellowship would like to meet up for dinner at the Raven Pub. They really miss getting together."

I stare at the mirror image of my eyes for a moment. "Would everyone be there?"

"Yeah. Except for Dr. Hughes. Zoe says she's in the UK for the summer. She promises we're just hanging out. It's not to pressure you into rejoining."

"OK. I've seen all of them except Dr. Hughes, anyway. I'll speak with her alone when she returns from Britain."

Tyler grins and takes a drink of his coffee. "Great. She will scream with joy. She misses you, Mom."

"I miss her, too." I frown as I reach for the doorknob. "I've really gotta go. Ms. Pritchard is a cantankerous old woman, and I don't want to be late. See ya later."

When I arrive at Agnes's house, I almost jump out of my Prius like it's my first day of school—a far cry from the first time I trained with Spence at Archie's house. Magic scared the shit out of me. But today, I'm ready for anything she throws at me. Stepping onto the porch, I notice a paper taped to the door. I pull on the screen and snatch the note. It reads: *This is your first assignment. Weed out the herb garden, and make sure you only pull out the weeds. I left gloves, a shovel, and a hoe for you. Don't bother me with questions. I'm busy. I'll check on your work later.*

How hard can weeding be? I stroll to the left side of the house and enter through the gate into the backyard. The herb garden has a chicken wire fence around it to keep out vermin, I'm sure. The butterflies and bees flit about like the first day I saw them. As I approach the garden, it becomes less magical. In fact, it's a mess of epic proportions. Vines and weeds wind in and out, interlocking the plants like snakes wrapped in continuous spirals.

I clip my hair to the top of my head, throw on my floppy hat, and get to work after lathering my skin with sunblock. It's a bitch trying to discern the herbs from the weeds, but I can't bother Agnes. The last thing I want to do is piss her off. And then where would I be? I grab the hoe and whack at the vines to break their tight grasp on the fragile greenery and pull long sections of the choking plants out, all the while disrupting the flight of the butterflies above me. The milk thistle scars up my arms with long, red scratches as I pull out the plants. After two hours, I've only cleared out about half of the garden and decide to take a break for lunch.

While I eat my hummus wrap in the shade of a nearby tree, I examine the leaves and the vein-like bark of the specimen providing me with a cool spot to enjoy my lunch. The beautiful, old tree appears to be an American Elm, which baffles me. So many died of a fungus on the DUB campus. This hardwood appears healthy with a silver shimmer emanating from its outer skin. A notification sounds on my cell—a text from Nick. He's inviting me to dinner on Monday. I consider Ronnie's advice and accept.

My phone rings with Tyler's name showing on the screen. "Hi, dear. What's up?"

"The Fellowship is definitely meeting at the Raven Pub for dinner. Will you be able to make it?" he asks. "How much work do you have left there?"

I examine the herb garden as air whistles between my lips. "A bit. And I don't know what else Agnes needs help with." If I finish the weeding in two hours, she should have about two hours to begin my training, giving me time to go home and shower. "I could make it by 5:30 p.m."

"Perfect. Zoe will contact everyone," he says. "Should I invite Archie?"

I suck in my lower lip. "Sure. Why not?"

"Great. Zoe has to work, so we may arrive a little later. See you there, Mom." The phone call ends, and I return to my work.

When I've cleared away all but the last quarter of the garden, a sense of excitement overwhelms me. As soon as I'm done, Agnes will take me on as an apprentice, and my magic schooling will commence. I extract the last of the weeds and finish hoeing the soil between the plants, stopping to inspect the leaves of the large herb plants—seven leaves on each stem. OMFG...Agnes is growing pot. No wonder she wanted me to weed. They need sun.

I leave the hoe and gloves near the entrance to the garden and walk back to the front porch covered in dirt. Another note hangs on the door, flitting in the warm breeze. The note states: *I'll check your work after dinner. Come back tomorrow.* I grind my teeth. No training? What the fuck! I exhale, march back to my Prius, and throw my lunch bag into the car. She must have known I'd be tired. I stare at the insides of my arms. Red welts from the Japanese hops and milk thistle resemble graffiti. This will spark an interesting dinner conversation.

The Raven Pub parking lot is full, unusual for a Sunday night. The first time I came here after the renovation, Ronnie dragged me to see a local rock band. I remember nothing about the visit, other than the band was so loud, it drowned out the obnoxious train running a hundred feet behind the building. It's too bad she had to work at the café tonight. Having her and Derek here would have made the gathering more comfortable. Upon entering, the smell of fresh popcorn invades my nostrils. I pass the bulky, dark-oak staircase welcoming visitors and walk through the short hallway to the main eating area.

As I approach the hostess wearing a black t-shirt with the Raven logo, I hear Spence screaming my name from a table in a secluded room to the right of the entrance. "Gwyn! We're in here!" He waves both arms above his head—always over the top, the only way he can be.

I meander around tables to the intimate room the Fellowship has reserved. Shane, Elijah, and Trinity are at one end of the long table while Skye and Spence sit on opposite sides at the other end chatting about a recent rock show. I find a seat near Trinity and Elijah.

"Hey, Gwyn! So glad you could join us!" Trinity shouts in her resonant voice.

"We haven't seen you in a couple of weeks," Elijah says. "I thought you'd make it to the shelter by now. Hope you can volunteer soon. We're low on help in the summers with the students gone."

"I've been kind of busy with work, but I'll try to get there." I wave to Spence and Skye. "Tyler and Zoe should be here soon, but she had to work today."

"Gwyn has been putting in a few extra hours for me, too," Shane says.

"You know we don't hold our breath waiting for Zoe," Spence says. "But maybe Tyler will light a fire under her butt." He passes me a menu. "Tanner's home, hand-holding a worrywart client, but you're blessed by the gods with my presence tonight."

Not long after, Archie arrives wearing a tight-fitting Henley shirt and worn jeans. "Hey, Archie!" the group shouts. Everyone knows we're dating again, but it's awkward.

"I see Zoe hasn't arrived yet. Want to bet on what time she'll bless us with her presence?" He sits down next to Skye and winks at me. I wish he wouldn't flirt, but the others are on their cell phones texting and don't notice. His phone pings several times. What's that about?

Trinity grabs my hand and pulls my arm out straight. "What the hell happened?"

"When I made a delivery to Agnes Pritchard, I noticed how infested with weeds her herb garden was," I say. "I spent the day weeding and got into a fight with a Japanese hops plant."

"A plant left those marks? With the scars on your palms and arms, you look like you've been fighting a..." She pauses. "Well, you know what I mean."

Archie stares at me with curious eyes. "So, you visited Agnes Pritchard's farm, after all."

"Yeah. It was the least I could do." I glare at him with pinched lips.

"Well, that explains why you haven't been to the shelter," Elijah says. "Agnes is getting older, and I heard she had another mild stroke. Left her weak on one side. Better you help her out for a while. Make it to the shelter when you can."

"Thanks for understanding," I say. "I'll volunteer as soon as I'm finished on her farm."

"You best be careful with that old woman." Trinity peers at me with a wrinkle in her mouth. "She's got some strange ideas about the world."

"Are you talking about the eccentric witch on the edge of town?" Spence asks. "Spill the tea."

"Shhh, Spence," Skye whispers. "Someone might hear you."

"Whaaat? She touts being a witch. No one believes her, though." He guffaws and slaps the table. "Go figure."

"That's very true," Skye says. "Hey, has anyone heard anything more about the collapse of the city building? Seems like they've cleaned up most of the rubble."

"I read they hired a couple of structural engineers to investigate," Archie says. "Seems like a sinkhole may have caused it."

I know what caused it, and it wasn't an air pocket in the ground.

"It was damn scary when it happened, being only a few doors down from the store," Shane says. "Gwyn missed the implosion by mere minutes."

"We're all relieved the collapse spared her." Archie smiles at me, and my cheeks flush. The man still makes me blush.

"Let's hope they figure it out," Trinity says.

Elijah nods. "The people on the streets are frightened. I'm doing all I can to allay their fears. I mean...what are the odds it could happen again?" *Zero, I pray to the gods.*

As Skye glimpses the time on her cell, Tyler and Zoe enter the room. "6:35!" She jumps out of her seat, swaying her arms in the air.

Shane groans, snapping his fingers. "Missed it by one minute again."

"Hey!! You did NOT bet on me again?" Zoe scowls at everyone.

"Don't let it bother you, Zoe," Elijah says, wrapping an arm around her tiny body. "You know we love ya more than Spence's tattoos."

"I heard you, Elijah," Spence says, pointing a finger at him.

Tyler cocks his head. "I don't get it."

Everyone busts out laughing as Zoe dances with no care in the world. The two of them find seats next to Skye and Spence.

"It's an ongoing joke we have, Tyler. It's OK," Zoe says with a wide-toothed grin.

"I don't know if I'm OK with the teasing." He snaps open his menu. "You've been working hard at being on time."

"You have, Zoe," I say. "Everyone, I think this should be the last time we tease her about her lateness. We can do better."

"Gwyn's right," Archie says. "It's gone on long enough, and I'm sorry I perpetuated it."

"Well said," Trinity says. "I know we all joke around, but let's strive to be more supportive." She's a genuine leader, and I have hope she can fight back against Leslie's Elder ways.

"I say we order since Zoe and Tyler are here," Shane says. "I'm so hungry I could eat a whole pecan pie."

It's like old times, eating together. Zoe talks about wanting to be a museum curator. Skye hopes to continue onto her Ph.D. Spence hints at being a forever student, whatever that means. Tyler's attendance foreshadows his potential future, but I'm hoping to put off telling him of his witch ancestry for as long as possible. He's never shown signs of emerging magic, so I'm optimistic. I'd rather he remain an Unremarkable if he can. We discuss the upcoming renovations at Mitchell Hall, but no one mentions the protection spell they put on the mansion and its gardens. We're in public, after all.

Two hours later, the noise in the Raven increases as the evening progresses. Soft chatter turns into bursts of raucous laughter and obnoxious shouting of expletives. The clinking of glasses increases, signaling the passing of a train behind the building. But there is no train. The floors rumble as the building appears to sway to and fro. The tables shake, and I grab my plate to keep it from sliding off the table.

I raise my head, and my fellow witches are goggling at each other. Plates slide and glasses roll off the table, crashing into pieces on the floor. What the hell is happening?

Archie's eyes flip back and forth, and he jumps up. "We have to get out of the pub. Grab your things and run." He shouts to the patrons nearby. "Everyone! Get out! The building may collapse!"

Patrons rush in a panic to the small hallway to exit in the front and through another door in the back. Fellowship members help the elderly and children, so they don't get trampled. I gesture to Tyler to get him and Zoe out of the pub. When the last of the Fellowship has exited, we dart to the exits, too. Except for Archie. He remains in the restaurant.

I dash back to get him. "Why are you still in here?"

"Get out of here, Gwyn." His eyes widen with fear.

"I'm not leaving without you." *Why is he doing this?*

He lays a hand on my face. "I know what I'm doing. Go."

I run out through the front double doors as the building sways and shakes. A bright light shines through the windows, and the patrons gasp and shout, "Fire!" from the street. The rumbling and quaking seem to go on forever, but only a couple of minutes have passed. And abruptly, everything becomes still. I glance down at my hands but discover no evidence of an amber glow. I didn't cause this.

Not far in the distance, sirens blare. The Fellowship members assist the frightened patrons, but I stand, grinding my teeth on a thumbnail, with my eyes glued to the pub entrance. The doors fly open, and my former lover walks out. My hands drop to my sides as my heartbeat relaxes from the palpitations. He smiles when he discovers I'm waiting for him alone in front of the crying and screaming crowd.

Archie approaches with a heaviness on his brow. "Are you all right?" He scans my body for wounds. "You appear to be un-harmed."

"I'm OK." I jump at him, wrapping my arms tightly around his torso. "Are you?"

He wraps his arms around me and presses his fingers into my back. "I'm fine."

He removes his arms and steps back. I stare up at his face, recognizing the allure he has as the evening breeze plays with his ash-blond locks. A few of the Fellowship members dart to us to check on him, too.

Spence gives Archie a quick hug and smacks his arm. "What the fuck were you doing in there? The entire building could have fallen on you."

"We'll chat about that later," Archie says. "Is anyone hurt?"

"A few minor abrasions. Lots of scared kids," Skye says. "But they all appear OK."

I search the crowd for the others. A small child rubs his teary eyes as Elijah consoles him on his lap. Shane is strolling through the distraught clusters of dinner patrons, stopping and offering his help. Tyler and Zoe are helping with the little kids. Trinity hugs an elderly white woman who's crying, and she raises her head. Archie motions for a few of them to join us, but Zoe and my son remain with the children.

Trinity marches in her spike heels toward us. "What the fuck happened, Archie?"

"We can't talk specifics here, but I can tell you it wasn't a natural occurrence." He glances back at the building. "I'm sure they'll have engineers check the structure for any damage, but I'm fairly certain I saved the building. And it was NOT a minor feat. I had to call on every bit of my witch energy to fight back against the...whatever it was."

"Please, tell me it's not another you-know-what," Spence says as he wipes his face.

Skye grimaces. "That would really suck."

The new Bearsden Coven leader eyes the Raven Pub and gives the order. "We need to have a summer meeting. I normally wouldn't call one without Leslie, but the situation demands it. I'll send a text to everyone to meet on Thursday. You're welcome to come, Gwyn."

I glance at Archie, not wanting to disappoint her, and he interjects. "I think we can manage without her, Trinity."

"The invitation is always open," Trinity says. "But I understand."

When the firetrucks arrive, the firefighters jump out in a frenzy and dash into the building, but they won't find a fire. A couple of EMTs rush to the patrons in the street and check on the wounded.

"So, what happens now?" Spence and Skye ask in unison.

Archie slides his hands in his pockets. "We go home. Let the first responders do their job. Better we're gone when the Bearsden Police arrive."

"He's right. Make yourselves scarce, and I'll be in touch," Trinity says.

"Let's go, Skye. See ya later, fam." The young witches run to their cars, and Trinity walks into the street to signal to the others to wrap it up.

Archie stares at me with those magnetic eyes. "Can I walk you to your car?"

"Sure." I wave goodbye to Tyler and Zoe from a distance. When we arrive at my Prius, he opens the car door when it beeps. I long to go home with him, but I shouldn't.

"I know it's last minute, but would you like to come for dinner tomorrow evening?" he asks. The light on the telephone pole illuminates his clear-blue eyes.

I glance down at my key fob. "I'm sorry. Nick invited me for dinner earlier."

"Maybe another night this week?" he asks, frowning.

"Sure," I say. "How about Tuesday?"

"Perfect." He touches the side of my face. "Be careful with that old hedge witch. I've heard she's extremely powerful, but untamed. The merging of those two qualities presents a highly volatile mix."

"I'll be careful." The evening breeze blows my hair back as I'm drawn to him. "Goodnight, Archie."

"Goodnight to you, Gwynedd." He walks to his home on Duncan Street.

Before I get into my Prius, I glance back at the Raven Pub. If I didn't trigger the building to fall, who or what did? And it occurs to me...maybe I didn't cause the city building to collapse, after all?

CHAPTER TEN

THE HEX FIX

IT'S A BEAUTIFUL MONDAY morning to start my training—not a cloud in the sky. And the humidity has dropped. I connect my phone to my Prius and call Ronnie on the drive to Agnes's farm.

"Hey, Gwyn! What the hell happened at the Raven?" she asks. "I got a text from Trinity calling for a coven meeting."

"We have no idea. The restaurant started with a mild rumble and graduated to full-blown shaking," I say. "Archie sensed someone, or something, was causing it, so he stayed inside to save the restaurant. His witch energy lit up the place like a blazing fire. The Bearsden Fire Department showed up to check it out."

"Be honest with me, woman. Was it you? Did you lose control of your witch energy?"

"No, I checked my hands. I didn't see or feel anything when the building shook, so please, don't tell the coven. While Archie was in there, I almost lost it. I worried he might not come out."

"Oh, my gods, friend." She blows into her phone receiver. "You're still in love with that man."

I hesitate to answer her, because I recognize the accuracy of her statement. But I also acknowledge the magnetism he has over me. Is it real or is it magic? I've got to figure it out. "Love was never the problem. Well, I'm at Agnes's farm now. I hope to begin my training with her today. And before you tell me to be careful, I promise I will."

"I hope so. Whenever I've talked to her, she's been curt and unfriendly."

"Oh, really? Gee, what reason would you have to talk with Agnes?" I chuckle into the car microphone. "Does it have anything to do with what she's growing in her herb garden?"

Ronnie cackles. "Oh, you found her secret garden?"

"Of course, I did. Don't worry. I know what I'm doing. Talk to you later."

As I park my Prius, I notice Agnes already has a new project set out for me. Four cans of exterior white paint and a brush rest on the porch with a note attached: *Paint the fence. Start at the left of the house. Paint both sides.* A sigh escapes my lips as I notice a raggedy Grateful Dead t-shirt dotted with paint the colors of a rainbow. After slipping on the t-shirt, I put my hair in a clip and don my floppy hat. I grab the paintbrush and paint before plodding toward the fence.

The burning sun beats down all morning without even a whisper of wind to cool me. Beads of sweat sting my eyes as they roll down my forehead. I bat at the flies, but killing one only seems to invite others. After six hours of strokes—up and down and up and down—my body aches all over. My back pinches, my grass-stained knees buckle, and my hands curve as if I'm grasping a brush. When I finish the dregs of the last paint can, my body relaxes with elation—another job done. Surely, Agnes will begin my training now?

I struggle to stand straight and stretch backward to ease the pain, but the pinching hurts worse than before. Weightlifting did nothing to prepare me for this excessive manual labor. I'm going to need a week to recover. I step up to the open door and tap on the wood screen. Agnes doesn't come, so I pull on the screen to go inside. It's locked. I knock using my molded hand. "Agnes? Are you in there?"

Pots and pans banging in the kitchen confirm she is. "Agnes, can you unlock the screen?" Cabinet doors and drawers slam shut while I stand hunched over on the porch. I press my face to the dusty screen and squint, hoping to catch her passing in the hallway, but I only glimpse her shadow. "I know you're in there. Please, let me in. I'm ready to train. We had a deal."

"Have you finished the right side of the house, too?" she asks in a gravelly voice. "There's more paint in the barn."

My mouth falls open. She expects me to do the other side, too? "I think I've done enough for one day. And I'm ready to train."

"I'll decide when you're ready," she says with a snarky tone. "Paint the fence, and then we'll negotiate."

Negotiate? We already negotiated! I grind my teeth as my face becomes hot as a chili pepper. "No! I'm not painting more of that fence until you've given me some training!"

"No painted fence? No training." Her shadow slinks back into the kitchen.

I beat the heel of my foot on the porch floor. Fuck it. I'm tired of people thinking they can control me. "Fine. You know what? Fuck your training. Fuck your magic. Fuck your curmudgeon attitude." I clench my teeth, and a hot flash erupts in the sweltering heat. "Fuck your worn-down house. Fuck your garden. Fuck your fuck-ing fence." I wipe the dripping sweat off my face and neck. "And fuck you, Agnes." I give her the bird with both middle fingers, pressing them against the screen. I turn toward the steps in a rage and shout for all the world to hear. "Fuuuck!"

As I take the first step, the screen door creaks open and claps shut. I swivel around, and Agnes stands on the porch. "Are you done with your rant?"

"What the fuck is all this about? Some kind of Karate Kid type pre-training to get me ready to practice the craft?" I ask.

"Fuck no. I just wanted you to paint my fence!" She guffaws, slapping her thighs and relishing in her accomplishment.

I frown. "Why would you do that? You know I would gladly help you out."

"Your momma hid her use of magic...and her mouth, apparently. She didn't have the guts to stand up to Leslie when the shit hit the fan. Instead, she chose to withdraw in shame...give up her magic in order to save you from something. Yet, here you are. An ancestral witch with powers you can't control with fear of a coven Elder you could so easily surpass." Agnes purses her lips with squinty eyes. "I heard more fight from you in that rant than I ever heard from Lowri. It was sort of a test to see if you had the strength in you to fight back. Because you'll need it."

I raise my head with a new respect for my mentor and gaze at her wrinkled, heart-shaped face.

Agnes grabs the porch handrail and hobbles down the steps carrying a straw hat in her hands, making her way to the left side of the house. She stops and motions to me. "Well, are you coming? Are you ready to train?"

"Fuck, yeah." I grin like a witch who's won the lottery as I run down the stairs.

I follow Agnes to the herb garden where the butterflies and bees frolic about the plants. She stops at the gate, inspecting my weeding prowess. I hoed between the rows of greenery, but the ground could use some mulch.

"Not bad. Now my plants will get some much-needed full sun," she says as she pushes the hair off her face.

"Especially the back quarter of the garden, right?" I ask.

Agnes snickers and walks through the gate. "A girl has to supplement her income, doesn't she?"

I chuckle and enter the garden, disrupting the butterflies. They flit off in random directions, and I'm careful not to anger the bees. "Why are we out here?"

"As good a place as any to see what you've got." She throws her straw hat on her head and hammers it down with a hand. "Summon your energy—only a smidgeon. Make your intention to give the herbs a warm glow since they've been missing the sun."

I raise my hand but fold it into the other. "Something bad might happen. I told you I've regressed since I left the coven."

"Oh, for fuck's sake." She flings a hand into the air. "You gotta start somewhere. Do it!"

Setting my palm facing up, I call on my witch energy, and the amber glow emerges with tiny tentacles of rays. The corners of my mouth raise a little. It's working. With my confidence boosted, I roll my hand over to radiate the plants. And it ignites an herb...and another...and another!

Agnes screams, "Fuuuck! For the love of the gods! You're gonna burn me down!"

"Oh, my gods! I'm so sorry! Where's your hose?" I say as I run to the gate.

She belly laughs and waves a hand at me. "I don't need no fucking water." She lifts her hands up, chanting softly, and clouds form over us. Out of nowhere, or somewhere I guess, bits of white fluff fall onto the garden where the fire blazes. Snow falls, and in seconds, the only thing left burning are a few embers.

"That was amazing." I gape at Agnes in awe of her power and arrogance to use those skills in the open. No wonder Leslie had issues with her.

"Yeah." She blows on her knobby fingers. "I still got it." Her eyebrows fall. "But you? Not so much."

"I told you. Why do you think I wanted to apprentice with you?" I stare at my hand in frustration and make a fist.

"Are you gonna hit me?" Agnes bursts out laughing, but stops abruptly and shuffles toward me, sniffing.

"Do you need a tissue?" I ask. "I always carry a travel pack in my pockets. Allergies."

"I don't have the sniffles." When she's right on top of me, she leans into me and inhales deeply.

"My B.O. must be bad, I know—sweating in the sun all day."

"I'm not sniffing your stink. I smell a hex. A witch played a practical joke on you. Or a mean trick. A wicked spell weakened control of your energy."

My lips part as I ponder who the culprit might be. "You mean Lindsey Hope's death wasn't my fault?"

"Never was. Some witch cast this hex to weaken your magic. You couldn't have caused the building to collapse," Agnes says. "Someone or something else caused its destruction."

"What do I do about it?" I ask.

"I'll cast a spell to remove it—call it a hex fix. It leaves a layer of protection, too. But you should probably figure out who's pissed at you. Got any ideas?"

I press my lips together. "Yeah. I do. Well, let's do whatever you have to do. Will it hurt?"

Agnes chuckles with a wrinkle on her nose. "Does it matter?"

"I guess not. Go ahead," I say.

I close my eyes and prepare for the hex fix. She chants softly in her gravelly voice. Pins and needles encompass my body and goosebumps appear at random on my skin. A tugging at my inner muscles pulls at my body, and I wince in pain. And snap! A rush of relief overwhelms me. I lift my eyelids.

Agnes's face is no more than an inch from mine. She sniffs once. "Damn, I'm good."

After a much-needed shower, I slip on a flowing, aqua sundress and apply a bit of eye makeup. I examine the wounds on my palms and knees complemented by the skin rash on the inside of my arms from the Japanese hops. Not all the makeup in the world will make me sexy tonight, and it's for the best. What am I doing dating a thirty-eight-year-old man?

As I drop into my car seat, every ache and pain surfaces. I can't cancel my date with Nick this late, so I drive to Main Street to his apartment above Roots of the Earth. Every muscle has tightened up, and I moan, rolling out of my car. I want to curse Agnes for what she put me through, but I'm too elated with the discovery I'd been hexed. It's such a relief knowing I wasn't responsible for Lindsey Hope's death.

As I climb the stairs to Nick's apartment, I contemplate who the hex giver is and where she's lurking—an investigation for another day. I tap on the door and footsteps come rushing.

"Hi, Gwyn. Come on in," Nick says. He's dressed casually in a loose button-down shirt and tight-fitting slim jeans. "Why do your arms have welts?"

My eyes widen with embarrassment. "Oh, I helped an old woman who has a farm on the edge of town—at the end of Manor Road. I weeded her garden and got into a fight with Japanese hops."

He chuckles. "Well, it looks like the hops won. Would you like something to drink? I've got beer and wine in the fridge."

"No, thank you. As worn out as I am, I'd go from sober to asleep in seconds. But you go ahead. A glass of iced water with dinner would be fabulous, though."

"Sure. Why don't you take a seat while I finish in the kitchen?" He gestures to the sofa.

I fall into the cushions and groan under my breath. A hot soak in a tub would soothe me right now, but I try to enjoy his company. "Dinner smells great."

"I'm not a stupendous cook, but I hope you like Mexican. I found a vegetarian recipe that uses tofu and quinoa." Nick walks into the living room, displaying a charming grin. "Ready to eat?"

"Sure," I say. "But you're gonna have to pull me off this cushion of comfort."

I grasp his hand, enjoying the warmth and firmness of it as he lifts me off the sofa. When I fall into him, he catches me crashing into his chest. I peer up at his dark-brown eyes as he hugs me.

"I couldn't have managed this if I had planned it." He stares at me with yearning in his eyes and leans down to kiss me. His lips are warm and gentle, but I whimper in pain. "I'm sorry. Did I hurt you?"

I chuckle. "Of course, not. I spent all day painting Agnes's fence. That, on top of weeding yesterday, has tapped me out."

We both grab a plate, serve ourselves from the stove, and take seats at the bar. There's no room for a kitchen table, but the cozy eating setup sparks memories of dates with my husband Richard—the early days when I mattered to him. The Mexican dish tastes scrumptious while the conversation touches on all the mundane topics of weather, work, and the upcoming makeover to Mitchell Hall.

"I assume they'll postpone the renovations while they finish cleaning up the collapse of the building on Main Street," Nick says. "So weird. I hope there isn't a problem with other city buildings. You heard about what happened at the Raven Pub last night? The building shook, but there was no evidence of an earthquake or problems with the old heating system. They have no clue what happened."

I stare down at my Mexican bowl. "Yeah, I was there. Some of the Fellowship members met for dinner."

"Ohhh," Nick says, averting his eyes. "I assume Archie was there?"

"Yeah, he was there." I lay my hand on his. "Don't let it bother you, Nick. If I didn't want to be here with you, I'd be sitting at home in Tyler's apartment, binge-watching a show on Netflix."

He gazes into my eyes for a stretched minute before sliding off his bar stool. "Let me take these plates to the sink, and we can go chat on the sofa. Go ahead, and I'll come in a minute."

As I slip off the bar stool, each muscle spasms. I'm going to regret not stretching after today's work. When I fall onto the comfy cushion, I moan with an open mouth as my ass sinks in.

Nick walks over to join me. "I heard you moaning in the kitchen." He sits down close to me with a flicker of desire in his eyes and takes another sip of his bottle of beer. "I'm really psyched you came for dinner. You must be exhausted, yet you came."

"My parents raised me to keep appointments even if not one ounce of energy remains," I say. "And despite how tired I am, I very much wanted to come."

Nick bends over my face and says in a breathy voice, "Well, I'm glad you did." A whiff of Victory beer enters my nose as he kisses me. This time, he's less nervous and isn't afraid to go further. He wraps his hand around the nape of my neck and presses harder on my lips, spreading his mouth and inviting me to do the same. His titillating tongue arouses me, and I rub my legs together as I wrap my arms around his torso. My back arches as he leans into me, and we fall back on the cushions.

He plants warm kisses on my neck and inches toward my ear. As a hand slinks along my inner thigh, I squirm. When he reaches my panties, I buck involuntarily, causing my back to spasm. I cry out and flail. "Aghhh!"

"I'm so sorry. Did I hurt you?" Nick asks.

"Nooo. My back is pinching. It's the injury from when I fell." I try to sit up, but I'm stuck there flat on my back.

"Give me a minute." He darts into his bedroom and returns with a tennis ball. "Let me help you onto your stomach."

Nick rolls me over. My dress has shifted up, exposing my panty-covered ass, but he adjusts the material to cover me up.

"I'm sorry about this," I say. "I mean, you are dating an older woman—emphasis on the older part."

"Don't worry about it. And the work you've done the past two days would hurt anyone." He places the tennis ball on my back and rolls it around. "Tell me when I've found the strain."

"A little downward. A bit to the left. No, too far. Go back. Ahhh." He presses the ball into my back, hitting all the right spots. "Thank you so much for doing this, Nick. I owe you one."

"I'll remember you said that." As Nick presses hard into the strained muscle, the relief overwhelms me. And it occurs to me. He alleviated my pain without magic. "I do this for my mom all the time when her hip joint acts up."

I squish my eyelids shut, cringing, but the ball massage has worked its magic, and I relax as he continues. While I enjoy the amazing kneading of my back muscle, my mind wanders to the night the coven banished the Sluagh back to the Otherworld—the last time my body hurt this bad...

I lift my eyelids and view Nick sitting in the chair across from the sofa. Oh, my gods. I fell asleep. "I'm sorry I dozed off."

"It's OK. I let you sleep since you were exhausted." He moves to the sofa and lays his hand on my cheek. "I had fun."

I burst out laughing. "Liar. I think I should go home and go to bed."

"I understand," he says as he places a kiss on my cheek. "But I wasn't lying. I had a great time. Gwyn, I like you a lot. I want to keep seeing you. If you want to, of course."

"If you're willing to put up with my old lady stuff, I'm game." I stand up with his help and go to the door to slip on my flats. "Next time, I'll skip manual labor the day of our date."

Nick grabs his keys and begins putting on his shoes, but I gesture for him to stop as I collect my purse and hoodie.

"I can walk to my Prius alone," I say. "The parking lot is lit like a football field."

"OK. If you insist." He bends over to kiss me again. "I want to do more of this next time."

"I wouldn't mind," I say, blushing. He opens the door for me, and I walk into the hallway. "Goodnight, Nick."

"Goodnight, old woman," he says as he closes the door.

I chuckle at his choice of a pet name on the way to my car and stop in my tracks. He never spoke to me about the translations of my mom's journal. And I realize it never crossed my mind either. A cool breeze blows my hair and goosebumps rise on my arms as I continue to the car. While I slip on my hoodie, footsteps echo in the parking lot. I turn around, but no one appears to be there.

When I'm almost to my car, the footsteps return. I snap my head around and observe a faint flash of light near the corner of the building. My witch energy appears to seep out in response, but contracts as quickly as it emerged—different from the first two times. And the footsteps dissipate as the person runs away. Enough. I'm paying a visit to the DUB Physics Department tomorrow.

Chapter Eleven
A Witch's Apprentice

Tuesday morning, I wake up early to hop into the shower before Tyler rises. As I dress in a V-neck tee and jean shorts, I contemplate the super-packed day ahead of me—first stop, DUB campus. I recall the night of the Winter Solstice Ceremony while shoveling my scrambled eggs into my mouth. That was the last time I saw Audrey Kenilworth. The Fellowship never uncovered the reason for her infiltration into our coven, but they sensed she had left the area. I place my breakfast dishes and flatware into the dishwasher and grab my purse from the kitchen chair.

Tyler's door creaks open, and he shuffles out with sleepy eyes. "Why are you up so early, Mom?"

"I've got too many items on my to-do list." I head toward the door, but stop when I notice the dour appearance on his face. "What's wrong, son? Didn't you sleep well?"

He peers up at me displaying a mini frown. "No, I haven't slept well for a week. I guess the deprivation has caught up with me."

"Why aren't you sleeping?" I ask with a crinkle in my brow.

Tyler shrugs. "I'm sure it's stress from work. Don't worry about me, Mom."

"You know that's not possible," I say. "If this continues, you let me know. And that's an order."

"Got it. See ya, Mom," he says, dragging himself into the bathroom.

I make my way to my Prius with worry camping out in my brain. As usual, parking is a bitch. Since the building imploded, maybe we'll finally get a parking garage in its place. Or was it demolished on purpose? The flash of light from the roof of the building had a distinct quality similar to the night I melted the Porsche. My hand vibrated with a magnetic-pull toward the building. Was Audrey lurking on top of the city structure? If so, why was she hanging with Lindsey Hope? And why was last night's encounter different?

With no other option, I park in the South Campus parking lot and make my way to Menzies Hall, where the Physics Department has offices and labs. The July sun beats down through clear-blue skies. Hot flashes only crop up once in a while now, but how would I even know? Delaware's humidity can be unbearable, and today, it has a real feel temperature of ninety-five degrees. I put my hair in a clip as beads of sweat roll down my barely visible cleavage and climb the steps to the double doors of the Georgian red-brick building.

I enter the Physics Department office and approach the lone receptionist who's busy typing on her computer keyboard. "Hello, I knew a student who attended DUB on a post-graduate research fellowship. I lost touch with her, but was hoping you might have an address for her?"

The woman with short brown hair stops typing and stares at me with skeptical brown eyes. "I can't give you her personal information. Confidentiality and all."

I glance at the watercolor painting of Menzies Hall hanging on the wall behind her. "Can you at least tell me if she's still on campus? I could hang out until I run into her."

"What's the name of the student?" she asks with an annoyed tone in her voice.

"Audrey Kenilworth. She was from New Jersey," I say.

"Oh, I don't need to search for her," the woman says. "I knew Audrey. She was odd, practically a hermit in the last semester. She left without updating her contact information. I'm sure you can find her if you search the internet."

"Thank you, anyway," I say.

I walk back to my car while disappointment gnaws at my stomach. Past searches found nothing. I drive back to the apartment and log my hours with the insurance agency. Even with Tyler at work, I have limited focus, but I complete the online forms.

When I've finished, I do a quick search for Audrey's name again. Like before, only her master's dissertation shows up, but I notice something else further down the page. The Kenilworth name appears in an old court filing, so I click on the PDF file. As I read, I learn Kenilworth is the name of a large developer in New Jersey. They must be her family. I can't imagine she went back to them after the way they treated her.

After a quick lunch, I rush over to the farm to begin my apprenticeship. Agnes is sitting on the porch when I pull up. She's wearing a tie-dye t-shirt, purple cotton pants, and bright yellow sunglasses—not the usual witchy attire. Her straw hat hugs her head.

"You dressed in colorful clothes today? Special occasion?" I ask.

Agnes grabs the porch railing and pulls herself up. "Fuck no. It's hotter than a fucking furnace out here. Black's impractical."

"Oh, I imagined you might be as excited as I am about starting." I chuckle and slap on my floppy hat.

"You must think a lot of yourself if you believe I'm happy about sharing all my witch secrets." She stares me down and chuckles. "Well, let's get a move on. I don't have all day." While we stroll back to the garden, she explains her philosophy of magic, which isn't much of a philosophy. "Perform magic however you want and whenever you want, if it gets you what you want."

I tilt my head. "Sounds quite selfish, Agnes."

"You're gonna insult me, are you?" she asks, squinting.

I glance at the grass near my feet, noticing a few caterpillars crawling on my shoes. "I'm sorry. You're right. How you practice the craft is none of my business."

"Isn't it now?" She smirks at me. "I'm only testing you, dear. I will train you, but you have to develop your own set of ethics regarding the magic you perform. That's the whole point. Your philosophy will develop differently from mine and other witches. But you have to respect each other's opinions. You can't expect a witch to conform to a single set of ideals. Not if you want successful collaboration."

"That's not a hypothetical," I say. "You're talking about Leslie and the Bearsden Coven, aren't you?"

"Never you mind. We have work to do, and the temperature goes up with every fucking unnecessary question you ask." Agnes bends over and scoops up about five caterpillars. "Your first task. Change these squiggly things into butterflies."

I frown with embarrassment. "I don't know an incantation for transformation. If you tell me what it is, I can attempt it."

"What? You're a fucking ancestral witch. You don't need to learn an incantation to do this."

"But the coven members told me I had to train at each level. I was only on level two, using incantations to cast spells, and I was barely competent."

"For fuck's sake, training on levels is for those who aren't born into magic." Agnes rolls her eyes around, and they land on mine with a blink. "Of course, you can learn an incantation and cast the spell like us lowly practitioners. Or you can use what the gods gave you through your family line."

"Why didn't someone tell me?" I ask.

"Hmph. Because they wanted to control you. Leslie's all about staying in control. She knows about the innate power Lowri had. Didn't want you to know, I'm sure. Now the others might not have known. But I hear there's an ancestral witch from Scotland in the coven. Been there for a few years now. Surprised you didn't go to him for help."

My eyes hop around the landscape. "I couldn't go to him."

Agnes snickers. "Of course. I sensed the trappings of lust floating around you when I mentioned him." She leans into me and sniffs. "I can smell the sex on you."

"I'm not having sex with him now," I say, rolling my eyes. "We're only dating."

"For now." She cracks up and slaps her thigh.

"Can we get back to the training?" I ask. "I don't know what to do."

"So, it's my understanding, from what Lowri told me, you create a focused intentional thought in your head—a super focus. Make a command with an intention and see what happens. You must have done this before, haven't you? I heard you fought back the Sluagh, and you didn't do it chanting incantations."

I recall the fight with the Host of the Unforgiven Dead and remember chanting the protection spell, but I only fought back with my intentions. She's right. "OK. I'm ready."

"Thatta girl! Now you're talking."

Agnes holds her hands in front of me as the caterpillars wiggle around in her palms. I lift both hands and spread my fingers. I'm inclined to chant, because it's all I know, but I hold my tongue and focus on an internal intention—speeding up the life cycle of the caterpillar. When I'm confident I've achieved the pinnacle of my concentration, I summon my witch energy and apply the amber glow to the caterpillars. I'm amazed as the young insects transform briefly into cocoons, and the wings of butterflies sprout from the silky cases and take flight. My lips part as they dance about us.

"Fucking amazing," Agnes says. "Told ya. Your mom would be proud."

"Would she, though?" I ask. "She raised me without magic for a reason, and I don't think wanting an Unremarkable life for me was the only one."

"I'll admit I was jealous of Lowri's ancestral witch power, but I got the impression she was proud of her ancestry. And you should be, too. When we're done with your training, you should have the skills to break the charm on your mom's letter. And then you'll know."

"I hope so." I gaze at the butterflies fluttering in the cerulean-blue sky.

"Enough chit-chat." Agnes spreads her mouth into a sinister smile. "Ready for more?"

"Yes, a thousand percent yes," I say.

We spend the rest of the afternoon perfecting the application of my intentions. I skip around the forest behind her house, conjuring green sprouts from tree limbs and ferns from the ground. Flowers bloom at the wave of my hands, creating a blanket of red, yellow, and pink. I giggle like a schoolgirl as I dance in a clearing, swirling twigs and fallen leaves around me like a mini tornado. All the while, Agnes basks in the joy of her teachings.

She attempts to push up from a log where she's sitting but slips to the ground. "Fuck this old body."

"Wait! Let me help you." I rush to Agnes and support her elbows as she stands. "Isn't there something a witch can do to counteract the effects of the stroke? You are a talented witch. Can't you cast a spell for old age?"

"You can't cheat death, my dear. I can chant an incantation or two...or three, but it only delays the inevitable. And there's the issue of doctors. The whole...how did I heal shit? I gotta mask some of it or they'll be coming after me. Ain't nobody wants to attract busybodies, am I right?"

"True. The last thing you want is for the authorities to come sniffing around here. Especially in your garden."

She snickers and waves at me. "Let's go back to the house." When we arrive at the porch, she stops. "Would you like to stay for dinner? I've got lots of fresh veggies. Better than anything you'll find in the store."

"I would love to, Agnes, but I've got a date. Let me take a rain check."

"Hmph. Eating with that Scot, I sense. I guess I see the attraction, if you like tall, blond, and buff. But I go for the lanky and brunette myself."

I help Agnes up the porch, and she turns to say goodbye. "This is only the beginning. Once I'm done with you, you'll be capable of anything. Can you come three times a week? I believe that'll give me enough time to cover everything and give you time for your...personal life."

"Absolutely. I can't wait."

I wave goodbye as I drive off. In the rearview mirror, I observe her blowing me a kiss before entering the house. Oh, Agnes. You're hiding a sweet, old lady underneath all those fucks.

As usual, dinner on Duncan Street impresses. Archie has the cooking prowess of a chef, and I've missed the savory meals. We discuss the warmer, humid weather and the class on Scottish folklore he's teaching. He talks me into playing checkers afterward, and we chat.

"So, you're happy Summer Session One is ending?" I ask. "I thought you were enjoying teaching again?"

"Aye, I love it, but I hadn't planned on jumping in as soon as I stepped down from the chair position." Archie sets up the checkerboard on the steamer trunk while I get comfortable on the sofa. "And I didn't step down completely. I've got to monitor the department while Leslie is in Wales. She'll be back in the middle of August."

"Oh, that makes sense. When does the session end?" I set up checkers on my squares.

"Seventh of July. Grades have to be in on the eighth," he says. "I have to enter grades online after you leave tonight."

"I'm sorry. You should have said no when I offered Tuesday." I peer at him with concern in my eyes.

He leans over the trunk and strokes my cheek. "I didn't want to wait any longer."

I glance down at the checkerboard and blush. How does he do this to me? Is it his touch? His magnetic-blue eyes? The aroma of his woodsy cologne? I break out in a sweat and grab a Celtic Folklore magazine to fan myself. "Shit."

"Hot flash? I'll be back in a jiff." Archie darts to the kitchen and returns with a bag of peas.

I chuckle. "What's this?"

"I don't have any ice packs in the freezer at the moment. It's the peas or the broccoli?" He cracks up as I place the bag on my neck.

"Ahh. Thank you. I hoped I'd gotten past the worst of them. But I hear they can come and go for years."

"So, I've heard. I remember the night I first kissed you, and your face combusted into the color of a blood-red rose. I thought I'd offended you."

"Hardly." I jump a checker and remove it from the board. "Your turn. It was one of the best nights of my life."

Archie smiles and hops over a checker piece. "It was for me as well. I just didn't realize it at the time."

After thirty minutes of losing every game to him, the clock dings the first of nine, and I surrender. "Clearly, I'm off my game tonight. I had a long day. I stopped by the Physics Department to see if they could tell me where Audrey Kenilworth is living."

"They can't share student information," he says. "Why are you snooping about her, anyway?"

"I wasn't going to talk about my training with Agnes, since we're trying to keep magic out of our conversations, but I need to confess something. The evening the city building collapsed, I saw a flash of light, and the amber glow of my witch energy seeped out of my fingers. It was like a magnet sucked my energy from me. And immediately, the building collapsed."

His eyes grow big. "And you fell. Did you cause the implosion?"

"When it happened, I worried I did. I only told Ronnie about it. When I heard they found Lindsey Hope's body in the rubble, I was beside myself."

"I imagine you were. But you're saying it wasn't your fault?"

"At the first lesson with Agnes, I started a fire by accident. Don't worry. It was only a little one. She detected a hex on me. She removed it, so I'm fine now. I think Audrey was on top of the city building with Lindsey Hope. I don't know how she got off. Maybe she flew away on her broomstick. But it didn't occur to me until the other night when I was leaving Nick's apartment." I stop but it's too late. "I'm sorry...I can't explain without mentioning where I was."

Archie's mouth twitches. "It's all right, Gwyn. Continue."

"I heard footsteps and turned around to catch a flash of light, which seemed to trigger my witch energy to seep out, but not much. And I didn't feel a magnetic pull on my energy at all. Agnes cast a protection spell on me to guard me against future hexes like the one she removed."

"And you think it was Audrey? Do you mind me sharing this information with the coven at our emergency meeting?"

"Of course not. I'm not hiding anything, since I know Lindsey Hope's death wasn't my fault." My back pinches when I attempt to stand. "I should go home and let you get your grading done. All the work I did for Agnes has aggravated the muscle strain in my lower back, so I need to lie down."

Archie moves to the sofa next to me and slides his hand along my back. Oh, how his touch relaxes me. He presses his hand over the strain, and a burning sensation appears. After a few seconds, he removes his hand and helps me stand.

"Better?" he asks.

I twist my back, and other than some sore muscles, the strain has disappeared. "Why did you use magic? You should have asked me first."

"Aye, but you would have said no, because you're a stubborn woman."

"Insults will get you nowhere. You know this, right?"

"I do." He follows me to the door and waits while I slip on my sandals.

"You've barely touched me since we started dating again." I sense the repressed longing burning brightly in his eyes. "It's OK if you want to."

"If I press my lips to yours and touch the supple skin again...I'll not be able to hold back." Archie brings his face to mine. "I'll take you right here on the wooden floor and dust it with you."

My eyes widen as he adjusts the bulge in his jeans. "I should go then?"

"That would be best," he says, opening the door. "If you change your mind about attending the coven meeting, let me know. They would be fine with you attending as a mere local witch."

"I'm not ready yet, but I'll let you know if I change my mind." I stare into his eyes once more. "Goodnight, Archie."

He strokes my cheek. "Sleep well, Gwynedd."

Chapter Twelve

Arduous Decisions

The next three weeks of July transform from warm and humid to downright sultry and suffocating. No matter what I wear, I can't escape the return of daily hot flashes. My underwear sticks to my skin so badly, I have to peel them off.

The city has brought in seismologists to test the area, but the investigators find no evidence of seismic activity. Of course, they didn't. It must be Audrey Kenilworth. For whatever reason, she wants to destroy our quaint town. But I can't imagine why she'd want Lindsey Hope dead. It's a mystery to the coven, too. Ronnie says the Fellowship remains on alert, but no similar incidents have occurred. Audrey hasn't stalked me again. Not that I'm aware of.

I juggle my dating between Archie and Nick with the finesse of a well-meaning klutz. Ronnie says I should take the plunge and jump Nick's bones once and for all, but I can't add sex with a new man to my emotional basket. As it is, the heavy necking with Nick plus his magical wandering hands has invaded my dreams, leaving me hot and sweaty like a construction worker—and frustrated.

The sexual tension harms the focus on my training, so I've cut back on how often I see them.

I squeeze in three days a week of training around my work at the insurance company and Shane's store, which allows for a few dates with the men, but not much more. Since she's a hedge witch, Agnes insists on being in nature, swearing it's the prime way to gain the skills I need—and do it quickly. When I screw up, which happens frequently, she loses her patience, but she perseveres. She instructs me to establish a routine to not only control my magic, but to allow it to evolve and grow exponentially.

"Wake up bright and early at the crack of dawn every day," she says in her gravelly voice. "Thank the gods for another day of life and open yourself to the spirits of the forest. Eat a substantial, healthy breakfast to fuel the day. Have an intention for everything you do. No intention? Don't do it. Seek inner peace. Without inner peace, you're of no help to others. Seek friendships that complement and support you. Those who ask for more than they give are not friends. And be creative. No witch developed a new spell without spreading their wings."

On our last day of training, the temperature rises to over one hundred degrees, so Agnes moves us indoors to the only space with a window air conditioner. A rather large room on the ground floor, her magic room has haphazard organization and emits a hodge-podge of the most pleasant herbs of lavender, cinnamon, and sage to the rank odor of dead carcasses. I cover my nose, wondering how I'm going to train here.

One wall has mismatched shelves containing vintage books, bottles of herbs, half-used candles, crystals, animal skulls, and pre-pared spell bottles for purchase, I assume. On the adjacent wall, I observe a shelf with several bowls, mortars and pestles, and various wooden spoons and sticks for mixing. Another shelf houses wine, liquor, and stone crocks. I imagine those spirits have a recreational purpose with something special stored in the crocks. A beat-up pine table sits dead center in the room with easy access to the shelves. A Victorian claw-foot piano stool guards the table.

"If we have to work inside, why don't we work on spells? If you're gonna crack the charm on your mom's letter, you need these skills, too," Agnes says.

I stand next to the table while Agnes meanders around the room, dragging her left foot and collecting the required items: a massive wooden bowl, oversized hardwood spoons, several bottles of herbs, etc.

"Don't just stand there like a statue," she says. "Make yourself useful. Grab those mortars and pestles."

"Sure. Anything else?" I ask, placing them on the table.

"Yeah. Grab the brandy from the booze shelf. And a couple of glasses." Once I've brought the items to the table, she grasps the bottle of brandy and pours a small amount into each glass. "Every time we're successful, we'll take a swig. Kinda like beer pong. Let's start with a protection spell. Easy-peasy."

"Oh, I'm good with protection incantations. They were the first successful spells I created." I complete the work in a few minutes, chanting and waving with a sleight of hand, and we both down the brandy.

"Fantastic. Let's move on." Agnes fills up the glasses again.

Together, we create and cast spell after spell until we're so tipsy we're throwing herbs into the air and sparking them with our witch energy, setting off tiny explosions of fireworks above us.

Agnes belches from the depths of her soul. "Excuuuse me." She belly laughs and sets the brandy aside.

"So ladylike." I crack up and set my glass on the table as my head spins. "I've had enough. And the alcohol triggered a hot flash." I stagger over to the bookshelf to snatch a loose piece of paper and fan myself in front of the air conditioner.

"We both know I'm no lady. And I agree. You're ready."

"Ready for what? I thought we were done?"

"Did you bring your mother's letter as I told you?"

I freeze as the AC blows my hair away from my flushed face. "Yes. It's in my purse." I stagger back and sift through my tote bag until I find the envelope marked Gwynedd.

"Now it's time to put your training to the test." Agnes holds onto the worktable as she stands and moves next to me. "Come on. Lay the letter down here."

I pull the letter from the envelope, unfold it, and lay it on the rough wood. "I'm scared, Agnes. What if I destroy my mom's letter in the process?"

"Then you'll be in the same fucking place you are now. Don't lose your confidence. If I say you're ready, you are."

My right hand trembles as I raise it above the paper. I summon my energy and the amber glow radiates, purring like a well-tuned car engine waiting for me to press on the accelerator. As I focus my intention on the unknown charm, letters spring from the page toward my hand. I smile while I continue with my intention. The letters begin as a blur but become clearer and SNAP! They spring back onto the paper. I close my eyes and grind my teeth.

"Stop it, Gwyn. You're gonna give up after one attempt? I thought you were tougher." She slaps her hand on the table.

I flinch, pull myself together, and try again. And again. Over and over. With each try, the letters fade back into the paper until they barely appear. I plop into the chair I carried from the kitchen. "All this work for nothing."

"What the fuck? Because you can't de-charm one letter, you've achieved nothing?" Agnes picks up her straw hat and slaps me with it.

"Stop! What are you doing?" I ask.

"I'm trying to smack some sense into that noggin you call a brain. You have come further in three weeks than I did in three years. I'm sure the ancestral witch background has a lot to do with your success, but I see so much more potential in your future. You'll become a more powerful witch than Lowri ever was. And she'd be damn proud. Your dad, too."

"I'm sorry. It's so disappointing. Now I'll never know what she had to say to me." My eyes become wet, and a single tear rolls down my flushed cheek.

"All is not lost, my dear." Agnes pulls the piano stool close and her face lights up with hope. "You still have options."

"What do you mean? Grovel back to Leslie for help?"

"Fuck no. You don't have to go back to the coven owing them anything. You're an ancestral witch. This lover of yours, the Scottish professor I've heard about. Didn't he tell you what it entails? The special connection you have with your ancestors to learn and perform the craft?"

"He shared some things, but not a lot," I say.

"You may need training from another ancestral witch to gain the skills to unlock the charmed letter. I would bet my life on it." She lowers her unruly eyebrows. "You know what that means, right?"

"Oh, shit. Archie is the only ancestral witch I know, but he's not my lover at the moment. Actually, I know two. But I don't think Audrey Kenilworth would help me, considering she lured the Host of the Unforgiven Dead from the Otherworld to kill me."

"What?" she shouts. "That's fucked up, Gwyn."

"You're telling me." I puff, displacing my fringe of bangs.

"Your former lover is your only option. Not a great one either, but he's all you've got."

"I know, and he's a member of the coven. They would expel him for training me."

"You're in that lovely space between a rock and a hard place. I'm glad I'm not you." Agnes cracks up and pours herself another brandy.

I frown at her and give her the bird.

The parking lot behind Shane's store has no spots left, and the street parking on Main Street is full. I text Spence to see if I can park in front of their house and walk from there. Since I gave myself extra time, I can stop for a quick visit. August is around the corner, and I've not seen most of my friends for weeks while I was training with Agnes.

The door flings open, and Spence hugs me with a tight squeeze. "It's been so long since we saw you last! You just missed Tanner. He stopped by for lunch but left about fifteen minutes ago." I follow Spence into the kitchen, and he gestures to the teapot on the stainless stovetop. "Want some tea? Water's heating on the stove now."

"Sure, but it's all I have time for. I have to walk to the Mystic Sage in this unbearable humidity and heat. Hot flashes have returned like an old, sinister enemy. Maybe I should put an ice cube in my tea."

"I could give you a small bag of ice to carry on the way." The teapot whistles, and he prepares my tea, setting a mug on the table in front of me. "So, what have you been up to?"

"Oh, working and dating," I say.

When I wave my hand with a faint amber glow, the spoon scoops up one serving of stevia and drops the sweetener in. I swirl my finger in a circle, leaving a spiral of amber streaks in the air, and the spoon creates a tiny whirlpool as it spins.

"And training." My Zillennial friend pulls up a chair and sits. "No way you're gonna keep this to yourself. Spill the tea. Right now."

"You can't tell Trinity or Dr. Hughes. Promise?" I ask.

He lays a hand on his heart. "May the gods strike me down."

"I spent most of July apprenticing with Agnes Pritchard," I say.

Spence grimaces. "The old hedge witch who shops at the Mystic Sage? I'm surprised she would even talk to you. But I see you were an excellent student. Look at you. Flaunting your magic. Dr. Hughes and Trinity would not be pleased."

"Well, they don't have a say. And if they want me to return to the Fellowship, they'll deal with it."

"Gwyn, you've become so sassy this past year. I love it. So, you're gonna come back? Everyone would be sooo happy."

"I have to clear up a couple of things first, but yeah. I'm thinking about it." As soon as I have a talk with Leslie and lay down my conditions. I sip the last of my tea, and a hot flash erupts.

Spence wets a paper towel with cold water. "Here, hot woman."

"Not funny." I lay the cold compress on my neck. "I guess I better get going. The stroll to Main Street takes a while. Thanks for the tea and tell Tanner I'm sorry I missed him."

"He'll be sad he missed you." Spence walks me to the door. "You seem a lot more confident. Is dating two men the reason?" he asks, wiggling his eyebrows.

My lips part. "Have you been talking to Ronnie?"

"Don't be mad. I had to pull it out of her. I'm glad you're playing the field. You deserve to be happy. And frankly, Archie screwed up. He should have to work for your affection."

"I appreciate your support," I say with a hug.

I begin my long trek to Main Street in my sneakers. The cold compress doesn't last long and becomes nothing more than an incubator. I clip my hair up, thankful I wore a tank top and shorts.

As I pass the Raven Pub, I notice what appears to be a team of engineers following up on the unexplained quaking event from earlier in the month. They won't find an answer, because she's not in there. Who knows where Audrey Kenilworth is hiding?

By the time I arrive at the Mystic Sage, I'm a sweaty mess and can't wait for the relief of the icy-cold AC in Shane's store. As I grasp the door handle, I notice Jeff speaking with an older woman with wavy brown hair, I'm guessing in her 60s. I pull on the door and catch the end of a conversation.

"Do as I say, Jeffrey. You don't have a choice." The woman chides him in a curt tone of voice. "You owe us."

I don't want to invade this heated, private conversation. "Hi, Jeff. I'll be in the back if you need me."

His eyes become bulbous, but he doesn't say a word. As I pass by, the woman glares at me with irate dark eyes—black like coal. I enter the crystals room and set my purse down and eavesdrop near the doorway. Not my usual behavior, but his gloomy face appeared to signal the coming of the reaper.

"Why didn't you tell me she might show up?" she whispers in a low-pitched, grating voice. Silence follows. "Do it, Jeffrey." The door slams with a ding.

I wait a few minutes before strolling nonchalantly into the front of the store. Jeff stares down at the counter. Avoiding my gaze, I suppose. Do I let it go or do I ask him about the argument? "Who was that woman? Do you want to talk about what happened?"

"It was my Aunt Edith." Jeff stares out the window as he talks. "Always giving me orders...things I don't want to do. She's paying for my education, so I can't say no."

"You don't have to tell me what it's about. But remember, you always have choices. If she's asking you to do something unreasonable, you can say no. You might lose their financial help, but you have friends who care about you. We would help you out. I can't offer you a place to stay since I'm sleeping on my son's sofa sleeper, but I'm sure Shane could put you up."

His eyes glisten with appreciation. "You guys are so nice. If things get worse, I may take you up on your offer."

I walk behind the counter and wrap my arms around him in a motherly hug, and he hugs me back, as if he's clinging to life itself.

The oppressive humidity hangs in the air as I stroll back to my car at dusk. When Mitchell Hall comes into view, I cross the street and observe the renovation preparation. The workers have nearly erected all the fencing. I scan the area for passersby, but no one is even close. So, I walk to the side gate to the Celestial Gardens. Feeling cocky, I raise my right hand and attempt to break the bubble the Fellowship cast on the gardens. The amber glow on my hand intensifies as I increase the razor-sharp focus of my intention. My witch energy springs back, knocking me on my ass.

"Shit." I stand and brush off my tush and notice I've got grass stains on my shorts. "Ugh. Nothing is going right."

I'm about to turn and leave, and a white glow lights up the mound. The Seelie Fae boy and girl eye me with big-toothed grins and skip to me at the gate. Their peachy skin and mint-green eyes shimmer as their golden-blond hair blows in the evening breeze. I wave as they approach me.

"Aunt Gwyn! Aunt Gwyn!" they shout. "It's been so long since we've seen you. We are so lonely here in the gardens without Momma Mitchell and Aunt Lowri. You said you would visit us!"

I kneel and place my hand against the invisible barrier. "I had to stay away for a while. And now I'm not allowed to enter to play with you. But I will soon. What are your names? I'd like to call for you next time."

"Shailagh," the girl says. "Aonghas," says the boy.

"Such beautiful names." Footsteps echo in the distance, and I say my goodbyes to the Seelie Fae. "I promise you. I will return, and we can play in the gardens. And you can tell me about Aunt Lowri."

The little ones wave and skip back to the mound. I stand and turn to find Bearsden police officer Braddock Wilson glaring down at me from his six-foot-nine frame.

"Ma'am, you shouldn't be in here," he says. "The city has construction workers prepping for the renovations. What are you doing?"

"Oh, I'm only snooping—excited about the renovations," I say, lying through my teeth.

"You look familiar. Do I know you from somewhere?" Officer Wilson asks in his deep voice. "Hey, I remember you. You were at the Bearsden homeless shelter last Thanksgiving when we got a call about the crushed body of a homeless man."

I bite my lower lip and peer up at him. "Yeah, I remember."

"Damn shame. We never figured out who committed those murders. The case is still open." He scratches his head. The Bearsden Coven knows, but I can't tell him. "Well, you better move along."

"Oh, I'm on my way home. Thank you." I move toward the paver walkway and turn back. "Have a nice evening, officer."

Officer Wilson tips his hat. "You, too, ma'am." He turns and strolls toward city hall.

On the way to the car, I mull over my next step. I must join the coven to enter the gardens, but I can't go back until I've read my mom's letter. When I arrive at my Prius, I notice the lights are dark at Tanner and Spence's house, so I hop into the driver's seat and sit for a moment. Agnes said I was stuck between a rock and a hard place. Time to remove the rock.

After the short drive to Archie's house, I sit in my car and stare at the living room window. The faint glow of the alabaster light splays through the sheer curtains. "Shit." I get out of the car and approach his front door and tap the wooden screen.

The door creeps open, and his eyes widen. "Gwyn, what are you doing here? You said you wanted some space."

"Can I come in?" I ask. "I've got something important to ask you?"

"Of course. Would you like a cup of tea while we chat?"

"I'd love some tea. I won't sleep; night sweats have been keeping me awake, anyway."

"Sorry to hear that. Let's go into the kitchen."

I sit down in the chair while he puts the kettle on and grabs cups from a cabinet. "This seems serious. Are you all right?"

"Oh, yeah. I'm fine. I finished my training with Agnes." An enormous grin brightens my sunburnt face. "I have confidence I never had training with the coven. Don't be offended."

He lifts a corner of his mouth. "I'm not. You didn't finish, remember?"

"Yeah, I know." I left them all in the gardens the night of the Winter Solstice Ceremony with the intention of never returning.

When the water boils, Archie prepares our tea and places it on the table, taking a seat next to me. "I'm listening."

I put my spoon in my cup and pause. Damn it. I decide when I'm going to use my magic. With a slight wave of my hand, the spoon spins in my cup.

"The old coot taught you a few tricks, I see. Be careful it doesn't become second nature. You wouldn't want Unremarkables to catch you performing magic."

"I know," I say with a roll of my eyes. "I only wanted to impress you."

Archie grins with a glimmer in his eyes. "You've done way more than mixing tea to impress me, Gwynedd. Come out with it."

"Even with all the training, I wasn't able to break the charm on my mom's letter." I sip my tea and tap my fingernails on the cup. "Agnes believes I need training in ancestral witch magic to cancel the charm."

He runs a hand through his ash-blond locks. "I'll do it."

"I haven't asked you anything yet," I say with a wrinkle between my eyes.

"It hardly requires guesswork. I'm your only option." Archie takes a drink of his tea and places his cup on the table.

"If Leslie or Trinity find out, they'll expel you. Especially after..."

"After my improprieties with the witches from other covens. I understand what the risks are."

"But I'm not sure I should ask. It's not fair to you."

Archie grasps my hand. "Gwynedd, I would do anything for you."

I gaze into his transparent-blue eyes. It's as if he's saying *I love you*.

CHAPTER THIRTEEN

SEEKING MY ANCESTORS

RONNIE SETS A CUP of jasmine green tea on the table for me and plops into the kitchen chair across from me. "Damn, woman. I've barely seen or heard from you these last three weeks!"

"I didn't mean to ignore you. The training with Agnes was grueling but fruitful." The tea has an intoxicating floral aroma, fresh from the garden.

"So, was she palatable?" Ronnie asks, chuckling. "'Cause she was always curt when I picked up my *herbs*."

"I have a new respect for Ms. Pritchard. She has many reasons for being so bitter." I decide not to share Agnes's past relationship with Leslie, even if Ronnie's my best friend. She confided in me. "But she was a great mentor, and I owe her my devotion. She's a witch of great power and taught me when no one else would."

My friend takes a sip of her black coffee. "I'm happy for you. Did you read your mom's letter yet?"

"No. Agnes said I need to apprentice with an ancestral witch to learn those skills." I lower my eyes to the teacup and stare at the tea leaves in the bottom, searching for a hint of my future.

"Gwyn, you only know one ancestral witch. You're dating him AND you've slept with him. Let's not even get started on how many rules he'd be breaking. I can only keep quiet for a while. You know I'm obligated to tell the coven, which puts me in a tough spot and isn't fair. If Leslie or Trinity ever find out, they'll fry Archie and serve him to the gods. You can't ask him to risk his membership."

I peer up at her through my fringe of bangs. "He offered before I could ask. I don't have any other choice. It's why I stopped by. I have to fetch a couple of my mom's witchcraft items—connections to her. I'm gonna start lessons with him this week."

"For fuck's sake." Ronnie shakes her head with hanging, crimson eyebrows. "Please, be discreet...for Archie's sake. Not that you owe him anything. Can I make a suggestion? Maybe keep your relationship platonic during the ancestral training?"

"Don't worry. I've already decided training needs to be my focus for now."

"You've not mentioned Nick at all. Have you seen him lately?"

"Not recently, but we're supposed to meet about my mom's grimoire. He's completed a few more translations. I had to stop seeing the two of them as often. My apprenticeship with Agnes came first."

"So, I can assume no hanky-panky yet?"

I blink twice. "No. But the last time I saw him, I wanted to rip his clothes off and get it over with. I think my hormones are way out of whack. He's invading my dreams night after night, and I'm waking wet all over...if you get my drift."

Ronnie bursts out laughing. "You may have to do something about that, or the dreams will only get worse. Think about it."

Think about it, she says. That's all I do.

A heat wave extends into August, taxing Tyler's window air conditioner. Even when I take a shower, I come out wanting to take another. I slip on a tank top, cotton shorts, and sandals for my training. At least the magic room in Archie's basement is cool. As I'm driving to his house, the phone rings through the speakers of my Prius. When I view Nick's name on the digital screen, I tap the green phone icon. "Hi, Nick."

"Hello, stranger. I've finished more translations and thought you'd like to come for dinner and go over them. Of course, I want to see you, too." Nick's voice has an eager tone.

I hate to turn him down, but my ancestral witch training takes priority. "I know we were supposed to get together, but these next two weeks are busy. Can I take a rain check?"

"Ahh, sure." The disappointment rings in his answer. "I'm not gonna lie. I really wanted to see you. It's been over a week since our last dinner."

"When I get past this busy time, I'll make time for you. I promise."

"I'm gonna hold you to that, Gwyn. Text me if you change your mind. We'll discuss these last few pages I translated."

Part of me wants to know now, but the translations and dinner will have to wait. "Bye, Nick."

I come to a stop in front of Archie's house on Duncan Street. My heart palpitates as I approach his door. So many emotions flow through me—relief, excitement, trepidation. I raise my fist to knock, but the door flings open.

He welcomes me with a wide grin spreading his goatee. "Are you ready for this? We could be at it for a few hours."

"I am, but I have one request." I enter the foyer and peer up at his chiseled face. "While I'm training, I don't want to see you in any other capacity. Can you put your emotions aside for now?"

"Aye. I can." He gestures toward the basement door. "Shall we?"

"As Spence would say, 'Absofuckinglutely,'" I chuckle.

I make my way down the steep stairs, and Archie follows. He shoves the boxes aside and opens the pine door to his magic room. It's been months since I practiced magic here. Familiar aromas of cinnamon, lavender, and mint permeate the hidden area, and I try to relax while he retrieves items from the shelves. I set my purse on the floor next to the long pine table and wait impatiently for him, tapping my foot to the rhythm of the opening of Beethoven's Fifth Symphony.

He sets crystals and a divination cloth on the table and glances at my feet. "You have no reason to be nervous. This will come naturally to you, assuming Agnes trained you as well as you say."

"I'm not so much nervous as eager. Patience isn't my forte." I move close to the table.

Archie snickers. "That's the understatement of the century."

I scowl at him and shift my gaze to the shiny black and white crystals. "Obsidian and selenite crystals. Where is the hanging stone for the divination cloth?"

"You'll not use a divination stone. The obsidian crystal will aid in rooting you to your ancestors. Use this selenite stone every time to connect with them. It fosters a direct line to break through all the clutter in your brain."

I chuckle and lean over the crystals to scrutinize them. "I'll need a lot of those."

"You've done extremely well in the past. At least when it mattered. Did you bring your mum's framed photo and other personal items?"

"Yeah." I pull out her framed photo and a dragonfly necklace she always wore from my purse, draping the necklace over the corner of the frame. "Well, tell me what to do."

"Stand directly in front of the cloth. I've placed the selenite between the larger obsidian crystals. This should help them blend as you pull on their magic. Place your palms above the crystals." I raise my hands, palms down, over the divination cloth and stones as he continues with my instruction. "Focus on a strong intention around connecting with your mum. If needed, gaze at her picture."

I spread my fingers and stare at the photo as the amber glow radiates from my hands. The crystals vibrate and a faint hum resounds. I tune out everything around me, including Archie. The crystals shake on the cloth as I intensify my intention, and my mother's picture falls flat with silence. My shoulders collapse.

"Gwyn, I told you this could take hours, days...even weeks. You were raised without magic. And your parents aren't here to guide you in your ancestral practices. I know patience isn't your virtue, but you must find a wee bit, or you'll not succeed."

"OK. I'll do it again." And again, and again...

While I'm sitting on the toilet, I nod off, nearly falling off the seat. I should give up and go home. Twelve days have passed, and outside of eating, sleeping, and working, I've done nothing but practice divination. I've barely seen Tyler, and he remains down in the dumps. Yet he won't tell me what's going on. Banging on the door makes me jump, and my heart takes off like a rocket.

"Gwynedd! Did you fall asleep in there? Get your bum moving. We have more to do. The night is young." Archie's footsteps dissipate as he descends the basement stairs.

Young? The mantle clock over the fireplace just finished dinging ten times. "I'm coming." I return to the basement and lean against the magic room doorway for a moment. "We should stop for the night. My focus flew out the basement window about two hours ago."

"I'm so proud of you. No matter how many times you've tried, you continue without fail. I know it's frustrating." Archie saunters over to me and stares into my eyes. "One more time."

"Fine." I shuffle over to the table and prepare my hands.

"Wait. Usually, we don't use herbs until an apprentice has achieved a bit of success with the crystals, but let's try." He scratches his goatee and walks over to the shelf to grab a jar and a small wooden bowl. "We're going to burn some mugwort. It will draw on the spirit of your mum. Be prepared. Viewing the ghost of a loved one can be traumatic, as you well know."

Seeing Richard's spirit come through the portal on Samhain nearly ripped me apart—until he pissed me off, and I sent him back to the Otherworld. "You worry too much. Let's get it over with so I can go to bed."

"All right." Archie grinds the mugwort and sifts the granules into the bowl. "Proceed."

I chant a blessing for my ancestors and fire up the herb using my witch energy. The scent has a mixture of bitter cedar and sage. I gag and cough, waving my hand in front of my face. He frowns and gestures to get started. My eyelids barely stay open, but I go through the motions, hoping this will satisfy him. I raise my hands, summoning the amber glow with a sliver of intention, and stare at my mom's beautiful face. A memory of her laughing as she tickles me appears in my head.

"I miss you, Mom," I whisper. Her image appears to float off the photo, reaching out to me. "Mom!" Her face disappears back into the photo as I touch the frame.

Archie lays a hand on my shoulder. "Gwyn, are you all right?"

"Fuck, yeah!" I jump up and down, laughing. "I want to try again!"

He chuckles. "I have a better idea. Let's stop for the night and drink to your success instead."

"Sure. Beat you up the stairs," I say.

I dash out of the room and run up the steps to the kitchen, and Archie's footsteps echo in the basement stairwell with a thud, thud, thud, ending behind me.

"Scotch whisky?" he asks, catching his breath.

"Yeah. This celebration requires something strong."

I rub my abdomen as my breathing becomes steady, and I fall into a kitchen chair grinning like I'm stoned—not that I've ever partaken of the herb. But Scotch whisky will suffice. My mentor brings the bottle to the table with two whisky glasses in hand and sits next to me.

"I've not had a dram with you for a long time." He smiles as he pours a wee bit into the glasses.

Archie sips his Scotch, but I down the entire amount. I grab my chest as the Scotch burns my throat. "Whoa! I'm not used to this."

"Another?" he asks with a wink. "But you should sip the Scotch."

"Sure, but I'll decide how I'm going to celebrate." I down another Scotch and grab the table. "Ohhh...that one burned, too. I'll need more."

He pours us another dram. "I'm so happy for you, Gwyn. You have a long path ahead of you, but with patience, you will eventually break the charm on your mum's letter."

"I just wish I could read her words now." The Scotch doesn't burn this time. "Another."

"Are you sure?" Archie asks as a wrinkle forms between his eyes.

I slam the glass on the table. "Yes! It's not like I do this ALL the time."

"That's what worries me. You'll not be able to drive home." He pours another dram into my glass and takes another sip from his glass.

"I'll call Tyler to pick me up. No biggy." I knock back another Scotch, and my face flushes enough to cure hypothermia. "Oh, my gods! I'm burning up!"

Archie darts to the fridge and returns with an ice pack. "That should be your last one, anyway."

"Are you cutting me off?" I ask as I lay the ice pack on my chest.

He leans back with a lascivious grin. "I am."

I stare into his magnetic eyes and realize the ice pack does nothing to quell my flaming cheeks. "Can we move into the living room and let this buzz wear off a little?"

"Of course." Archie stuffs the cork in the bottle and stands as if he hasn't had a drop of Scotch.

I push up from my chair, and the room spins around me like a merry-go-round, prompting me to clutch the edge of the table. "Ohhh, I didn't feel a thing until I stood up."

"Let me help you to the loveseat." He reaches for my arm, and I pull it away.

"I'm sure I can walk 'cause I'm not drunk." I straighten my back and stagger toward the doorway, running smack into the doorjamb. "Ouch."

"You stubborn woman." He grasps my arm and guides me to the loveseat, where I stumble and fall.

I burst out laughing. "I'm thirsty now. Can you get me a glass of water?"

"Sure." He smiles and returns to the kitchen.

I sit up, and the room wobbles back and forth. The mantle clock dings, the first of eleven if I'm reading the clock right. My head pounds as it rings, and I would throw my shoe at it if I could get up. Archie returns and sits next to me and passes the glass of water.

"You're probably dehydrated," he says.

"Thank you so much." I take a swig of water. "Why aren't you staggering? You don't even waver when you walk."

He snickers. "You're supposed to sip Scotch, and I can hold my liquor. But you're more than a wee bit drunk."

"No, I'm not…I'm only a little tipsy." I attempt to place the glass on the steamer trunk and spill water down the front of his light-blue t-shirt.

"Whoa, it's cold!" he yelps as he rips off his shirt. "It's only water. No worries."

"I'm so sorry," I say.

In my drunken stupor, I pull off my V-neck tee and blot the beads of water off his chest, leaving me in my light-gray bra. I stare at his buff chest and stroke my fingers across his firm muscles, grazing his nipples. When I raise my head, Archie's eyes burn with desire as the room swerves. My lips part to speak, but the words tumble in my head, trying to find a pathway out. I caress the side of his warm face.

In one swift motion, he pulls my head to meet his, locking his tender lips on mine. I'd forgotten how his kisses lit a fire inside of me, and how the gentle touch of his skin removed the stress of the world, making me feel whole. Whiffs of woodsy cologne make my head spin with memories of better times, times without the thrill of magic.

I grab his shoulders, a poor attempt to balance, and fall back with him on top of me. As our tongues continue to play, the bulge in his jeans swells, pressing against my leg. It's more than I can take. So, I reach for his belt buckle. When I unfasten the leather and pull down the zipper of his jeans, I become wet with anticipation. But my hands fumble with the button.

And suddenly Archie tears his mouth from mine. "Stop, Gwynedd." He moves my hand from his bulge as he pants. "I'm so sorry for stealing a kiss. It was wrong of me."

"It's OK. I wanted you to kiss me." When I wrap my hand around the nape of his neck, I recall his warm lips. "I *want* you to kiss me."

He cups my face and gazes into my eyes as his bare chest rises and falls. "I love you, Gwynedd. I love you."

"What?" Did I hear him right? I must be drunk—hallucinating.

"I've never felt this way with any other woman, witch or Unremarkable. The yearning, the wanting, the aching for you. You were right. It hurts. Headaches like a hammer pounding away with a vengeance so bad, no healing spell would work." Archie lowers his eyebrows and chuckles. "I had to go to a fawking doctor."

He leans his forehead against mine. "I know I love you every time I reach for you in the morning when I wake, and you're not there in bed next to me, illuminating the room with your smile. You cast a spell on me no magic can break." He pulls away from me and zips up his jeans with difficulty. "I broke my promise as your mentor. It won't happen again."

As I salivate over his bulging...everything, I can't believe he's turning me down, so I sit up and grab my woozy head. He said the three words I'd waited so long to pass through his lips. I want to believe him, but it must be the Scotch talking. The ticking of the mantle clock gets louder with each annoying tick while I search for a response in my inebriated brain.

"I should go," I say.

"You're too drunk to drive. And Tyler has gone to sleep by now. I'll sleep here on the loveseat. You take the bed upstairs."

"Can you help me?" I wobble all the way as Archie assists me to his bedroom.

Falling onto the bed, I finally recognize what a state of drunkenness I'm in and have trouble removing my cotton shorts. With a quick tug, he pulls them off and slides the sheet over my torso.

"Goodnight, Gwynedd." He strokes my cheek with a finger.

I gaze into his icy blues with droopy eyes. "Goodnight, Archie."

Chapter Fourteen

THE ELDER WITCH RETURNS

My head throbs like a bitch, and my ears hum. I raise my hand to block the sun's rays from blinding me and glance at the empty glass case on the wall where the ancestral dirk used to rest. I rub my temples as I recall what happened last night. Did Archie actually say he loved me, or did I dream he said those words? I slide out of the bed, landing on the wooden floor in my bare feet, and walk to the bathroom for my morning pee. After pulling on my shorts, I tiptoe down the stairs and peek into the living room. He's still passed out on the loveseat with his long legs hanging over the edge.

I sneak in and grab my V-neck tee and slip it on. He appears so peaceful. I go into the kitchen and check the fridge, taking out eggs, spinach and peppers. Cooking breakfast is the least I can do after these grueling two weeks of training. I prep the pan with a bit of avocado oil and scour the drawers for a small knife.

"Toast may be all I can handle this morning," the Scottish voice says. "I may pass on the eggs and veggies."

I turn around to find him leaning against the kitchen door-jamb. He's definitely looked better. "Why don't I make toast first? Maybe it'll settle your stomach. Want some tea?"

"Yes. Black tea would be great." He slides into a chair and scratches his goatee. "How long have you been awake?"

"Not long. Got up a few minutes ago." I put a couple of bread slices into the toaster and fill the kettle with water. "I thought I'd give you a break and cook breakfast. You've been so patient training me for the last two weeks. I can't thank you enough." I wish I had eyes on the back of my head, so I could observe his face. Get clues about what happened last night. Unless he brings up the topic, I'm not saying anything.

Archie clears his throat. "We need to talk about last night."

My eyes bulge out, but he can't see them. "About what? I was pretty drunk. About my success with the divination?"

"Don't be evasive," he says with a thicker brogue. "You know damn well what I mean. Are we not going to discuss the elephant in the room?"

Oh, my gods. It wasn't a dream. I inhale and hold it for a moment...and turn around. "More like a whale, I would say."

"So, you remember everything I said to you?"

"The gist of it, I think."

The kettle whistles, and I prepare our tea, setting the cups on the table. I sit down and peer up at him.

"I meant every word, Gwynedd." He leans into me and stares into my eyes. "You told me you needed space, so I stayed away. As each month passed, I longed for you more. When the revelation of my love for you became clear, I wanted to shout it at the world. But when you said you were seeing Nick, I decided I should remain quiet. If being with an Unremarkable makes you happy, then you should do what brings you joy. I want you to be happy."

"Archie, I want to believe you. But you drank a lot of Scotch last night, too." I take a sip of my tea.

"I shouldn't have told you yet, but it's done. Until your training is complete, we'll not speak of this again."

Does he think I can forget what he said? Lover, you can't put the genie back in the bottle. "You expect me to just ignore what you said?"

"Yes, if you're going to finish your training. You said as much yourself." Archie gets up from the table and ambles to the toaster. "Would you like me to cook your eggs? I'm feeling better now."

"No, thank you. I think I'll go home." I stand and walk to the hall tree to retrieve my purse and slip on my sandals. His footsteps follow close behind. "When will I train again?"

"Let's take a break for a few days. You could use the time to refresh."

"Are you trying to avoid me now?"

"No, Gwyn." He touches the underside of my chin. "I want you with me every day. Leslie returns today, and she'll want to meet with me about the Celtic Studies department. And she'll want an update on what's happened to the town."

"I need to speak with her, too," I say.

"You should wait until she's recovered a bit from jet lag. It's much harder at her age. Don't expect the answers you want. If she's kept her secret this long, I imagine she's not eager to share now."

"But she'll know I'm aware she's hiding something. That could come in handy down the road."

"Do not underestimate Dr. Leslie Hughes. I've been on the receiving end of her wrath." He opens the door. "I'll be in touch in a few days, and we'll continue your ancestral apprenticeship."

"Thank you." I step out the door onto the stoop, and the screen door claps shut. I glance over my shoulder at Archie, and he shuts the door.

Before I drive home, I text Ronnie, letting her know I need to see her for lunch. When I enter the apartment, Tyler and Zoe are necking on the sofa in their pajamas. At least they're dressed?

"Sorry, guys. I expected you'd still be in bed," I say.

"I hope it's OK I stayed over." Zoe sits up, snickering. "Since you didn't come home last night."

"Zoe," Tyler mutters. "I told you not to mention it." He peers up at me. "Sorry, Mom."

I chuckle. "Wipe those dirty thoughts out of your head. It's not what you're thinking."

"You've been spending so much time with Archie, we figured…you know," Zoe says.

"He's been helping me with…some studies." I glare at Zoe and roll my lips inward.

Tyler's eyes shift back and forth between us girls. "But you're not taking any classes this summer, are you?"

"No." I scramble for an answer in my hungover head. "He's been helping with some research to prepare for the fall. It was late, and I fell asleep at his place."

Zoe snickers. "So nice of him to offer."

"Yes, it was." I glare at her. "I'm meeting Ronnie for lunch early to avoid the crowds, so I've got to take a shower. Is it OK for me to jump in?"

"Sure. Zoe, let's go hang out in my room until she leaves." They get up and stroll toward the bedroom.

"Tyler, can I talk to you for a minute?" I ask with concern in my voice. "You've appeared sullen lately. I know I've not been around a lot. Is there something wrong you need to share with me?"

"You know the stress at work has affected my sleep. The situation hasn't improved. But we should finish the new updates soon," he says. "I'll be OK, Mom. Don't worry about me."

"I wish there were something I can do," I say.

Your mom interfering with the rhythm of your love life can't be helping either. I put off looking for a place to live while I was training with Agnes, but now it's time. As I hug my son, a temporary solution leaps into my head like an uninvited enemy.

I tap my nails on the wooden table as I scope the patrons of the Sunshine Garden Café. If Ronnie hadn't put a table aside for us, we'd have to eat in the back. The clinking of the plates and glasses cuts into my ears as I rub my temples.

Ronnie darts through the kitchen doors and drops into the booth seat. "What's so important you had to meet me for lunch instead of texting? One of the cooks got sick, so I've gotta help in the kitchen."

I lean over the table and open my mouth, but the words don't form.

"Are you OK?" she asks, staring into my bloodshot eyes. "You look like shit. Spit it out."

"You know, I've been training with Archie recently." I roll my lips inward but blurt it out. "He said he loved me."

"Oh. My. Gods. And what did you say?"

"I don't remember. I think I replied with 'what?' He blurted it out after he kissed me."

"Oh, for fuck's sake, Gwyn. You've wanted him to tell you he loves you for how long and you respond with 'what?'" She raises her crimson eyebrows. "Or is it because you don't know how you feel?"

"I don't know. And I was drunk. He was drunk. I had success with my ancestral divination, so we celebrated with a few drinks of Scotch." My head pounds as the chatter in the café rings in my ears. "And I spilled water on his t-shirt, so he ripped it off. I think you can fill in the rest."

She snickers. "So, you finally got laid."

"What? No. He stopped and pulled away. He apologized and said it won't happen again. At least not while we're training."

"Wow. Archie had the chance to get laid after all these months of celibacy, and he threw in the towel? He must really love you, woman."

I swallow and glance at the menu. "I don't know what to do, Ronnie. If he'd said it months ago, I'd be all over him. But after what happened, and now I'm dating Nick? He's an Unremarkable. This could be my chance at a normal life." As if that could ever happen.

"Hmph. Take some advice, friend. Dating, loving, and living with an Unremarkable has huge drawbacks, too. Once you achieve the success you need to read your Mom's letter, do you really think you can turn the magic off?"

"I'm so confused." I rub my throbbing temples. "What do you think I should do?"

"Hey, lady. You know better than to ask me. I just got my shit together this past year with Derek. You'll figure it out. For now, have fun and don't overthink the situation."

"Have fun? There may be a rogue witch with a vendetta out there, and I'm not at full capacity as an ancestral witch yet. AND my mentor just told me he loves me." I swipe my hands across my face. "All this fun may kill me."

Dr. Leslie Hughes—acting chair and professor of the Celtic Studies department, the Elder witch of the Bearsden Coven, and my former professor—has had three days to recover from her trip home from Great Britain. And I'm not waiting any longer to confront her.

I stand in front of the tiny Tudor house on Drummond Lane, grinding my teeth. The last words I spoke to Leslie were "fuck destiny." But it appears destiny might have won this round. I stroll up the driveway and stand on the side porch, rapping on the door. Part of me hopes she's not home, but the rattling of the knob ensues.

Leslie opens the kitchen door and glares at me with copper-brown eyes. She's dressed for the blazing heatwave wearing a loose blouse over cotton capri pants with her silver hair wrapped tightly in a bun on the top of her head.

"Gwynedd, what a pleasant surprise." The slight scowl on her face would beg to differ. "Please, come in. It's good to see you after all this time. Excuse my appearance. I was cleaning."

I notice a bucket full of suds in the sink as I enter. "Thank you for inviting me in, Dr. Hughes. I know our last conversation was curt and vulgar on my part."

"There's no need to call me Dr. Hughes," she says. "I'm not your professor any longer. Please, call me Leslie, as you used to. What can I do for you, Gwynedd?"

"Can we sit down?" Leslie's chimeric cat familiar with a black and ginger coat slinks into the kitchen and rubs against my leg. "Hello, Mr. Yeats. Glad to see you're still looking after Dr. Hughes."

Leslie gestures toward the hallway. "Let's go to my office."

I follow her to the book hoarder's paradise, Mr. Yeats in tow, and am taken aback when I enter. "Wow! Your office looks…"

"Organized," she says with the slightest of smiles. "Mr. Yeats was a great help, especially after the large donation of books I made to the DUB library."

Over half a year ago, her office had books stacked everywhere, and her shelves behind the desk were a haven for dust bunnies. The sliding shelf hiding the entrance to her magic space even has new baskets to store items. Mr. Yeats scuttles over to the entryway and lies on the floor, staring at me with his yellow and powder-blue eyes. Leslie sits behind her desk and motions to a chair on the other side. I set my purse on her desk as I sit and glance over my shoulder at the familiar. He's purring and swishing his tail.

"How was Wales?" I ask—procrastination for the win.

"It was lovely. But you didn't come here to discuss my annual summer trip, I suspect."

"No, I didn't." I peer at her placid face and get on with it. "Leslie, I know why my mom left the coven."

Her copper eyes grow big. "Indeed. And what is this revelation you learned?"

"I already knew about the opening of the great portal in the mid-'60s. But what you didn't tell the coven, or me, is my mom didn't want you to do it. She begged you not to, and you still went through with it despite her pleadings. It angered her so much, she withdrew from the coven and magic for good."

The professor's eyes narrow on her wrinkled, pale face. "Are you finished?"

"Almost. I know you have a secret you're keeping from me and everyone." I glare at her with fire in my eyes. "You need to tell me, Leslie."

She glances at Mr. Yeats, and he scuttles out of the office. "I cannot tell you. For the benefit of the coven, I will never divulge the reason. And you must put this behind you for your benefit as well."

"That's unacceptable on so many levels," I say.

"Who have you been speaking with? There are only a handful of witches who took part and know what transpired."

I blink. "That's for me to know and you to find out."

"You've spoken with Trinity. But she was a teen and wasn't present all evening." Her silver eyebrows fall into her eyes. "Have you approached Agnes Pritchard?"

I figure now is as good a time as any to show off. With a focused intention and a slight wave of my hand, the door to her office slams shut. "I've done more than talk to her, Leslie."

Her eyes bug out. "You apprenticed with Agnes Pritchard?"

"I sure as hell did. As you can see, she taught me a few tricks." I move toward the office door and place my hand on the knob, almost forgetting my other objective.

"Agnes is an impulsive, disorganized, and undisciplined witch. It wasn't the best path for you to learn." She stands and stares down at me as she straightens her spindly body.

"Maybe not, but she didn't require a commitment to a coven and its rules." Or a pledge to not defy her like you require. "That being said, I'd like to make a proposal to you. I haven't decided whether to return to the coven yet, but I'm considering the possibility. Meanwhile, I have no good place to practice the craft living in Tyler's apartment. Plus, I need to move out. Would you consider renting me a room? Only for a few months while I figure things out."

Leslie purses her lips and peers back at the magic room. "Yes. Moving in here is a wonderful idea."

I cock my head at the professor. Well, that was easy. And her eagerness to accept my offer alarms me.

"Dinner was wonderful, as usual. I'm sorry I've been so aloof in the past few weeks. I've been preoccupied with work and...studies.

Preparing for the fall semester," I say as Nick moves closer to me on the sofa. "I promise you it's not the company."

I gaze into his dark-brown eyes with a flirty smile, thinking I shouldn't have avoided him these past two weeks. He wraps an arm around me and leans in to press his lips on mine. His kisses are so tender and loving, not full of the passion I remember with Archie, but his life lacks the drama of the supernatural world.

"Before we get too hot and heavy. I don't want to forget about the translations I completed." He picks up his tablet off the end table and hands it to me. "What do you make of this?"

While I read the words, I swallow to suppress my desire to shout "holy shit." This is an obvious hex. "Interesting."

"That's all you have to say. This reads like the definition of an evil spell—a hex. I'm certain this is an antiquarian book of witch's spells called a grimoire. Were your ancestors into something wicked?"

"Hell if I know. I mean, my mom never mentioned it."

"I'm intrigued." He takes the tablet from my hands and sets it on the end table. "This is some badass historical shit. I assume you want me to continue with the translations?"

"Oh, yes. There may be more than spells and hexes in it. I'm still rooting for a soup recipe," I say.

Nick bursts out laughing. "I love your sense of humor, Gwyn. It's only one of the many reasons I like you."

I wrap my hand around the nape of his neck and pull him toward me, pressing my hungry lips against his. When he offers his tongue to me, I happily reciprocate. He pulls away and removes his shirt, inviting me to do the same. I pull up on my tee but stop when my right bicep pinches. "Oh, my muscle hurts. You may need to help me."

"No problem." Nick whisks my shirt off and lays it carefully on the back of the sofa. "Let me massage it. You probably strained the muscle lifting." He kneads the painful area.

"Ohhh. Your hands feel so good." I peer up at him with lust in my eyes and stroke his chest with my other hand. "Stand up, Nick."

His brow wrinkles as he complies. I shift on the sofa so I'm sitting directly in front of him. I gaze into his dark eyes with a simper and unclasp the button on his jeans, which are expanding exponentially. He sighs as I slowly pull on the zipper. A dream of him replays in my head, and my stomach churns with nausea. Archie's confession joins the replay as I lean back against the sofa and catch the disappointment on his face.

"I'm sorry, Nick," I say.

"It's OK." He zips up his jeans and sits next to me, stroking my cheek. "You're not ready. Take whatever time you need."

"That's not it. I like you a lot, Nick. So much more than I expected to. I want to have sex with you. But my heart's not in it."

"It's Archie. You're in love with him."

"I don't think I ever stopped loving him. It's not fair to you." Suddenly, a rumble encompasses the apartment, and the building begins to quake. "We need to get out of the building, and fast!"

"This happened at the Raven Pub a few weeks ago. It will probably pass, but let's not chance it," he says.

I grab my shirt and slip it on. We snatch our shoes and run down the stairs, exiting through the emergency door. The ground continues to shake while we fumble to put on our sandals. The apartment building appears fine, but we hear screaming near Mitchell Hall. And fire alarms blare.

"We should go see what's happening," I say, with knots churning in my stomach.

"I agree," he says. "Maybe we can help."

Nick leads the way as we run down Main Street toward the crowd. As we get closer, dust floats past the glow of the lampposts. We both cringe at the sight. One entire side of Thomas Hall, an old red-brick building housing the DUB alumni organization, has fallen to the ground. A couple of mangled bodies lie in the pile of brick and wood while two students scream for help from the exposed second-floor rooms.

"Holy shit," Nick says.

I scan the crowds, searching for a woman with wavy brown hair and inky eyes, but there are too many people gathering under the spill of the lamppost. Within minutes, the area has accumulated locals from the Raven Pub, the campus, and the nearby neighborhoods of Old Bearsden. When the city police and fire engines arrive, the firefighters jump off the trucks and run toward the rubble of Thomas Hall.

"I wish we could do something," I say, continuing to scour the crowds.

Nick puts his arm around me. "Let the first responders do their jobs. We'll only be in the way. Are you OK?"

"Yes, I'm fine," I say.

He kisses me on the head. How could I have led him on like this? It wasn't fair to him at all, but right now, I have more important issues to worry about. I inspect the crowds and start an intention to sense magic in the area. A buzz twitches across my skin, and I snap my head around, hoping to catch Audrey Kenilworth in the act.

Instead, I find Archie standing in the distance, staring at bare-chested Nick and me. He shoves his hands in his pockets and walks away with his head down. And my heart sinks.

Chapter Fifteen

Like Mother, Like Son?

The next day, rescue trucks, local police, and first responders continue to sift through the rubble, blocking the end of Main Street. So far, the news has reported two deaths and several wounded—mostly students. The heat must be unbearable in the gear the rescuers are wearing. It's so horrifying. I can't believe Audrey could cause this amount of destruction, but none of us know her true identity. She could be capable of anything.

A phone call rings over my car speakers. "Hey, Ronnie."

"Did you hear what happened to Thomas Hall?" she asks. "I was gonna call last night, but I knew you were at Nick's. Didn't want to interrupt anything."

"Yeah, Nick and I walked down there. The building looks decapitated on one side, like someone actually took a knife and sliced it right down the middle."

"Oh, my gods. I read two students died. So sad. So, I can assume you didn't jump Nick's bones last night, then?"

I hesitate. "No, I didn't. I tried, Ronnie. I got as far as undoing his zipper. And the bulge in his pants was inviting. But I became nauseous, and Archie's face popped into my head."

"I think your heart's deciding for you." Derek's voice rattles off words in the background. "I'll be right there, honey! Hey, I gotta go, but I wanted to ask you. And you can say no. Would you consider coming to the Fellowship meeting tomorrow evening? Trinity has called a meeting, and I know she won't ask you." She waits for me to respond, but I don't. "Are you still there?"

"I'm thinking. I'm going to rent a room from Leslie. Give Tyler back his privacy, so I might as well." And Agnes said I was ready.

"Moving is great, but into Leslie's house? Oh, my gods," she cackles. "Derek's waiting for me in the car. Talk to you later. Love ya."

The phone disconnects as I park in Archie's driveway, and I walk to the porch. I stand at his front door, dripping in sweat in my tank top, jean shorts, and sandals. Another hot and sticky August day awaits, but I'd almost rather melt on this porch than enter his house. I suck in the humid air and knock.

"Good morning," he says as I enter. "We should get started right away. I've got a busy day ahead of me."

I can barely look him in the eye. "Me, too. I've got to work at Shane's store this afternoon." I flip off my sandals and set my purse on the hall tree.

"We all do, I imagine." Archie glances at the mantle clock in the living room and returns his gaze. "Trinity sent out a message to the coven when she heard about the partial collapse of Thomas Hall. She didn't include you, because she wants to respect your boundaries. But I'm asking you, as your mentor and friend. Will you at least come to the next meeting and consider returning to the Fellowship? If only to address this issue. The coven is down by three members. It takes a year to recruit new bodies. The coven needs you."

Are he and Ronnie conspiring together? "I already told Ronnie I would go, but I'm worried I won't be able to stand up to Leslie."

"Gwynedd, you're ready." He leans into me. "I heard about your wee exhibition at Leslie's."

"Only a wee flex." I wrinkle my nose.

He chuckles. "Flaunting your magic will get you into trouble someday. You haven't achieved the level of success you need to read your mum's letter, but you're more than ready on a magic level. The rest has to do with confidence. And your *wee* flex proves you have that as well."

"I've also asked Leslie if she'd rent me a room, so can I move out of Tyler's apartment. He needs his privacy, and I'd be able to keep tabs on her. What makes you think I can stand up to her?"

"I don't call you a stubborn woman to piss you off. You've earned the title. Moving in with her is a double-edged sword at best, but it's not an awful idea."

"You're meeting tomorrow night?" I ask.

"Aye. At the Pumpkin House. Think of it as a family reunion." Archie checks the mantle clock again. "We should get started. We only have the morning to practice."

I wait a few seconds and decide to go there. "About last night..."

He gazes at me with a flat mouth. "You owe me no explanation. I told you before, I have no claims on you."

I shift closer and stare into his transparent-blue eyes. "Don't you?"

"You know how I feel." He shoves his hands into his pockets. "Don't make this harder for me. The teasing isn't appreciated."

"Archie, I'm not seeing Nick anymore, other than meeting to discuss the translations of the grimoire."

"I'm a wee confused. When I saw you both in the street, I noticed Nick was shirtless and assumed..."

"Maybe you shouldn't assume. I'll admit, I was...how would the
young ones put it? Thirsty for Nick. But I didn't sleep with him,
Archie."

The mantle clock ticks while he pauses. "We should get to the
magic room. The morning is flitting away." And he smiles.

I straighten my back and walk toward the basement with a cocky
grin.

The parking lot behind the Mystic Sage is full again, so I park in
front of Spence and Tanner's house. I tap on the front door, and
Spence flings it open. "Hey, stranger. What's up?"

"I'm not coming in. Gotta get to work, but I wanted to make
sure it was OK to park out front." I gesture to my Prius.

Spence throws his palms up. "Sure? This was YOUR house."

"But I don't pay the mortgage anymore," I say.

He bursts out laughing. "Neither do I." We both laugh together.

"You know you're spoiled by that man of yours, don't you?" I
ask.

"Don't I know it?" He puts a hand on his hip. "The Fellowship
is having an emergency meeting tomorrow night. I know it's not
fair to ask, but would you come if I asked you? Pretty please? Some
kind of shit is going down, you know?"

"Ronnie and Archie already asked. I'll be there," I say.

"Oh, thank you, sis!" he shouts, hugging me. "It'll be like old
times. I can't wait."

"Me neither. Tell Tanner I'll see him tomorrow night. I'll be too
tired to stop in when I finish work."

"Will do. But you're not leaving until you tell me what's going on between you and the professor. And don't tell me you're only friends."

I chuckle. "Never you mind. I'll see you tomorrow."

He grimaces and gives me the bird.

As I trudge through the afternoon heat to the store, I regret not buying a personal fan. I clip up my hair and enjoy the relief of the warm breeze on the back of my neck. When I get to the end of Manor Road, where it transitions to Main Street, the rescue and clean-up crew are working on what's left of Thomas Hall. I sense a foreboding strolling past the area from across the street—so close to Mitchell Hall. And my worries jump to the Seelie Fae children in the Celestial Gardens. If it weren't for the protection spell the coven cast on the Mitchell's property, it could be next.

Shane is stocking the shelves when I arrive, which surprises me. I usually take over for Jeff. Ahh, the air conditioning is glorious.

"Hey, Shane. Can I help?" I ask, setting my purse behind the counter.

"Sure. There's an entire box of herbs in the box. Agnes bought me out of a bunch. Something about a fire in her herb garden." He has a twinkle in his laughing eyes.

My brow crinkles. "Has Agnes been gossiping?"

"Darling, that old curmudgeon woman does not gossip. She just says it like it is."

"Oh, my gods. She told you what happened? I can't believe it. The woman barely spoke in complete sentences when she came to the store."

"Seems she's slightly more cordial these days. I wonder if a certain apprentice has anything to do with her friendly demeanor," he says, placing jars on the shelf.

"She's not so bad," I say, grinning. "In fact, I kinda like her. She has spunk."

"Not unlike another witch I know. I gotta hand it to you, Gwyn. I've never seen Agnes so happy as the last time she shopped. She was full of smiles, going on about you."

"We didn't start out too well, but we ended on a positive note."

The door dings, and Jeff enters the store. Shane whispers, "We'll talk more later." He raises his voice. "Good afternoon, my son from New Jersey. How did the economics test go? Jeff is finishing up a special Summer Session course."

Jeff grins. "Got an A! Thank you so much for helping me study, Shane."

"No problem. I'm available anytime to help you study for an economics exam that will do absolutely nothing to prepare you for the actual business world." Shane laughs and grabs his belly.

Jeff frowns, and I admonish my boss. "Sha-ane. You're bad."

"Being good is no fun." He grins, exposing his yellowed teeth, and turns to empty the box he's working on.

"Jeff, you know he's joking, right?" I ask.

"Yeah, but he's right. I wouldn't even bother with this degree if it weren't for my aunt." Jeff's face morphs into a somber expression. "I attended both Summer Sessions, so I can graduate early. It's why I could work in the store all summer."

"More problems with your aunt?" Of course, I'm intruding. Someone has to help this young man.

"The usual. It's OK. I only have one more year, and I'll be done with them. I can find a job and start my life." He nods, showing a trace of optimism on his face.

"Remember, we're here for you if you ever need an intervention," I say. "Family isn't determined by blood. You choose your family by finding the ones who truly love you."

"Thanks. I'll remember your advice." He walks behind the counter to set up.

Shane checks a side pocket of his cargo shorts for his wallet, I assume. "Gwyn, I'm heading home. The store is in your watchful, caring hands."

"Bye, Shane." I wave to our boss.

I spend the rest of the afternoon in the back room going through inventory while Jeff mans the cash register. The door dings all afternoon with the steady rhythm of a trending song until a sudden silence occurs. Good. My colleague deserves the break. About thirty minutes passes, and the door dings again. Terse voices snap back and forth, so I sneak to the doorway to eavesdrop.

"What are you doing here, anyway?" Jeff whispers.

A woman with a low-pitched, grating voice replies, "You haven't been answering your phone."

"I'm sorry. Classes have kept me busy all summer," Jeff says in a defensive tone. "I finished my finals a few days ago, so I'm done."

"I expect you to be responsive from now on. The family has much to accomplish in the next couple of months, and you owe us, Jeffrey. Remember that," she says.

"Yes, ma'am." The clicking of high heels resounds, and the bamboo chimes clank when the door shuts.

I ache for Jeff but decide it's too intrusive to admit I heard any of this conversation. He *owes* them? For the love of the gods, what does he owe her? He's their nephew. She should have been happy to take him in. I wish I still had the house, so I could offer him a place to stay. I tiptoe to the back room and continue with the inventory. When Jeff leaves for dinner, I take over the cash register until closing and lock the store.

Passing the remnants of Thomas Hall, I notice the work crews have gone home for the night, so I sneak past the road blockades to get to Mitchell Hall to the left. I dart to the entrance of the Celestial Gardens and search for the Seelie Fae children and find them dancing under the moonlight. I grin and wave at the fairies as they skip toward me, their golden-blond hair floating on the wisps of a breeze.

"Aunt Gwyn!" they shout. "Did you come to play?"

"No, I'm still not able to break the invisible protection bubble. But I will the next time I come." I lay my hand against the barrier, and they press their tiny hands on mine. "Shailagh and Aonghas, you need to listen to me. Very soon, people will show up to work on Momma Mitchell's home. You must remain hidden, especially during the day. Will you promise to wait until nighttime to come out and play?"

The Seelie Fae children squint at each other and giggle. "We'll try, Aunt Gwyn."

"I have to go now. Play in Momma Mitchell's garden but hide when people come." I wave as they run through the gardens, catching fireflies.

The walk to my car seems to take forever in the heat, and I slap at mosquitoes the entire way. Manor Road is never this empty. The quiet on the road is creepy, and I imagine footsteps following me, only to turn around and find no one is there. I recall the night the Sluagh appeared to follow me home, and a shudder seizes my body. "Get yourself together, Gwyn."

As I quicken my pace, I observe a flicker of light from behind me and twist my head around. Nothing. But a faint glow appears on my hands and disappears within seconds. Is Audrey trying to put a hex on me again? Thanks to Agnes's protection incantation, I don't have to worry about an evil spell anymore. I search for her in the distance and smirk.

By the time I arrive at the apartment, Tyler appears to have gone to bed. It's only 9:30 p.m. He'll jump for joy when he hears the news about my move. I go to the bathroom to wash up and brush my teeth and slip into my PJs. I should do push-ups before I go to bed, but I'm pooped. When I pull out the bed from the sofa, the damn thing drops hard, landing on the floor with a bang. Damn it.

The bedroom door creaks open, and Tyler shuffles out, scratching his head. "Hey, Mom," he says, dragging his feet into the bathroom. He appears so sleep-deprived. The toilet flushes, and he walks out. "Goodnight."

"Tyler, since you're awake. Can I talk to you for a minute?" I ask.

His face says no, but he says, "Sure." He staggers over like he's hung over.

"Are you intoxicated?" I ask.

"What? No. Why would you think I'm drunk? I'm just exhausted."

"Sit down next to me. We need to talk."

He sits but falls back on the sofa bed. "Go ahead."

"I wanted you to know I found a room to rent, so I'll be moving out. And you'll finally have the privacy you need."

Tyler sits up straight with bulbous eyes. "That's a terrible idea."

"What? I assumed you'd be happy. You don't need me cramping your style anymore."

His eyes swell up with water, and a tear rolls down his cheek. "I don't want you to go, Mom."

"Tyler, this isn't like you. Only a few weeks ago, you were ready to kick me out. Why the sudden change?"

He wipes the tears with the back of his hand. "I need to tell you something. I thought things would get better, but they've gotten worse. It's why I'm not sleeping. Work has nothing to do with it."

"Oh, Tyler. What's happening to you?" I ask, wrapping my arm around him.

"I'm so scared, Mom. A few weeks ago, I began noticing some strange things. It got worse, and now I'm seeing them all the time."

My eyes pop out. "What are you seeing?"

"Things that aren't there. I'm hallucinating, and I don't know what to do." He opens his hands and stares at them with fear in his eyes.

My heart enters tachycardia mode. "What exactly are you seeing, Tyler?"

"A strange light on my hands. I told Zoe about it, and she acted strangely. I think I've lost her." He raises his right hand, and an amber glow radiates on his fingers. "Aghhh! It's happening now. I'm losing my mind."

"Oh, my gods, Tyler." I gape at my son.

"Wait. You see it, too?" he asks. "What the hell is happening to me, Mom?"

"I need to show you something." I raise my right hand and summon my witch energy, and the amber glow appears. "You're not hallucinating, son."

His mouth falls open as the tears dry up. "What the fuck?"

I swallow. "I have to tell you about Nain and Taid. And you're not gonna believe me."

Chapter Sixteen

Making Frenemies

"I didn't sleep at all last night. How can any of this be true?" Tyler sits across from me at the kitchen table, staring at his hands. "This must be a dream, and I can't wake up."

I grasp his hand. "It's a shock, I know. But you'll get through this, I promise."

"When did you find out?" he asks.

"The night of the Samhain Celebration. I wasn't supposed to be there. I snuck in and peeked at their ceremony. Archie and Ronnie told me they were witches, and I didn't believe them."

His eyes widen. "You mean the Fellowship is a..."

"Coven." I roll my lips inward and wait for cogwheels to turn inside his head.

"Zoe is a witch?" He squishes his eyes shut. "No wonder she got weird when I told her."

"She didn't know what to do, I'm sure. There's so much I have to tell you. But you need to get to work. I've got to get insurance documents completed for the company today. And then I've got a Fellowship meeting tonight. I'm going back."

"What made you leave? Some kind of shit went down at the Winter Solstice Celebration, and something tells me it wasn't faulty fireworks."

I spill the tea. "Witches and magic aren't the only supernatural elements. Fairies are real and cross through portals. And not only the cute, mischievous kind. There was an evil Unseelie Fairy who tried to kill me at the behest of a malevolent witch who had joined our coven. We don't know why, and she's still out there somewhere. It was called a Sluagh, but it's the Host of the Unforgiven Dead. We sent it back through the portal."

Tyler's mouth hangs open, and he blinks. "A fairy tried to kill you. And you didn't tell me?"

"I wanted to, but part of me preferred to say goodbye to a life of magic for your sake. And then the city building fell, and I thought I'd caused it and killed Lindsey Hope. But then I apprenticed with Agnes Pritchard, a local hedge witch who discovered I'd had a hex cast on me. She removed it, though."

"I don't think I wanna hear anymore. I gotta take a shower." He stands and turns toward the bathroom. "Did you leave Archie because of magic?"

"Not the only reason," I say, shaking my head. "Turns out, he slept with a plethora of witches he had recruited for other covens and ours."

"Oh, I can see how that would have bothered you." He cocks his head. "But you've been going to his house a lot. Are you dating again?"

"Eh, it's complicated. Nain was a Welsh ancestral witch. She left me a letter to read, but it's charmed. So, I'm training with Archie now, but you can't ever tell Zoe. It's against the Regional Book of Shadows to train a witch outside the coven. The leaders would expel him. But it won't matter after tonight, anyway. Since I'm returning."

Tyler stands there frozen, blinking, so I continue.

"But there's so much more. Nain's family witch stuff is in that old steamer trunk I'm storing at Ronnie's. I'll want to show it to you at some point. Meanwhile, I've already arranged for movers to take my bed, nightstand, and a few other items from storage to Dr. Leslie Hughes's house. I'm going to rent a room from her so you can have privacy."

"I'm taking a shower." He walks into the bathroom and slams the door.

I scratch the back of my head. Did I share too much?

"Fifty-eight, fifty-nine, sixty." I end my push-ups and roll over on my back to do some bridges, finishing my exercise session with a few planks. I can't wait for the semester to start, so I have access to the fitness center. Body-weight exercises blow. But I have to keep them up or my lower back pain might return. I hop in the shower and dress for the meeting, changing my outfit twice. What am I doing? I don't need to impress them. I throw off my dressy clothes, replacing them with a comfortable tank top, jean shorts, and sneakers.

When I arrive at Archie's, he's sitting on the porch step in a t-shirt and shorts, waiting for me. As I lock my Prius, he approaches me sporting an enthusiastic smile.

"Ready to face the wolves?" he asks.

"I think you mean wolf. The only person to object to my conditions will be Leslie. And maybe Trinity." I fan myself with a piece of junk mail advertising gutter replacements. "I can't believe the humidity. The air is like a wet rag."

It's so muggy out, I twist my hair and clip it. The stroll on campus sparks so many memories—the evening Archie flirted with me under the Kissing Arch, the night he took me to his house after I fell at the Old Men oak trees, our indiscretion against Menzies Hall. But they weren't all pleasant. The Host of the Unforgiven Dead attacked me right here on the Green.

"Penny for your thoughts?" he asks as we continue our trek to the Pumpkin House.

"I'm remembering events that happened here on campus, not all of them good." I increase my stride, and he follows to keep up with me.

"In a rush, are we?" He grasps my hand and squeezes. "You're remembering the night the Sluagh attacked you."

"But it doesn't scare me anymore. If it ever crosses, I know I can defend myself. And your family's dirk provides a level of comfort, too." I peer up at him and smile. "Tyler knows."

"He knows what?" He stares at me for a moment and his eyes grow big. "What does he know?"

"Everything. Last night, he broke down in tears, telling me he was experiencing hallucinations. He showed me his hand, and an amber glow appeared."

"Fawk," he exclaims. "How did he take it?"

"OK, considering. He didn't say much this morning. I think I talked too much. He seemed overwhelmed."

Archie presses his lips together. "I imagine so. Would you like me to talk to him? It might help."

"At some point. For now? Let's wait. The revelation has to sink in first."

I wring my hands as we approach the steps of the Pumpkin House, the Victorian house with orange siding and ornate trim. After the Winter Solstice Ceremony, I vowed never to enter this house again, yet here I am. We enter the foyer, and the Fellowship bursts into applause.

My face flushes, and I take a bow. "Please, it's not like I haven't seen all of you recently."

"Don't act like this isn't a big deal," Spence says, giving me a hug. "Because you know it is."

"It feels right having you back. I hope you stay," Tanner says.

Skye and Zoe are grinning from ear to ear, and the older members smile with hopeful eyes. Ronnie puts her hand over her heart. It's not as awkward as I imagined it would be. The air conditioner makes a whining sound, struggling to cool the space, but my fellow witches have dressed in loose tops and shorts, anyway—even our leaders. We all find seats in our witch's circle as our coven leader stands to begin the meeting.

"That's enough, witches," Trinity says as we quiet down. "We're all overjoyed Gwyn has returned, but the coven has a lot to discuss tonight. Thank you all for attending at the last minute." It's strange having Trinity lead the meeting, but it feels right, too. "Leslie will lead tonight's discussion."

With a tap of her Elder staff, Leslie stands with a serious face. "I want to welcome Gwynedd back to the Bearsden Coven. With the recent incidents on Main Street, her skills will greatly improve the success of the coven..."

"Stop." I stand and address the group. "Before we proceed with the meeting, I need to make a statement. When I left the coven, I had no intention of returning. I'd had enough of magic, fairies, and secrets. But I realized there was no pathway back to an Unremarkable life. So, here I am—back in the fold. But I have conditions. And if you can't agree to these conditions, I'm outta here."

Leslie's eyes narrow, and she raises her chin. "State your conditions?"

"One. No more secrets. If you or any of the older members have information the younger witches should know, you must divulge it. Two. With my recent training, I don't need to study through any more levels. I'm accepted back at a level three status. And three." I stare into Leslie's cat-like eyes. "I understand every group needs leaders to function, but the current organization isn't working for me. From now on, the coven votes on all decisions as equals without the Elder overriding them."

Leslie's withered, pale face turns red as a beet as her pinched lips disappear inward. I swear I can view steam exiting her ears. The metal chairs creak as the members shift in their seats, and I catch Elijah, Shane, and Ronnie covering their smiles. The younger members' eyes flit back and forth, but they don't utter a word. I think we're all waiting for the Elder's head to explode.

And Leslie speaks. "I accept your conditions."

My fellow witches move in their chairs and mutter to each other. I raise my head. "Fabulous. Then I'm back." When I sit, the young members woohoo, and the older members applaud.

Leslie taps her staff two times. "Silence. We have much to do. As you all are aware, a third incident has occurred on Main Street. Although the investigations by the Unremarkables point to unusual seismic activity, we now know the town is being targeted. Archie will recap the prior meeting." She sinks into her seat.

Archie stands to address us. "At the prior meeting, we discussed the strange event at the Raven Pub. I sensed the magical attempt to destroy it. Not knowing who or what was behind the failed hex, I used my ancestral magic to cast a protection barrier spell on the building. The destruction of Thomas Hall confirms whoever or whatever is behind this has an agenda. Gwyn has a hypothesis we should consider."

As Archie sits, I stand and browse the anxious faces of my fellow witches. "My skills became weak over the past few months with the lack of training. When the first building fell, I thought I caused the implosion. I believed Lindsey Hope's death was my fault. But I found out a witch put a hex on me to weaken my magic skills further."

"Why didn't you tell us?" Trinity asks, scowling. "This would have helped the coven decide a path forward."

Ronnie interjects. "Let her explain, Trinity. She didn't keep it a total secret. She told me, but I'm bound by friendship before the coven. Sorry, not sorry."

"Thanks, Ronnie. I'm telling you now, Trinity," I say. "I saw a flash of light when the city parking building crumbled to the ground and when I went to my Prius behind Shane's store. It triggered my witch energy to seep out, like a magnet was pulling at my internal magic. Similar occurrences have happened several times since then, but without the magnetic pull. Those attempts failed, of course. I'm pretty sure it's a who and not a what. The most recent incident occurred last night on the way to my car in front of Tanner and Spence's house."

"Why didn't you come in and tell us?" Tanner asks.

"We could have helped you go after the culprit!" Spence shouts.

"Frankly, I was too tired," I say. "And I'm pretty sure I know who it is. I think it's Audrey Kenilworth."

The coven breaks out in babble, and Leslie taps her Elder staff on the wooden floor. "What makes you think it's Audrey?"

"I mean, who else would do this? The destruction of the buildings must be some kind of revenge on the town for discovering she was a fake and tried to kill me for whatever reason." I fall into my chair and a discussion follows.

"Makes sense to me. She was after you," Ronnie says.

"It absolutely sounds like her," Elijah says. "There was something odd about that girl from the start."

"I'll admit," Shane says, petting his beard. "She had me duped. But I think there's more to the story."

"But could Audrey do this on her own?" Trinity asks. "She's an ancestral witch, but she's a young one. It would take more magic than what she can wield to destroy these buildings."

Archie scratches his goatee. "No, she couldn't. But a group of witches could produce enough power to implode a building."

Skye bends forward in her seat. "But you guys have always said formal covens won't hurt others. The whole do-no-harm thing."

"I didn't say it was a coven." Archie leans back in his chair, and the Fellowship members glance at each other around the circle. "I believe a closed-practice ancestral witch family may be involved."

"What is a closed practice?" Zoe asks with wide eyes. "It doesn't sound good."

"I ran into one of these closed-practice families in Scotland when I was younger. They don't adhere to any Regional Book of Shadows much like lone witches and can be quite dangerous. They inherit their witchcraft like Gwyn and me, revering and worshiping their ancestors to cultivate their skills. But they won't collaborate with others...some hoarding their magic for personal gain."

Leslie tilts her head. "I've never heard of such practices. Does a coven like ours have the power to fight off an attack from this type of group?"

"Absolutely, if we're at full capacity. But with the removal of Courtney Davies and Audrey, we are at risk," he says. "Gwyn's return is opportune, especially with her level of magic."

Trinity shakes her head. "And we don't have the time to do any formal recruitment. That will take at least a year."

"Basically, we're fucked." Spence throws his hands up.

"Oh, don't be so doom and gloom, hon," Tanner says. "We sent the Sluagh back through the portal without either of their help."

"Have faith, Spence," Elijah says. "We've always defended this town somehow. We'll come through this time, too."

Leslie clears her throat. "But from what Archie has explained, we are dealing with an entity more powerful than an Unseelie Fairy."

"Great. Then we're absolutely fucked." Spence wipes his face with his hands.

I stand again, thinking Tyler may disown me for this. "What if we can recruit two existing witches to fill the coven to its full capacity of thirteen? Hear me out. I know of two witches who may need a little coaxing, and one is quite fresh, but we can prepare the neophyte."

"Who are these witches you are suggesting?" Leslie asks.

"Yeah. I'm all ears, Gwyn," Trinity says. "Unless you've been hanging out with some out-of-towners I don't know about, I can't imagine who they are."

"I found out last night Tyler has inherited my ancestral witch powers. He was so upset...thought he was hallucinating until I told him I saw the amber glow on his hands, too. Then he really freaked out. I guess hanging around Zoe triggered his magic." I glance at her. "She knew but didn't tell anybody."

Zoe throws her palms up. "I didn't know what to do with you being out of the coven and not wanting to talk about magic. Don't be mad."

"It's OK, Zoe. But your next date is going to be a little awkward," I say.

Spence cracks up and slaps his thigh. "No shit? That's lit with a thousand light bulbs."

"It would be fire to have him join the coven," Skye adds. "All in the family, right?"

"I'm not sure he'd agree with you right now, but I'll work on him." I twist an earring. "He's overwhelmed at the moment."

"Fantastic," Ronnie says. "Now you don't have to worry about hiding your magic from him."

Archie gestures to the young witches. "I or any of the younger members could talk with him to allay his fears."

"And number thirteen?" Shane asks with a twinkle in his emerald-green eyes.

Ronnie's eyes pop out like one of those animated cartoon characters, and her head quivers like a rattlesnake.

My eyes hop from one witch to the next, and I blurt it out. "Agnes Pritchard."

"Absolutely not!" Leslie shouts in her raspy voice. Her face turns scarlet red, and she slams her staff on the floor.

Elijah rubs his jaw. "She's not exactly friendly. And she hasn't been in a coven for years."

"Nope, nope, nope," Spence says. "She's stranger than strange, if you know what I mean."

"Listen, I got to know Agnes this summer, and she's not that bad," I say.

"I can concur," Shane says. "Agnes has been friendlier since Gwyn trained with her. She comes into the store singing like a lark."

Skye laughs. "Whenever I've been around her, she smells like a frat party."

Everyone chuckles, including me, and I glance at Ronnie. "Well, an old woman has to make a living, right?"

"Agnes provides a service." Ronnie cackles and winks at me.

"I don't think we have any other options, do we?" Archie asks. "Gwyn, do you think you can convince her to join? She left this coven decades ago. What would make her come back?"

I glare at Leslie. "Oh, I may know of a way to convince her."

Trinity puts her hands on her hips. "This all sounds fine and dandy, but what concerns me is how the targeted buildings get closer and closer to Mitchell Hall. Thank the gods we cast a protection barrier spell on the property. And by the way, they begin renovations tomorrow. I sure hope those Seelie Fae children keep to their mound."

"I talked to them," I say. "Don't worry. I was careful. And I spoke to them through the barrier."

"I think we've accomplished all we can this evening. Remain alert, everyone." Leslie taps her Elder staff three times, and we disband. "Gwynedd, may I have a moment?"

While the others put the chairs away, I talk to Leslie. "I'm sorry if I appeared demanding, but I appreciate you relenting to my conditions. I'll be reasonable."

"It's done," Leslie says. "I want to speak to you about Agnes Pritchard. You'll not be successful. When she left the coven, she vowed never to return. And she did not. Nothing has changed."

"Did you ever ask yourself why she hasn't returned?" I ask. "Tyler won't be much help, even if he's comfortable with the idea. But we could use Agnes's skills. She may practice magic by the seat of her pants, but she's powerful, Leslie. And she's lonely."

Leslie looks away and clears her throat. "Do what you must. I won't stop you. When will you move your furniture and personal items to the house?"

"I'll let you know. This week sometime. Archie and Tyler will help. Goodnight, Leslie."

"A restful night's slumber to you as well, Gwynedd."

A smile almost cracks her placid face. Who would have guessed we'd become frenemies?

Chapter Seventeen

PROMISES TO KEEP

I sigh as a warm breeze provides relief on the stroll back to Duncan Street. "Ahhh, the wind feels sooo good. This August heat needs to find another place to take a vacation."

"Aye. This is the worst summer since I moved here. I guarantee it's cooler in Scotland," Archie says. "You're more than a wee bit happy with yourself. Quite cocky, if you ask me."

"I worried she would strike me with a witchy thunderbolt or worse," I say with wide eyes.

"I can't imagine there would be much worse than a bolt of witch energy, but I'm happy she spared you." He eyes something past me and stops. "I swear I saw a burst of light over there between the two sciences buildings. Hopefully, no one blew up anything."

"I hope not, too." I glimpse an amber glow on his hands. "Oh, Archie."

His eyebrows fall as he inspects his hands, shaking them until the glow disappears. "I felt something pulling at me...like a magnet, but it failed. We need to get back to my house quickly. No time to waste."

"But shouldn't we go after her? Audrey or whoever it is?" I ask.

"NO. We don't know the power of whomever we're dealing with."

"I've never seen you this worried. Not even when we had to banish the Sluagh back to the Otherworld."

Archie grasps my hand, and my heart beats like a drunk drummer as we rush to his house. He scrambles to unlock the front door, and we enter, panting. After a quick scan of the street through the screen, he shuts the door and sets the deadbolt.

I kick off my sneakers. "Are we even safe in here? The witch could have followed us."

"Aye. But I cast a protection spell on the house a while back when you first told me about the hex," he says.

"I've gotta get home. Tyler's in danger." I bend over to put my shoes back on.

"Gwyn, no. You can't leave. If you go to the apartment, it will only put Tyler in more danger. The aggressor witch likely doesn't know about Tyler's emerging magic. Better to stay put."

I pull out my cell phone. "I have to tell him something...say I'm staying to practice the craft late."

"Good idea. I'll text Zoe and suggest she drop by and check on him. Will that allay your concerns?"

"Not really, but I'd feel more comfortable if someone was with him. And I'm sure they'll talk most of the night after I revealed the *big lie*."

Archie chuckles. "To be a fly on the wall." He sends Zoe a text while I call Tyler.

"Hi, Mom. I thought you'd be home by now." Tyler's voice has an anxious tone to it.

"Hi, dear. I'm gonna spend the night at Archie's. Try to get more ancestral witch training in. It's gonna be a late one, so I'll crash here. But I won't stay if you're still unsettled. I imagine you are."

"Uhhh, it's OK," he says. "I got a text from Zoe saying she's stopping by. Probably better you're not here for the confrontation."

"Go easy on her. She didn't know how to handle the situation. You can ask her anything now, and she can explain how everything works. I'll see you in the morning. And Tyler, I love you."

"I love you, too, Mom." The phone goes silent, and I shove my cell into my jeans pocket. "Well, what now?"

Archie rubs the tip of his goatee. "We could go to the magic room and practice. It's not too late."

"Eh, I'm too revved up to focus on divination tonight." The mantle clock over the fireplace ticks like a time bomb, reminding me why I'm here.

He glances out the front window and pulls the shade down. "Want some tea? I could put the kettle on?"

"Nah. The caffeine will keep me up, not to mention I'd have to pee in the middle of the night." I collapse onto the loveseat and rest my feet on the steamer trunk, removing my socks to let my feet breathe.

He sits down next to me, doing the same, and wiggles his toes. "Aye. I remember. It's too early to go to bed. A game of checkers?"

"No, I'm too wired for games. Standing up to Leslie gave me a shot of adrenaline. My confidence level is sky high." I turn toward him and rest an arm on the back of the loveseat. "I can't believe she agreed to my demands."

He shifts onto the loveseat and faces me. "I was quite shocked. But you gave her an ultimatum, and she knows you wouldn't back down. Are you sure it's a good idea to rent a room from her?"

"Yeah, I do. She's keeping a secret from me, and renting a room gives me access to snoop. There must be an answer hiding in her magic room. I'll find it."

"You'll not have an easy time with Mr. Yeats spying on you. He'll report every impropriety to her."

"Maybe? What he doesn't see, he can't report." A whiff of his woodsy cologne passes my nose. "How can you smell so good after sweating all day? With the heat and hot flashes, I'm shocked you can get this close to me and not gag."

"I took a shower before the meeting. And I assure you, your scent does not make me gag." Archie moves closer and his nose grazes my neck. Goosebumps rise on my chest and arms, and my heart palpitates with his touch. When he pulls back, he stops close to my face. "No gagging."

"I showered, too, but the humidity makes me...wet. Maybe we should go to bed?" My heart tugs at him with invisible fingers.

"I'll take the loveseat again," he says. "Surprisingly, it's rather comfortable."

"That's not what I meant." I peer up at him and bat my eyelashes.

"I'm a wee bit confused." He cocks his head and squints. "You want the loveseat?"

His magnetic eyes draw me closer. We're inches apart, and my lips part as I plan my next words. But I hesitate.

"Cat got your tongue?" he asks with longing in his eyes.

My heart leaps toward my chest as I pant. "Kiss me, Archie."

His mouth spreads into a wide, exuberant grin. "Are you testing me? I promised to keep things platonic until you've completed your training. I broke my commitment once, but we were both intoxicated. There's no need to test me."

"But I'm not drunk. In fact, I'm wide awake. I'm not testing you. Kiss me, Archie."

"I won't. You may not be drunk, but you're high on the night's events. You'd regret it in the morning and blame me."

"Yes. I'm high on everything. Tyler finding out he's a witch. Returning to the coven. Standing up to Leslie." I stroke his chest and fondle his nipples through his black t-shirt. "I'm high on you. Addicted without remorse. And it's not the magic. I love you, Archie. I never stopped loving you. Kiss me."

He places his lips only a breath away. "But a promise is a promise. I don't want to lose you again. We're not finished with your training. You'll lose your focus."

"Lose me? You're all I ever think about. It affects my focus. Kiss me, Archie." I grab his t-shirt.

"This isn't fair, Gwyn. Once I kiss you, I won't want to stop. It took all my will to stop the last time." His eyes burn with a fiery yearning, and his heart beats heavily in his chest under my fingers.

I curve my mouth into a bawdy smile. "I'm banking on it. Kiss me, Archie. Kiss me."

He removes the clip from my hair, allowing the strands to cascade across my shoulders. His full lips barely touch mine, testing the waters, and I dig my nails into his chest as his devilish goatee titillates my skin. He presses hard against my mouth and offers me his tongue, which I consume completely. I was too drunk to remember much about the kiss the night we celebrated my divination skills, but I savor this moment, enjoying each stroke of our tongues intertwining. We fall back on the loveseat, and he comes up for air.

"When you left me after killing the Sluagh, I thought I'd lost you forever." He gazes into my eyes and swipes his thumb across my lips. "I never knew what love was. Before I met you, I went through the motions in relationships."

"Like on a conveyor belt?" I ask.

He scowls at me, and his Scottish brogue thickens. "You're mocking me, witch."

"No. I wouldn't do that." I entice him with a naughty smile.

"Aye. You're mocking me," he says. "I should spank you."

"Promise?" I kiss him as I run my hands through his wavy hair.

Archie stands up and adjusts the bulge in his pants. "Apparently, I can't keep my promises." He offers me his hand. I grasp its firmness, and he pulls me off the loveseat. "Shall we go to bed?"

"I thought you'd never ask." I burst out laughing and yank at the belt loops on his jeans. "Beat you upstairs."

I dart over to the stairway and run up the steps in my bare feet, and he laughs behind me on the way. He makes it to the bedroom doorway about the time I throw back the comforter and jump on the bed, kneeling. I glance at the empty glass case on the wall, recalling the night I first glimpsed the glow of the dirk inside. He pulls off his t-shirt as he slinks to the bed, and I scoot on my knees to the edge. As I stroke my hands across his rounded shoulders and firm chest, I stop and fiddle with the springy blond hairs on his pecs.

"It's like being let loose in a candy store after swearing off sugar for a year," I say.

"You think I've had an easy time?" he asks, stroking my chin. "I'm using every ounce of will to keep from ripping your clothes off."

"What's stopping you?" I lick my upper lip.

"You're a tease, Gwynedd." Archie bends down and kisses me while I caress the swelling in his jeans.

When I come up for air, I whisk off my loose tee and throw it toward the end of the bed. "I missed you so much. I want to feel you inside me again."

He smiles, and lust enters his eyes like a long-lost lover. As he reaches around to unclasp my bra, he whispers in my ear, "I'll be happy to oblige."

Archie plants kisses behind my ear and works his way down my neck as he removes my bra. The whiskers of his goatee titillate my skin, making my nipples erect.

"I never thought I'd have you in my bed again." He cups my face. "May the gods send me to the Otherworld if I ever do anything to hurt you. I love you with all my soul, Gwynedd."

I shift back on the bed while he climbs on, and I unbutton his jeans, unzipping them to release his bulge. He chuckles and leans back on a pillow while I tug at his pants and boxer briefs, tossing them over my shoulder with a flip of my hand. A sexy grin forms on his mouth as I crawl toward him, placing wet kisses on his thigh and grazing his skin with my warm lips. As I inch closer to his erection, he wraps his hands around the back of his head, flexing his arms and chest.

While I relish in the beauty of his physique, I exhale and wrap my hand around his firmness. He closes his eyes and moans as I take him in my mouth. I missed his hardness and tease him with my tongue.

Archie lays a hand on my head and whispers, "Oh, Gwynedd. I don't deserve you. And if you keep that up, I'll have nothing left for you."

He grasps my upper arm and urges me to come to him. While his eyes flare with desire, I unzip my jean shorts and slip them off, pulling off my panties with them. As I climb over him, I position my knees on either side. He presses my hips down, and I slide onto him. I claw his shoulders and lunge at his mouth, as if to consume his inner soul. I want to devour him, take in everything he's offering, and never let go.

When I lean back, I raise a hand, and I gesture for him to do the same. I touch my palm to his and summon my witch energy. The amber glow radiates from our hands and spreads throughout our bodies. Sending a wave of his magic through me, he penetrates my body with the heat of his passion and brings me to the peak of my arousal. And I fall onto his chest, quivering.

Archie grunts with his release and holds me tightly against his chest. "I missed pleasing you like this. I want to make love to you forever if you'll allow me the honor."

"Promise?" I ask, panting.

He strokes my cheek. "I promise."

CHAPTER EIGHTEEN

THE PRANKSTERS

WHEN I AWAKEN, I gaze upon my Scottish lover. While Archie finishes his slumber on his stomach, my lecherous eyes roam his muscular body, ogling the definition of his back muscles down to the Horned God tattoo on his buff ass. I'm so bad, but I can't help myself.

He stirs, and his eyes open, catching my gaze. "Good morning. What are you doing?"

"Good morning." I brush my hand down his back, stopping on his ass. "I'm ogling your body. Do you have a problem with that?"

"Not if you kiss me." He grabs the nape of my neck and pulls me to him, pressing his lips to mine. "Mmm. You taste like sex."

"We're both musky," I say. "I should brush my teeth and wash up before I go back to the apartment. I don't want to embarrass Tyler."

"It's not like he'd be shocked after walking in on us Thanksgiving weekend." Archie rolls onto his side and rests his head on a hand. "I'm so chuffed you stayed last night. Why don't you come back tonight?"

"I have so much on my plate today. I've gotta talk with Tyler and explain more about our ancestral witch history. How the magic works. Show him the items in my mom's steamer trunk—the grimoire and her letter. And I've got to convince him to join the coven only days after finding out he's a witch." I press my face against my hands. "Aghhh. And I've gotta stop by Agnes's farm and beg her to come back to the coven. That's gonna be worse than pulling taffy—more like stretching wood."

"If anyone can convince her, it'll be you."

"I'm gonna tell you something. You already know Agnes, Leslie, and my mom were members of the Fellowship in the early days. Leslie spoke about the coven opening up a large portal on Samhain. What she never shared was my mom didn't take part in the ceremony. Trinity was there as a teenager and heard them arguing about it. Leslie never told Agnes why it upset my mom, and she refuses to tell me."

"Why did Agnes go along with the ceremony to open the portal if your mom was uncomfortable with the event?"

"Here's the clincher and hold on to your hat. Leslie and Agnes were lovers."

Archie's jaw drops. "No fawking way. Well, it explains a lot. A chain of bitterness hangs around Leslie's neck."

"And Agnes's. She left a girlfriend for Leslie and never had another. I think Leslie was the love of her life. But Leslie wouldn't tell Agnes why my mom didn't want a portal opened. Agnes was jealous of Leslie's friendship with my mom. So, she left her, the coven...life."

"So very sad for both of them. I can see how Agnes wouldn't want to return after all these years. You have a laborious task to fulfill." He kisses me again. "I'm sure you'll find a way to convince her."

I sit up and scoot toward the footboard. "You have more faith than I."

"Where are you going?" he asks. "Stay in bed for a wee bit longer."

"I'd love to, but I've really gotta pee." I jump off the bed and head to the bathroom.

"You're so romantic," he says. "Wash up while you're in there, too. And I'll use the hall bath."

When I exit the bathroom, Archie has returned and is resting against the headboard with his body relaxing like an Italian Renaissance painting. I slip on my bra and panties and carry the rest of my clothes with me to the bed.

He pats the edge of the mattress, and I sit close to him. "I wish you could stay."

"Me, too. But it's not like I'm never coming back. I have to train." I kiss his cheek and remember the move. "Oh, damn. I forgot I have to move my things to Leslie's house, too. Too much is happening this week."

"Don't move into Leslie's," he says. "It won't end well."

"It's the best solution for now. Tyler has put up with me for months." I stroke the side of his stubbled cheek. "And I'll be closer to you."

"Facts, as the students would say. But I have an even better suggestion. Move in with me."

"What? Oh, Archie. Don't misunderstand me. I'm happy about us, but it's too soon for me. With everything that's happened this past year, I need my space."

"I understand." He lifts my hand to his mouth, placing a soft kiss on my fingers. "Know the invitation is always there."

A smile sneaks onto my mouth, and I kiss him. "I love you, Dr. Cock-burn."

"I suppose I asked for that." He strokes my lips with a finger. "I love you, Ms. Crowther."

While I drive down Main Street to get home, I notice the crews sifting through the piles of brick and timber—the remnants of Thomas Hall. They'll probably condemn what's left of the historical home. But a crowd gathers in front of Mitchell Hall next to a Bearsden City Police car. Trinity, Ronnie, and Derek huddle away from the police.

I pull into a metered parking space across the busy street, pay for fifteen minutes online, and stroll over to them. The humidity lingers like an unwelcome relative, overstaying their visit with the start of school right around the corner. DUB must be inundated with phone calls from students and parents over the situation, asking if it's safe on campus. What can the authorities say? To the Unremarkables, these incidents appear to be seismic or geological related to the underground springs that snake under the city.

"Hi, friends. What's going on?" I ask.

Trinity wipes sweat from her brow. "Police answered a call from the foreman heading the renovation on Mitchell Hall. Apparently, vandals got into the house somehow."

"Oh, what happened?" I ask, with a wrinkle between my eyes.

Ronnie contorts her face into a you're-never-gonna-believe-this expression. "Tools and materials strewn all over the place, for one."

"And two of the evening workmen who stayed late to clean up?" Derek asks. "They found them tied up in chairs...in their underwear." Ronnie cackles, and Derek admonishes her. "Babe, it's not funny."

"Actually, it is a little. They weren't hurt. It was only a prank," she says.

"A prank?" I ask. "Like juveniles broke into the work area?"

"Damn straight," Trinity says. "But the workers swear the kids were tiny, like elementary-aged students."

My eyes widen, but I avert my gaze so Derek doesn't see my reaction. I've got to have another talk with Shailagh and Aonghas.

He bends down to kiss Ronnie. "Gotta get to the gym. Do you need a ride back to the café, babe?"

"No, prince charming. I can hobble back very well on my own," she says.

"I get the hint. Meet you at the café later. Bye, babe." He strolls toward Young's Fitness Center, his personal business.

When Derek has walked far enough to be out of hearing range, Ronnie and I crack up. But Trinity sends us a leader's scowl. "I'm sure glad you both find this so humorous. This presents a HUGE problem. What if they do this every night? What if the city installs cameras and actually catches those pranksters on surveillance?"

"I'm sorry," I say. "You gotta admit. Finding the workers in their underwear at least deserves a snort. I'll speak to Shailagh and Aonghas, and remind them how dangerous it is to commit these pranks."

"You know their names?" Trinity asks. "Developing close friendships may not be the best way to go, Gwyn."

"I disagree," I say. "They remember my mom and call me Aunt Gwyn. They're more likely to listen to me if they feel an attachment."

"Whatever you say." Trinity inspects my clothing. "Isn't that the same shirt and jean shorts you wore last night at the meeting?"

"Maybe? Is it a problem if I wear my clothes two days in a row?" I ask. "Saves on laundry."

"Right," she says. "But most people don't wear clothes multiple days with the wicked heat and humidity we've had. But who am I to judge? Well, I've gotta meet Elijah at the shelter. I'm late already. Gwyn, keep me updated on the progress with Agnes. I know it's gonna be a tough row to hoe."

"I will, Trinity." Our coven leader walks to her car as I gape at Ronnie. "Oh, my gods. Last night..."

"You slept with Archie, didn't you?" Ronnie asks. "You've got I-got-laid-last-night splattered all across your face."

"Oh, for the love of the gods, I hope the expression slides off before I get back to the apartment." I fan myself with a hand. "It's disgusting out."

"A typical August day for Delaware, though. Spill the tea, woman. How did you end up in bed with the professor?"

"We walked back to Duncan Street through the Green, and he saw a burst of light between the buildings housing the science labs. Archie figured some students had caused a minor explosion. Then an amber glow radiated on his fingers, and we knew a witch was trying to hex him, too. He'll tell Trinity and Leslie what happened. We rushed to his house, because he had cast a protection spell on it. He didn't think it was safe for me to go home in the dark, so one thing led to another and..."

"You can tell me the details later. I'm sure you're eager to get back to the apartment. Last night was probably not the time to leave your son alone."

"I was worried about him being by himself, so Archie sent Zoe a text. She went over there. I have no idea what I'm walking into. They could have argued. Tyler could be an emotional mess." I wipe the sweat from my neck. "I'll let you know."

"Sure thing. Don't worry, Gwyn. I know this wasn't what you hoped for, but the silver lining is, he knows. And you don't have to lie to him anymore."

I inhale and hold the sticky air for a moment. "I'll be in touch."

Ronnie limps a bit as she heads back to the café, and I drive home to the apartment. I expect the worst as I push the door in, but no one is around. It's after ten. Tyler must have decided he could handle work. But I flinch when his door creaks open, and he walks out in a t-shirt and lounge pants. He shuts his bedroom door behind him and gestures to the kitchen. I follow him in there.

"Zoe is still sleeping," he says in a soft voice. "We were up pretty late. Thanks for asking her to stop by."

"I can't take credit. Archie texted her, but I'm glad she came." I examine his demeanor, and he appears rational and in cheerful spirits. "I hope you and Zoe didn't fight over this. She was following coven rules."

"No, we didn't argue. She explained more of the hidden world to me. Told me what *in the knowing* means, who Unremarkables are, what happened at the Winter Solstice Celebration, which apparently wasn't an actual celebration. You went through all of that without my support. I'm proud of you, Mom. After what Dad put you through."

"Yeah, well, there's more to the story, but I don't wanna talk about your dad now. Later." I catch him glancing back at the bedroom door. "So, everything went OK with Zoe."

"Oh, yeah. After we talked things out, she calmed me down." He pushes the side of his mouth out with his tongue, attempting to squash a smile.

"Oh, really." I say. "Did witch energy sex have anything to do with that?"

"Mah-om! I'm not gonna answer that." He frowns at me and tilts his head. "Your cheeks seem pretty rosy this morning, too, if you ask me."

I snatch a magazine from the kitchen table and fan myself. "Hot flash."

He snickers, and the bedroom door flings open. Zoe plods into the kitchen, wearing Tyler's robe. How can such a tiny woman have the footsteps of a four-hundred-pound man?

"Hi, Gwyn!" She shuffles over and gives me a hug. Her black hair flops all over, and she makes an ill attempt to pat the strands down. "So, you stayed at Archie's last night?"

"Yeah. Thank you for coming to be with Tyler," I say. "I imagine you were worried about how he was going to act after...you know. But he told me everything's OK."

She wraps her arms around his torso. "Yeah. I was so scared he'd break up with me, but the opposite happened." Her eyes hop between Tyler and me several times. "So, last night turned out to be a great night, right? 'Cause we all got laid."

Tyler and I lock eyes.

After a tepid shower, I log some hours for the insurance agency and eat dinner. The twilight skies display strokes of pink and orange as I depart for Mitchell Hall. With the reduced parking on Main Street around Thomas Hall, I decide to park at Tanner and Spence's house again. It still feels strange to knock on the front door.

"Hi, guys. You heard about the vandalism and assault at the Mitchell's mansion?" I ask.

Tanner nods. "I heard about it at work."

"Yuppers," Spence says. "They found two of the workers in their underwear. I know it's not funny, but..."

"I've gotta talk to the Seelie Fae children again. Make sure they understand why they have to stay out of the house." I tap my fingertips. "Would you mind going with me?"

Spence crosses his arms. "Please, don't tell me you're frightened of a couple of silly fae children."

"Dude, not cool. Gwyn has good reason to worry about them." Tanner says. "We'll be happy to go."

"Thank you, guys, but I'm not scared of the Seelie Fae. I'm worried about the witch who's been stalking me. And whoever they are, the witch tried to hex Archie on the Green last night when we were walking back to his house."

Spence's eyes become animated. "Oh! Do you think it was Audrey?"

"No idea. The witch never shows their face." My face contorts into a cluster of wrinkles. "But it means the coward may come after all of us."

Tanner grimaces. "That's not cool. We'll change and join you."

On the brisk walk to Mitchell Hall, Spence grills me on the prior evening's activity. "So, you went back to Archie's house last night?"

"Well, I parked at his house." I try to redirect the conversation, but he's not buying it.

"You specifically said you walked back to his house," he says. "Why would you go there? Since it was so late."

I stare straight ahead. "He didn't think I should go back to the apartment after the witch attack. I don't know why you're making so much of it. We've been dating some."

"Dude, don't harass her," Tanner says. "Gwyn can do what she wants."

"Sure, she can, but she should spill the tea to her friends, and she's hiding something." Spence scrutinizes my reactions.

I blink at his inquisitive face. "What?"

"Oh, my gods. You did." Spence shimmies as he walks.

"Dude. Stop needling her," Tanner says, coming to my rescue.

"You slept with Archie," Spence says. "I see it in the smile you're trying to hide."

"What smile. I'm not smiling," I say with tight lips.

Tanner slaps Spence's arm with the back of his hand. "Stop, hon. You're embarrassing her."

"For fuck's sake. Is it plastered all over my face?" I ask, wiping the sweat off my nose.

"Yeah. It kinda is," Spence says. "I'm happy for you, sis. Oh, we're here. Looks like they've locked up the fence. Good thing their security won't keep us out. Allow us, Gwyn. Help me out, Tanner."

"Whatever you want, hon." My two young friends chant over the lock, and the latch falls open.

"You guys are handy on a break-in." Spence and Tanner follow me toward the opening in the iron fence. I push on the gate and amble right through. What a relief. "I don't see Shailagh and Aonghas."

Tanner cocks his head. "You know their names?"

"Yeah, they told me, but from the other side of the gate. Since I wasn't a member of the coven, I couldn't enter because of the…"

"Protection barrier," Spence says. "Never crossed my mind you'd want to get back in here when the coven cast the spell."

Tanner gestures to the mound. "The portal's opening."

A bright light appears. Shailagh and Aonghas grin when they notice I'm there and come running over with their golden-blond hair flying behind their heads. "Hi, Aunt Gwyn. We're so excited. You brought friends!"

"Sort of, yes." All three of us kneel. "These are my friends Tanner and Spence. They came with me to say hello."

"Hey, what's up?" Spence raises his hand to fist bump their tiny fae hands.

"Spence, I doubt they fist bump." Tanner offers his hand. "Nice to meet you…"

"I'm Shailagh, and this is Aonghas," the Seelie Fae girl says.

"Hi, Tanner and Spence," Aonghas says with a tooth-filled grin.

"Can you stay and play with us?" they ask. "We can dance around the gardens."

"We don't have enough time to play." I extend my arms to touch them, but they dash toward the corner where the hawthorn tree once stood.

"Catch us if you can!" they shout.

Tanner stands and huffs. "We can't chase after them all night."

"I know, but what's our alternative?" I ask as I stand. "Let's play catch, boys!"

The three of us dart around the Celestial Gardens under the moonlight in different directions, trying to corral the mischievous Seelie Fae. Each of us nearly captures the pranksters, but they disappear when we try to snatch their tiny arms. After fifteen minutes of dashing back and forth under the twinkling stars, I'm out of breath and collapse on a concrete bench.

"This is getting us nowhere. I'm too old for this shit." My heart pounds in my chest as I steady my breathing.

Tanner and Spence stop where they are and catch their breath. They search the gardens for the little ones, but they've disappeared.

"We're gonna get caught if we don't get out of here soon," Tanner says.

"Witches, I have an idea." Spence skips toward the gate, gesturing for us to follow him.

I fill my lungs up with the damp night air and push off the bench. As I trudge toward the gate, Tanner strolls behind me.

Spence shouts, "I'm pooped. Let's go home."

"Yeah. I'm done for the night, too. Bye." I wave my hand without looking back.

When we've almost arrived at the gate, the mischievous fae appear and plead with us. "Please, don't leave."

"You'll have to stand still to talk with us. Will you do that?" I ask.

Shailagh and Aonghas glance at each other. "We will, Aunt Gwyn."

"Come here, and we'll rest and chat." I motion for them to join us.

The Seelie Fae children skip to us, holding hands. "What do you want to chat about, Aunt Gwyn?"

"We heard about the practical joke you played on two workers in Momma Mitchell's house. It wasn't a nice thing to do," I say.

Their sparse eyebrows fall toward their mint-green eyes. "But those mean men tore the pretty paper off of Momma Mitchell's walls. We had to stop them."

"Ohhh. I understand why their work bothered you." I grasp their hands. "You have to understand Momma Mitchell doesn't live there anymore. The building is being improved for the benefit of our community. Momma Mitchell would want these improvements. You can't go into the building again. Promise?"

Shailagh and Aonghas pout as their eyes become wet with light-green tears. "We promise. Will you come back to play again?"

Tanner interjects. "It's dangerous right now for us to come in here, but we'll come back when we can. IF you stay out of the house."

"We will. We love to play," they say.

Spence stands up and dances around, throwing his hands in the air. Shailagh and Aonghas giggle while they dance with him.

"We should go," Tanner says, eyeing the gate.

"Shailagh, Aonghas. I have one question before we leave. Guys, go on, I'll be out in a minute." While Tanner and Spence head toward the gate, I ask them the question that's floated in my head for quite some time. "Do you remember the last night you saw Aunt Lowri?"

"Yes," Shailagh says. "Aunt Lowri was angry. She screamed at a woman with brown hair to close our door...forever. We cried. We thought Aunt Lowri cared about us."

"I believe she cared about you both. But she was scared." I squeeze their tiny hands.

"Why? We didn't do anything bad to her. Why was she scared of us?" the Seelie Fae ask.

"I don't know, but I'm gonna find out. You should go back through the portal now. Get some rest. Even fairies need sleep." They skip off and disappear into the mound. Why did my mom want to close the portal?

When I arrive outside the gate, Tanner is on the ground, knocked out, and Spence is kneeling over him, crying.

I dart to them. "What happened? Is Tanner all right?"

"I don't know," Spence cries. "He's passed out. Two witches, a man and a woman in the shadows, threw a magic fireball at him. I can't get him to wake up."

I place my hand on Tanner's chest and summon my witch energy, concentrating on a healing intention.

His eyes twitch and open. "Am I on the ground?"

Spence slaps him. "That's for the scaring the shit out of me!"

"Dude, I'm OK." Tanner sits up and hugs Spence. "Where did they go?"

"They took off toward DUB campus." Spence hugs me tightly. "Thanks so much for healing him."

I pat his arm. "You're welcome. Tanner, can you get up?"

"I think so." Tanner stands with Spence's help.

"Did either of you see their faces?" I ask.

"No. It happened too fast. We should tell Trinity, Dr. Hughes, and Archie." Tanner rubs the back of his head.

"Let's get you home, hon," Spence says. "And into bed."

As we depart from Mitchell Hall, I glance at the head of the Green and notice two shadowy figures running in the distance.

CHAPTER NINETEEN

RECRUITING A HEDGE WITCH

SATURDAY HAS ARRIVED, AND it's finally time to leave Tyler's abode. I lie on the sofa bed browsing my social media feeds, procrastinating the morning away. Convincing Agnes to return to the coven will be a heavier load than moving my furniture, but failure isn't an option. Especially after the attack on Tanner and Spence last night. Tyler comes out of the bedroom and scoots into the bathroom—my signal to get up. When he enters the living room, I'm stripping the sheets off.

"I'll throw these into the washer, so you don't have to. How do you feel about me moving out?" I ask.

Tyler messes with his hair. "Believe it or not? I'm a little sad, Mom. I got used to you being here. And now...I kinda need you more than ever."

"Oh, don't worry. You're not getting rid of me. I just won't disrupt your love life anymore." I throw the sheets into a pile and pick up the end of the bed.

"Let me help you." Tyler grabs the edge and shoves it back into the bottom of the sofa, and we replace the cushions. "We make a good team, don't we?"

I grin at my offspring. "We do. I only hope you're willing to join the coven. Did Zoe ask you? I wanted to wait a couple of days."

"Yeah, she mentioned it. I don't know. It's all so soon."

"I know how shocking all of this was for you. The same thing happened to me on Samhain. And I didn't react too rationally."

"What did you do?" he asks.

I recall the indiscretion against the brick wall of Menzies Hall and snicker. "Never you mind. We should get moving. Archie is meeting us at Leslie's. I'll text him when we've arrived with the rental truck. Why don't you get dressed while I cook breakfast? It's the last time for a while, at least."

"Sounds good, Mom."

As I wait for Archie on the front stoop of Leslie's house, a notification shows on my cell—a text from Nick. I feel bad I haven't contacted him since our last date, the night Thomas Hall collapsed. He wants to meet with me, but I hope it's not a quest to continue dating. I read the text as Archie approaches me. I've chosen the hottest day of the summer for my move-in. Gotta love Delaware's weather—NOT.

"Could it be any fawking hotter?" he wipes sweat off his forehead. "Who texted you?"

"Nick Evans," I say. "He wants to go over more of the translations."

"It's all right, Gwyn. If you want to keep seeing him, I'll be none too happy after Thursday night, but I'd understand."

"I told you I'm not seeing him anymore except to go over the translations." I kiss his damp mouth, and a whiff of B.O. enters my nose. "You need a shower already."

"No doubt." He kisses me back at about the time the door opens, and Leslie stares at us with disapproving eyes.

"Good morning, Dr. Hughes," I say. "You can still say no."

"Nonsense. Is there anything I can do to help?" She spies Tyler, who's opening the back of the rental truck.

"Don't trouble yourself, Leslie," Archie says. "Gwyn isn't moving in much. Maybe get the door to limit the flies from entering the house."

"Splendid." I think she's actually happy I'm moving in. I sure hope she's not expecting a girl's night every week.

Archie lowers his voice a bit. "I suspect you didn't tell Tyler about the attack last night?"

"No, I didn't." I peer at him through the storm door. "I didn't wanna freak him out. Let's keep it to ourselves for now until I find the right time to tell him. Shh, he's coming."

Tyler enters the house, and I introduce him to Leslie. She appears quite taken with him—or is it a vulture coven Elder eyeing her prey? It takes about two hours to move my boxes and set up my bed in Leslie's spare bedroom.

"Thank you, guys," I say. "The move went much faster with the two of you helping."

"We make a good team." Archie shakes Tyler's hand. "I haven't had a chance to speak to you yet about training. Expect a call soon."

"I look forward to it," he says.

I'd dreaded the moment Tyler would find out he's a witch, but it's all worked out. And I trust putting my son in Archie's capable hands.

"Tyler, hang on for a minute while I say goodbye to Archie." I leave him with Leslie, who appears to be dominating the conversation as I walk my lover to the door. "Thank you again."

"Will I see you later?" he asks, wrapping his arms around me.

"I think I should stay here tonight," I say. "Chat with Leslie a bit. But I want to."

"Good to know." He leans forward and kisses me goodbye. "If you go out, please be aware of your surroundings."

"Don't worry. I will." Archie leaves, and I return to my bedroom where Leslie continues to talk my son's ears off. "Leslie, I should show Tyler your magic room."

"Splendid idea," she says. "I'll leave you to it."

Tyler lifts his eyebrows. "Magic room?"

"You'll see. Follow me to the end of the hallway. She has an office there." We enter Leslie's newly organized office. "This is where we practice witchcraft?"

My son glances around the room. "Looks like a regular office to me."

I move to the glass-enclosed shelf with the bottles and roll it to the side. I motion toward the doorway for him to follow me in.

"That's her office. This...is her magic room. I practiced witchcraft here, and you will, too." I sneeze from drying herbs in the hanging baskets.

"Gesundheit, Mom." Tyler eyes Mr. Yeats over as he scuttles by and jumps up in the corner chair. "Hey, Dr. Hughes has a cat." He walks to the chimera cat with half-black and half-ginger fur. "He's got one yellow eye and a light-blue one. So, cool." The familiar rubs his head against my son's hand.

I bend over and glare at Mr. Yeats. "You be good. He found out he was a witch only a few days ago."

"Will you be here to help me?" His eyes jump around the room from the shelves, storing bottles of herbs, crystals, and bones to the long table with the tools of a witch: wooden bowls, mortars and pestles, knives, and a crystal ball.

"Of course. I'm living here. But you'll train in Archie's basement, too. Spence is quite talented at witchcraft despite his appearances. He trains the students, so Zoe will be there with you, too. And Ronnie. She's only level two. Before you ask, I'm level three, but that's a recent designation. All the time I spent helping Agnes on the farm was in exchange for training. I'll tell you more later when we visit Ronnie's, and I'll show you Nain's streamer trunk and the letter she left me."

"I'm a little overwhelmed." Tyler strokes Leslie's old leather-bound grimoire. "Spell book, I assume?"

"Yeah, I bet you are, son," I say. "We have a grimoire, too. It's as old as this one, but smaller, and the spells are written in Welsh. I asked Nick Evans to translate it for me."

"That's why you were seeing him. I thought it was odd," he says.

"Oh, really. For the record, I was actually dating him," I say. "But thanks for the support."

Tyler grimaces. "Sorry. Wait. He's an Unremarkable, right? Wasn't it dangerous to give an Unremarkable an old grimoire? I'm only asking, because I don't know about this stuff."

I frown. "Everyone's a critic. Even my son."

He glances toward the chair and jumps when he sees Mr. Yeats's human form in the chair. "Where did you come from? And who are you? I didn't see you come in here."

I remember that face with a narrow jaw and pouty lips. He has switched sides for the part in his brown hair and is wearing his usual dark-gray three-piece suit. The familiar has a look of bewilderment in his dark-brown eyes. He adjusts his spectacles and fluffs up his antiquated black bowtie.

"Surely, you're going to introduce me, Ms. Crowther?" Mr. Yeats asks.

"Tyler, this is Mr. Yeats," I say as Leslie's familiar extends his hand. "This is my son, Tyler Wolfe."

My son grasps his hand in a firm grip and stares into his eyes. "Uhhh, you've got a yellow eye and a blue... What's. Going. On. Here?"

"Mr. Yeats is Dr. Hughes's familiar—a magic assistant who has both human and cat presentations," I say. "He can be an enormous help in creating spells. But he can also be a nuisance. Like showing his human form to my son when I asked him to be good. Don't let him scare you. At best, he's innocuous. At worst, he's a royal pain in the ass."

"Ms. Crowther, if you're going to insist on insults, I'll be forced to leave." Mr. Yeats crosses his arms.

I hike my eyebrows. "Don't let me stop you."

"Hmph." He adjusts his spectacles and walks into the office, transforming into his chimeric cat form as he scuttles through the doorway.

"He just turned into a cat." Tyler shakes his head. "I think I'm going to go now, 'cause I need a dose of...I was gonna say reality."

I hug my son. "Welcome to the real world, dear."

Beads of sweat roll down the nape of my neck as I wait for Agnes to come to the door. The temperature has reached 90 degrees with a real feel temp of 102 degrees. Please, Delaware, stop trying to be Florida.

The door flings open, and Agnes grins with wickedness in her eyes. "How the hell are you, Gwyn? Come in, and I'll pour us a glass of cold iced lemonade."

"I'd love a cold drink." I follow her into the kitchen and sit in a chair, noticing the coolness of the air. "Did you have air conditioning installed in the entire house?"

"I've put it off for years since I'm the only one who lives here. But after the July we had, I said 'fuck it.' You only live once...or maybe twice? I'm rooting for my good deeds to come back to me threefold. Karma, you know?" She sets glasses of lemonade on the table and takes a seat.

"Wouldn't that be awesome," I say. "How have you been? You seem to be moving around with a little more pep in your step."

"Decided it was time to give in and do some physical therapy. My doctor's been nagging me for a couple of years." Agnes peers at me through fallen strands of salt and pepper hair. "In case you hadn't noticed. I can be a teensy bit bullheaded."

"Teensy?" I laugh and take a sip of my cold drink. "Ahh, the lemonade tastes so good, Agnes."

"It's the magic I sprinkle in it." She nods with an arrogant grin.

I sniff the contents of my glass. "You put magic sprinkles in my lemonade?"

"Nah." Agnes bursts out laughing. "I'm fucking with you. Why did you stop by? Are you having trouble with your ancestral training?"

"Not exactly. It's progressing slowly and requires more patience than I usually have, but I'll get there. Archie and I are back together. So, I'm hoping I'll be able to focus better."

She takes a swig of lemonade. "Unresolved love...takes its toll on the heart and the mind. I've had a life of learning that very lesson."

My eyes roam around the kitchen at the worn cabinets while I contemplate how to broach the subject of her lost love. "Your cabinets would be so beautiful with a coat of paint, don't you think?"

Agnes stares at me. "Out with it. You didn't stop by to offer me a paint job."

"No, I didn't." I hold the side of the cold glass against my cheek. "The town is in danger. You already know about the witch Audrey Kenilworth infiltrating our coven last year. Well, we're not so sure Audrey was the one who hexed me. Last night, Tanner Jones, Spence Huxley, and I visited the Celestial Gardens to chastise the Seelie Fae children for tying up those two workmen in their underwear."

She cracks up, nearly spitting out her lemonade. "That's what happened. Classic."

"Luckily, it was too dark for the workers to identify the pranksters as anything other than juvenile delinquents. But after...two witches, a man and a woman in the shadows, attacked the men. Tanner was knocked out, but I used magic to heal him."

"And you're coming to me for help? Why isn't the coven doing something?" she asks with a dubious eye.

"One reason the Fellowship came after me last fall was because of my mom's ancestral witch status. They knew I had the potential to add great power to the coven, especially since I completed the needed thirteen. But we lost two witches. Audrey Kenilworth was a mole, and her friend Courtney went along with the whole thing. They were both expelled." I drink the last of my lemonade.

"What do you expect me to do about it?" she asks. "I have no say in the coven or its recruitment."

"Archie thinks the witches could be in a closed practice, where they draw only on the spirits of their ancestors and form a select family coven, amassing unlimited powers. I found out recently my son Tyler has inherited my family's ancestral magic, but he's spanking new and needs training." I hesitate. "If we could fill the thirteenth spot, we'd be at full capacity and possibly have a fighting chance."

Agnes's face scrunches up into a scowl of epic proportions. "Not happening. Why would you think I'd consider returning to the coven with my history? Give me one good fucking reason I should?"

"I know you have no reason to return. I felt the same way. When I left the coven, I swore off magic. I was so sure I'd never cast another spell. Then I discovered my mom's steamer trunk and her charmed letter. I decided I could compromise. Go back and transform the coven."

My eyes tear up. "When Thomas Hall collapsed, all I could think was...what if Tyler had been in there? If it was only the coven, my friends, even Archie, I wouldn't ask you, Agnes. But now my son has magic running through his veins. What if these witches come after him? I'd never forgive myself if I hadn't at least asked you to help us."

Agnes pushes up from the table, displaying a curmudgeon's face, and shuffles to the counter to pour herself another glass of lemonade. "Does Leslie know you're asking me to return?"

"Yes, she does. I told her I was going to ask if she approved. She gave me the go-ahead."

"No. If Leslie wanted me to come back, she'd have asked me herself."

It's no wonder they've not spoken to each other since the breakup. They're both so obstinate. "And what about the town? My son and me? Shane? Do you not care about anyone but yourself?"

Agnes walks back to the table and sits. "Did Leslie agree to give all witches an equal say in the coven?"

"Yes, the new rule is in place now," I say. "It was one of my demands for returning."

"Thatta girl." She slaps my arm with the back of her hand and becomes quiet—completely out of character for her. "I've not been around people for a long time, Gwyn. It's hard for me."

"I'm sure you'd be fine, and I'd be there to support you. I owe you so much. You're not anxious about all the people. Only one in particular."

"Ahh, fuck that. It's been too many years."

"Did it ever occur to you Leslie might have similar feelings? You'll never know if you don't lower the barbed wire surrounding you." I sigh. "Will you at least think about it?"

She squints at me with pinched lips. "Hmph."

While Agnes fiddles with her long, unruly hair, I recognize this was an uphill battle. It's not like I didn't try. But I want to thank her in a more personal way.

"Do you have any scissors in the kitchen?" I ask.

"Sure. Got some in the junk drawer. Third one down. Why?" she asks.

I amble to the drawer, grab the scissors, and rummage through my purse for a comb. "When was the last time someone cut your hair?"

"What? I don't need a fucking haircut." Agnes swats at the strands falling onto her face.

I gaze into her eyes full of regret. "Let me do this for you, Agnes. You've done so much for me."

"For fuck's sake...if it will shut you up, go ahead," she says.

Snip, snip, snip, and twenty minutes later, I've cut at least ten inches off the ends of her salt and pepper hair and shortened her bangs so they swoop across one side of her face. I take my compact out of my purse and hand it to her.

"Take a look," I say.

Agnes's mouth opens and closes with a smile. "Thank you, Gwynedd. No one has treated me this well in thirty years."

"Well, if you hadn't tramped around like a hermit with a chip on your shoulder, people might have seen the wonderful woman you're hiding." I swipe her bangs with my fingers. "A sexy, old witch."

She snickers. "Now you're just fucking lying."

"I don't think that's what Leslie would say." I wink at her.

"You're a troublemaker," she says, passing me my compact.

"I've been told that on occasion." I bend over and wrap my arms around her tattooed arms. "Thank you for everything. Let me know if you change your mind about the coven, but I respect your decision."

Agnes turns around and scans her kitchen. "About my cabinets...what color do you plan to paint them?"

Chapter Twenty

A Friend to Cherish

I LIE IN BED with my eyes closed, relishing the comfort of my mattress. How I had missed the way the memory foam molded to my body, yet supported my weak lower back. I moan out loud. "Ahhh, nothing like one's own bed to guarantee the perfect night's slumber."

"I completely agree," a man's Irish-accented voice declares.

"Aghhh," I exclaim. My eyes snap open to find Mr. Yeats sitting on the edge of my bed, crossing his arms. "What are you doing in here?!"

"I always rest in this room on Sunday mornings." He blows air on his spectacles and wipes them with his handkerchief. "Why should your occupation of this room change any of my routines?" He places his antiquated glasses on his nose.

"Because this is MY bedroom now. So, get out." He glares at me and doesn't move, but I push at his arm. "Shoo!"

Mr. Yeats stands and smooths out his coat. "Well, I never. Hmph." He shuffles toward the door, transforming into his chimeric cat form as he exits.

"He's gonna be a problem." I sit up, stretching my arms to the ceiling and twisting my back as the cracking steps up my spine, vertebrae by vertebrae. As I recall my night at Archie's, I chuckle to myself. Living this close provides easy access to my lover now. I should plan an excursion to his house soon.

I slip on my short satin robe and amble to the kitchen, shutting my bedroom door behind me. Leslie sits at the tiny table for two in a cotton robe, sipping her coffee. The sun peeks through the window, lighting up the daffodil-yellow walls.

"Good morning, Leslie," I say, smiling.

She lifts her chin displaying an authentic smile. "And to you, Gwynedd. I trust you slept well."

"Yes, thank you for asking. I'd forgotten what my mattress felt like after months of sleeping on a sofa bed." I cross my arms. "We've gotta talk about Mr. Yeats. I woke up to him sitting on my bed."

"That is unacceptable," she says. "He should know better. I will have a talk with him about proper etiquette. As you can imagine, he's not used to houseguests."

"Thanks." My eyes roam around the kitchen. "I spoke with Agnes yesterday."

"Indeed." She takes another sip of her coffee. "And what was her response?"

"She's not coming back," I say. "Too many unpleasant memories, I guess."

"I'm not surprised. She was never much of a collaborator. Lowri and I had to coax her to join the coven. She was so obstinate." Oh, that's rich. Leslie could offer a course in pigheadedness—and arrogance.

"I tried to convince her. Told her I'm scared the rogue witches will go after Tyler. And I couldn't live with myself if I didn't try everything to bring her back. But she wouldn't budge. I guess it's just too hard for her. She's too nervous about seeing you again."

Leslie drops her cup on the saucer with a clink. "What did she tell you?"

"Everything," I say.

She picks up her cup and saucer and moves them to the sink without a reply, and her hands shake with an uncontrollable tremor. "The addition of Tyler may not provide enough power to fight off these witches who refuse to show their faces."

"I've never seen you this concerned." The time on the clock reminds me I have to get ready for brunch with Nick.

"I have some apprehension about the time we have to prepare," she says. "But I have faith."

"I've gotta take a shower. Nick Evans asked me to meet him for brunch at the Raven Pub. He's been translating my mom's grimoire. As you probably remember, it's all in Welsh."

"Yes, I do recall. Are you sure that was a wise decision?"

"Too late now. He's almost done. All he knows is it's an antiquarian book I found in my mom's belongings. He thinks I should auction it off for a bundle of money."

"Indeed." Leslie presses her lips together.

"Don't worry. Once he returns the grimoire, I'll put it back in the steamer trunk. Have a wonderful day, Leslie."

"And you as well, Gwynedd."

I take a shower and throw on a sundress for the muggy weather but erupt in a hot flash when I dry my hair. Why do I even bother? I drive to the Raven Pub and am lucky to find a spot. The hostess shows me to a table for two in the main area against the wall under the encased stuffed raven. Oh, joy.

"Thanks for agreeing to meet for breakfast." Nick flashes a smile over his menu as I sit. "I thought it would be less awkward."

"At least you tried." I return the smile and glance at the stuffed raven in the glass case. How did we luck out being seated below this carcass representing Poe?

"I would be lying if I said I wasn't disappointed, but I'm glad you're willing to remain friends."

Nick's voice is barely audible over the morning chatter in the large open area. The aroma of freshly baked waffles and pancakes permeates the restaurant, a contrast to the odors of evening beer and popcorn.

"I cherish our friendship, Nick. You've been such a help to me, and I love having a friend who knows so much about the Welsh language, culture, and history. For convoluted reasons of their own, my parents deprived me of my heritage. Sometimes I feel a sense of loss and having someone to talk to about everything Welsh fills the emptiness. What I'm trying to say inadequately is...thank you for being that friend."

"You're welcome. Can I ask...why did your parents forgo sharing your Welsh ancestry?"

He's being invasive, so I glance at the stuffed raven. "Personal reasons I'd rather not share."

Nick pulls his tablet out of his backpack. "I'm almost done with the translations. When I've finished, I'll let you know and arrange the return of your family's journal. Or should we call the antiquarian tome by its true identity? A grimoire."

"You're sure that's what the journal is?"

"Oh, yeah," he says with a lowered tone of voice. "Read these translations."

Nick passes me the tablet and observes my reaction as I read the first couple of pages. I swallow several times as I decipher the words describing macabre spells, promoting easy incantations for "ridding oneself of unwanted enemies."

"This is quite alarming," I say as my heart peaks to new heights.

"No other explanation. Or it's a book of recipes on how to win over lovers, protect yourself from attackers, and kill your enemies."

"That would be some kind of recipe book. I can't imagine why my mom held onto it." I hate feeding him white lies, but what else can I do?

"Well, good thing she did. It's incredibly valuable. You could auction this book off for a lot of money someday." Nick waves to our waitress to come and take our order.

"I'll keep it in mind." I read over my menu one last time. "Let me know when you've finished, and I'll come by DUB and pick it up. Classes start soon, anyway. I'll need to come to campus to check out where my classrooms are."

"Or I can drop it off." Nick lays his soft hand on mine. "If you ever need anything...another translation, an ear to bend, anything, don't hesitate to ask. I'm here for you."

While I'm at the Mystic Sage on Wednesday, Trinity sends a text reminder about Thursday's meeting, encouraging us not to walk alone at night. Soon after, another text notification vibrates my cell.

Archie: *You received the text from Trinity, I assume?*

Me: *Yeah. Don't worry, I've been careful. After the attack on Spence and Tanner Friday, I'm not taking any chances.*

Archie: *That comforts me, stubborn woman.*

Me: *LOL. I wish we knew who they were, so we could defend ourselves better.*

Archie: *Aye. That would be optimum.*

Me: *Ronnie would like us to meet her and Derek for dinner at the café before the meeting tomorrow night. Interested?*

Archie: *Aye. I suggest arriving by 5:30 p.m. I'll stop by Leslie's, and we can walk from there.*

Me: *Sounds good. See you tomorrow.*

Archie: *I can't wait to see you, my love.*

"Your phone has been going off for the last ten minutes." Jeff sets a box in front of me so I can restock the herb baskets. "Big date?"

"You're funny. Actually, I have a date, but not tonight. I'm eating dinner with my friend Ronnie, her boyfriend, and my..." My what? He's definitely my lover now, but does he qualify as my boyfriend after sleeping with him not even a week ago?

"Your what?" Jeff asks, ripping open the box.

"My boyfriend, I guess." The mushy spot in my heart ignites, and I grab a loose piece of cardboard to fan myself. The man raises my temperature even when he's not in the room.

Shane enters the store, wearing a tie-dyed t-shirt and cargo pants, and he's dripping in sweat. "Woo-hoo! Nice and cool in here. I had to park past the Raven Pub. I sure hope they get Thomas Hall torn down soon. Main Street could use those parking spaces the demolition crew has roped off. It's a damn shame to watch that old house come down. And it saddens me every time I think about those poor students who lost their lives."

Jeff returns behind the counter and lowers his eyes.

"Did you know any of the students who died in the building?" I ask.

"No, but I don't want to talk about it." He sits on the stool and folds his hands.

He reacted oddly, but maybe he's got family issues again. I follow Shane into the back room for some privacy.

"You received the text from Trinity?" I ask.

"Yes, I did." Shane places a hand on my shoulder. "I'm truly frightened for our small town, Gwyn. And all of us. You be careful going home tonight. Do you want me to walk with you to Leslie's?"

"You'd have to stay until closing, Shane. After being here all day. I'll be OK. The Green is well-lit. And I can always call Archie." I walk back into the front of the store and finish stocking the herb baskets.

Shane swings his small backpack over his shoulder. "Have a wonderful evening, you two, and I'll see you tomorrow, darling. Stay cool!"

"Bye, Shane!" Jeff shouts as I wave goodbye.

The next three hours pass in a blink of an eye while the unexpected deluge of customers stops by to peruse the occult items. After a slow day of sales, the uptick should bring a grin to Shane's mouth. Around five to nine, I turn the sign to closed.

"Jeff, why don't you sign off the register and get ready to go? No more shoppers will show up now." I gather my belongings and wait for him at the door.

"This is great," he says. "Classes start in another week, and I'd like to get home early to relax. Once the semester starts, I won't have any time."

I lock the door of the Mystic Sage, and we stroll down the sidewalk until we hit the opening where Main Street intersects with the Green. As I turn toward the steps leading to the extensive area of grass and paver walkways, Jeff becomes inquisitive.

"Where are you going?" Jeff asks, chuckling. "Are you living in the dorms now?"

"Nooo. I'm renting a room from Dr. Hughes, the Acting Chair of the Celtic Studies department. She lives on Drummond Lane."

His eyes grow big. "Oh, I thought you lived with your son."

"Not anymore. And I'm sure he's enjoying his freedom again. Thank you for walking with me this far, though. I appreciate the escort. Enjoy the rest of your night. Kick back and play some video games."

"Thanks, Gwyn. Goodnight."

"Goodnight to you, too. Jeff."

I continue down the steps toward Victorian Row, pass the Pumpkin house, and cross onto the lower section of the Green on the north side of campus. The lampposts have a hazy glow in the thick-as-mud humidity, but the bright lights spill onto the maze of paver walkways and grass.

I pass the occasional student on the way to their dorms. As I approach the Old Men oak trees, a déjà vu of the night I fell overwhelms me. The aura prompts me to clutch my stomach, and I become dizzy. I glance at my hands. No amber glow. Must be the heat. Once my head clears, I snap my head around, sensing a witch. I scour the Green but observe no one, not even a single student.

"Audrey?" I yell out into the void but receive no response. "Audrey, do you wanna talk?"

Footsteps clomp in the distance and stop. A young woman with wavy brown hair wearing a sundress is standing near a lamppost, but I can't make out her face. She clasps her hands together, turns around, and runs away. Her shadow dissipates in the alleyway between the red-brick buildings facing the Green.

CHAPTER TWENTY-ONE

NOT QUITE A REUNION

THE CLINKING OF PLATES and glasses rings throughout the Sunshine Garden Café as we attempt to carry on a conversation in our booth. Ronnie sits next to me, so the men can catch up after all these months.

"I'm not gonna lie, Gwyn." Ronnie nudges me. "I miss double dating, so I hope things work out this time for you and Archie."

"So far, so good." I gaze across the table at my man. "But I'm approaching the relationship with open eyes this time. I believe he loves me, but love isn't always enough, you know."

"I understand, friend. But I can be happy for you now." She whispers in my ear. "Are you going to tell the coven about your encounter with the mole last night?"

"Yeah, but I'm uncertain the young woman was Audrey," I mutter. "I never saw her face."

"Well, who else could the witch be?" she asks.

I shrug. "What are you men talking about? The benefits of weightlifting?"

They both flex their biceps, and we laugh. Derek sets his forearms on the table. "Nope. We were discussing the seismic activity that's been plaguing our town. Seismologists are coming from all over to examine the locations where the buildings collapsed and investigate the ground the Raven Pub sits on. I was mentioning to Archie I find it strange the restaurant had no damage when it's one of the oldest buildings in Bearsden."

"I told him a minor quake wasn't enough to do any damage," Archie says.

Derek lowers his eyebrows. "I don't know about that. The rumble spread far up the other end of Main Street."

I change the subject. "So, Derek, Ronnie says a bunch of new people have registered at the fitness center. Those will keep you busy."

"Oh, yeah. And Ronnie doesn't need my help much now." Derek drinks from his water glass. "That new assistant professor Nick Evans stopped by, too. He already gets access to the DUB employee fitness center but wants a personal trainer. He's a thin guy. I hope he isn't expecting miracles from me."

"I'm sure you'll do wonders, babe." Ronnie blows him a kiss.

During dinner, we discuss the upcoming renovations on Mitchell Hall and how long it's taking the crew to dismantle Thomas Hall. Archie glances at me with those shimmering blue eyes and winks while I play footsie with him under the table. Once we've finished dinner, Ronnie hugs and kisses Derek goodbye, and we walk to Victorian Row.

Archie glimpses irritation on Ronnie's freckled face. "Something bothering you?"

"There sure as hell is," she says. "I'm fed up with the secrecy. Derek already suspects fireworks weren't the cause of my injuries. Gwyn's right. We should have more choice in the decisions of the coven. I want to propose allowing us to vet and divulge our coven and magic to Unremarkables, especially our loved ones."

Archie hikes his eyebrows. "Exposure to Unremarkables could come back to bite us in the arse, Ronnie. I'm not saying I'd vote against the idea. Only that we should be absolutely sure about the ones we expose our true identity to. For now, I'm asking you to table the proposition until after we've resolved the threats to the town."

"Whatever you say." My friend throws her palms in the air. "Gwyn, is Tyler coming tonight?"

"Yeah. I finally told him about the attack on Tanner and Spence. He's coming with Zoe. She's been giving him some mini-training lessons." I grab Archie's hand. "I figured it would give him a head start. Make him more comfortable."

"That's fine," Archie says. "We don't always follow the rules."

Ronnie cackles. "You sure as hell don't."

We arrive at the Pumpkin House, and the others are already setting up the chairs. It's about to turn 7:00 p.m. when Tyler and Zoe come running across the street. I motion to Archie and Ronnie to join the circle while I wait for them.

"Sorry, Mom. We had trouble finding parking." My son pants as he runs a comb through his hair.

Zoe taps her chest. "It was my fault. My shift at the library ran over. We're setting up for the new semester."

"You're right on time." I hug my son. "You'll be fine. You know most of the people in the Fellowship already."

Tyler smiles as Zoe grabs his hand, dragging him to the circle in the parlor. I wait by the door for a few seconds, tapping my foot. I'm hoping my mentor might have changed her mind, but there's no sign of Agnes. Asking her to face her old flame after all these years was too much.

As I close the leaded-glass door, a faint voice calls out my name. "Gwyn!"

My mouth stretches into the most joyous grin ever as Agnes hobbles up the steps, and I shut the door after she enters.

"Parking was a bitch!" she shouts in a gravelly voice. "How is an old as fuck woman supposed to get anywhere?"

I chuckle. "Perhaps we should get you a handicap parking tag?"

"Fuck no. I can walk. Just not fast." She catches her breath, and her hands tremble as we approach the chatter in the parlor.

I wrap my arms around her and squeeze. "Thank you so much. I know how hard this is for you. Are you ready to face her?"

"Sure. Let's go," she says, but trepidation suffuses her face.

Agnes follows me into the parlor, and everyone becomes quiet as mice. She peers up through her bangs, scanning the circle until her eyes stop at Leslie. The two women lock eyes and stare at each other with no sign of emotion. This is NOT how I imagined it would go down.

Leslie taps her staff two times and clears her throat. "Everyone, this is Agnes Pritchard. She has incredible, cunning magic skills that will solidify our chances of fighting these witch aggressors attacking our town. Please, give her a warm welcome."

My fellow witches hoot and holler with a few of the younger ones, whistling through their teeth. Agnes nods as I help her to an empty seat next to Skye, and I sit next to Archie. Ronnie, Tyler, and Zoe wave to Agnes from across the circle.

"We are so fortunate to have you join us. Thank you so much, Agnes," Elijah says.

Ronnie nods. "Ditto."

"I've known Agnes for years now," Shane says. "And I can happily say it's a gift to have you return to our coven."

"It's so great to have you. Thank you for helping us," Tanner says.

Tanner nudges Spence. "Oh, it's lit to have such a talented witch back in the group. I'm psyched you're here."

"Are you speaking English?" Agnes asks.

We all laugh, and Skye explains. "It's just Zillennial slang, Ms. Pritchard. You'll get used to it."

"Don't call me Ms. Pritchard. I'm not YOUR fucking grandmother," she says.

We all crack up again as Trinity pushes up from her chair. "Agnes, we are all indebted to you for coming here. I, for one, can't thank you enough, and I'm overjoyed to be collaborating with you again."

"Thank you for the warm reception. Before we proceed, I want to be clear I expect my suggestions to have significant weight in our decisions." Agnes glares at Leslie. "Although I am not an ancestral witch, I have acquired many unconventional methods that could come in handy. This fight ahead of us will require us to think and react outside the box of anything you've ever dealt with before."

"Agnes is not off the mark here," Archie says. "Even I am uncertain how to fight a closed-practice ancestral witch family."

"True words, Agnes," Trinity says. "And with the new rules, you have equal say. Everyone, I've done some digging into the rumors circulating last year when we were fighting the city council to stop the demolition of Mitchell Hall. Gossip spread about a shell corporation making huge donations to a couple of city council members—and Mayor Manley. If we can discover who's in the shell corporation, I think we'll find the witches who are destroying our town."

"I could help you research, Trinity," Skye says. "But the semester begins soon. I'd like to get started."

"I wanna help!" Zoe exclaims. "You can depend on me now."

"You're welcome to join us, Zoe," Trinity says. "The three of us will dig into it."

Archie turns his head toward our coven leader. "So, you're saying witches own this shell corporation?"

"Damn straight. Makes perfect sense," Trinity says. "And I believe the target is Mitchell Hall."

The witches babble among themselves, and I notice Tyler's anxious face. I catch his gaze and smile, trying to allay his fears, but who am I kidding? We're in deep shit.

"I agree, Trinity," Archie says. "It would explain the proximity of Thomas Hall and its destruction."

Elijah shakes his head. "Damn shame what happened to the students. At the wrong place at the wrong time."

"Why Mitchell Hall? What would be the reason?" I ask.

"The portal mound," Agnes says. "They want access to the Otherworld to call on more malevolent fae and demons."

"Agnes has a point. The portal in the mound is small, but it's still an access point," Leslie says.

"The mound is an issue, but I believe there is another underlying reason to destroy Mitchell Hall," Trinity says. "Acquiring the portal or causing its destruction could unleash an opening into the Otherworld we have never seen. We must figure out what their end game is."

Folds form in Archie's brow. "We must make this our number one priority, but I also want to remind you the semester will begin soon, and many of us will become extremely busy. I recommend we be proactive and get our work done early so we can prepare for any surprise attack."

"Do we even know how they will strike us?" Tanner asks.

"They'll probably throw amber bombs." Spence shoots fake amber shots from his hands like he's holding an assault rifle. "Those two witches who fired at us on Sunday night weren't messing around. But we aren't either."

"I doubt they'll be using witch rifles, Spence." Shane pats his slight paunch.

"We should practice our craft daily," Elijah says. "Be prepared for the worst, friends."

"Preparedness is key," Archie says. "Each of us should follow Elijah's plan. Be at your best."

When I glimpse Tyler's face, he's staring at the floor. Have I made a mistake thinking he could handle this? The entire reason for begging Agnes to return was to limit the danger to him. And I've thrown him into the witch's brew kettle.

Leslie stands. "Despite the issues at hand, I want to remind you of the Delaware pagan conference scheduled for the weekend of Mabon this year. The local covens in New Castle County are aware of our issues and have offered their assistance, but I felt we already owed them enough for their help with the banishment of the Sluagh. Go in peace, my friends."

The coven Elder taps her staff three times. We stack the chairs and make our way toward the front door with despondent faces. Agnes glances over at Leslie but drags her feet to talk with the young witches who are welcoming Tyler into the coven. Leslie collects her belongings without even a peek at Agnes. Archie finishes a chat with Trinity and walks over to me.

"They're not even speaking to each other," he says.

"They haven't spoken for fifty years," I say. "Both too stubborn to give an inch."

"Can you fathom a woman being that obstinate?" he asks, scratching his goatee.

I cross my arms. "You think you're funny?"

He chuckles and kisses my cheek. "They didn't yell obscenities at each other during the meeting, so that's promising."

"Imagine not seeing the woman you loved for fifty years?" I ask.

"I did." Archie strokes my cheek. "It was unbearable."

While I grasp his hand, Agnes walks to us. "So, this is your man, I take it?" she asks.

"Yes, I suppose he is," I say with a bashful smile. "Agnes, this is Dr. Archibald Cockburn."

"I'm honored to meet you, Agnes," he says. "Gwynedd has told me of your incredible magic skills. And please, call me Archie."

She attempts to suppress a smile, but she's hardly humble about it. "I do my best. I'm exhausted, so I'll say goodnight."

"Thank you again for coming. See you at the next meeting," I say.

While Agnes shuffles to the foyer, I catch Leslie gazing in her direction. Once Agnes exits, the Elder ambles over to us.

"I thought the meeting went quite well, don't you?" she asks. "We accomplished so much this evening. Shall we go?"

"Archie is going to escort us to the house," I say.

"Splendid." Leslie dashes toward the door, leaving us in the dust, and turns her head. "Are you coming?"

We follow her, trying to stay in step with her brisk pace. The heat continues to hang in the 70s at night, but a cool breeze has broken through on our moonlit walk.

"You seem pleased with the addition of the new witches," Archie says.

"The additions raise our level of success. So, yes, I'm pleased." She doesn't even acknowledge Agnes by name as we arrive at her house. "I'll let you say your goodnights without the burden of my eyes. Goodnight, Archie."

"A restful night to you, Dr. Hughes," we say as she ambles up her driveway.

Archie hugs me. "She's acting calm for a woman who just saw her old love after decades."

"It's that emotional barrier she's built all these years, and they have a lot to iron out. I don't have faith Agnes won't screw it up somehow…or Leslie." I stare up at his eyes, shimmering in the moonlight.

"Let's hope they don't, for the town's sake. It's been a week since I woke with you in my bed."

"I know. This was a very busy week for all of us. Why don't I stay tomorrow after Tyler's first training?"

"I look forward to it. You know you can't hover over him like a helicopter mum, right?" he asks with a thicker Scottish brogue.

"Yeah, I know. He wants me present for support. I can't believe it's only been a week since he found out." A face peeks out of the living room window, and I chuckle. "I guess I better go in. She won't go to bed until I do."

Archie kisses me and squeezes a butt cheek. "Something to dream about. Sleep well, my love."

"Pleasant dreams." I stroke the whiskers of his goatee.

He releases me and strolls down Drummond Lane, disappearing into the shadows.

Chapter Twenty-Two

How Unremarkable

I open my bedroom door to the suit-wearing familiar, nearly running into him. "Why are you standing here?"

"I have a message from Dr. Hughes." Mr. Yeats adjusts his bow tie. "She hopes you have a pleasant day and wishes you much success with your son's training."

"Oh, so nice of her to say." And unusual. "Can you move out of my way now? I have to shower and get to my friend Ronnie's house to meet Tyler."

He adjusts his spectacles. "Anything I can do to help?"

"Are you flirting with me?" I ask in a high-pitched voice.

The familiar blinks, as if a spec of lint is in his eyes. "Ms. Crowther, I do not flirt."

"Yeah, I've heard that line before." I push past him into the bathroom and lock the door—twice.

When I arrive at Ronnie's, Tyler's black sedan sits in the driveway behind my friend's red SUV. That's one conversation I wish I hadn't missed. I enter Ronnie's kitchen as her cackle of a laugh reverberates in the kitchen. My son is laughing so hard, he's hyperventilating.

"What are you guys laughing about?" I set my purse on the counter and put the trunk lock key in my jeans pocket.

Tyler's laughter calms to a chuckle. "Ronnie told me what happened at the Samhain Celebration."

"What did you tell him?" My heart thumps toward my ribcage.

"That you thought they were a cult and didn't believe them until a spirit crossed over from the Otherworld. And then you screwed it all up and shut the portal by accident," he says. "Way to go, Mom."

"Well, I was as shocked as you were when you found out," I say. "Can we go into the spare bedroom so I can show Tyler the trunk?"

"Sure," Ronnie says.

She pushes up from her chair, and we follow her into the room she uses as an office. I turn the key and open the lid, gesturing for Tyler to kneel next to me.

"All of this was Nain's, I guess. And her ancestors," I say. "I went through most of it and threw out old gross shit and kept the important items."

"This is amazing, Mom." He lifts the black hooded capes and strokes the soft material. "They used to wear these?"

Ronnie plops on her butt next to us. "They stopped wearing them a few years ago, because the students said they were creepy and outdated."

"I can see why. What's this?" He picks up the envelope bearing my name.

"The charmed letter I told you about. It's why I started training with Archie. He's the only ancestral witch in our area other than us, of course. I didn't have time to practice this past week. Eventually, I'll break the charm and find out what she wanted to tell me."

"I have faith in your mom, Tyler," Ronnie says. "She saved the whole town."

"I'm proud of you, Mom," he says. "Who thought you'd turn out to be a badass? But one thing I don't understand. Why did Nain and Taid give up magic in the first place?"

"Something happened fifty years ago on Samhain, and your grandparents raised me without magic. Dr. Hughes knows, but she won't tell me. My only hope of finding out is in Mom's letter." I pass my fingertips over the paper.

"Have faith, Gwyn," Ronnie says, squeezing my arm.

Tyler lifts Archie's family dirk from the tray. "Oh, Archie gave this to you in March. Why is it in your mom's trunk?"

"Because his dirk has special powers. It's made of iron and can kill fairies." I take the precious gift from Tyler's hands. "I used it to banish the Host of the Unforgiven Dead to the Otherworld."

"Ahhh, now I understand what happened," he says. "You are a badass, Mom. How does it work exactly?"

"I'll show you." After removing the dirk from its leather sheath, I wrap my fingers around the handle. "I have to summon my witch energy and trigger the transfer of power using an intention. You'll learn about intentions tonight."

"Don't just hold the thing. Show him, Gwyn." Ronnie nudges me.

"I didn't want to show off in front of my son, but OK."

As I raise my hand in the air, I focus on an intention. An amber glow seeps from my hand onto the dirk and radiates toward the ceiling. The gem on the handle shines in all directions.

"I wasn't sure I could trigger it again," I say.

Tyler's eyes beam with amazement. "That's fucking lit!"

The door swings open abruptly, and Derek walks in with Nick Evans close behind. They stop and gape at us. The three of us freeze since we're at a loss for words. My eyes pop out of their sockets while the rays from the dirk light up our side of the room like a Broadway show.

"Oh, shit!" Ronnie attempts to stand, falling on her ass, before grabbing the trunk to help herself up. "I can explain, Derek."

Derek shakes his head with his eyes closed, only to open them to the same scene. "I thought maybe I was seeing things. Do you see what I see, Nick?"

"Like the Christmas song says." He locks eyes with me.

I try to speak, but my vocal cords are on strike.

Tyler smacks me. "Mom, maybe you should, you know..." He points to my hand, holding Archie's family heirloom.

"Oh..." I shake my hand repeatedly, and the amber glow won't subside, so I pull the dirk out of my right hand using the left, and my witch energy fades away. "I guess we should explain." I shove the dirk into the sheath and place it back in the trunk tray.

Ronnie shuffles toward Derek with a slight limp, and he backs away. "Oh, for fuck's sake. You've been sleeping with me all this time, but NOW you're scared of me?"

I close the lid of the steamer trunk, and Tyler helps me stand. When I look at Nick, he's examining me with the eyes of an academic searching for the footnotes.

Derek crosses his bulging arms. "Go ahead, babe. Explain away."

"So, the short story is, we're witches. Real live witches. And we're part of a coven. We protect the town. Gwyn only found out about her witch ancestry on Samhain last year. Tyler found out about a week ago. The steamer trunk has her ancestral witchy stuff stored in it. She was showing Tyler." Ronnie gestures to my mom's trunk. "The long story...I'll need to tell you later when we're alone. We're sworn to tell no one or risk being expelled."

"So, what exactly happened at the Winter Solstice Celebration to injure you?" he asks. "The fireworks cover was ridiculous."

"Yeah, well. The coven couldn't think of another explanation." She extends her hand, and he wraps his burly fingers around hers, yanking her toward him.

"Did you think I was a stupid jock?" he asks. "I know you've been covering up something all this time, but I didn't expect this."

"Well, now you know. I've wanted to tell you for so long, but the coven leaders wouldn't allow it." She kisses him. "Don't be mad."

My heart pounds with palpitations. How the hell are we going to explain this to Archie...to the coven? Nick stands there with a gaping mouth, blinking. I elbow Tyler.

"We should go." I bend over and close the lock on the trunk. "Nick, why don't you walk out with us and leave them alone? They've got a lot to chat about."

"And so do we." He glares at me with a flat mouth. "Derek, this was an awesome way to meet your girlfriend. Ronnie, it was nice to meet you."

"You, too, Nick," she says. "I hope we meet under different circumstances next time."

Nick follows Tyler and me out of Ronnie's house without saying a word. What am I going to say to him? When we get to my son's car, Tyler breaks the silence.

"I've gotta get back to work. That lunch lasted way longer than I planned. Glad I got to meet you, Dr. Evans." Tyler gets in his car and leaves.

I peer up at Nick's dark-brown eyes and melt. "Like Ronnie said...I couldn't tell you."

"What did I just see in there?" he asks while he fiddles with the straps of his backpack.

"Magic," I say. "The dirk has special powers."

He cocks his head. "What kind of powers?"

"I can't tell you, Nick." I avert my eyes.

"Well, it clears up some questions I had, but I wish you had trusted me enough to tell me." Nick takes off his backpack and pulls out my mom's grimoire. "I finished the translations and sent the files to your email. When I finished training with Derek, he said you were stopping by for lunch at Ronnie's. So, I tagged along to give the journal back to you."

I grimace. "We both know it's not a journal...or a recipe book."

"I knew something was up when I translated the last spell." He opens the grimoire and flips the pages until he gets to the last entry, pointing to my mom's handwriting. "I'll translate it for you. 'This may be my last entry. An incident has occurred that could trigger danger to Gwynedd's life. From this day forward, I must never practice witchcraft again.' The rest of the pages are blank."

"Were you planning on confronting me about this entry?"

"I don't know. I figured it wasn't any of my business."

"But now it is," I say as I fiddle with an earring. "We call non-witches Unremarkables since you're not *in the knowing* of all things supernatural. But you know now. I would be indebted to you forever if you could promise to keep this revelation a secret."

"Forever?" Nick's dark eyes twitch. "I'm going to hold you to that."

"I really am sorry, Nick." As I rub the palm of my hand, I regret the forever remark.

"I do have one question. Did you stop seeing me, because I'm a...what did you call me? An Unremarkable?"

"No. I liked you very much. Part of me wanted the balance of an Unremarkable in my life. But I wasn't being true to myself...to my heart."

"I better get back to campus." He flings his backpack into his car. "I don't think I should see you for a while."

Nick gets in his car and drives off. This is bad…really bad. What if he stews over this and tells someone? Tyler sends me a text from work.

Tyler: *Are we in trouble?*

Me: *I don't know, but we're gonna find out. See you at Archie's.*

I grind my teeth on my thumbnail while I lean against the kitchen counter, waiting for Tyler, Zoe, and the others to arrive. You'd think this was his first day of kindergarten. And if I remember correctly, my son came home sporting a face full of smiles and arms full of craft projects. I, on the other hand, spent the day checking my voicemail for messages of his demise.

Archie puts the kettle on for the cinnamon tea and wraps his arms around me. "Why are you so nervous? Tyler appears to have taken the news of his witch status well."

"You don't have children." I lay my hands on his rounded shoulders. "Mothers never stop worrying about them, no matter how old they are."

"True. But I read people fairly well. He's an intelligent young man. I'm sure he'll succeed as well as his mum." He kisses me, and the doorbell rings. "Brilliant. They've arrived."

I follow him into the foyer, and he flings open the front door. "Good evening, everyone. Come on in."

Tyler and Zoe enter, laughing. My son throws me an enthusiastic smile as they flip off their sneakers at the hall tree. Spence, Skye, and Ronnie follow in after them, flinging their flip-flops onto the pile.

"Are you training with us tonight, Gwyn?" Ronnie asks.

I grimace. "No. I'm not allowed."

"Good," Tyler says. "I don't need you critiquing my every mistake."

Zoe flashes him a tooth-filled grin, and the others laugh.

"Don't worry, Mom," Spence says. "I'll take good care of him. Archie, did you put water on for the tea?"

"Of course. It should boil any minute," he says, and the kettle whistles.

"Fantastic. I'll get it and meet you guys downstairs." Spence darts into the kitchen.

Skye motions toward the basement door. "Follow me, Tyler. Archie's magic room is downstairs in a musty, cold, damp room."

"You're actually dissing my magic room?" the Scottish professor asks.

"Well, she's being kinda accurate." Ronnie grimaces and pinches her nose. "The room bothers my allergies every time we practice there."

"I never wanted to say anything before, but the mold makes my nose run," Zoe says.

"Points taken," Archie says. "I'll see what I can do for the next practice session."

Spence walks out of the kitchen with the teakettle and a cup. "You guys are still up here? Let's go! We don't have all night!"

"It's Friday," Zoe says. "We do have all night."

"Really? Backtalk?" Spence asks. "Archie, I'll let you know if we need anything."

They file in line to descend the stairs, and Tyler looks back at me. "Don't worry, Mom. I'm good."

"Have fun, son." I grasp Archie's hand as they make their way into the basement.

"What shall we do while they're schooling?" he asks, reaching for his tablet. "Want to stream a show?"

"Hell, no," I say. "I'm not gonna strain my eyes looking at a minuscule screen. I can't believe you still don't own a T.V."

"My academic and personal life don't allow much time for viewing. My tablet and laptop serve well enough." He sets the tablet back on the end table. "We could play a game? A rematch of checkers?"

"Oh, all right," I say.

I sigh and drop my butt on the sofa while Archie retrieves the checkerboard. He sets the game on the steamer trunk, and we both set up the checkers on our squares. I remember the time he kissed me, leaning over the trunk, and my face flushes. The AC must be on, but my body needs a freezer. I grab a magazine from the other end table and fan myself.

"I wish this late summer heat wave would break," I say.

"Do you want me to turn down the air conditioner?" he asks. "I don't mind."

"No. You'd freeze out everyone." I glance at the open doorway when laughter trickles up the stairwell.

He lifts a corner of his mouth. "Sounds like training is going well."

"I'm elated Tyler knows, but deep inside I was hoping he'd remain an Unremarkable." I jump two of his checkers and snatch them up.

He leans over the steamer trunk and gives me a quick kiss. "That's not fair. You're distracting me with all this nonsense."

"It's the only way I can win," I say.

For the next two hours, Archie obliterates me, winning all but one game. I just have too much swimming in my head to concentrate, especially after the incident at Ronnie's house. We've got to tell him what happened and hope he doesn't freak out. I tap my fingernails on his steamer trunk in time to the tik, tik, tik of the mantle clock.

"You don't regret your training with Agnes and returning to the coven, do you?" he asks.

"Not now." I walk to him and straddle his legs in the chair. "I'm happy I returned to you, too. The months without you were so lonely, but I couldn't get past your history."

"You know how sorry I am I hurt you. I'll never cause you pain again."

He cups my face and kisses me tenderly and rubs his nose against mine. He kisses me again with an open mouth, and I moan as our tongues roam. And the smoke alarm in the basement goes off, blaring throughout the house like a screeching banshee.

"Fire spells!" we shout in unison.

I jump off of him, and we run downstairs to the magic room. Smoke slithers through the doorway, and we hack as we enter.

"I promise it wasn't Skye and me this time!" Ronnie declares.

Skye adds, "Zoe was trying to impress Tyler with her recent prowess and...oops."

Spence coughs and waves the smoke away from his face. "Before you yell at Zoe, I allowed her to do a heating spell. I didn't know she'd overestimate the level of heat. My bad."

"I'm sorry," she says. "I guess I wasn't ready yet."

"It's all right," Archie says with a proud smile. "I'm glad you're taking more risks, Zoe. You won't improve without making a few mistakes."

"How did your first training go, Tyler?" I ask, as if it's his first day of high school.

Tyler wraps his arm around Zoe's shoulder and smiles in my direction. "I did OK. It was my first session."

"He's being humble, Gwyn," Spence says. "Accomplished level one in minutes. Dare I say his initial training went better than yours? Must be your age...no offense, sis."

"Offense taken, but I'm overjoyed." I hug Tyler, but he grimaces. "I'm sorry. Am I embarrassing you? My bad."

"Your momma is proud. Deal with it," Ronnie says.

"I trained with Tyler tonight. He's gonna jump levels quickly." Skye glimpses the time on her cell phone. "Should we clean up now? I'd like to make it to the Raven Pub for band night."

"That sounds like a brilliant idea." Archie winks at me.

"OK, students," Spence says. "Let's put the herb jars back on the shelf and wipe down the worktable."

Everyone finishes cleaning up and rushes through the doorway, except for Ronnie. We stare at each other, and our tongues are tied as tight as a constrictor knot.

"Why are you both so quiet?" Archie asks as he organizes the jars.

Ronnie wrings her hands. "I'll tell him."

"Tell me what?" he asks, putting the wooden bowls on the shelf.

"Tyler stopped by the house on his lunch break, so Gwyn could show him the contents in her mom's trunk. He saw your family dirk in there and asked about it, how it worked."

Archie's eyes shift back and forth between our guilt-ridden faces. "Go on."

"I was explaining how the power of an ancestral witch controls the dirk, and Ronnie suggested I show him." I hesitate. "So, I did. I put my hand in the air and summoned my witch energy. The magic impressed him extremely when the amber rays lit up the room."

"Naturally. How is that an issue?" he asks.

Ronnie grimaces. "Because the door opened, and Derek and Nick Evans entered the room."

"Fawk!" Archie's face contracts into a look of constipated angst.

"As you might guess, they were shocked at what they saw," I say.

"Fawk!" He wanders around the room, running a hand through his hair. "Fawk! Bloody hell!"

"It's not as bad as it seems," Ronnie says.

He turns around, and his Scottish temper seeps through. "And how is that possible, exactly?"

"Derek was cool with it. We even joked about it afterward," she says while fiddling with a mortar and pestle. "He'd had his suspicions something was up all along after what happened at the Winter Solstice Ceremony. You don't need to worry about him. He loves me and will keep our secret."

He glares at me with fiery eyes. "And Nick? What the fawk do I do about him? I work with the man, Gwynedd."

"I don't think he'll tell anyone," I say. "He really likes me and values my friendship. I think Nick could be an asset to the coven. In fact, I think we should be more open about our witchcraft to other Unremarkables—vetted first, of course. But he was a little pissed."

"Great." He sucks in the musty air of the basement and holds his breath until his face turns beet red. "I'll contact him and set up a meeting...smooth things out if I can."

"I'm sorry, Archie," Ronnie says. "It's my fault. I didn't think I needed to lock the door. Derek wasn't supposed to come home until the dinner hour. But I'm glad he did. I was tired of lying to him." She shoves the mortar and pestle to the back of the table. "I'm gonna head home. He's waiting for me and has a lot more questions. Goodnight."

Ronnie's footsteps dissipate, and the front door slams shut. I peer up at Archie, pouting. "Don't be mad. It wasn't intentional. But I admit we were lax."

"I'm not angry. Not much, anyway. But my heart rate jumped a few hundred beats." He strokes my cheek. "I could never remain angry at you, stubborn woman. But this presents a situation. Do I tell Leslie and the rest of the coven? The Elder will snap her staff."

I step toward him and stroke his arm. "We can discuss the Fellowship later, can't we? We should go to bed and work off the stress?"

"My mood for sex has tanked for the night." He brushes a hand through his hair. "I have so many knots in my stomach, I'll need a forklift to remove them."

"OK. I'll head out and let you figure out what we should do." I turn toward the doorway.

"I wasn't asking you to leave. Please, stay the night. I miss not having you in bed next to me."

"OK, but I can't promise to keep my hands to myself."

He grins from ear to ear. "Have I told you recently how wonderful you are?"

I smirk. "Yes, and flattery will get you...everything."

CHAPTER TWENTY-THREE
UNEXPECTED VISITORS

ARCHIE'S JUST RETURNED FROM an 8:00 a.m. meeting with Nick at the department while I lounged in bed, beating the pillows. It's the next morning, and we're setting up for an ancestral divination practice session. He has a dehumidifier running in the magic room. I can't possibly have successful divination with that damn thing humming.

"I'm so glad Nick agreed to meet with you on a Saturday morning. How did it go?" I ask with clenched teeth.

"Awkward. Neither of us knew what to say." He lays out the divination cloth. "I finally told him I knew he was aware of the coven and begged him not to tell any other Unremarkable. He says he'll keep our secret in his pocket. I only hope he doesn't pull it out for a favor someday. My class load in the fall semester is full."

"I trust him. Don't worry about it." I suck in my lip, recalling my *forever* comment. "Did you tell Leslie?"

"Not yet," he says. "Maybe never."

I stand facing the picture of my mom and drink my cinnamon tea. The divination cloth has selenite and obsidian crystals placed as before, but my confidence is waffling. This is the first time I've tried to contact my mom since I slept with Archie. What if I screwed up my focus? My foot taps to the rhythm of "Another One Bites the Dust."

He chuckles as he moves next to me. "Do you need to pee?"

"No, but the Earl Grey will kick in soon. I meant to tell you. Thank you for the wonderful breakfast." I knead my fingers while I gaze at my mother's photo. "I'm worried I messed up the progress I made."

"Maybe if you worried less, you could focus more…and have less gray hair to color at your next appointment," he says with a kiss on my cheek.

"Like you don't have silver swimming through your waves." I slip my fingers through his locks and kiss him on the mouth.

"Stop procrastinating. If you want to develop the skills needed to transcend the charm on your mom's letter, you must proceed."

I focus on the intention to connect with my mom, pulling energy from the crystals. As I raise my hands, they radiate with the amber glow, and I face my palms toward the picture. I focus on the lines around my mother's face, wishing I could talk to her about my new life—about Richard, Tyler, Archie, the coven, and magic. How I wish Lowri Crowther were here.

"That's good, Gwyn. Now Think about your mom, what you want to say to her." Archie shifts away from me, allowing me space to concentrate.

"Stop. Talking. To me. I can't focus." Yellow lines form around Mom's pretty face as I recognize myself in her image. "Come forth, Mom. Talk to me. Meet me halfway? Please?" The yellow outline morphs into a three-dimensional vision protruding from the picture, growing until a life-sized form is directly in front of me. I pant as the vision becomes more defined.

"Mom?" The vision of Lowri Crowther attempts to speak to me using a slow-moving mouth. "I can't hear you, Mom. Can you turn up the volume or something?" Her face morphs in and out of clarity, and I struggle to discern what she's saying. As her face fades away, I snatch up the framed photo. "No. Talk to me, Mom."

Archie lays a hand on my back. "You were amazing, Gwyn. It's the closest you've come to making a genuine connection."

"I'm so frustrated," I say. "But I want to try again."

He kisses my cheek. "Take a break and try again later this week. You must build your ancestral divination in small increments, like the break you give your muscles after you work out. Time to heal and refresh."

"Aghhh! You know I'm not patient." I place my mom's picture on the shelf.

Archie folds the divination cloth with the crystals inside and places the bundle next to my mom's photograph. He wraps his arms around me from behind.

"And that, my love, adds to your focus issues. It's difficult to conjure the spirit of such a close ancestor. We normally reach further back, but your lack of training since childhood inhibits the depth of your reach. It's why I recommended connecting with your mother. But seeing her can bring forth powerful emotions."

"On the one hand, I want so badly to find out what she wrote in her letter. But on the other hand, the contents might scare the shit out of me." I turn and rest my head on his firm chest and sense the beating of his heart, slow and relaxing. "Well, I better get home. Leslie will probably give me the evil eye coming in at 10:00 a.m. And Mr. Yeats...he's like a mother hen."

"I don't know how you live there, but it's your choice. My bed always has a vacancy with your name on it, flashing in neon pink over the pillow."

I grin and walk toward the stairs as Archie turns out the light in the magic room. When we get to the foyer, I put on my sneakers and grab my purse.

"I'll call you when I'm free next," I say. "Thank you for being so patient with me."

"Anything for you, my love." He pats my butt and kisses me goodbye.

The minute I step onto Archie's porch, I notice the heat wave has finally broken. Temps in the upper 70s mimic air conditioning compared to the prior stint of 90-degree days. A cool breeze displaces my bangs as I enjoy the sunny stroll to Drummond Lane. When I turn the corner, I notice Trinity's large SUV in Leslie's driveway. I dash to the side door, nudging it with my hip. Once inside, voices trickle down the hallway, so I kick off my sneakers and shuffle to the office with Mr. Yeats scuttling alongside me.

"That's alarming, Trinity," Leslie says, sitting at her desk chair. "Very disconcerting."

Trinity sits on the edge of the desk tapping a pencil. "It certainly explains a lot."

"What's going on?" I ask as Mr. Yeats transforms into his human persona. "Stop appearing so close to me. It's creepy."

"It's not creepy. I'm just being...me." He walks into the magic room with a poetry book in his hand.

"I don't know how you live here, Gwyn," Trinity says. "He's part of the reason I moved out when I started at DUB. But I'm indebted to you, Leslie, for being there for me when I needed support."

"Of course, Trinity." Leslie smiles and pats her hand.

"So, is someone gonna fill me in?" I ask.

"I did some digging into those rumors about a shell corporation paying funds to a couple of city council members and Mayor Manley," Trinity says. "One of the council members, I won't say who, delved into the shell corporation. It's called the Williams Development Group. A little more digging revealed who owns the assets inside the group. The council member had to break some rules to uncover that information."

Leslie lifts her chin. "The assets belong to another entity in New Jersey—the Kenilworth Development Group."

"No, shit," I say. "They're the family of ancestral witches. So, what was their endgame?"

"Take your pick," Trinity says. "Maybe they paid off the crooked council members to solidify a bid. They knew our coven existed and were tweaking the outcomes of the votes on the city council."

"And they sent Audrey to infiltrate the Bearsden Coven—to spy on your plans, I assume." I shake my head. "Hmph. And bringing me into the coven to help with the spell of influence ruined their scheme, so she had to do what she could to remove me, even if it meant killing me."

"Our success must have enraged them," Leslie says. "They retaliated against the entire town. Destroyed as much as they could."

Trinity nods. "With Mitchell Hall as their ultimate aim."

"Why, though?" I ask. "So, it would be gone, and they'd finally get the parking garage contract? To have access to the portal mound? To get even with us?"

"All the above, Gwynedd," Leslie says. "Evil witches do not have one motive. They have an agenda with an extensive list."

"Now what?" I ask.

"I'm calling for an emergency meeting tonight." Trinity pushes off the desk. "Leslie, I hope you enjoy dinner at Agnes's."

My eyes widen. "You're having dinner with Agnes?"

"We must discuss plans for the coven," she says. "She asked if I would join her for dinner before tonight's meeting. The coven does not need to be subjected to our arguments."

As Leslie exits the office, Trinity and I squash our smiles, but we follow our coven Elder into the kitchen and say goodbye. Outside, I broach the subject of Audrey's recent behavior.

"The last time I came in contact with Audrey was on the Green," I say. "I couldn't make out her face, but I sensed it was her. She could have attacked right there, but she didn't. Not even a spark. Does that sound like an evil ancestral witch trying to kill me?"

"Doesn't make sense, does it?" Trinity asks. "I wanted to murder that young woman when she tried to kill you and hurt Ronnie using the Sluagh, but you wouldn't let me. You said she was being controlled and stepped in to protect her. But why would the parents of an ancestral witch have to put a masking spell AND a controlling spell on her? Two plus two doesn't equal four."

I inhale and collect my thoughts. "No, it doesn't add up."

"I'll see you tonight at the Pumpkin House, Gwyn."

While Trinity walks to her car, I run all the permutations through my overloaded brain. Was I right about Audrey all along?

Trinity towers over us with foreboding on her face and delivers the news. My fellow witches chatter like chickens over the revelations about the shell corporation being a cover for the Kenilworth Development Group.

"So, let me get this straight. Kenilworth is the name of the group that wanted to build a parking garage? That's Audrey's last name." Spence throws his hand into the air. "Is she responsible for all of this?"

"I doubt a woman of her age runs a real estate development group, Spence," Archie says. "It's probably her family."

"We can assume they were furious about losing the contract for the parking garage." Leslie peers at Agnes and nods.

Skye chimes in. "Audrey always professed her parents kicked her out, and she certainly fooled me, but maybe it was all a front."

"She fooled all of us," Elijah says. "There was always something off about her."

"We found out she was working for someone. She basically confessed as much." Tanner leans forward in his chair.

"But was she working for others, or was she being controlled?" I ask. "Or both? We know she had a spell cast on her to keep her from divulging who sent her to infiltrate the coven. The other night on the Green, she could have attacked me, but she didn't. What's that about?"

Tyler grimaces. "You walked home through the Green by yourself? That wasn't very smart, Mom."

"You won't convince her otherwise," Ronnie says.

"Never mind," I say with a wrinkle between my eyes. "I only wish she had approached me and talked."

Agnes flings a hand in the air. "Forget about Audrey. These witches must be stopped. We must act to save the town."

The screen door claps shut in the foyer, and squeaky footsteps follow. Our mouths snap shut. We should have locked the door. Jeff Williams enters the parlor, where we're sitting in our coven circle. His face has a look of anguish, mashing his lips together and wringing his hands.

Shane jumps up out of his chair. "Jeff, what's wrong? You're supposed to be at the store! Did the building fall?"

"No. I locked the store. It's fine." He lowers his head and closes his eyes. "I'm so sorry, everyone. My aunt and uncle demanded I come here and introduce them to you."

"What is this about?" Ronnie whispers.

Jeff's aunt walks in with a man near her age, most likely in his mid-50s. He's wearing a black suit and tie and has long silver hair pulled back into a ponytail. Jeff's aunt has one side of her wavy, brown hair clipped behind her ear and has on a black jumpsuit. Her charcoal eyes exude hatred from the depths of the Otherworld. And she's standing as if someone shoved a broomstick up her butt. The coven members gape with bewilderment.

"This is my Aunt Edith and Uncle Edmond," Jeff says.

Leslie stands with a crinkle in her brow. "This is a private community meeting. Not to be rude, but you aren't permitted in here. If you have questions for the Fellowship of Associated Pagans, you may contact me or Trinity Johnson tomorrow."

"May I interrupt?" I ask. "I've seen Jeff's aunt stop by the store. Mrs. Williams, I'd be happy to talk with you tomorrow."

Jeff's aunt bursts out laughing. "My name isn't Williams. My name is Edith Kenilworth."

As my eyes bulge out, the members shout, "What?!" "Why the hell are you here?" "How dare you show up at our meeting!" "Get the fuck outta here!"

Edmund interjects while the shouting continues. "We will leave when we've made our demands."

The Fellowship quiets down enough for Edith Kenilworth to speak. "This coven has interfered with our business transactions, and we've had enough. But the city council is still willing to grant us the contract if Mitchell Hall should suffer the same demise as Thomas Hall."

Archie stands and glares at them with steely eyes. "You're here to ask us to lift the protection barrier from the Mitchell Hall property. Why would we comply with such a request?"

"If you do not remove the barrier, we will destroy more buildings in your town," Edith says. "One. By. One. Is that what you want?"

My fellow witches chat among themselves. Archie walks to Leslie, Agnes, and Trinity and whispers to them. I observe lots of nodding and worried faces. What the hell are we going to do?

Edith snaps. "We don't have all night. What is your response?" Her husband Edmund crosses his arms and glares at us with dark, threatening eyes.

Archie, Trinity, Leslie, and Agnes finish their discussion and return to their seats. Our coven Elder grabs her staff and stands.

"We will accept your demands," Leslie says.

The coven erupts in anger. You can almost see the lava flowing from their heads. "Dr. Hughes, no!" "Don't give in to this, Leslie!" "We should fight!" The Kenilworths smirk at us while the Bearsden witches continue to shout with angst.

"It's done," Archie says. "It will take some time. The city has fenced in the property for renovations, although they suspended them until the cleanup of Thomas Hall is finished."

Trinity stands and glares at the Kenilworths with laser eyes. "You vow not to touch our town if we give you Mitchell Hall?"

"Of course," Edmund replies. "We had no issues with your pathetic little coven until you interfered with our...affairs."

Spence jumps out of his seat, his arms flailing about. "You're gonna let them do this? We're supposed to protect the town."

"We don't have a choice, dude." Tanner wraps his arm around Spence's shoulder and encourages him to sit.

"I think we're finished here." Edith and Edmund turn toward the foyer.

I stand and shout, "Wait. Why isn't Audrey with you?"

Edith turns around and sneers. "Come on, Jeffrey."

Jeff peers at us with a distraught face and follows the Kenilworths out the front door. With the clap of the wooden screen, the babble begins.

"We're supposed to protect our community," Zoe says, hopping out of her seat. "That's what all of our shenanigans were about."

"I am perplexed beyond words," Shane says. "Jeff has been spying on us all this time. Why didn't Gwyn and I sense his witch energy?"

"He never gave us a reason to question who is," I say. "I knew his aunt was a bitch, but I never imagined she was a Kenilworth. And I'm not sure Jeff was doing this willingly. He's complained about her controlling him since I met him. And he didn't appear too happy about introducing them. They must hold payment for his schooling over his head."

"But why are we giving up so easily?" Skye asks. "Aren't we better than this? And we're all supposed to have a say. New rules and all."

"Seriously, Trinity. How can you just roll over for them?" Ronnie asks.

"Hold on," Trinity says. "Elijah, before I explain, would you check the front door and make sure the Kenilworths are gone?"

"Will do." Elijah darts to the foyer, and the sound of the entry door shutting echoes. "No sign of them anywhere. And I didn't sense any evidence of their presence."

"We're not going to, witches. Give us some credit," Trinity says.

"I'm confused," Spence says. "You just told those creepy as hell ancestral witches we're gonna remove the protection barrier on Mitchell Hall."

"We are," Archie says. "But Agnes knows of a protection spell to put a barrier on the entire town."

"Well, aren't you the sly ones?" Elijah says.

"No way in all the Otherworld would I do as they want," Trinity says. "We agreed to their demands to buy us time."

"Putting a protection barrier on the entire town sounds daunting," I say.

"And scary as hell," Ronnie whispers to me. "What if we fail?"

Agnes stands to address the circle. "Casting a spell of this magnitude will be extremely difficult, but I'm sure we can do it with a coven of thirteen, especially having three ancestral witches in our group."

Tyler raises his hand. "Ms. Pritchard, I've known I'm a witch for barely two weeks. I think you're putting a lot more faith in my neophyte skills."

"I trained your momma, Tyler," Agnes says. "You'll do just fine."

I stare at my son with a proud smile. "Where will we cast the spell?"

"We'll have to break into the Mitchell Hall property and perform the casting in the gardens." Archie scratches the tip of his goatee. "We have to cancel the first one and quickly cast the other before the Kenilworths are aware."

Agnes lifts her hand. "I want to warn you. This incantation is old, and I've never performed it. There could be repercussions."

"What sort of repercussions, Agnes?" Shane asks.

Leslie scans the circle. "Many years ago, we cast a fertility spell to help Rose Mitchell conceive. The intent was to increase her chances of acquiring a child. The incantation triggered weeks of rain, and the mound formed, bringing with it the Seelie Fae children."

"That was a big oops!" Spence snorts.

Agnes grimaces. "Well, shit happens."

"It sure does," Trinity says. "Archie and I will check out Mitchell Hall, and I will confer with Leslie about a good time to sneak in and cast the spell. I'll send everyone a text."

Leslie taps her Elder staff three times, and we stack the chairs. A few of the Bearsden witches hang out on the porch and discuss the task ahead of us.

"Do you actually think we can do this?" I grind my teeth on my thumbnail.

"Agnes has accumulated many years of successful witchcraft." Leslie observes Agnes as she makes her way up the street. "I trust her judgment."

"It's late," Trinity says with a yawn. "Charlie is probably wondering where I am. Goodnight everyone and get some rest." She clicks in her stilettos as she descends the steps.

"I'll walk you and Leslie home," Archie says.

We head home on the Green, our eyes roaming the campus, leery of the sinister shadows along the way. An overwhelming sense of dread makes me shudder, and Archie wraps his arm around me. Leslie plods with long strides, and her breathing appears labored. When we get to the house, she proceeds toward the side door. But I remain at the bottom of the driveway. She stops and turns her head.

"Gwynedd, will you be staying at the house tonight?" she asks.

"I think so." I glance at Archie, and he nods. "If we should need him, he's only one street away."

"Goodnight to you, Archie." Leslie ambles to the door and enters her house.

I grasp his warm hand. "I've never seen her this scared. Not even when the Sluagh was murdering those homeless men last year. Do you think we'll have enough power to cast a protection spell over all of Bearsden?"

My lover strokes my cheek. "We're about to find out."

He bends down to kiss me, and I stroll to the side door as he looks on—my protector. As I nudge the door, I ponder over Audrey's absence. Why didn't she come with her parents to the Pumpkin House?

Chapter Twenty-Four

An Ounce of Protection

Trinity checks with the city regarding the renovations on Mitchell Hall on Monday and discovers we have one week to cast a protection spell on the town. She schedules the spell casting for Wednesday night and sends a text to everyone, asking us to show up around midnight. Shane hasn't heard from Jeff Williams since the coven meeting and has no one else to work on Tuesday evening. So, I offer to help him out. Students don't show up on campus until the end of the week.

"I still can't believe Jeff was working here to spy on us." I wipe down the counters, feeling duped. "But he seemed unhappy. I don't get why we didn't sense his magic."

"Gwyn, he was doing as he was told, with no other option on his plate," he says. "As far as the magic, maybe his aunt cast a veil over it."

I scowl as I count the money in the cash tray. "Maybe. But he always had options. He knew he could depend on us." I slam the register closed.

"It's easy for us to perceive his life from the outside. We don't know what they were holding over his head." Shane walks toward the glass front door. "Thank you so much for working tonight. I would have been here twelve hours if you hadn't agreed to come in."

"That's what friends are for, boss," I say.

"Have a wonderful evening." He pulls on the door, and it dings. "You be careful walking home tonight."

"I will, Shane. Enjoy your dinner and evening."

I wave goodnight to my friend as he exits, and for the next thirty minutes, relish the hum of an empty store. The shoppers trickle in throughout the night, and I'm elated when the clock turns to 9:00 p.m. on my cell phone. I turn off all the lights, set the security alarm, and lock the door.

My chestnut strands tickle the side of my face as the sultry air toys with them. You can sense the calm before the storm when thousands of students will invade the campus from out-of-state, lugging bulky backpacks and entitled attitudes. The lampposts emit their hazy glow and cast eerie shadows from the branches of the Old Men oak trees, but I no longer fear them. I veer off the main paver walkway and enter the alleyway between Menzies Hall and Campbell Hall. Suddenly, my entire body buzzes and tingles—a witch!

I twist my body around and come face-to-face with Audrey Kenilworth. She's wearing an old t-shirt and frayed jean shorts, and her wavy brown hair flits in the breeze as her inky eyes stare back at me. I don't know whether to scream, run down the alley, or smack her with an amber glow ball, so I stand there, staring back at her, and swallow.

Audrey rolls her lips inward, and the tears drip down her cheeks. "I'm sorry, Gwyn. So sorry for everything I've done to you. My parents were controlling me all last year, but in May, I ran away."

"Really?" I say, squinting. "And I'm supposed to believe you, because?"

"You have no reason to believe me. I know that." She wipes a tear from her cheek, and a bit of amber glow seeps from her fingers.

I step back from her. "I'm level three now, Audrey. Don't try anything."

"No, I'm not. I didn't want to join the Bearsden Coven and hurt anyone. My parents cast an old ancestral spell on me to make me comply. I wasn't myself." She opens her hands and stares at them. "When I returned home after the coven expelled me, my parents punished me for my failure. They removed the other spell but put a hex on me. I can't control my magic. The hex also affected the magic of others when I got near them."

My mouth falls open slightly as I recall the day the city building fell. "Is that why it felt like someone was pulling at my magic before the building collapsed?"

"No," she says. "I wasn't there. My parents cast the destruction spell. Since you happened by, my mother cast a hex on you to weaken your magic. They did it again from the roof of the Mystic Sage. I know they went after others in the coven, too—Archie, Tanner, and Spence. Jeffrey told me everything."

"Why was Lindsey Hope on top of the city building?" I ask.

"My mom blamed her for siding with the others on the city council. So..." Audrey lowers her head. "I wanted to warn all of you, but I knew if I got too close, my hex might affect your magic skills, anyway. When I tried to approach you in the parking lot of Roots of the Earth, I realized it was too soon. I waited this long to talk to you, so I could work on removing the rest of the hex. It's not completely gone, but I'm not affecting you now."

"Agnes Pritchard, you remember the old eccentric witch on the outskirts of town? She removed the hex your parents cast on me and put a protection spell in its place." I observe my hands, and they're unaffected. "You should come back with me to Leslie's house. I'm renting a room from her. And I bet Agnes could do something."

I have mixed feelings about my former foe. She seemed so evil. How can I be sure she's telling me the truth? What if this is another trick?

"I don't want to affect anyone else if there are remnants of the hex," she says. "I've already caused so much pain to all of you, and I worry about Jeff." Footsteps reverberate on the Green, and she snaps her head around. A student runs by the opening of the alleyway, and Audrey relaxes. "And please, don't hurt my cousin. My parents are controlling him, too. He has no magic to fight back."

"Jeff is an Unremarkable?" I ask.

"Yes. His mother was my mom's sister, but his dad was an Unremarkable. He's just trying to graduate and disappear somewhere they'll never find him. I need to go. My parents can sense when I'm near, and I don't know where they're hiding."

"Did you know they demanded we take our protection barrier spell off the Mitchell Hall property? So, they can destroy it and finally get their parking garage contract?"

"Oh, Gwyn, you must stop them. They don't care about anybody but themselves. Please fight them. I have to go." Audrey turns around and runs toward the Green, and the pitter-patter of her feet echoes in the distance.

I call Archie on the way home and share what transpired. "What do you think? Is this another trick?"

He hums into the phone. "Hard to say. You must trust your judgment. Did she sound sincere?"

"The most authentic I remember." I run up the steps of the side porch. "I'll tell Leslie when I get inside. Audrey said Jeff is an Unremarkable. I wish we could help him."

"One step at a time. We need to protect the town first. Then we can discuss Jeff. Try to sleep, Gwyn. Don't let this stress you out."

"That's unlikely." I pause, picturing the chiseled face of my lover at the other end of the phone. "I love you, Archie."

"And my heart is yours, my love."

As we sneak into the Mitchell's Celestial Gardens on Wednesday at midnight, Ronnie can't stop repeating, "I can't believe she's telling the truth."

"Elijah always said there was something off about her. And a controlling spell would explain most of her actions." I scan the gardens for Tyler under the moonlight. "She was probably trying to fight the effects of the spell the entire time. I truly feel bad for her."

"I'm going to speak with Trinity, Leslie, and Agnes," Archie says. "You and Ronnie find a place in the circle."

The gardens are lit by a partial moon, providing us with enough light to identify each other. I find Tyler hanging with the young witches and catch his wandering gaze. He smiles and waves. I can't tell if he's nervous or not, and I won't ask. Everyone appears to be here. We join Elijah and Shane, who are chatting about Audrey.

"I always had a feeling in my gut Audrey was good deep down," Shane says. "Imagine the life she's led, a pawn of her parents."

Elijah's cavernous voice reverberates in the gardens. "I never imagined she was just an extension of her mother, reaching us through her. Still, I have a hard time trusting her actions."

"We all do," Ronnie says. "But Gwyn was the one who spoke with her. We have to trust her gut feelings."

I chuckle and grab my stomach. "I'm not sure it was my gut. It might have been the new chocolate bars at the Mystic Sage."

"Oh, darling. I'm sorry. I know they're sweet. But not as sweet as you," Shane says, hugging me.

I grin at my boss and notice Archie, Trinity, Leslie, and Agnes joining the circle. Tyler and the other young witches spread out and join hands. Archie moves between Tyler and Tanner, relieving this mom's stress about his first spell casting. I have to say our dress is comical compared to the night we banished the Sluagh. The temps were so bad, we wore several layers. Tonight, most of the young witches are wearing t-shirts, shorts, and flip-flops—hardly practical for a casting. The rest of us have worn casual shirts with jeans and sneakers, but Agnes and Leslie are decked out in full black witch attire. If it weren't so hot, they'd have thrown on hooded capes, too.

Leslie begins. "Thank you all for taking on the enormous task of protecting our town. We will remove the protection barrier from the property, and I will pass the staff to Agnes to cast the new protection spell."

"Leslie's actually going to give Agnes her staff?" Ronnie whispers. "I guess there's a first time for everything."

"She must trust her." I smile at Leslie, admiring her willingness to let go. Or maybe she's admitting Agnes is more skilled?

We all join hands, and Leslie directs us to summon our energy. The amber glow radiates throughout the circle, lighting the gardens in a halo of orangey red. I observe the whites of Tyler's eyes springing out from their sockets as he stands rigid as a two-by-four. Archie whispers in Tyler's ear, and my son nods. I have no idea what Archie said to him, but I'm grateful. I remember how overwhelmed I was the first time. Leslie continues to chant and in seconds, the glow dissipates.

"Now Agnes will lead us in the new incantation." Leslie relinquishes her staff.

"Witches, we have to be quick about this!" Agnes says in a loud, gravelly voice. "I want to warn you, the power we will summon could bring on repercussions. Be prepared for anything. Bring forth your energy!"

Spence shouts, "Hellz, yeah! Let's do this!"

"Dude, let her do her work," Tanner says.

"Sorry, Agnes," Skye says. "We're excited."

"OK, OK," Trinity says. "Let the witch do what she's gotta do."

Agnes flashes them a disapproving stare and raises the staff above her head. The clear crystal on the top of the staff lights up, sending rays of white light in all directions. She chants so fast the words are unintelligible. We squeeze our hands together and wait for her instructions.

"Raise your clasped hands in the air and chant with me! Oh, wondrous Dagda, please protect our town of Bearsden. Safeguard us from the evil attacks of the Kenilworth family. Protect our town of Bearsden. Protect our town of Bearsden..."

As we continue to chant, billowy, gray clouds swim in the sky above us, and heat lightning flashes above. The winds pick up, blowing debris from the withered gardens in all directions. Everyone stands transfixed on the unexpected formation of the storm above us as it intensifies with thunderclaps and menacing clouds.

"Bring forth every ounce of power you have left, witches!" Agnes shouts in her gravelly voice. "Only a little while longer."

My fellow witches and I squint as plant refuse stings our faces. And with the deafening crack of thunder, the winds abruptly stop. While we stand frozen with our hands interlocked, I observe Agnes. She opens one bulbous eye, and then the other, scanning the sky above us. The threatening, gray clouds dissipate, allowing moonbeams to shine on our circle once again. She shimmies her hips and shakes her fists in the air.

"Yes! It worked, and no repercussions. Well, not that we know of, anyway." She bursts out laughing, and the rest of us crack up.

"Thank you for leading us in this endeavor," Leslie says. "This should keep the town safe from any attack by the Kenilworths."

"They won't be happy about this. What if they're pissed?" Zoe asks, clenching her teeth.

Spence waves a hand in front of his torso. "Let them be pissed. They can't do anything about it."

"I don't know, Spence," Skye says. "Outside the town protection barrier, they could still come after any of us."

Tyler's eyes skip around the circle. "That sounds scary."

"Don't you worry, Tyler," Trinity says calmly. "After the success of this protection spell, they wouldn't dare come after any of us."

"Excellent work, my fellow witches," Leslie declares. "We can all sleep well tonight. Go in peace."

The coven disbands, and we all sneak out of the gardens. Archie locks the fence employing a moderate wave of his hand, and we go our separate ways. Tyler and Zoe approach us.

"My first spell casting was... eye-opening. I wish I had been better prepared," Tyler says.

"You did well." Archie grins and pats him on the back. "Truly incredible. Keep up your training, and you'll build confidence."

"I'm so proud of you, Tyler. And the coven is so thankful you jumped into this so quickly." I hug my son and Zoe. "Goodnight, you two."

Archie and I walk with Leslie to her house, and I decide to spend the night with him. We enter through the back of the house and kick off our shoes in the tiny mudroom. I amble into the living room, cracking my knuckles and shaking my hands.

"I can't go to sleep yet," I say. "I'm too wound up."

He hugs me and places his warm lips on mine. "I was hoping you weren't tired. It's been so long since…"

"What? No. I'm even too wound up for sex." My eyes roll around, knowing what I need to do. "I'm gonna go to the basement and try to cast a divination spell on Mom's letter."

Archie drops his arms. "Gwyn, you've made astounding progress, but it's too soon to perform a divination on the letter yet. Your power could be too intense and wipe out the words along with the charm. Please, don't try."

"I have to. I need to know what's in the letter. There could be important information in it for Tyler and me. Knowing we're fair game for the Kenilworths outside the town frightens me. I'm willing to take the risk."

He bends down and kisses me on the head and gestures toward the basement door. "I guess we're going to perform a divination." He glimpses the time on his cell phone. "At 2:00 a.m. in the morning."

I kiss him, and we trot down the stairs. Archie sets up the divination cloth with the crystals and places my mom's picture behind it for influence. I pull the letter out of my purse and lay it out over the cloth. I rub my hands together, shaking like a leaf, and suck in all the musty air. As my lungs deflate, I raise my right hand over the shimmering letters and call on my mother's spirit.

"Mom, I ask for your guidance. Please, help me find the power to break through your charm. When I was younger, I didn't always appreciate you enough. I didn't understand the lengths you took to shield me from this unpredictable and dangerous supernatural world."

Archie looks on with a supportive smile as I continue. A faint glow projects from my mother's picture, and a small arm extends out over the letter while she smiles. He encourages me with a nod, so I summon the amber glow on my hand. I'm careful to control the strength of my intention since I don't want to fry the thing.

As I lift my hand, letters pull up from the paper, and I stretch them out slowly, increasing their visibility. On the last pull, the letters leap off the paper and dance in the air—shimmering in gold and swirling on their path to resolution. I gape in wonder and chuckle at the amazing sight. And all at once, the letters tumble onto the page, and the gold transforms into blue ink. When I view the words, tears roll down my cheeks.

"Gwyn, what's wrong?" Archie asks as he examines the letter. "Oh, my. I'm so sorry, my love. This never occurred to me." He wraps an arm around my shoulder.

I lift my eyelids and stare through wet eyes at my mom's handwriting. Why in the hell would Mom write the letter in Welsh? She knew I didn't speak Welsh. I wipe the snot dripping from my nose with the back of my hand, and he grabs a tissue from the shelf for me.

"What am I going to do?" I ask.

"I may know enough to break down some of it, but my knowledge of Welsh is limited," he says, rubbing my back.

"Nick could do it. He translated the entire grimoire." I peer up at Archie as I wipe my nose.

"Don't even think about it," he says. "Translating the grimoire was one thing. Spells, incantations, and the like. But you have no inkling of what's in the letter. It could contain family ancestral secrets meant only for your eyes. Promise me you'll not give him this letter."

I stare at my mother's picture and stroke her face with my fingertips.

"It's nearly 3:00 a.m. We should get some sleep. It's been a long, exhausting day." He grasps my hand and strokes it tenderly. "I'll contact some witch academics I know in London. You should be leaping like a frog over this. You broke the charm and made contact with your mum. This is only a wee setback. You know, you could ask Leslie."

"What? I can't trust her. If my mom's secret is in it, Leslie would make something up to keep it hidden. I'm so disappointed. Let's go to bed."

"Don't fret, Gwyn. We'll find someone trustworthy to translate it for you."

While Archie is brushing his teeth, I collapse into the bed and groan as my head sinks into the pillow. I turn off the volume on my cell phone and notice a text from Nick.

Nick: *I'm sorry how I left things on Friday. It really bothered me you couldn't trust me enough to confide in me. I don't want to leave things this way. Could we meet for coffee sometime this week and hash this out?*

I pause for a moment while my lover slides into bed. And I type into my cell phone.

Me: *Sure. Let me check my schedule.*

CHAPTER TWENTY-FIVE

FALL ASSOCIATIONS

FOR THREE WEEKS, THE Bearsden Coven stressed about a possible backlash from the Kenilworths, but our little town marched on without a care. And we plodded, too. Temperate weather finally arrived, sending the heat wave packing. Potted chrysanthemums of orange, purple, yellow, and white decorate the front steps of homes, and tree leaves are turning the shades of mustard and squash. Fall waits right around the corner. The renovations on Mitchell Hall continue with only one minor disruption from the Seelie Fae children, and the clearings of the city building and Thomas Hall rubble have left barren lots.

I started fall classes at half-time status to fit in work and enjoy life. I never thought I could be this content. Archie shows unending devotion to me, and I trust him again. His class load has eaten into our personal time, but I don't mind. The days and nights we spend together are worth the wait. I've settled into my room at Leslie's and have come to terms with the fact she may never divulge her secret about my mom. But I'm hopeful I can change her mind once we've developed a better relationship.

Tyler has settled into the coven, and it's a joy to see him at the circles every Thursday night as we plan for the Delaware Conference for Pagans, a cover for our network of covens throughout the state. The fall equinox is a fantastic time to have the conference. As I primp in the bathroom, I go over my packing list in my head. Delaware's weather in September encompasses all the seasons except winter, and often they happen over the span of four days. How do I pack for that?

When I spin around, Mr. Yeats scares the shit out of me, standing in the doorway with a crooked nose and his arms crossed. "Where are you going, Ms. Crowther?"

"None of your damn business." I push him out of my way as Leslie walks out of her office carrying her leather satchel.

"We are both attending the Delaware Conference for Pagans in Lewes, Delaware. You will be on your own for the weekend. Enjoy your time alone," she says. "Scuttle along."

The familiar scowls and transforms into his cat presentation as he enters her office. He's such a busybody.

"Don't mind him, Gwyn," Leslie says. "He gets anxious when I leave. I think he worries I'll leave him someday, and he'll be back on the streets alone."

"But he can be so annoying." I smooth out my loose V-neck blouse and my capri pants. "Are you sure you won't ride with Archie and me to Sussex County? We have room."

"No. You two don't need me tagging along. I've made other arrangements. Enjoy your ride south. It's a beautiful, sunny day."

"For now. Did you see the forecast for the weekend? It's 82 degrees today, 75 on Saturday, and 65 and rainy on Sunday. A storm is brewing. At least the temperature will be perfect on Saturday for the Mabon celebration."

Leslie smiles. "Indeed."

There's a knock on the kitchen side door. "I better grab my stuff. See you down there." I throw my large travel tote bag over my shoulder and grin when I see Archie on the other side of the storm door.

"Are you excited?" he asks, rubbing his hands together. "These conferences are a bundle of fun, especially the large Mabon celebration."

"I am," I say with an exuberant smile. "I haven't been to the beach in a few years. It'll be nice to stroll on the sand. But we better take a walk today. A storm is moving in—cool temps by Sunday."

"Sounds wonderful." He puts my travel tote in the trunk, and we settle in for the drive.

Once we pass the congestion on the freeway, the drive provides picturesque scenery of farmhouses surrounded by soybean and corn fields. To avoid the traffic of the Rehoboth and Lewes resort areas near the beach, the DCP has used the same grand Victorian farmhouse for decades. The owner, Clyde Wiggins, leads the Sussex County Coven and offers his property as a secluded sanctuary to keep out Unremarkables—the only way to remain hidden. The house has three stories and a wide wrap-around porch with an enormous back lawn protected by forests on all sides. As we pull up, members are mingling.

Archie parks his Tesla in the cleared field next to the house, and we stroll over to find the other Bearsden Coven members. We pass by a few witches, and they eye my lover up and down, making lascivious comments to him as we pass by. "Hiii, Archie. How have you been?" "Hey, lover. It's been a looong time." "We should get together later, handsome."

When we enter the foyer, I throw him a side-eye. "Can you at least warn me? How many witches at this conference have you slept with? Don't be shy."

"I'm sorry," he says with a thicker Scottish brogue. "I thought if they saw me with you, they'd back off, and I can't give you an exact number, Gwyn."

"You can't do anything about it now. But it's good to be prepared," I say.

Archie leans down and kisses me on the cheek. "I truly don't deserve you. But I'm elated to call you mine."

"Hey, witches!" Spencer shouts from the other side of the grand foyer. "Get on over here!"

Tanner's with him as well as Skye, Tyler, and Zoe. They carpooled together. I'm so happy Tyler adjusted well to his new life and friends. And he's excelling at his magic training, maintaining a level two status.

"The drive wasn't too bad for us. How about you?" I ask.

"Not bad at all," Tanner says. "Once we got off the freeway."

Tyler observes his surroundings. "This house is enormous, but I wish it were closer to our hotel."

"We came straight here," Archie says. "But the hotel is close to the beach. That'll be nice at sunset."

"Trinity, Shane, Elijah, and Ronnie are out back. We'll all gather there in a few minutes," Skye says. "They'll introduce and welcome new witches into the conference."

"How many witches are here?" I ask.

"I'm guessing," Archie says. "But I'd say nearly one hundred thirty for all three counties."

Spence's mouth drops. "That's gonna be a big fucking circle on Mabon."

"Please, tell me we won't have to share, like last year." I roll my eyes.

Zoe counts her fingers. "That would take hours."

Archie chuckles. "No. We'll not share, and there won't be a circle. Too many of us."

Leslie and Agnes walk into the foyer together, and Spence snickers. "Well, well, I thought they were sworn enemies, only working together for the good of Bearsden."

I smile at the former lovers. Maybe there is hope for them.

"Let's head outside to the gathering, shall we?" Archie motions toward the double-French doors leading to the backyard.

Thick woods of loblolly pine, sugar maple, and American holly surround the massive grassy lawn behind the house. The woods create an important barrier to the world of the Unremarkables, so we can practice witchcraft without the worry of being discovered.

Clyde Wiggins, a man in his 80s with white hair and a long nose, opens the conference by giving a long, drawn-out speech. But who's going to stop him? It's his house, after all. When he finally gets to the introductions, he announces the new members from the covens of East and West Sussex Counties, Smyrna, Dover, and Frederica in Kent. When he introduces the new members in New Castle County, the members from Kent and Sussex grumble at how long it takes, because a representative witch from each coven takes over the microphone.

I recognize the reps who helped us expel the Sluagh: Riley Shaw of Middletown, Gareth Thomas of New Castle, Brayton Harris of Wilmington, Elizabeth Wang of Greenville, and Laura Lovelace of Hockessin, an old flame of Archie's who caused a ruckus before the Winter Solstice Ceremony. I glare at her with the intensity of a thousand hexes.

My eyes wander to the trees, hoping to catch a few deer skipping quietly through, but no luck. Out of the corner of my eyes, I catch movement in the thicket. I swear I glimpsed people running, but on closer inspection, I realize it's a deer prancing through. Darn.

"What are you looking at, Gwyn?" Ronnie asks. "Nothing but trees out there and poison ivy. Elijah and I walked through there earlier." She scratches at her forearms. "He must be immune."

"Sorry," I say. "You should stop at a drugstore and get some poison ivy scrub."

"Witches from each of the covens take turns to monitor the woods," Trinity says. "Shane and I have the next round."

Shane strokes his white beard. "I sure hope I don't brush up against that evil plant at this conference. The last time it took weeks to get rid of the rash."

"Where's Derek, Ronnie? Didn't he come with you?" I whisper.

"Oh, yeah," she whispers back. "He's back at the hotel. He'll join us for the Mabon Celebration, since Unremarkables can attend."

"We should find seats for dinner," I say.

When Leslie's turn arrives, she takes the microphone and introduces us. "I am overjoyed to announce three new witches have joined our Bearsden circle. The first two are mother and son—Gwynedd Crowther and Tyler Wolfe."

We smile as the Bearsden Coven hoots and hollers, humbled by the introduction. Tyler and I wave at everyone.

"The third witch is someone special to us. She helped grow the coven in the early days before she sought solitude," Leslie says. That's one way to put it. "I proudly present the return of Agnes Pritchard, a local hedge witch who brings much talent and skill."

The entire conference whistles and cheers, and Clyde grabs the microphone. "We will break for lunch, and I encourage all of you to check into your hotel rooms and enjoy the sands of Rehoboth Beach. We are blessed by the gods to have one of the most bewitching beaches on the East Coast. Peace be with you all."

We all check into the hotel on Coastal Highway and relax until dinner. The young witches, including Tyler, join a few of the other

Gen Z and Zillennial witches they met at the conference and scout out the local pizza place known for its thin crust. Derek, Ronnie, Archie, and I find a quaint vegan café off the avenue leading up to the boardwalk.

"Be honest with me, Derek. How are you handling all of this?" I ask.

He laughs and shakes his head. "It was a lot to take in. And I was pretty pissed she'd kept it from me." He glares at her sweet, freckled face.

"His anger didn't last long," she winks. "I made up for the dishonesty."

Derek bends to kiss her. "You sure did, babe."

"Get a room, you two," Archie says.

"Puh-leeze," Ronnie says. "As if you and Gwyn haven't displayed...cough...affection in public. And I think you know what I'm talking about."

I grimace as I peruse the menu. "I don't know what you're referencing."

Archie bursts out laughing. "She's in denial. Derek, at first, I panicked. We must remain under the radar of the town, or we can't be effective. But now, I'm elated you're *in the knowing*. And can carry on these conversations without white lies."

"I am, too," he says. "Now I understand what transpired when Ronnie got hurt. I only wished I'd been there to help her."

"You would have gotten hurt. It's better you weren't," I say.

"How about this Kenilworth family?" Derek asks. "Is the town safe from them now?"

Archie nods. "We've had no incidences, other than the Seelie Fae children breaking into the Mitchell's mansion again. I think we're safe from them. They've moved on."

"I certainly hope so," Ronnie says. "It would be freaking great if we could have one year without drama in our town."

"Wouldn't that be awesome?" I glance at Archie, and he winks at me. How could life be any better than this?

After dinner, Ronnie and Derek go back to the hotel, but I'm eager to take a walk on the fine sand of Rehoboth Beach. Archie and I stroll along the water's edge. The salty air of the Atlantic Ocean blows our hair and fills our nostrils with the magic of the sea. There's nothing like the mushy feeling of your feet sinking into the warm wet granules, but the ideal weather won't remain for long. By Sunday, the incoming storm will usher in fall with the slap of chilly winds and downpours. But I'll enjoy this moment while it lasts.

We approach the area where Rehoboth Beach meets Dewey where the beach is empty, passing only one couple who are necking on a towel. He pulls my hand to his mouth, and he places a warm, soft kiss on my pale skin.

"I love you, Gwynedd," he says. "Please, don't worry about the witches I've been with. I can't remove them from my past. But I swear to you, they'll never be part of my future."

I bend my head to kiss him as the sea air dances through our hair, and I open my mouth to invite his tongue. He gazes at me with those magnetic-blue eyes and drags me across the sand by the hand to the space between two rental sheds housing beach chairs and umbrellas. I press my mouth against his, and he slowly guides me back toward the side of the shed. After he slides a hand under my bra, he fondles a nipple, and I moan in delight.

"Let's go back to the hotel. I want you so bad." I run my slender fingers through his hair as my eyes lust for him in the shadows of the moonlight.

Archie slides a finger across my lips. "Then you don't need to wait, my love." He unsnaps my capri pants and pulls the zipper down while he explores my mouth with his tongue.

"What are you doing? We can't do it here. Someone could walk by."

"This area of the beach is vacant." He yanks my pants and panties off and kneels in front of me. "Doesn't the humid night air feel invigorating?"

He spreads my legs and finds me while I lean back on the cool wood of the shed. I wrap a leg around his back and press back against his wet mouth. The warm breeze blows across my bare skin as he arouses me. And the waves crash in the distance.

"Oh, Archie. Please, can we go back to the room?" I ask.

He continues to pleasure me until I can't restrain my voice any longer, and I yell out his name as I reach the peak of my arousal. Archie peers up at me with glistening lips.

"That should hold you over, then." He stands and kisses me. "Let me help you put your pants on."

I slide my fingers inside the top of his pants. "Maybe I changed my mind?" I unbutton his jeans and slide the zipper down, allowing the bulge in his pants to breathe.

"Ahhh, much better," he chuckles.

I point to the ground. "Lie down on the sand."

When he's on his back, I climb on top of him, moaning as he enters me. He slides his hands under my shirt again and pinches my nipples. I find a rhythm, matching the rolling and roaring of the foamy waves, and savor every thrust until Archie grunts with his release. As I lay my head against his firm chest, his palpitating heart beats against my face. He finds my hand and intertwines his fingers with mine.

"I wish I knew what gods sent you to me, because I want to thank them profusely," he says, stroking the back of my head.

"Who says it was the gods?" I ask.

"I fathom it must be otherworldly. How could I have found you otherwise?"

"You don't actually believe that, do you? Of course, you always said there are no coincidences."

"Naw. I don't believe in fate, but I'm chuffed to bits you came into my life." He kisses me tenderly as we relax in our afterglow on the fine sand.

"I am, too," I say.

I lay my head on his chest again. He's right, though. It's as if an unknown entity brought us together.

Chapter Twenty-Six

WITCH SCHOOL

AFTER A LONG NIGHT of lovemaking, Archie sleeps dead to the world beside me. I'm too excited to sleep anymore, so I disconnect my phone from the charger and bring up the conference agenda for today. So many fabulous workshops. There are classes for every type of witch: green, ancestral, hoodoo-based, crystal, eclectic, kitchen, house, and sea. In fact, Rehoboth Beach has a Sea Witch Festival around Samhain.

My lover stirs next to me, rolling over on his back, and his eyelids lift. "What time is it?"

"It's almost eight. We've gotta get in the shower and eat breakfast." I lean over him and plant a kiss on his gorgeous face. How can he be so handsome after a night of frolicking?

"I don't want to get up," he says, rubbing his eyes. "I'm getting too old for these late nights."

"Oh, come on. I'm older than you, and I was awake thirty minutes ago."

He rolls over on me, a mischievous smile peeking through his goatee. "If you're so awake, can I interest you in a little playtime?" His erection presses into my thigh.

"As enticing as your offer is, I don't want to miss the first class on ancestral divination." I rub my nose on his, and he falls to his side.

"Wow. I've lost out to a divination class."

I chuckle as I jump out of bed. "I can have you anytime, but a good divination class only happens every two years. Join me in the shower instead."

"Now that I can compromise on." He follows me into the bathroom and hugs me. "Are you hoping this class will help you strengthen the connection with your mum?"

"That's the hope," I say.

"I've contacted a few witches in Wales we can trust to translate your mum's letter. Be patient."

"I'm working on my relationship with Leslie, too, you know. She's bound to tell me her little secret, eventually."

"Don't put too much faith in that." Archie slides a finger across my lips. "You know what today is?"

"Workshops and the Mabon celebration," I say. "Am I missing something?"

"We made love for the first time on Mabon. Remember?" He rubs his nose on mine.

I smile coyly. "Of course, I remember. It was one of the best nights of my life. And then the next morning, I found out you had screwed Courtney Davies in the study room."

He grimaces. "I'm sorry I mentioned it."

"It's OK," I chuckle. "But it's hard to remember one without the other."

"Very true. Let's make fresh memories of Mabon tonight. Ones you'll never forget." His eyes turn lascivious.

"Hmm, I like that idea." I pat the tattoo on his butt cheek as we hop into the shower.

This day couldn't be more perfect—sunshine and mid-70s with a slight breeze. We drive to Clyde Wiggins's Victorian house and mingle with witches from other covens for a few minutes before heading into the designated rooms and areas outside on the back lawn.

Archie attends a couple of coven leadership workshops while I sit in on an ancestral divination class and a class on hexes. Time flies while I learn the intricacies of calling on one's ancestors for their knowledge and power. We can't try it out, of course. Because we all need our own special altar. That's a bummer.

The hex class turns out to be a blast, but it's standing room only and taught by a kitchen witch, the type who incorporates magic into their cooking and baking, choosing herbs for their magical properties. She performs an incantation on a volunteer who barks like a dog every time one of us says the word bone. Another volunteer hops like a bunny whenever we shout carrot. It's all so silly and juvenile, but she clarifies these spells can be dark and evil but occasionally necessary for our survival.

On the way to meet Archie and the rest of the Bearsden Coven for our lunch roundtable, I pass Laura Lovelace in a tight hallway. She smirks at me as she struts by. Get over yourself, Laura. He's mine now. At lunch, we share our experiences in the morning sessions. I smile at Tyler's excitement as he shares his success at performing a protection spell with the young Bearsden witches at the adjacent table. Leslie and Agnes are eating with Clyde Wiggins and other witches in their 70s and 80s at the long table. Probably laughing about the old days. I'm happy to see the former lovers being cordial with each other. It's a start.

Ronnie nudges me. "I see you eyeing your son, proud momma."

"I'm glad he's having a good time," I say. "All of this happened so quickly for him."

Trinity says, "He jumped right in when we needed him and didn't blink an eye. Your son is a strong young man."

Archie smiles, and I blush at all the compliments. When you consider the man his father turned out to be, I'm lucky Tyler grew into such an awesome person.

"I'm not surprised," Elijah says. "If I remember correctly, you jumped right in, too. I still remember the look on your face the night of Samhain when, you know..."

Everyone laughs, recalling my screaming tirade at Richard's spirit. "Well, it was a shock."

"Gwyn, I'm so glad you snuck into the ceremony," Shane says, giving me a hug. "You've made all the difference for this coven—and our town."

"She's made a difference to all of us, Shane." Archie winks at me.

We clean up after ourselves and plan for our afternoon agendas. The young witches have plans to take part in a circle in the field next to the house with a group of baby witches—another name for neophytes. The older witches scatter around to workshops on crystals, herbal uses, and divination.

"I'm off to a divination class, Gwyn," Ronnie says. "Don't forget to meet me in the woods for our assigned monitoring time."

Archie chuckles. "Sounds so clandestine and mysterious."

"It's a tramp through the swampy forest. Hardly mystifying." I wave to Ronnie as she leaves for her workshop. "What class are you attending this afternoon?"

"I'm really feeling last night's activities. I think I'll go back and take a nap. Refresh for Mabon."

"I approve. Meet you back at the room around four?"

"Perfect. Enjoy your workshops. I'm elated you're having such a good time." He kisses me goodbye.

"How were your afternoon workshops?" I ask Ronnie as we slosh through the thick underbrush of the forest.

"Fantastic. I attended a class taught by a cosmic witch." She gestures toward the sky. "All about astrology, the stars, and the moon cycles. A lot of science-based stuff, too. I think I've found my niche. How were yours?"

"Mine were OK. Not as much fun as the morning sessions, but I learned new things. Of course, being a practicing witch for less than a year, it's all new."

When I turn my head, I catch movement out of the corners of my eyes. I'm almost positive I saw people in the distance, but a survey of the area finds no one.

"I keep seeing things," I say. "It's probably animals, but I swear I had a glimpse of people over there."

"Eh, don't worry about it. They've had this conference here for decades. They've never had Unremarkables spy on them."

I glimpse the time on my cell phone. "Our shift is over. I told Archie I'd meet him in the room in fifteen minutes. Is Derek meeting us for the Mabon Celebration dinner?"

"Yeah, he dropped me off this morning. He went for a run on the beach. I think he had the better day. See you at dinner."

I catch a ride with the young witches back to the hotel, hoping to have a few minutes to clean up before the ride back for the celebration. I give Tyler a hug and drag my tired legs to the room, wishing I'd come back with Archie for a nap. With a click of the key card, I press the lever handle and push on the door.

I hyperventilate at the sight. Laura Lovelace's bare-naked body is pressing against my lover's torso with a hand on the nape of his neck, kissing him as deeply as I ever have. He catches me gaping at him in his peripheral vision and pushes Laura away.

"Gwyn, this is not what it seems!" he shouts as Laura snickers in jubilation.

I turn around and exit the room, flying down the hallway in tears. Archie screams my name from behind, his voice getting louder with each of my steps until he grabs my arm.

"Gwynedd, stop!" he yells, panting. "Nothing happened."

"Ha! I know what I saw, Archie! You think I'm an idiot."

"Gwyn, I don't think you're an idiot." He extends his hand to touch me again, but I yank my arm back.

"I trusted you. You said you loved me." Drops of disillusionment roll down my cheeks.

"You have every reason not to believe me. I was not forthcoming about my past, and I tried to make amends for my unsavory behavior. I worked so hard to regain your trust and love, Gwynedd. Why would I betray you? In a hotel room we're sharing? Why would I do that?"

"I don't know what to believe." My heart pounds like a jackhammer in my chest.

"Laura has been after me for a long time. I could have bedded that woman anytime I wanted. Why would I bed her here?" He brushes a hand through his hair. "For the love of all the gods and demons in the Otherworld, I still had my fawking clothes on."

I pinch my lips and squint at him. "How long had she been there?"

"Five minutes. She knocked on the door and told me she had a surprise for me from the Hockessin Coven. I told her she'd have to be quick about it. She came in and ripped off her clothes. And kissed me. You walked in and saw me push her away. End of story."

"I want to believe you, but it's hard." I stare down at the geometric-patterned carpet of the hotel hallway.

Archie moves closer and cups my face. "I love you, Gwynedd. I'll submit to a verity spell if that's what will convince you. But I hope I don't have to. You're everything to me. My friend, my lover, my soul mate."

"You would submit to a verity spell for me?"

"Yes. Just don't let Trinity do it. I want to keep my faculties. Her verity spells can be a wee jarring."

I gaze into his eyes, sensing his truth, and place a hand on his cheek. "You don't need to. I believe you."

"Thank the gods." Archie sighs and lays his forehead against mine. "I've got a wicked past, Gwyn. She won't be the only witch to come after me in the future. My mistakes will haunt me forever."

The cogwheels turn in my head as I pull away from him, and I turn toward the hallway to return to our hotel room.

"Where are you going?" he asks, following behind.

I stop and turn to him. "To deal with the mistakes of your past."

"Are you going to fill me in?" he asks.

"Follow my lead," I say, opening the door to our room.

Laura is lying on the bed on her side in the buff, primping her hair. "What are you doing back here?"

"This is my room. So, it's time to get dressed and leave," I say.

Archie leans against a wall, his arms crossed and his lips sealed, but he appears to be enjoying the show.

"Why don't you admit it?" she asks in an arrogant tone. "You can't keep your man. He wants me. Why else would I come to his room?"

"Because you want something you had a taste of, and you know you'll never have again," I say. "Get out of here, Laura. And if you ever try something like this again, I'll file a letter of impropriety with the entire Delaware Conference. They will bar you from every coven in the state. Go...before I throw you out myself."

"Archie, are you going to let her talk to me that way?" Laura asks as she slips on her clothes.

My Scottish lover shrugs. "Apparently, yes. Gwyn does what she wants."

Laura grabs the rest of her belongings and dashes out of the room in a huff. When the door slams, the room is silent except for the panting from our enraged emotions. Archie walks to me and gazes into my eyes with the lust of a ferocious beast.

"Watching you fight for me with such haughty confidence was so hot," he says.

He grabs the back of my head as he suffocates me with his mouth. Our clothes fly off, piece by piece, as we tumble to the floor, and he enters me with heightened fervor. He folds his hands around mine and summons his witch energy, intensifying our arousal until my body is consumed by the heat of the amber glow. I break out in a hot flash with beads of sweat dampening my entire body—drips of my lover's passion. How will he top this after the Mabon Celebration?

CHAPTER TWENTY-SEVEN

A MABON TO REMEMBER

"Ronnie, you look stunning as usual," I say. She has on a bright-orange dress with elbow-length sleeves and a plunging neckline. Her boyfriend looks handsome in a russet dress shirt and black trousers. "Derek, you look great, too."

"Thank you," she says. "I love your forest-green dress. And your black pumps are fabulous."

"Archie, will I see magic performed at the celebration this year?" Derek asks.

"No," he replies. "There are many Unremarkables here who are unaware of the supernatural world around us."

"Ahhh, gotcha," Derek says. "Because they're not *in the knowing.*"

"Exactly," Archie says. "It's why we won't monitor the woods tonight. They won't see anything unusual."

My lover leans down to place a kiss on my cheek. His light-blue dress shirt accentuates the color of his eyes. I wish he would wear it more often. It's wonderful to have Derek join openly in our magic discussions. Ronnie became impatient, so she told Leslie and Trinity Derek was *in the knowing*. But we're still hiding the secret about Nick Evans since the Elder flipped out at the news.

I notice my son and the young witches arriving in the enormous backyard. I catch his wandering eyes and wave. Trinity and her wife, Charlie, are chatting with a few witches from Sussex County while Shane and Elijah hang with a couple of Wilmington witches. Agnes and Leslie walk through the back door to the patio, where they stop to speak with Clyde Wiggins.

The round white tables that dot the green lawn have small pumpkins and dried husks of corn in the center with a cluster of candles to light when the sun sets. The aroma of barbecued meat permeates, which turns my stomach, but at least the conference has vegetarian offerings.

When we sit down to dinner, Clyde Wiggins goes to the microphone to give the blessing for Mabon. "Welcome, everyone, to the Delaware Conference for Pagans. I hope you have enjoyed your learning sessions today. Normally, we share in our circles, but that would take many hours. Instead, please accept this blessing for balance and harmony in your life on this Mabon. Enjoy your dinner."

The young witches from our coven are eating at a table with other witches of similar ages from Dover. The rest of the Bearsden Coven sits at another table.

"Charlie, it's wonderful to see you again." I jab a fork into my kale salad. "I haven't seen you since the last Mabon. How have you been?"

"I've been doing well," she says. "Especially since you all put protection on the town. But I lament for all those poor people who died."

Trinity gives her a hug. "No worries now though, hon. We took care of their overreach. They can stay in New Jersey."

"True dat," Elijah says as he shoves in a slice of chicken. "They had some nerve trying to trash our town."

Shane cuts into his beer-battered fish. "I place blame on the city council members and Mayor Manley, the ones responsible for selling out to the Kenilworths."

"Some witch should hex that criminal," Agnes says. "He's a blight on our town."

Leslie gives Agnes the side-eye. "You agreed to no hexing when you returned to the coven."

"I'm kidding," Agnes says.

"We should do something about it next year," I say before sipping my white wine.

Archie sets his wineglass on the table. "Are you referring to the special election to replace Lindsey Hope?"

"Yeah," I say. "We need to find someone trustworthy to put in that seat."

"How about you, Gwyn? Would be great to have a mole on the board." Ronnie cuts through her falafel.

"That's a fantastic idea," Elijah says, gesturing with his knife. "She could take a slice out of their control."

"It's not a bad idea." Derek places a piece of tofu on his tongue. "Give them a taste of their own medicine."

"You'd be great, and we'd have control of the vote," Ronnie says.

"We'd have a much easier time protecting the town," Shane says. "Think about it, Gwyn."

"That's never gonna happen." I'm disgusted they're even suggesting the idea, and I grimace.

Archie chuckles at my expression. "I don't think you know what you're asking. Even if Gwyn was willing, she's not much of a compromiser. Have you forgotten how principled she is?"

I give my lover a hex-filled glare and shove a piece of tofu in my mouth.

"And Gwyn made her principles well-known when she returned to the coven," Trinity says. "We'll discuss this at length in a future meeting."

"Indeed." Leslie peers at me with an expressionless face.

Agnes gazes at the sky with piqued interest and points at the billowy clouds forming. "The storm is brewing as we eat. I sure hope we don't get drenched."

While I gaze at the threatening clouds, they swirl in front of the partial moon. An icy breeze blows through, foreshadowing a sense of doom. I slip on my sweater as the trees sway eerily, and a shudder rips through my body.

"Are you cold?" Archie asks. "Take my hoodie if you need it."

"You don't feel that? Something's not right, and I see it in the trees." I stand up and begin walking toward the forest.

He jumps up from his chair. "Wait, Gwyn. I'll come with you."

He follows me as I tiptoe toward the edge of the forest, attempting to keep my heels from sinking into the sandy ground. I scrutinize the openings between the trees where the moonbeams peek through branches, spotlighting the clearings. I must be paranoid. Or it's the creepiness of the shadows from the moonlight.

"There's nothing here. Only the eerie shadows of the trees. But since I have you here hidden from roaming eyes, let's take advantage of the opportunity." Archie wraps his arms around my shoulders and kisses me, melting away the sense of dread.

"I love how your kisses remove all my anxiety and make me feel safe."

I wrap my arms around his torso and lay my head against his firm chest, closing my eyes to relish the moment—so calm with the slow beating of his heart. The chilly wind blows around us, rustling the leaves on the tree branches, but I'm warm in his embrace.

When I open my eyes, Jeff Williams is staring at me through the thicket. "Jeff?"

"What?" Archie asks, turning his head. "What are you doing here?"

"This was the soonest I could get here." Jeff's face twists into a guilt-filled grimace. "I wanted to warn you. I'm so sorry, but I don't think I arrived soon enough."

"Warn us about what, Jeff?" I ask.

In the far distance, we view a faint amber ball, radiating with a tail like a comet. With every nanosecond, the sphere of fire expands until it's the size of a small boulder. I'm frozen in my spot, mesmerized by the beauty of the flames. People rush toward the house, scattering in all directions. When the magic fireball strikes the back lawn, it illuminates the entire area. And the screaming begins.

"Tyler!" My heart beats against my ribcage as we run back through the thicket of the forest.

"The Kenilworths must have planned this attack, knowing we would be unprotected out here," Archie says.

"I'm so sorry, Gwyn. Let me help." Jeff follows close behind, crying.

"I think you've done enough, Jeffrey!" I yell.

As we approach the scorched earth, I survey the area. The grassy center of the lawn burns black with yellow and orange flames flickering. Everyone huddles together in small groups, crying and assessing their injuries. Some witches tend to a few others with severe burn wounds on their extremities. Others have blistered faces and singed hair. A few tables and chairs are charred to a crisp. And I panic.

"Tyler!" Tears drench my face as I dash from group to group, trying to find my son or any members of the Bearsden Coven.

"We're wasting time darting around," Archie says, pressing my shoulders. "We have to plan for their next attack. Jeff, are they trying to destroy all of us? Or only the Bearsden witches?"

Jeff swallows and clears his throat. "I overheard Aunt Edith and Uncle Edmond talking. They're really pissed you put a bubble over Bearsden. They're coming after all of you, and they don't care if others get hurt."

"I have to find Tyler. Make sure he's not hurt," I say, trembling.

A male voice calls out, "Mom! Are you OK?"

I spin around and tears of joy overwhelm me. My son is alive. And so are my young witch friends. Their faces and arms have cuts and bruises from broken plates and glass, but they appear well otherwise. They were sitting farther away from the impact.

Tyler hugs me tighter than ever before. "I couldn't find you. I thought you were dead."

"This is some bullshit!" Spence shouts. "We gotta do something. They're gonna come back."

"The Kenilworths are enraged—out of control," Tanner says. "What happens now?"

Archie fills them in on what Jeff told us and focuses on our defense. "Closed-practice ancestral witch families have enormous power, but harnessing a fireball that large would have drained their magic for a while. They'll need to regenerate."

"We should find the others," Skye says, tying her fire-red hair into a ponytail. "We'll need the entire coven to fight them."

Zoe kneads her hands and weeps. "What if they're dead?"

"Then we'll ask for help from the other covens," Archie says. "Let's split up and search for the others. We'll meet back at this spot. You only have a few minutes. Go."

"Jeff, if you want to help, go to the injured." I peer at his sullen face and lay a hand on his arm. "I'm sorry I yelled at you. You did what you could, being an Unremarkable."

"I wish I could have done more, but I was so scared." Jeff rushes to the injured while we discuss what to do.

Archie scratches his goatee. "We've got to find the older witches. We can't fight ancestral witches with only the young ones. The Kenilworths will kill all of us. And then they might finish off the rest of the Delaware covens."

We rush from one group to the next. Most of the witches have severe injuries and share our horror as we explain who attacked us and why. But everyone appears to be alive. My heart palpitates with an irregular beat, and I struggle to breathe in the dense smoke. My friend with crimson hair runs toward us alongside her handsome boyfriend in tow. Her face is bleeding, most likely from blowing debris, and his shirt has tears and bloodstains. I clutch my chest.

Ronnie wraps her arms around my shoulders. "I don't know how I would have survived without you. I'm so glad you're not hurt."

"What's the plan, Archie?" Derek asks. "I don't care if I'm not a witch. I wanna fight with you. They don't scare me one bit."

"I appreciate your desire to help," Archie says. "But I'm afraid this is one fight you're not capable of winning. There are so many injured witches. Could you assist the others in moving them inside the house?"

"Sure thing." Derek turns toward Ronnie and kisses her on the mouth. "Don't get killed, babe."

"I'll do my best, lover." Ronnie hugs him goodbye.

When I turn around, I observe the rest of the witches in the Bearsden Coven walking toward us, with Trinity leading them in the front. She's so angry, fury burns in her eyes, and a bloody gash seeps onto her cheek. Half of Shane's beard is singed, and he's limping. Elijah's face has second-degree burns, but his left arm is worse—exposed pink and bloody skin with open wounds. Leslie appears to have minor abrasions on her face and arms, but Agnes is bleeding from her forehead. We form a compact circle.

"I know we're all hurt, but at least we're alive," Trinity says. "And I guess I was wrong. The Kenilworths didn't go back to New Jersey without a vendetta."

Spence snickers. "Can I mark this day on the calendar?"

Trinity smirks at him. "Don't be a smart ass." Her spike heels sink into the dirt, so she yanks them off and throws them, prompting Ronnie and me to do the same. "I assigned Charlie a task—gather all the Unremarkables in the house and keep them there. They can't witness what happens from here on. Derek and Jeff Williams will help corral them. I don't know how we're going to explain the fireball."

"Excellent idea, Trinity," Leslie says. "Edith and Edmund Kenilworth may have caught us off guard, but we'll be prepared for their return. Once we show our strength, they'll stay away."

Agnes wipes the blood trickling into her eyes. "I wouldn't count on it. Going by the size of that fireball, they want us dead. We must prepare to do the same."

The young witches gape at each other. They didn't sign up to kill witches. And neither did I. But what choice do we have?

"So, what's the plan?" Tanner wraps his arm around Spence. "We'll do what we have to."

Tyler, Skye, and Zoe join in. "We're in."

"I'm proud of you, young witches," Elijah says. "When I was your age, I didn't have half your courage." He fist bumps all of them with a special one for Zoe.

"We should focus on an intention," Archie says. "It must be specific, if you know what I mean."

"You're saying we should shoot to kill, aren't you?" Shane asks.

"Exactly what I'm suggesting," he says.

Leslie tilts her head. "We swear to do no harm. How do we follow the Regional Book of Shadows and do what you're asking?"

"Fuck the Book of Shadows," Agnes says. "It also says we must fight evil. Edith and Edmund Kenilworth represent the most nefarious witches I've ever come across. The world would be a much better place with them gone."

Leslie turns her head away from Agnes. So much for a rekindled friendship.

"Trinity, you decide, and we'll commit," I say. "Personally, I don't think we have another option."

Clyde Wiggins hobbles over to us. A glob of garnet-colored blood from a gash on his forehead has matted his hair. "I've spoken to the other coven leaders. After wounding witches from our covens, they all agree we should assist in your defense."

"We appreciate your support, Clyde," Trinity says. "Archie, you're the most experienced ancestral witch. How should we proceed?"

"The Bearsden Coven must form a tight circle," Archie says. "The covens of Delaware should remain behind us and form a barrier, in case the Kenilworths try to move past us. Since the amber bomb came at us from high in the air, I can only assume these witches can levitate. We'll need to focus our intention on a barrier first to wear their power down. On the next pass, we will combine our energies into one stream to attack them before they hit us. We may only have one opportunity for this without the barrier."

As we set up our circle with the Delaware Conference behind us, we prepare for the Kenilworth's next attack. The storm front has moved in with dense, ominous clouds veiling the skies for our enemies. I stand with my friends and family, ready to fight for our lives, and send these wicked witches to their demise. A fleeting thought flows through my head. What about Audrey and her cousin Jeff? This could help them, too.

The clouds move, taking different shapes, and we scan the skies all around us. Edith and Edmund Kenilworth could attack from anywhere, so we snap our heads side to side and all around, scrutinizing the billowy clouds.

"There! Do you see that?" Zoe points toward a split in the gray haze.

The Kenilworths, dressed in black, zoom toward us with fiery balls of amber in their hands and send the spheres at us with the wrath of an enemy scorned. The Bearsden Coven summons their witch energy, joining their magic to create a protective barrier. When the amber bomb bounces off and lands on the ground nearby, the Kenilworths veer off into the woods. The witches of the Delaware Conference cheer behind us as we examine our bodies.

"Is everyone OK?!" Trinity shouts.

"Hell, yeah!" Spence replies. "These witches are going down!"

Everyone chuckles at Spence, but we recognize it as nervous comic relief in a stressful situation. The other Bearsden witches seem prepared for another attack. Yet I worry about Leslie and Agnes. They are powerful witches, but age isn't on their side. I can't stop panting. The adrenaline flows through my body, sending my heart thumping, and perspiration beads on my upper lip.

"What now?" I ask.

"On the next pass, they should be weaker," Archie says. "This time, focus your intention on the dangerous task at hand."

"We can do this, everyone!" Trinity yells. "Set your intentions now!"

We peer up at the dismal skies, and the Kenilworths break through the billows of gray. Their coal-black eyes shine with vengeful fury as they approach us, but this time, they combine their energies and form a massive fireball, slinging it toward us before we can form a barrier. We scramble to create another magic bubble above us, but we're too late. The amber ball strikes our circle, knocking half of us on our backs as Edith flies off with her wavy, brown hair slithering in the air. Edmund follows her through the clouds.

When I sit up, my head throbs, and my ears hum. I inspect my fellow witches in the circle. Skye and Tyler are rolling on the ground with the help of Tanner and Spence, extinguishing the fire on their clothes. Zoe is jumping all around, screaming my son's name. My heart goes into full tachycardia mode, and I attempt to get up.

"Gwyn, are you all right?" Archie grabs my arms and helps me stand. "I'll have some wicked bruises in a few days."

"My back hurts like a bitch, but I think so. I'm a little stunned and bruised as well." As my heart continues to leap toward my ribcage, I stagger over to my son with Archie's help.

"I'm OK, Mom," he says. "I have some second-degree burns, but I'll recover." Zoe wraps her arms around his torso.

I hug him, too. "Thank the gods. Skye, are you OK?"

"Yeah. Same as Tyler, but I've got a bitch of a headache," she says, rubbing her temples. "Good thing Spence and Tanner acted so quickly."

"Well, when you see fire, your ass goes into overdrive," Spence says.

Tanner gestures to the older witches who are crouching over someone. "Who's hurt over there?"

The witches of the Delaware Conference gasp and shout behind us as we dash to the others, but we motion to stay back. The Bearsden witches are rubbing their heads and backs as they lean over a body. Archie and I shove between Elijah and Shane...and gasp. Agnes is lying on her back with a few burn marks on her right cheek and arm—bubbling and oozing blood.

Leslie bends over her, saying her name in a stern voice, "Agnes, get up. Damn you, this is no time to cop out on us. Get. Up."

I can't tell if Leslie is concerned or pissed. As I grasp Agnes's hand, I call to her. "Wake up, Agnes. Please, wake up."

The others all shout at her. "Come on, Agnes." "You're too strong to leave us." "We need you."

Agnes squeezes my hand, and one bulbous eye opens. And she snickers. "Gotcha."

"For fuck's sake, Agnes." I pull my hand from hers.

"I'm still hurt, numbnuts. Help me up," she says.

Elijah and Shane help Agnes stand, and the rest of us huddle together.

Leslie pinches her lips together and stands. "The Kenilworths will be back anytime. We must regroup."

"Agnes, those aren't just flesh wounds," Trinity says. "Can you fight?"

She sneers. "I'll be fine, but I'm fucking pissed. They burned my favorite tattoos."

"Stand next to me, Agnes," Archie says. "We can't afford to lose you. Let's prepare, everyone. And this time, we must act quickly."

We drag our battered bodies into a circle formation and wait for the Kenilworths to attack again. I peer across the circle at my son with wet eyes. Asking him to commit murder breaks every ethical code I raised him on. I rejoined this coven with the objective of improving our codes. Ending the lives of two murderous, closed-practice ancestral witches seems like the right thing to do, but I'll have no principles to stand on after this.

Eyeing the dreary skies, the moon peeks through the clouds as they roll by. Minutes pass with no sign of their return. I rub the palm of my hand while my chest rises and falls sporadically.

"Perhaps they have rethought their offense," Leslie says in her raspy voice.

Agnes calls out. "Not a chance in all the Otherworld! They came here with a purpose and mean to kill us!"

"And here they come!" Tanner yells. He points toward two bodies approaching us on the back lawn.

"I believe we've weakened their power," Shane says. "They're on foot now."

Spence does a little dance. "We've grounded the bitches!"

"This is it, everyone," Archie says, waving a hand. "If you cannot follow through with the intention, leave the circle now. No one will fault you."

Ronnie and Skye raise their fists in the air. "Let's do this."

Trinity nods at all of us, giving us the go-ahead. And we prepare our intention. Raising our hands with our palms up, we chant, focusing on the intensity of our power. Edmund and Edith are only a hundred feet away when they lift their hands with an amber glow and attempt to send rays of amber magic toward us. But we combine our witch energy and strike at them first, knocking them down as their rays deflect toward the sky.

My heart pounds in my chest, hoping they are down for the count. But their bodies move, and they stand with rage in their black eyes. Panic ensues, as the coven recognizes we may not have the magic to destroy them. I notice the trembling in my fellow witch's hands.

"Give up, Bearsden witches," Edith and Edmund Kenilworth cry out. "You can't win."

Elijah bellows. "We do it again. As many times as we need to, friends."

Archie stares at me, and for the first time, fear emanates from his eyes. "We go again." He whispers in my ear, "I love you, Gwynedd."

"I love you." I turn my focus back to the intention, pulling on the anger within.

As Edith and Edmund raise their hands, they summon their witch energy, and Agnes screams, "Now, witches!"

We stream our magic into one beam, directing it toward the Kenilworths, and a stray ray of amber joins us, lighting up our foes in a bubble of red-orange glow.

"It's Audrey!" Skye shrieks. "She's on the left side of the lawn near those woods."

As the Kenilworths collapse on the ground, Edith sends out one last shot of amber light, zapping her daughter. Audrey collapses onto the ground. In the distance, Jeff screams her name and runs toward the woods where she fell. Derek follows, and Shane bolts to join them.

"I should go to her," I say. "Are the Kenilworths gone?"

He eyes their lifeless bodies. "I believe so. Of course, go check on her."

Archie hugs me, and I dash over to the area near the woods. A few of the witches from New Castle County hover as Shane and Derek examine Audrey's body.

Jeff bends over his cousin, sobbing. "Please, do something. She's the only family I have who cares about me."

"Shane, what can we do to heal her?" I ask.

"I've already tried, Gwyn," he says. "Her mother hit her with every ounce of rage she had left."

"That was one helluva hit she took." Derek shakes his head.

Audrey's eyelids lift, and she notices Jeff. "You're OK. I hoped they hadn't hurt you."

"I took off before they traveled here, hoping to warn the Bearsden Coven, but I failed." He sniffs and wipes his nose on his shirtsleeve.

"Are Edmund and Edith dead?" she asks in a faint voice.

I glance over at her parents where the others are examining their bodies and look back at her inky eyes—not so demon-like now. "I think so."

Tears roll down her face. I can't imagine the mixed emotions she's experiencing. She grasps Shane's hand. "Will you help Jeff until he's settled? He has no one else."

"Absolutely, darling," he says, placing a hand on Jeff's shoulder. "He can stay with me for as long as he wants."

"Gwyn, I wish I had known you before my parents cast spells and a hex on me," she says. "You were the mother I wish I'd had."

My not-so-faux daughter closes her eyes for the last time. Jeff falls onto his cousin's body, weeping, and I rub his back as a tear rolls down my flushed cheek. I gesture to Shane to remain with him while I amble over to the other Bearsden witches gathered around the dead bodies of the Kenilworths. Clyde is talking to them.

"That's the dumbest explanation I've ever heard of." Trinity squishes her face like a prune. "No one will believe that shit, Clyde."

"What?" I ask. Someone has covered the magic-beaten cadavers with a bloodied white tablecloth.

Archie shoves his hands in his pockets. "Clyde said the Unremarkbles who aren't *in the knowing* were told to leave before the second attack, and all the coven leaders have accounted for all their witches and guests. It's a minor miracle the initial attack killed no one. But we still need an explanation for the first flying ball of fire."

"Clyde said Sussex County hosts a festival down here every October," Spence says. "People build all kinds of cannons, trebuchets, and other crazy machines to shoot huge pumpkins. The one to fly the furthest wins."

Ronnie agrees. "I think it's a fantastic cover. The competitors practice all year, and it's pretty wild."

"I vote we go with the story," Elijah says. "Silly enough for most to believe it."

"If we call the cops in, there will be an investigation," Tanner says, kneading his hands. "The covens can help with the coverup of the first fireball, but those Unremarkables who saw the attack may spread rumors about what happened."

"That's for certain," Clyde says. "And stuff gets around down here by word of mouth, if you get my drift. We'll discredit them the best we can using the pumpkin-shooting festival explanation. If the police come snooping, that's what I'm going to tell them. Other witches in my coven will back me up."

Trinity rolls her eyes. "OK. I guess we're going with the pumpkin-shooting cover."

Zoe points at the covered bodies of Edith and Edmund Kenilworth. "But what do we do about them?"

Leslie nods. "We can't have rumors floating about. Suggestions on what to do with the bodies, my friends?"

"I say we dump the Kenilworth's corpses in the woods in Dagsboro." Agnes groans while Shane heals her wounds a bit utilizing his amber glow.

Trinity grimaces. "Agnes, we can't go dumping cadavers willy-nilly. It's too risky."

"Then what do we do?" I ask. "We can't bury them here on Clyde's farm."

Tyler raises his hand like he's in class. "Only one thing we can do."

"And what's that, Tyler?" Archie asks.

"I got you, Tyler," Elijah says. "Burn all the bodies into ashes. Only way to get rid of the evidence."

Trinity rolls her head all around and wipes her face. "Oh, hell."

I glance back at Audrey's body. Shane has covered her face with his hoodie. "What should we do about Audrey?"

"Gotta burn her, too. No other option," Trinity says.

Elijah wraps his enormous arm around my shoulder. "We'll buy an urn for Audrey's ashes, so Jeff can have her near him."

"Jeff will have to file a missing person's report on all of them…to cover this up," Archie says. "We can guide him through the process."

"Clyde, the Bearsden Coven owes you much thanks for your assistance," Leslie says. "We will never forget the help you gave us tonight."

"You're most welcome, Leslie. Let's get busy," Clyde says. "Only a few of us should handle this. Everyone else should go back to the hotel and sleep. We can clean this mess up in the morning."

Trinity, Archie, Elijah, and Shane take care of the dead bodies, and the rest of us return to our hotel. We're all so upset, and the drive back is silent. When we arrive, the young witches decide to hang out in Tanner and Spence's room to decompress. Leslie and Agnes walk separately to their rooms without a word to each other. Ronnie invites me to go with Derek and her to their room to chat, but I want to be alone.

A couple of hours later, the door key clicks, and Archie enters. His chiseled face has aged since the attack. He falls onto the bed, a solemn expression blanketing his face, and wraps an arm around me. "Are you all right?"

"Not really," I say, leaning my head on his shoulder. "You took care of…"

"Aye. Trinity says she'll scatter the ashes somewhere in New Jersey." His chest rises and falls as if he's pushing up bricks.

"I don't think I'll ever forget this," I say.

He kisses my cheek. "I promised you unforgettable memories of Mabon."

"Maybe the memory of you screwing Courtney in Stewart Hall isn't so bad after all."

CHAPTER TWENTY-EIGHT

THE SECRET

THE NEXT MORNING, IT'S raining cats and dogs as we clean up Clyde's back lawn. The storm has brought cooler temperatures, which doesn't help our mood as we pick up the broken plates and glass scattered all over the wet grass. By the time we're finished, I want to crawl back into bed, but we've got a two-hour ride home. We all thank Clyde for hosting a memorable event and apologize profusely for bringing terror with us.

I hug Tyler and tell him to text me later once we've rested from the horrible experience. Archie and I wave goodbye to everyone as we all settle into our cars for the lengthy drive back to Bearsden. I gaze out the window through the raindrops spotting the glass, wishing none of it had transpired, but I'm thankful the man who loves me sits only inches away.

"What are you thinking about?" His hand grasps mine, and I turn my head to find his gorgeous face smiling at me.

"Lots of things. The actions of the coven. The Kenilworths. Poor Jeff. Audrey." I twist an earring. "I hoped Leslie and Agnes might actually find love again. But after this weekend, I have little faith."

"Don't fret about them. What will be, will be." He squeezes my hand, and I lay my head back and fall asleep to the pitter-patter of the rain on the roof of his Tesla. If only dreams could remove memories?

When we arrive at Archie's house, I wake and stretch my arms. He peers out the car window at the front door. "I wonder what Nick wants? I hope students didn't badger him while I was at the beach."

Nick stands on the porch, a steady rain pouring around him. The hood of his zippered sweatshirt protects him from the downpour while he holds his arms against his body. How long has he been waiting for us? I throw my hood over my head and run alongside Archie toward the door. When we get to the porch, he pulls out his key.

"Hey, Nick," Archie says. "I sincerely hope this doesn't mean there's a problem. I thought the classes went well."

"No. DUB classes were awesome. I didn't mind filling in on Friday at all. It was fun," Nick says on the way into the house. "I need to talk to Gwyn."

"Gwyn? What do you have to discuss with her?" Archie hangs his hooded jacket on the hall tree, and I put mine on a hook below. "Please, let me take your hoodie."

"Oh, sure." Nick removes his jacket, and Archie places it on another hook. "I finished a translation for her and wanted to get it to her right away."

My mouth falls open. "Do you have it on you?"

Nick nods and pulls my mother's letter from his backpack. "I'm sorry it took so long. The start of the semester was more time-consuming than I planned."

"What did you have translated? I thought Nick finished the grimoire?" Archie cocks his head, and his brow wrinkles. "We agreed that wasn't a good idea."

"You said I shouldn't, but I decided you were wrong." I press my lips together and peer back at the assistant professor.

"Stubborn woman." Archie exhales and gestures to the living room. "Please, come in and sit down."

I sit on the sofa with quivering hands. Archie pulls a chair up for his colleague and takes a seat next to me. Nick remains standing with an angsty face.

"Well? What did you find out?" I ask, twiddling my fingers.

"I didn't think I should send the file in an email, so I brought a couple of hard copies with me." Nick hands me a paper with the translation. "At first, it seemed like your typical letter, but the ending—well, you read."

"Archie, will you read it to me?" My hands are shaking so badly, I can't read the words.

"Of course, my love." As he reads, I recall the last time I heard my mother's voice—the day before the car accident stole my parents from me.

"*Dear Gwynedd, I know how you hated being called by your given name, but it's a mother's prerogative, right? If you're reading this letter, I can only imagine what you have been through if you've arrived at this juncture. You have discovered your witch ancestry and are practicing witchcraft, but still have many questions. I hope this letter will clear up the biggest one. Why did your father and I give up magic and withdraw from the only existence we knew?*"

"*We never planned to live the lives of Unremarkables, but so many worries about your survival led us to this decision. Your life has always been in jeopardy. From my early teens, your Nain warned me of our ancestral tale. Generations ago, our ancestors mingled with the Tuatha Dé Danann. Some call them fae. Others call them gods.*"

A witch killed one of their children by accident, and they made a demand. In a hundred generations, a female offspring must submit to a Tuatha Dé male as a reparation. My sweet Gwynedd. The offspring is you."

My lips part as I stand and shuffle to the fireplace, fixated on the painting on the mantle. "Keep reading."

"We moved to the United States to remove you from the dangers of the mounds, only to find that peril here as well when my friends Agnes Pritchard, Leslie Hughes, and I accidentally created a portal mound in the Celestial Gardens of Mitchell Hall. We figured it was too small a portal for large fae to enter and agreed to monitor the Seelie Fae children who crossed over from time to time. Everything was fine for three years until Leslie wanted to open a large portal on Samhain. I told her it was too dangerous and would put you in danger, so she promised me she wouldn't attempt it."

"Trinity was only a teen when she came to warn me Leslie was planning a secret Samhain ceremony in the gardens. I begged my best friend not to open the portal, but she refused to listen to me, and the others went along. Only Leslie knew my secret of the Tuatha Dé. So, we withdrew from magic and our witch friends to protect you."

"Gwynedd, I know you must be frightened and upset by this news. Now that you are practicing witchcraft, the Tuatha Dé can search for you. Please, be careful, sweetheart. And work at ancestral divination, so we can speak again someday. Oh, how much your father and I look forward to that moment. We love you, daughter."

I spin around, my face flush with anger. "Leslie knew. All this time, she kept this information to herself, knowing she was putting me in danger."

Archie darts to me and wraps his arms around my shoulders. "It's unforgivable, yes. I swear to you, Gwyn. I knew none of this. No one in the coven was aware."

"Agnes knew Leslie was hiding something important. That's part of the reason she left Leslie years ago. Agnes thought Leslie was protecting my mother. But she was really protecting her own interests." I push him away and march toward the front door. And slip on my sneakers.

"Gwyn, do you want me to drop you somewhere?" Nick asks, reaching for my hand.

"Stay out of this, Nick." Archie rushes to the door. "These are dynamics you aren't privy to."

"I'm sorry," Nick says, averting his gaze. "I'm just trying to help."

Archie rubs my back. "Perhaps you should sit and chew on this news for a wee bit. Go to her when you aren't so emotional."

I glare at him. "I've never been more rational in my life. Nick, thank you for letting me know as soon as you could."

Nick lays a gentle hand on my arm. "When I read the warning about the Tuatha Dé, I figured you should know right away. I'm sorry I didn't translate the letter sooner."

"You couldn't have known what was in my mother's letter." I scowl and turn the doorknob. "I have an immediate appointment on Drummond Lane."

After I exit the house into the pouring rain without my hoodie, I take a shortcut through a neighbor's yard to get to Drummond Lane. The tachycardia exploding in my chest increases with every step. When I arrive at the side door, I bang it open with my hip and tramp into the house.

"Where are you, Dr. Hughes? We need to talk!" No reply. Mr. Yeats scuttles by into the office and hisses at me. "Screw you, too, you busybody."

Leslie's bedroom door is closed. So, I pause for a moment. She must be napping after the exhausting events of the weekend.

Maybe Archie is right. I should go back to his house and cool down first. Oh, screw her nap.

"Dr. Hughes, I have a beef with you," I say as I push the door in.

And there they lie—Leslie and Agnes in bed with their sagging breasts exposed above the sheets. As I drip onto the wooden floor, I mutter, "Fuck."

Agnes takes a hit of her joint using her bandaged arm and blows out slowly, hacking and coughing as the smoke passes between her lips. "Nah. We already did that." She cracks up and passes the joint to Leslie, who partakes.

My jaw drops. "I'm sorry. I'll come back later."

"You appear quite upset, Gwynedd. Please, talk to us." Leslie inhales from the joint and passes the weed back to her lover.

Agnes pulls up the sheets to cover their boobs. "You appear pissed on like an outhouse. You better tell us what's bothering you."

I cross my arms and glare at Leslie with fire in my eyes. "Agnes, I discovered the secret your girlfriend has kept from all of us, especially me."

Leslie's eyes bulge out like an animated cartoon character. She swallows hard and says nothing.

"Well, don't hold back," Agnes says, taking another hit. "Come out with it."

"My mother, Lowri, entrusted Leslie with a tale about our ancestors. Many generations ago, an ancestor of ours accidentally killed the child of a Tuatha Dé Danann. To make reparations, my ancestors promised the daughter of a future offspring to a male of the Tuatha Dé. Apparently, that offspring is me."

"For the love of the gods, Leslie," Agnes scolds. "That's why Lowri was so scared about the mound portal and flipped out when you opened the larger portal on Samhain. It's why she left the coven. How could you betray your best friend and put her child at risk?"

Leslie raises her chin. "Because the need to strengthen the coven outweighed Lowri's family issues. I made the necessary choices."

"Oh, for fuck's sake!" Agnes frowns and slaps Leslie on the arm. "You haven't changed one damn bit." She slides out of the bed and puts on her clothes as she leans against the bed. "Gwyn, I know very little about the Tuatha Dé, but I bet they've been sniffing you out all this time and tracing your magic scent. What about the portal mound? Should we plug the thing?"

"Is it even possible?" I hike my eyebrows.

Agnes grimaces. "We opened it. We can close it. Never had a reason to find a spell to do it before now. Let me search through my grimoires, and I'll call you. It could take months or years to discover the right spell."

"Where are you going, Agnes?" Leslie asks.

"Home. You need to take a hard look at yourself. Is this really how you want your life to play out? All to save your precious coven?"

Leslie presses her lips together and lowers her head. "It is my life."

"Hmph. Don't call me until you're ready to put your witches first. I love ya, woman, but you have to do better." My former mentor hobbles out of the bedroom.

I stare at Leslie with knots tightening in my gut. "I don't know if I can ever forgive you for this."

CHAPTER TWENTY-NINE

WHAT'S IN A PICTURE?

I ENTER ARCHIE'S HOUSE through the back door, shivering, and remove my soaked sneakers. The temperature may be in the 60s, but the cold and wet together have me shaking as if it's raining icicles. He stops drinking his tea and rushes over, grabbing a couple of tea towels on the way.

"Dry yourself off." He hands me one while he blots my hair with the other.

"The rain hasn't let up at all," I say. Suddenly, a deluge of water pounds the roof of his house—a gloomy day to top a catastrophic weekend.

"I'll put the kettle on," Archie says. "Some hot Earl Grey tea will warm you up straight away. Why don't you rest on the loveseat while I fetch you a proper towel?"

I shuffle into the living room and check my bottom before sinking into the worn leather cushion. My head falls back, and I gaze at the painting over the fireplace. The young woman in the meadow sensed the storm coming. Why didn't I?

He dashes down the stairs and hands me a warm, fluffy towel. And the teakettle whistles. "I'll be right back with your tea, my love."

I pat my hair and wrap the soft towel around my upper body. Light flickers in my peripheral vision, and I turn my head toward the painting on the mantle. But there is no illumination—so odd. Archie returns with my tea and sits next to me on the loveseat.

"Mmm, it smells so good." I savor the hot Earl Grey and swallow. "Thank you, my Scottish savior."

"I don't know about being your savior." He chuckles and leans back. "You do quite well defending yourself. Are you going to tell me what happened? Or do I have to drag it out of you?"

"I walked in on Leslie and Agnes." I snicker, and it occurs to me, incidences do happen in threes.

"What do you mean? Were they arguing?" He sips his tea.

"NO." My eyes grow big, and a wide grin brightens my face. "They were in bed...together. And smoking a joint."

Archie drops his cup on the saucer with a clink. "That was a wee unexpected. I imagine Mr. Yeats was a tad upset, too."

"Yeah. He hissed at me from the office. He's a jealous soul. But I figured after this weekend, any chance of true reconciliation had passed." I sip more of my tea and bask in its warmth. "But it was short-lived. Agnes got pissed when I told her the secret Leslie had kept from me—from all of us. She got dressed and went home. But she's going to dig into her spell books for an incantation to remove the portal mound."

"Maybe I can help her. What did you say to Leslie?" Archie asks, stroking my back.

"I said I may never forgive her." I'd hoped for a closer relationship. But how do I trust her now?

"Would you like me to run you a hot bath?" he asks. "I could join you?"

I smile at his gorgeous face. "Sure. You can make up for last night."

"Remember, I had no control over murderous ancestral witches. But I'm more than happy to oblige you." He kisses me. "I'll start the water."

As Archie ascends the steps, he stops for a brief second to blow me a kiss and continues to the bathroom. I finish the last sip of my Earl Grey and stand to stretch. When I roll my head around, I'm sure a glimmer of light emanates from the picture like I noticed once before. But rain pelts the house as if the Kenilworths are stamping on it from the Otherworld. I examine the room for the culprit—glare from the ceiling light or the ricochet of a stray beam off the mirror on the wall. Nothing. I shrug and walk toward the stairwell.

"Gwynedd," a woman's voice whispers from behind. I twist my body around, and I'm face to face with my mother—well, a shimmering, gold impression of her.

"Mom?" I gape at the vision of Lowri Crowther, a younger version of herself projecting from the painting. "Are you actually here?"

The golden vision of my mother smiles. "Yes, dear. It's me."

"But how? I didn't call on you?" I'm both petrified and ecstatic.

"I sensed you were here and needed me," she says. "This object has allowed me to cross, so I can speak with you. I don't understand the magic, but it has a familial presence."

"I read the warning about the Tuatha Dé Danann in your letter. What do I do? How can I protect myself?" I ask.

"Continue your ancestral divination and develop stronger con-nections with your ancestors. Build your strength with the help of the Bearsden Coven. I assume you have joined the Fellowship." Her face shimmers in and out of focus. "Before I left Wales, your Great-Aunt Gorawen said she would send a protector for me and my children. I thought little about it at the time since she was so angry I was leaving. But there may be a witch who is watching over you—someone hiding in the shadows."

"Will I recognize the protector? Will she be someone unexpected?" I ask. Is it Agnes? It's definitely not Leslie!

"I don't know, dear daughter." The vision of my mother fades. "I must go now, but we will talk more in the future. And with increased ancestral connections, your father will appear also."

My head quivers, and I fight to hold back joyful tears. "I would love to talk with Dad. Please, tell him I think about him every day. I love and miss you both."

"Take care, Gwynedd." Lowri Crowther's shimmering face dissipates as I reach for her.

I stare at the painting of the young woman in a field of flowers, chasing a storm. The picture calls on me, drawing me toward the fireplace mantle like a magnet. I spy the lower-right corner again. Sometimes the artist's name is part of the strokes, but I discover nothing. Grabbing the sides of the frame, I lay it on the floor to inspect the other side. The brown paper backing has come loose in one corner, so I lift the covering to take a peek. The paper pulls off a bit, so I figure, what the hell? And begin ripping more.

Archie hollers from the stairwell, "What the fawk are you doing, Gwyn?"

I gape at him. "The painting attracted me, pulling at my inner soul to come to it. And then Mom's face appeared—shimmering gold like floating magic."

"I thought I heard you talking to yourself," he says, walking to me. "That's wonderful. What did she say?"

"She said there is something special about the painting allowing her to cross over to speak to me." I peer up at Archie with a hopeful heart. "Sometimes the artist signs the back instead of the canvas. I need to know."

He runs a hand through his locks and sighs. "What the fawk. Go ahead and rip it off."

I pull the paper back as carefully as I can. My lips part while I tear up, and I stroke the name with my fingertips—Gorawen Thomas.

"Archie, where did you find this painting?"

"At a wee antique shop in a Welsh town called Buckley, not far from Chester, England. I was attending a university conference there. I saw it resting against a wall in a tiny corner of the store. The oil canvas leaped out at me, almost begging me to snatch it up."

I stare at the painting. "My mom said my great-aunt would send me a protector."

"What does that have to do with this painting?" he asks.

"Gorawen Thomas is my great-aunt. The woman in the painting must be my mom. Oh, Archie, did she cast a spell on you with this painting? To send you to be my protector? It means none of this is real. The love you feel for me is only an illusion."

"Gwynedd, my love for you is NOT an illusion." He kneels next to me and cups my face. "I don't doubt she may have lured me here, but I fell in love with you of my own volition. Though I suspect you cast your own magic on me. You had me the moment you called me Dr. Cock-burn."

I chuckle and gaze into his transparent-blue eyes. "I love you."

"And I love you, Gwyn." He kisses me and lays his forehead against mine.

"I need to go to Wales to see if Aunt Gorawen is still alive and discover what she knows about the Tuatha Dé tale. I have to do what I can to prepare for his coming."

Archie looks away for a moment, takes a cleansing breath, and strokes my cheek. "I guess we're going to Wales."

ACKNOWLEDGMENTS

Many thanks to my entire family for your continued support through my author journey. You are my rock!

Special thanks to my editor Christopher Barnes at Cissell Ink. Your expertise is outstanding.

To my book cover designer Charles Clark, I am so lucky to have you on my team.

Many thanks to my ARC Reader Team. I consider you an integral part of my book publishing process. Thank you so much!

About the Author

J.C. YEAMANS is an author of paranormal fiction. A former public school teacher based in Lewes, Delaware, she writes about all things witchy to find the inherent magic in life's journey of discovery and love—all while making blunders along the way. Her prior career revolved around the performing arts. As the owner of Reed Shore Press, she also publishes fiction and nonfiction works for others. She is married and has two adult children. When she's not putting pen to paper (or more aptly, fingertips to keys), she spends time biking, hiking, and weightlifting.

Sign up for J.C. Yeamans's newsletter at jcyeamans.com to download a free backstory and stay in the loop!

OTHER BOOKS

The Bearsden Witch Series

Secrets of a Midlife Witch

Schooling of a Midlife Witch

Stalking of a Midlife Witch

Trials of a Midlife Witch
(December 2023)